THE THREAT

I looked across the boat to see Michael coming toward me, his eyes glowing with a rapacious, demonic intensity. Fear totally possessed me and I started to back away from him.

"Elizabeth!" he cried. "Don't move . . . don't move!"

Ignoring his command, I continued to move backward as he raced unsteadily across the wet, slippery deck, a crazed expression on his face. I did not want to die a watery death like Isabel. I wanted to live!

Michael lunged at me, again crying my name, and I felt the wet wood of the rail press painfully into my back as his hands roughly grabbed my shoulders. My hands and arms flailed at him, uselessly, for he was a powerful man with a tenacious will. I shut my eyes and went limp, expecting to be tossed into the dark, turbulent sea. . . .

THE LOST WIVES OF DUNWICK

BEVERLY C. WARREN

ZEBRA BOOKS
KENSINGTON PUBLISHING CORP.

ZEBRA BOOKS

are published by

Kensington Publishing Corp.
475 Park Avenue South
New York, NY 10016

First printing: July, 1988

Printed in the United States of America

One

It was late and I was on my way to my bedchamber after kissing Papa good night when the brass knocker on the entrance door rapped loudly and persistently. I hesitated on the landing of the first floor and looked down toward the spacious marble foyer as the steady cadence of Charles's measured step clicked along the marble floor.

As Charles reached out to turn the ornate brass knob, curiosity rooted me to the spot as the door opened and a tall, broad-shouldered man entered. Removing his hat, he handed it to Charles, then untied his cape as Charles deftly took the black wrap from those wide shoulders. Though the raven-haired stranger was impeccably clad in a black dinner suit with a ruffled white-silk shirt, his face commanded my attention. A livid bowed scar raged its way from the side of one cheekbone to his jaw, momentarily holding my gaze before my eyes coursed over a narrow high-bridged nose, wide thin lips flanked by deep crevices along his prominent cheekbones, a strong, square chin and ebony eyes set under dark, arched eyebrows. Each feature, if taken separately, was rough and jagged, yet molded together they gave an overall impression of distinctive handsomeness despite the scar. Not only did he fascinate me, but I felt a peculiar attraction toward him, an indefinable allure.

"Mr. Whitter is waiting for you in the library, Lord Tyrone," our butler, Charles, said.

A lord? Why would a lord be paying so late a call on my father? I thought I knew most of my father's acquaintances or at least had heard their names before. But the name Tyrone was completely unknown to me. As Charles hung the cape on the mirrored clothes rack and placed the hat on one of its multi-shelves, I watched the tall, mysterious stranger walk directly toward the library as if he had been there many times before.

As he was about to pass under the landing, his head snapped up as if an inner sense told him I was standing there. I felt like a bird in flight suddenly impaled by those dark, piercing eyes. I ventured a quick, little smile, but the expression on the stranger's proud face remained implacable, almost austere, and my smile faded under a powerful apprehension.

When he passed from view, I lifted my skirts and raced down the hall to the first-floor sitting room where I knew Mrs. Berrey would be working on what seemed to me an endless petit point design.

When I was born seventeen years ago, Mrs. Berrey had been hired as my nanny. She didn't know that only two years later she would become my surrogate mother and thus achieve a rather notable position in the household. Her status as a servant gradually diminished, elevating her to something akin to mistress of the household. It became habitual for her to take her meals with Papa and me if only to keep me company and on my good behavior.

"Mrs. Berrey, who is Lord Tyrone?" I asked breathlessly.

"Lord Tyrone?" She lowered her needlework to her lap as she peered at me over the wire rim of her glasses. "I'm sure I have no idea, Liza. Never even heard the name before. Why do you ask?"

"A Lord Tyrone just went into the library to see Papa." I walked to the fireplace and stretched my hands over the coals glowing in the brazier.

"Your father deals with a vast number of people. It would be impossible for either of us to know all of them." Mrs. Berrey went back to her petit point as if she had given me the definitive answer.

"But most of Papa's business associates and friends are not of the peerage. Why should a lord want to see Papa?" I was persistent if nothing else.

"Isn't it past your bedtime, Liza?" asked Mrs. Berrey, who always changed the subject when she thought I was becoming too dogged in my queries.

"I'm not a child to be sent to bed, Mrs. Berrey. In a few weeks I shall be eighteen and perhaps betrothed," I said with an air of haughty defiance.

"Well, until you are, I suggest you go to bed, for the hour is quite late. Shall I have Mary come up to assist you?"

"No. I can do it myself," I replied petulantly. Besides, I suddenly wanted to be alone. The idea of my impending birthday ball at which Papa would announce my betrothal to a man he deemed suitable presented a wealth of idle daydreaming. There were a number of eligible young men who made a show of courting me. And one or two were almost handsome. On the other hand, I am exceedingly plain of face and horribly shy in the company of men, the latter quality marking me as prudish and vacuous, neither of which I am. "Good night, Mrs. Berrey," I said quietly and fondly as I bent and kissed the papery, wrinkled cheek.

"Good night, Liza."

I closed my bedchamber door quietly behind me and leaned against it as I let my mind drift to the candidates who had been courting me over the last year or so. Who would it be? For the most part, they were dashing young men, yet I didn't feel particularly attracted to any one of them. Mrs. Berrey said that love comes after marriage. Melvin Winchester popped into my turbulent mind. Good Lord! Don't let Melvin Winchester be the one who gets my father's wholehearted approval. The Winchesters were almost as rich as my father, but that didn't enhance their insipid son in my eyes. I staunchly dismissed the possibility. Papa loved me too much to inflict that immature toady on me.

Snuggled down under the covers, the room darkened, I let my fancies wander aimlessly among the aspirants for my hand until dreams replaced my conscious thought. But my dreams did not hold the elation I had expected. They were constantly disrupted by an ominous form cloaked in black with blue-black hair that tossed wildly about a saturnine, scarred face. The bright light of morning finally washed my brain clean of the disturbing dreams.

Papa and Mrs. Berrey were already in the dining room when I entered. After a quick good morning, I retrieved my plate from its usual spot on Papa's left and took it to the sideboard to lade it with rashers of bacon, fried eggs, fried green tomato, and two sausages.

As I sat down, I glanced at Papa, who had finished his breakfast and was now reading the paper, occasionally taking a sip of his coffee. I knew he didn't like to engage in any conversation when his paper was at hand, but my curiosity was fast bubbling to the surface and I was powerless to stop it.

"Who is Lord Tyrone?" I asked before plopping a forkful of eggs into my mouth.

The widespread arms clashed the paper together with a crunch as my grim-faced father stared across the table at me. "Where did you hear the name Tyrone?" he asked lightly.

"Last night when Charles let him in," I replied, my china-blue eyes wide at his gruff manner.

"Why weren't you in bed? You had left the library an hour before, telling me you were going to bed." His ruddy face scowled as he absently smoothed his thick white mustache.

"I remembered I had left my reticule in the drawing

8

room. When I went to get it, I spied a new issue of *Punch* magazine and stopped to thumb through it," I replied defensively.

"Young ladies do not thumb through *Punch*," my father said.

"And why not?" I asked, noticing Mrs. Berrey shaking her head ruefully.

"It satirizes things you couldn't possibly understand. And it is a bit too risqué at times."

"I think some of the cartoons are quite amusing." I loftily raised my chin. I could be as stubborn as Papa.

"In the future, I'll have Charles make sure the magazine isn't lying around the house." His arms stretched out the paper once more, signifying an end to the conversation.

"You still haven't answered my question, Papa."

With an audible sigh of annoyance, he gathered the paper in one hand and let it drop over the side of his chair. "What question is that, Elizabeth?"

"Who is Lord Tyrone?"

"Michael Tyrone is a business acquaintance of mine."

"But you don't usually conduct business so late in the evening," I persisted.

"This was an exception. Now . . . have I answered all your questions? I would like to finish the paper before I have to leave."

I nodded and turned my attention back to my breakfast. I suppose my inquisitiveness sounded trivial to my father, who had so many business concerns to contend with. He was a prominent member on a number of boards—banking, commerce, mining, and probably a half dozen more I knew nothing about. He owned a large shipping line, tons of stock in the railroad, and a new factory that produced machinery. His interests were so varied and widespread, I had only a cursory knowledge of them. I did know we were immensely wealthy and owned one of the finest homes in London.

9

I was fully aware that I, as Papa's only child, would be the sole beneficiary of all that wealth, and I understood his careful scrutiny of any and all suitors who sought my attentions. I was even aware that on several occasions Papa had hired a detective to investigate some of my would-be swains.

Papa folded his paper and placed it on the table, then rose, coming to kiss me perfunctorily on the top of my head before leaving.

"I want you and Mrs. Berrey to go to the drapers today and pick out the material for your ball dress. You've put it off for far too long and the ball is only two weeks away. Do I have your promise, Elizabeth?"

"Yes, Papa." I dreaded the selection of material for the seamstress. There was always so many beautiful fabrics in the drapers that it was next to impossible for me to select one. It was easier to have an entire wardrobe made. A certain boldness came over me as I grasped Papa's hand on my shoulder. "Will my betrothal be announced at the birthday ball?" I asked anxiously.

"It most certainly shall," Papa replied.

"Who? Oh, please tell me who," I implored, gripping his hand tightly.

"You shall know at the proper time."

"What if I don't like him?"

"I trust you have enough faith in me to select a suitable candidate for your husband."

I hesitated. Papa was a good judge of people. He wouldn't have come as far as he had in business if he wasn't, I thought. Yet I was apprehensive enough to blurt out, "It isn't that horrid Melvin Winchester, is it?"

Papa had a booming laugh, and I swore the china rattled as he let loose with a resounding guffaw. "My dear Elizabeth, I wouldn't wish young Winchester on any woman, so set your mind at ease on that score." He patted my hand fondly, then removed his captive one from my shoulder as

10

he said to Mrs. Berrey, "Make sure she gets to the draper's today."

"Yes, Mr. Whitter," Mrs. Berrey replied, giving me one of her "don't-give-me-any-argument" looks.

After choosing the material for my gown and dancing slippers, and between fittings, French and piano lessons, the days slipped by with increasing speed. As the day of the ball drew closer, my mind raced over the names and faces of all the gentlemen callers who had visited me for tea or strolled in the park with me, my chaperone several feet behind. I was sure Papa would tell me who I was to marry on the morning of the ball, giving me a chance to offer my objections if there were any. I surmised he was playing the waiting game to increase the excitement of the day.

On the morning of the ball, I searched the house for Papa only to be told he had unexpected business to attend to and would be gone for most of the day. Filled with disappointment, and with servants scampering about like inmates of Bedlam and Charles gliding through the spacious rooms like a serene ray of light, I quickly sought the solace of the first-floor sitting room, hoping to find Mrs. Berrey. I had forgotten that she, along with Charles, was overseeing the arrangements for the ball. I settled down in a plush Queen Anne chair with a copy of *Great Expectations*. It had been out for a while and, even though I was a great fan of Charles Dickens, I hadn't gotten around to reading it. I opened the book, started to read and soon became so engrossed, I didn't notice Mrs. Berrey enter with a luncheon tray.

"I thought it best we have a solid lunch, for there'll be no tea today. Even with all the extra help, cook is in a pother and the kitchen is a madhouse," Mrs. Berrey exclaimed, setting the tray on the low table in front of the divan, then sinking wearily onto the divan with a low sigh.

"You know how Papa is, Mrs. Berrey. He never does anything halfway. French wines and champagne. Caviar imported from Russia. Enough food to feed the entire Napoleonic army, and the finest musicians in all of London," I said, inspecting the tray of sandwiches, scones, marmalade, and tea, then settling on the divan next to her. "Of all days for Papa to go off on business! He knows how important this day is to me." I laded my plate with some of the tempting morsels. I hadn't realized how hungry I had become.

After lunch I tried to read again but it was useless. My father's prolonged absence was making me apprehensive and I was beginning to feel he had done it on purpose. I no longer heard Mrs. Berrey's chatter as my mind shut out everything except the ball and the announcement Papa would make. I was growing angrier by the minute. It wasn't fair! I had a right to know in advance who my intended husband was. Resentment filled me and I decided to reject out-of-hand any man Papa had chosen for me. I would sneer, lift my skirts and stalk from the ballroom with head held high. Mrs. Berrey's voice finally penetrated my illusions.

"Liza . . . Liza, child."

I turned, surprised to see Mary, my maid, standing in the middle of the room.

"Didn't you hear me, Liza? Mary has your bath ready."

I nodded, then headed for my bedchamber, Mary in tow.

The hot, scented bath did little to soothe my frayed nerves and calm my rising excitement. Even Mary's competent fingers moving over my scalp didn't have their usual tranquil effect as she washed my long auburn hair.

I was standing in my chemise as Mary tossed the petticoats over my head when Mrs. Berrey entered, looking quite elegant in her plum bombazine gown. For a woman approaching her sixties, she seemed quite stylish in a refined way. She went to the bed and scooped up my blue silk

12

gown.

"We must hurry, Mary. The guests will be arriving shortly and Mr. Whitter will want Miss Elizabeth by his side to greet them," she said, handing the gown to Mary, who quickly slid it over my head, then fastened the tiny hooks.

I put my hands on my small hips and glanced sideways into the large mirror over my dressing table. The silken bodice was snug and daringly low-cut, revealing the rounded swell of my bosom. Though I knew I should have chosen a white fabric, the blue gown shimmered with a translucent light, and its color did indeed reflect the cornflower-blue of my eyes as I had known it would.

With the matching slippers on, I sat at the dressing table for Mary to coif my hair. She brushed my long tresses until they crackled with a healthy glow. Then, with experienced fingers, she dressed my hair atop my head, drawing tendrils of curls out to frame my oval face. I looked in the mirror, feeling quite mature. Though certainly not beautiful, I thought I looked fairly comely. Mrs. Berrey's running account of the food to be served was beginning to make my stomach rumble with pangs of hunger. But a fist pounding at my door immediately washed away any thought of food, for I knew it was Papa.

"Elizabeth!" the familiar voice boomed as Mrs. Berrey went to open the door.

Papa never came into a room. He made an entrance. He was a big man, who was showing signs of a rapidly developing paunch. His white mustache and thinning white hair gave him an air of distinction as he strode across the room, impressive in his formal attire.

"Stand up, Elizabeth, and turn around for me," he ordered, and I complied, whirling the full-skirted gown for his inspection. "Ah . . . you look lovely . . . beautiful, in fact. Your birthday present," he said, extending a red velvet case in my direction.

13

I opened the lid and gasped at the exquisite sapphire and diamond necklace that lay on the white velvet inside. "Oh, Papa, it's beautiful!" I exclaimed, flinging my arms about his neck and kissing him on the cheek.

"Here now . . ." he said, holding me from him. I knew the gesture pleased him even though he tried to pretend a certain reticence. "Let me put it on."

I fingered the delicate treasure as he clasped it about my throat. It was the first piece of jewelry with gemstones I had ever owned. I had pearls and lockets, but nothing that sparkled so brilliantly.

"Well, my dear, are you ready to go down?" he asked.

"Yes," I replied, enthusiastically fluffing the tiny puffed sleeves of my gown that lay slightly off my white shoulders.

As we descended the wide staircase, my arm securely through his, I said, "You've been avoiding me all day, Papa, and now I want to know the name of the man you have chosen for my husband." I tried to sound firm and unwilling to brook any sidestepping of the issue.

He patted my hand and gave me a condescending smile. "I promise you'll not regret my choice."

"You're being evasive, Papa. Who is he?" I asked impatiently. And when I thought I was finally going to get a straightforward answer, Charles opened the front door and the guests began to arrive.

The glitter of jewels and a kaleidoscope of colorful gowns soon filled the house, along with an undulating drone of voices. I had expected to be quickly swamped with admiring young men, but, to my disappointment, the first to my side was Melvin Winchester. I should have realized that at any affair where Maude Archer was in attendance men would scarcely rush to me. I was certainly no match for Maude and her dazzling blond beauty. My bright blue eyes were much too large for my small oval face, and my thin, retroussé nose wasn't very patrician. My lips were wide and full, not at all fashionable like Maude's tiny rose-

14

bud lips. Even though she was a year older than I and outshone me in any group, we had become quite friendly as her father did a good deal of business with mine. Yet, for all her vanity, I liked Maude. Although she was conceited and selfish, and never pretended to be otherwise, I think it was that odd strain of honesty in her that created the basis for my friendship with her.

I quickly dispatched Melvin to fetch a plate of food for me while I went in search of Maude. She had a marvelous faculty for securing the latest gossip in London, then embellishing it until it made a fascinating tale. I never took her stories seriously, but they made delightful listening. Before I could find her, Melvin had returned with my plate of food along with one for himself. There was nothing I could do except to find a settee on which to sit and devour the food. The champagne I had secured from a passing tray had made me a little lightheaded, and the food took priority over Maude.

"Do you think Prime Minister Gladstone will pacify Ireland as he claims, Miss Elizabeth?" Melvin Winchester asked.

"What?" I really hadn't been listening to him. I was too busy eating and searching the vast room for Maude.

"Gladstone. The Disestablishment Act and the Irish Land Act."

"I'm afraid I don't keep up with politics, Melvin."

"You should, Miss Elizabeth. There is so much going on, what with new laws and all." He paused to consume a portion of the food on his plate, then continued, "Isn't it sad about the Queen still in seclusion over the death of the Prince Consort?"

"I think it is an absolute disgrace. Victoria is Queen, first and foremost, and should act as such, tending to her duties and subjects instead of indulging herself in grief-stricken solitude," I stated rather strongly, amused by the shocked look on Melvin's face. Serves him right, I thought. Melvin

15

was the one man I was never shy with. I suppose my irritation with him erased my innate timidity. Relief surged through me when I saw his father, Robert Winchester, signal to his son. Melvin saw the gesture also.

"Do pardon me, Miss Elizabeth, but I must leave you for a moment. Don't forget to save several dances for me." Melvin rose, plate in hand, gave a stiff bow, then left to join his father, who was in concentrated conversation with some prestigious-looking gentlemen.

I left the settee, put my empty plate on a passing tray and went to find Maude once again. I was intercepted by two suitors, one of whom swept me onto the dance floor to the strains of a Scottish, while the other vowed to wait for the next dance.

After three dances, I was quite breathless and excused myself from accepting another, especially since I spied Maude heading my way. I went to meet her.

"I've been looking for you all evening, Elizabeth. Happy birthday," she said, kissing the air by my cheek. "You look positively enchanting tonight. And so daring! Wearing blue! How shocking! But it does become you. And that necklace! It must have cost a king's ransom. Is it from one of your swains?" Maude gushed with a knowing smile on her face.

"My father gave it to me as a birthday present," I replied.

"Well . . . it is beautiful just the same." She slipped her arm through mine and started to steer me toward one of the settees lining the spacious ballroom. "I'm exhausted. All the men seem to think I can dance every dance without the least respite," Maude declared, flopping down on the settee. I took a seat beside her. She flung her fan open and sliced it through the air with the verve of an overwound metronome. "That Bobby Thatcher is a charmer, but a little too forward, if you know what I mean." She gave me a sly wink and a mischievous smile. "He is handsome, though. What do you think, Elizabeth?"

16

I shrugged. "I suppose he is handsome, but I don't know him all that well. Is he your new beau, Maude?"

"Gracious no! Although . . ." She pursed her rosebud lips as if savoring the idea. "Perhaps I should give it more thought," she said in a drawl, then quickly shook her pretty blond head. "No . . . I mustn't. Daddy is quite vexed with me as it is. He claims he is tired of all these young men plaguing him. He says I must make up my mind and settle on one before the year is out, or he'll chose one for me. Is your betrothal going to be announced tonight?" she asked eagerly.

"Yes."

"You must tell me who it is. You must," she pleaded.

"You'll have to wait like everyone else, Maude." I couldn't admit I myself didn't know. It was too degrading and embarrassing, especially in front of Maude, who was always allowed far more freedom than I. She wouldn't understand that I was not allowed to choose my own husband, for Papa believed there was too much at stake to allow any juvenile flights of romantic fancy to make a binding decision like marriage.

"You're being cruel, Elizabeth Whitter. I'd tell you, and you know it," she said peevishly.

"Then, why don't you tell me who you're favoring these days?" I knew the simplest way to divert Maude's train of thought was to bring the conversation back to her.

"Well . . . right now . . . if I'm pressed to it, I think it would be Harold Payne-White. He's the richest and has the most beautiful estate in Kent, besides a sumptuous townhouse in London. And he's sooo very handsome."

"Yes, he is," I agreed, remembering the tall, lean, blond man with the cool gray eyes.

"Now, there's one I'd marry in a minute, whoever he is. No, Elizabeth! Don't turn around. He's glancing this way and I wouldn't want him to think I was talking about him. You must know him. He's talking quite avidly with your

17

father.

"Extremely tall . . . extremely handsome . . . superbly dressed . . . a real man," she exclaimed, a flush rising to her cheeks. "He's looking this way again. I do believe he is trying to flirt with me, the devil."

She took my arm as I was about to see for myself who could cause Maude to quiver so.

"Elizabeth, don't look now. They're coming this way." Suddenly, she grimaced in repugnance. "Oh, how awful!"

"What is it?" I asked with anxious curiosity.

"I just saw the other side of his face. It's gruesome. A long ugly scar all along his cheek," she whispered in my ear, the spread fan covering the lower part of her face.

"Elizabeth," Papa's voice boomed. "I'd like you to meet Lord Michael Tyrone of Dunwick."

I quickly turned, startled at the name, and gazed into the face I had gotten a brief glimpse of several weeks ago. It still held the same fascination for me as his dark eyes wove a web of seduction around me. I judged him to be in his mid-thirties, even though lines of hard living and sophistication were etched sharply on the angular contours of his face. Though I had been duly impressed that night I viewed him from the landing, I now found him most formidable in his highly fashionable evening attire. Though my father was a striking man, Lord Tyrone was awesome. While my thoughts raced, I somehow managed to greet him and raise my hand to his.

"My daughter Elizabeth, Michael," Papa continued.

"My pleasure, Miss Whitter."

He bent low over my hand, his lips almost grazing my skin, sending a strange warmth careering through my body. I didn't dare speak at that moment lest I betray the quaver rising in my throat.

"And this is Miss Maude Archer. Her father is Sir Malcolm Archer. I'm sure you've heard of him, Michael."

"Yes, I have. But I never knew he had so beautiful a

18

daughter."

For some reason, my heart sank as I watched him bow and take Maude's proffered hand, his lips performing the same ritual as they did over mine. Rationally, I knew it meant nothing, a gentlemanly display of social amenities. Yet, I do believe I felt a twinge of jealousy, an emotion that had always been a stranger to me.

"Why, thank you, Lord Tyrone," Maude said in the sweetest possible voice, her eyelashes fluttering as quickly as her fan and her smile so broad it creased her dimples deeply. "Oh, they're starting to play a waltz. My favorite dance."

"Mine also, Miss Archer." His dark eyes suddenly sought mine. "May I have the honor of the dance, Miss Whitter?"

"I would . . . would be delighted," I stammered, bewildered by his invitation. Whenever it came to a choice between Maude and me, invariably Maude was chosen. I stood and took his arm, noticing the smug expression on my father's face.

On the dance floor, Lord Tyrone was a graceful master of the waltz. With his strong arm around my waist, I danced as I never had before, whirling and spinning round and round the vast, ornate ballroom. I was in heaven. Admiring eyes soon turned our way and my self-confidence expanded a hundred-fold.

I gazed up at my dancing partner, happiness radiating from my eyes while his fastened steadily on mine with an enigmatic, hypnotic stare that made tremors race along my spine to my toes. For the moment, I was a dazzling jewel who blinded all those who dared to gaze at me—at least I thought so.

Even though the dance ended all too soon, the evening had come alive for me. I truly felt the birthday girl and queen of my own ball.

Lord Tyrone pulled my hand through his arm and held it there with his free hand as he led me across the dance floor to a settee on the opposite side of the room. I sat down, carefully smoothing the silken folds of my voluminous skirt. I could feel the weight of my birthday necklace as it rose and fell on my heaving bosom. Lord Tyrone sat beside me, at an angle, as if he might flee at any given moment. His face was an impenetrable mask.

"So, you are eighteen years of age today, Miss Whitter. Do you feel any older or wiser?" he asked, his voice low and resonant.

"No, I don't think so. I don't think birthdays really change anyone — inside, that is." I smiled, trying to hide my nervousness and wondered if I sounded too stoical. I took a deep breath and plunged ahead, my desire for him to stay, greater than my shyness. "Have you known my father long?"

"For a very long time, Miss Whitter."

"I don't believe I've seen you at the house before."

"Most of my contact with your father was conducted through the mail. On those rare occasions when I was in London, my visits here were usually late at night and you were in bed. However, we did meet on one occasion," he said, his dark eyes roaming my face.

"Oh? I'm sure I'd remember." I sent my brain spinning through my memory, only to find no recollection of the intriguing man sitting beside me.

"It wasn't a very happy occasion. I came to attend your mother's funeral. You were only two years old at the time, and I, a brash young man of nineteen. You sat on my lap for five whole minutes, fascinated by my watch fob." A flicker of an indulgent smile started to form on his lips, but vanished before it fully developed.

A hot flame flushed my cheeks at the thought that I had once sat on the lap of Lord Tyrone. Feeling oddly embarrassed, I sought to change the subject. "How long do you plan to stay in London, Lord Tyrone?"

"A month. Perhaps two."

"What part of England are you from?" I couldn't stop asking questions. I was afraid that if I did, he would leave, and I couldn't bear the thought of it. Every time he spoke in that deep, mellifluous voice it was like a lingering caress.

"I'm not a resident of England, Miss Whitter. My home is in Ireland. Northern Ireland."

"Belfast?" It was the only city in northern Ireland I could think of at the moment.

"No. My home is at Dunwick. About twenty-six miles northeast of Londonderry. However, by train, Belfast is not too far away. Have you ever been to Ireland, Miss Whitter?"

"No. Father likes to stay close to London and he's really much too busy for traveling. But Mrs. Berrey and I have holidayed in Brighton and Bath. Even went to Canterbury and Dover once."

"You'd like Ireland. God created it when He was in one of His better moods. it is a rare feast for any eyes, especially for eyes as beautiful and blue as yours."

I lowered my eyes to my lap. I knew his flattery was nothing more than gallantry extended to a daughter of an old-time friend. Nonetheless, it elated me.

"Do you ride, Miss Whitter?"

"Yes, I do," I replied, once more lifting my eyes to his.

"Then perhaps you could be persuaded to come riding with me during my stay in London."

"I'd like that very much." My heard was racing erratically at his unexpected invitation.

"Ah . . . there you are, Michael. I wonder if I might have a word with you in private. You'll excuse us, won't you, Elizabeth?" Papa asked, not posing a question but stating a foregone conclusion.

I nodded as Lord Tyrone bowed and departed with Papa. I watched them move through the host of people until they were lost to my sight. With the imposing image of Lord Tyrone still clouding my vision, I didn't notice Maude sitting down next to me.

"Well . . . you certainly were the center of attention out there on the dance floor with his lordship. But I don't see how you could bear to look at him with that ugly scar. Makes him look like something Mary Shelley would dream up," Maude exclaimed.

I felt a giggle starting. "Remember when we were children, how we used to sneak that book back and forth to each other under everyone's dire threats that we were not to read it? Papa used to hide it on the top shelf, behind the other books, never dreaming I knew exactly where it was."

Maude's laughter tinkled like fragile chimes. "I never really liked the book, but it seemed so naughty at the time. Who wants to read about monsters and all that when there are more exciting things to read about." Her voice dropped to a low, conspiratorial tone.

"I liked Mary Shelley's creature. He was such a sad character," I half sighed.

"You would. I swear, Elizabeth, sometimes I think you are hopelessly naive. But I could give you the names of some books that would flutter your stomach."

"Oh, Maude, how you do talk. If your mother or Mrs. Berrey ever heard us talking like this they'd have a massive attack of the vapors," I said with laughter in my voice.

"The world is changing, Elizabeth. Who ever thought we'd have divorce laws? By the way, did you see that article in the *Times* about Lady Pelham-Crofts?" Maude's blue eyes glinted with excitement.

"No." I stiffened, giving Maude my complete attention.

"Well . . . it seems she kept this diary . . ."

"May I have the honor of this dance, Miss Maude?" Harold Payne-White asked.

"I'd be delighted," Maude said after tossing me a sly glance.

Of all times for Harold Payne-White to appear! Why couldn't he have waited a few minutes? My curiosity had been piqued and I felt cheated. Fortunately, I was asked to dance, which helped to take my mind off Maude's unfinished tale. Later, and to my dismay, I was trapped into dancing a Scottish with Melvin, which suddenly brought back to mind the question of my betrothal. A quick terror filled me as I realized I didn't want to be married. I didn't want just anyone for a husband. I wanted to wait until I found someone who could make me feel as Lord Tyrone made me feel. I had to talk to Papa, and quickly, for the evening was rapidly slipping away. I danced the Scottish mechanically, thinking it would never end. Every time Melvin looked at me with that supercilious smile of his, my blood froze. I began to wish that the musicians' instruments would disintegrate in their hands.

The music stopped and I pleaded extreme fatigue, causing a certain amount of concern in poor Melvin. He fluttered about me like a guardian angel. Finally, Mrs. Berrey came to my rescue.

"Liza, child, what is wrong?" she asked in all innocence while Melvin's head swiveled from me to Mrs. Berrey, then back to me.

"I feel a bit faint and dizzy," I fibbed, hoping it would send a pathetic-looking Melvin out of my sight. Mrs. Berrey saw to it that Melvin went on his way so that I could be left entirely to her ministrations.

"Perhaps it would be best if you went upstairs to lie down for a while," Mrs. Berrey suggested as anxiety clouded her eyes.

"No . . . no. I'm feeling much better now. Really I am. But I must find Papa and have a talk with him. Have you seen him?"

"Why . . . no. I have no idea where he is. I still think you ought to lie down," Mrs. Berrey insisted, taking my hands in hers.

"I have to talk with Papa. It's very important."

"Charles might know where he is." She looked at me

warily as I withdrew my hands. "Liza, I think the champagne is a mite too strong for you. You haven't been imbibing too much, have you?"

I shook my head, swiftly kissed her on the cheek and went in search of Charles. I thought the most likely place to find him would be in the long dining room where the buffet was constantly being served and from where the waiters loaded their trays with full glasses of champagne. My suspicion proved to be correct. As soon as he finished supervising the cutting of the large roast of beef, I drew him aside and put my question to him.

"I'm afraid that Mr. Whitter cannot be disturbed under any circumstances, Miss Elizabeth."

"It's of the utmost urgency that I speak with him, Charles. Where is he?"

"He is in the library with his solicitors. I believe the door is locked, Miss Elizabeth," he replied tonelessly.

I knew there was no use pursing the notion. When Papa locked the library door, no one — but no one — got in, not even me. With a sigh of defeat, I went back to the ballroom, but not before I made a small gesture of defiance. I boldly took another glass of champagne.

As I skirted the ballroom floor, stopping to chat now and then with the guests, I saw Maude in her white satin gown, swirling about the black and white marble floor in the arms of Harold Payne-White. They made a picturesque couple, both of them light blond, uniquely attractive and perfect in body. They moved in such graceful unison, it seemed they were destined to be man and wife. I fervently wished Lord Tyrone would ask me for another dance before the music ended for the evening.

I fell in with several young women about my own age, joining them in a lively discussion concerning the newest fashions from Paris. However, the conversation soon deteriorated into a gossipy session which, for the main part, consisted of jealous and hostile remarks about Maude.

24

They were resentful that their own beaux were devoting an inordinate amount of attention to the beautiful Miss Archer. As I considered Maude my friend, I was not about to stand there and listen to their insults, especially when they wouldn't listen to my strong words of defense. I walked away.

Putting my empty glass on a passing tray, I brashly took another freshly filled one, then guiltily looked around to see if Mrs. Berrey was watching me. But she was nowhere in sight.

When I was asked to do what promised to be a very lively Scottish, I put my half-empty glass on one of the many small tables next to the settees and was eagerly led to the dance floor. My partner and I were swept up in the dance, and as we began to feel the full force of the rhythms, the music abruptly stopped. Everyone, even those who were not on the dance floor, turned toward the musicians. I swallowed hard, then held my breath. My father was standing on the slightly raised dais in front of the musicians.

My heart beat so strongly and rapidly I was sure everyone in the room could see the quickening rise and fall of my breast. My splayed hand went to my throat. I was sure I was going to stop breathing at any moment.

"May I have everyone's attention," my father began. "I'm sure you all know the reason for this happy occasion is that my daughter, Elizabeth, has attained her eighteenth birthday. But tonight is a doubly happy occasion, for I am pleased to announce my daughter's engagement to a fine, upstanding gentleman." Papa looked down at me, for I was standing directly in front of the dais. There was a smile on his face that did not extend to his eyes and I trembled inside, images starting to blur.

Two

Strong hands gripped my shoulders, but I was too paralyzed, waiting for my father's next words, to turn and see who dared be so bold as to put his hands on my bare shoulders. And, to be truthful, I was somewhat glad for the support.

"My daughter will soon be the bride of Lord Michael Raymond Tyrone," Papa announced with hauteur. Applause rippled around the room and Papa signaled the orchestra to commence a waltz, the last dance of the evening.

The hands tightened on my shoulders and spun me around. My new fiance's inky eyes captured mine and held them for a moment, his hands gently kneading my shoulders before one slipped around my waist, the other holding my hand outward as he smoothly led me around the empty floor. For once, I was not embarrassed to be the focus of everyone's attention. All I could see, all that existed for me, was the tall, strong man who was to be my husband. I knew there was a happy radiance on my face as I looked up at him.

"Disappointed?" he asked as other couples drifted onto the dance floor.

"No." How could I express the elation I was experiencing? I never dreamed I would be marrying a man so exciting, so handsome, so sophisticated in every way. And a man so compelling that the attraction I felt for him was immediate and devastating. I felt my pride swell, knowing that, despite his scar, he drew the eyes of every woman at the ball, especially the older women. At first I wanted the dance to last forever. But that, I soon realized, would only postpone my wedding day. And I did so want the wedding day to come quickly, especially the night.

Lord Michael Raymond Tyrone said nothing more while we danced, but continued to gaze at my face with an extraordinary glint in his eyes, a glint which I hoped was love.

I was thrilled when Michael joined Papa and me in bidding the guests good night. I received an awesome look from Maude, which held the promise of an early morning visit.

When all the guests had departed, Mrs. Berrey insisted I take myself to bed, but I wanted to spend every minute with Michael.

"Michael, I see no reason for you to stay at the hotel. We have more than enough rooms here," my father blustered, as only he could when his mind was set on something.

My eyes silently pleaded with Michael to accept my father's invitation. How marvelous it would be to have breakfast with him. Perhaps, during the night, he would steal into my room, gather me in his arms, his lips upon mine and then . . . then what? I really didn't know. I resolved to ask Mrs. Berrey first thing the next day what a wife was expected to do on her wedding night.

"Under the circumstances, John, I think it better that I remain at the hotel," Michael replied to my dismay.

"Well, since you've made up your mind . . . " Papa waved his hand in a gesture of resignation, as if he knew Michael was a man who could not be dissuaded when his mind was made up. Then, steathily glaring at Michael, he said, "You do understand I want the wedding to take place within the prescribed two weeks after the banns are posted, which I shall attend to tomorrow."

Michael's eyes shifted to me and his expression softened. "I fear two weeks isn't sufficient time to court a young lady properly, and I wouldn't want to deprive Elizabeth of the wooing stage. She is at a tender age where the little amenities can mean so very much."

Papa looked at me, then at Michael. "Two weeks is enough time to court."

"I think a month is more in order, John," Michael said in a tone that would brook no argument.

With a flourish, Papa pulled his handkerchief from a pocket and dabbed at his forehead. Then, he smoothed his mustache and quietly said, "Whatever you say, Michael."

My attention quickly snapped to my father. It wasn't like him to back down so readily. Papa always — always — got his own way. I couldn't understand why he was acceding to Michael Tyrone's demands so easily. What influence, what power did this Michael Tyrone have over my father? A doubt was beginning to gnaw at me, but then Michael gazed at me with those dark eyes, put his hands on my shoulders once more and kissed me lightly on the forehead, causing all doubts to drift into oblivion. I was totally unaware of Mrs. Berrey putting her arm around my waist and leading me up the staircase to my bedchamber where Mary was waiting to help me out of my elaborate gown.

It had been a long and exceptional day. I knew I would not sleep. In fact, I doubted if I would ever sleep again until the day I married Lord Michael Tyrone. Michael . . . the very name stirred my senses beyond endurance as I snuggled under the downy softness of the sheets and comforter. Automatically, my eyes closed, only to have visions of Michael Tyrone holding me in his arms to the strains of the waltz. As he whirled me around, the marble floor gave way to a grassy knoll, then to the very heavens themselves. I was to be Lady Elizabeth Tyrone!

I grabbed the pillow and placed it over my head to stop the cruel light from bringing my pleasant dream to a conclusion.

"Your tub is ready, miss."

To my annoyance, Mary's voice penetrated the pillow lodged on my head. I vaguely remember murmuring, "Go away." But deep down, I knew she wouldn't and that I should get up. "What time is it?"

"After ten, miss."

Dressed and downstairs, I thanked Charles heartily for having cook fix me a belated breakfast of poached eggs, two sausages, toast, and coffee. I ate more quickly than I should have, but there was so much to do to prepare for the wedding—my wedding to Michael Tyrone. Oh, how I loved the sound of his name.

Having finished breakfast, I went in search of Mrs. Berrey. The first priority was to make plans to go to the most fashionable house of design in London and have them create an exquisite wedding dress for me, then a complete trousseau. Guest lists, invitations, the reception . . . At the moment, it all seemed beyond me. There would never be enough time to accomplish all that needed to be done. I sat on the divan in the drawing room, deciding to straighten out my thoughts before confronting Mrs. Berrey.

"Miss Archer, Miss Elizabeth," Charles announced as a wide-eyed Maude bustled past him with a set smile, her hands outstretched.

"Why, you sly old devil, you," she exclaimed as I rose to grasp her hands in welcome. Charles discreetly left. "Letting me think you were going to be engaged to one of London's dandies, when all along you had an Irish lord lurking in the background. And scar or no scar, he is an intriguing man. So tall. So powerful! Why didn't you tell

29

me?"

"I found it difficult to make up my mind," I fibbed as we sat down on the divan. Of all people, best friend or not, I wasn't about to let Maude know the decision had been out of my hands. I had too much pride for that.

"A lord no less. I want to hear all the details." Her eyes sparkled with curiosity.

What could I say? There weren't any details. And when it came right down to it, what did I really know about Lord Michael Tyrone? "Oh, Maude, he's everything I had ever hoped for in a husband."

"I should think so. I heard some of the remarks made by the older women at your birthday ball."

"Speaking of the ball, you and Harold Payne-White made the perfect couple," I said.

"Oh, that Harold is quite a rogue. He whispered things in my ear that no gentleman would dare give voice to," Maude said with a coquettish gleam in her blue eyes.

"Like what?" I asked anxiously, hoping to learn what followed an embrace, a kiss.

"Oh, Elizabeth, with a man like Lord Tyrone for a fiancé you shouldn't have to ask such questions."

My cheeks flushed. How could I know anything? In my entire life I had never experienced anything more than a kiss on the hand, a kiss on the forehead, or a kiss on the cheek. A rebellion stirred within me. I couldn't let myself be pictured as a naive ninny in Maude's eyes. I had to play the sophisticated lady now that I was engaged. "I know that. I only wondered if Harold Payne-White was as romantic and exciting as Michael." For the first time, his name rolled off my tongue aloud, and it filled me with novel, delightful sensations.

"What does he say to you?" Maude asked as she leaned closer.

"Now Maude . . . that's between Michael and me."

"But you can tell me," she implored.

30

"I don't think Michael would approve."

"My . . . you are besotted with him, aren't you?"

"If I weren't, I wouldn't be marrying him. By the way, you will stand up for me, won't you, Maude?"

"I was hoping you'd ask me. And do remember, Elizabeth, peach is my best color."

"I will," I replied as Charles made his presence known by loudly clearing his throat.

"'This just arrived by messenger for you, Miss Elizabeth," he said in his usual clipped, cool tone as he handed me a long white box gaily tied with a large red ribbon. Then, in a martial stride, he left the drawing room.

I placed the box in my lap and tackled the ribbon. Once the lid was off, my eyes beheld what seemed a bower of red roses. Ignoring Maude's gasp of surprise, I quickly picked up the small white envelope, slipped out the folded note, flipped it open and read it greedily.

"My dear Elizabeth,

If you find yourself unoccupied this afternoon, I should very much like to accompany you on a ride in the park. Shall we say two this afternoon at St. Catherine's Lodge in Regent's Park? I shall be waiting for you.

                                    Yours,
                                    Michael"

"Who are the flowers from? What does the note say?" asked an eager Maude.

I handed her the note, then lifted the roses to bury my face in the soft, scented buds.

"Are you going?" Maude handed the note back to me.

"Of course. Why shouldn't I?"

"A feigned attack of the vapors or a debilitating headache shows a man you have control of any situation and helps to maintain your air of mystery," Maude declared.

"Don't be a goose, Maude. I have neither the vapors nor a headache. I only want to be with Michael, not control a situation or be mysterious." I laughed.

"Well, don't say I didn't warn you. Men like to think their women are helpless and mysterious; otherwise they soon tire of them."

"You've been reading too many of those novels, Maude," I chided her.

"You mark my words, Elizabeth Whitter. It takes guile and cunning to hold a man." Maude rose and smoothed her skirts. "I must be getting along. Harold is calling on me this afternoon."

I slipped Michael's note into the pocket of my skirt, then cradled the roses in my arms as I walked with Maude into the foyer. Her good-bye was stilted, almost curt, as if she were angry with me. But I was much too happy to be concerned with Maude's fluctuating moods. Besides, I didn't have much time to get ready and keep the rendezvous with Michael. Dashing up the stairs, I nearly collided with Mrs. Berrey on her way down.

"Liza, child, whatever is all the fuss about?" Her hand flew to her chest in astonishment.

"I'm going riding in Regent's Park with Michael. Here . . . take these and put them in water for me, please." I thrust the roses at her and once again picked up my skirts to dart up the stairs to my bedchamber. I rang for Mary, then fumbled with the fine buttons of my cotton shirtwaist, my fingers functioning as though my brain no longer had any say over what they did.

"Oh, Mary, do give me a hand. I seem to be all thumbs," I said as she entered the room.

"Something wrong, miss? You seem all flustered," she said as she deftly undid the buttons and helped me to undress.

"I received an invitation from Lord Tyrone to go riding with him at two this afternoon, which doesn't give me much time. I would appreciate your assistance."

"I'll be happy to do whatever I can, Miss Elizabeth." She smiled warmly.

Whether it was intuitive, a natural characteristic, or my father's training, I always dealt with the servants as though they were human beings and not objects whose only purpose in life was to serve me. I made a point of requesting their assistance and not ordering it.

"The royal blue habit will do nicely, Mary." The deep blue velvet lent a pink glow to my clear complexion, which was my best feature. The matching velvet hat was trimmed with yards and yards of pale blue tulle which was wrapped around the crown and trailed down the back. A very feminine outfit, it made me feel prettier than I actually was.

With Mary's aid, I was dressed in record time. While I completed last minute touches, I sent Mary to have Mrs. Berrey prepare for our journey to Regent's Park and to tell Charles to have the carriage readied.

I set my stylish hat atop my thick auburn hair, carefully coaxing wisps of curls from underneath it to frame my face. Pinching my cheeks a bit for color, I glanced at the watch fob pinned to the snug velvet jacket. Counting the length of the carriage ride, I knew I would be at St. Catherine's Lodge precisely at two o'clock. My heart began to beat capriciously with anticipation. To see Michael again, to come to know him, were the only thoughts that my mind would entertain. I would have to think about the details of the wedding later, much later.

During the ride to the park, I hardly heard Mrs. Berrey's sensible discourse on the order of priorities regarding the wedding. I glanced all about but saw nothing. My mind was clogged with thoughts of Michael. I clasped and unclasped my hands in my lap, for the carriage ride seemed interminable. When we finally arrived at the Lodge, the blood was pounding at my temples with such ferocity I didn't know if I could get out of the carriage. But as

Michael approached and extended a helping hand, serenity filled me. When his hand firmly held mine, I could feel the steady flow of his strength seeping into my body.

Mrs. Berrey decided she would go on to Queen Mary's gardens and would return in two hours.

"You look lovely, Elizabeth. The very flower of English beauty," Michael said as we strolled to where the groom held the reins of a full-bodied black stallion and a smaller roan mare.

"You are too kind, Michael." I blushed, but didn't fail to notice how magnificent and commanding an air Michael presented.

The groom assisted me onto the mare, while Michael's long legs swiftly put him astride the huge stallion. In moments, we were cantering side by side down the well-trodden horse path.

"Thank you so much for the roses. They were very beautiful," I said demurely.

"A small token, I assure you. But I am happy they pleased you."

"Will we be living in Ireland or here in London?" I asked lightly, for I really didn't care where I lived as long I was with Michael.

"In Ireland. You will be the mistress of Dunwick."

"Where is Dunwick?"

"In the northeast of Ireland. The estate straddles the three districts of Ballymoney, Moyle, and Cloeraine. We are about twenty kilometers from the sea. It is extraordinarily beautiful, Elizabeth, and I'm sure you'll feel quite at home."

"Will we be going there directly after the wedding?" My curiosity knew no bounds. I was about to enter a new world that I knew nothing about. Michael smiled obliquely at me and there seemed to be a glow of pity on those dark eyes. But I was sure I misread his look. It was fondness, not pity in his eyes. Yes, fondness . . .

"I wouldn't dream of depriving my lovely bride of her wedding holiday. We will settle in Dunwick after touring Italy and Greece. With the exception of Ireland, there is nothing more breathtaking than the Greek Islands."

"Oh, Michael, it sounds so . . ." I wanted to say romantic, but I didn't want him to think he was marrying a foolish child bride. ". . . so exciting," I finished.

He glanced briefly at me, then quickened the pace and we soon found ourselves in a stimulating gallop. I had no trouble keeping up with Michael as I was a good horsewoman, having ridden since I was six years of age. I had the feeling I would have to put this skill to good use once at Dunwick. Dunwick . . . the very name conjured up visions of multi-turreted castles and moats. I felt like a princess racing in the breeze alongside my prince.

We slowed our pace as the riding lanes became congested with other riders seeking the relaxation or practice of horsemanship. Michael reined his steed closer to my mare.

"Elizabeth, I believe there is someone behind us who is trying to get your attention."

I reined in the mare, my head swiveling as Michael came to a halt beside me. Coming up the path behind us was Maude in her riding finery. She was accompanied by Harold Payne-White.

"Isn't that the young lady you were sitting with when your father introduced us?" Michael asked.

"Yes. Maude Archer. And that's Harold Payne-White with her. His father is the Duke of Kent, a title Harold will inherit someday. He is an only son," I explained, wondering why Maude, after reading Michael's note, had decided to ride in Regent's Park at the precise time he and I would be riding there.

"Elizabeth, fancy seeing you and Lord Tyrone here," Maude said sweetly, moving her horse as close as possible.

"Miss Archer." Michael tipped his hat.

Harold drew his skittish horse alongside, and I made

cursory introductions. As always, Harold was dressed elegantly. In my opinion, he carried his fastidious and decorative attire to extremes, almost to the point of appearing foppish. His gray eyes glittered brightly in his handsome patrician face, and his long fair sideburns gave only a hint of the wavy blond hair under his black silk riding hat.

"Lord Tyrone comes all the way from Ireland, Harold," Maude purred, her eyes constantly scanning Michael's powerful, masculine form.

"Does he? I've never been to Ireland and doubt if I'll ever be lured there. Much too provincial and savage a land," Harold said with disdain, as though even speaking of the country would soil his spotless clothes.

From the corner of my eye, I saw Michael's hands tighten on the horn of his saddle. As my glance moved up to his face, his expression was implacable, but his scar appeared to be a bit redder.

"Have you set a date for the wedding yet, Elizabeth?" Maude asked, continuing to gaze at Michael.

I looked questioningly at Michael and was thankful when he answered for me.

"The wedding will take place before the oppressive heat of the summer months are upon us, Miss Archer."

"Then it will be soon." Maude's blue eyes twinkled as her long eyelashes fluttered like the wings of a hummingbird.

"It sounds a bit of a rush-rush to me," Harold drawled, attempting to stifle a yawn.

"When one is betrothed to a lovely creature such as Elizabeth, one does not want to let a moment of unmarried life slip by," Michael replied, causing my cheeks to flame at his suggestive words.

"You are fortunate indeed, Elizabeth, to have so gallant a suitor," Maude remarked, her smile tight and frosty.

"I know. Michael is a man above all others," I replied, gratified to see Harold stiffen and one fine, light eyebrow arch with displeasure.

36

"Why don't you and Lord Tyrone take tea with us later?" Maude asked while Harold took his watch from his pocket, studied it, then politely covered another yawn with his hand.

"It's nice of you to ask, Maude, but I promised Mrs. Berrey I would have tea with her at her favorite tea shop. After that we are to go to the dressmaker's," I said, knowing Mrs. Berrey's day would be ruined without her special cream cakes.

"Well, will we see you two at Edwina's party tonight?" Maude persisted.

"I'm afraid I'm the one who must decline that pleasure," Michael said. "I have a good deal of business to attend to in London before Elizabeth and I can leave on holiday after the wedding."

"Oh? Where are you planning to go?" This time, Maude looked directly at me.

"Italy and the Greek Islands," I announced, glowing with pride.

"Maude, love, I do believe we should be going. All this healthy exercise is fatiguing me and I do want to be at my best for Edwina's party tonight," Harold interjected with impatience.

"You're right, Harold. I, too, will need a rest before the soiree. I'll talk to you later, Elizabeth. And it was so pleasant meeting you again, Lord Tyrone. I'm sure we'll be seeing a great deal of each other from now on."

"My pleasure, Miss Archer," Michael said, thoroughly ignoring Harold.

Maude smiled sweetly and Harold tipped his hat before they rode off down the horse path.

"I find it difficult to believe that Miss Archer is your best friend," Michael commented as we urged our own horses along the path.

"Why?"

"The two of you are so totally different."

37

"When you have known Maude for as long as I have, you learn to take her the way she is. Though she is far more socially inclined than I am, we have had some good times together. She does love her parties and clothes and the company of young men, which, I must confess, does not hold the same fascination for me. But, over the years, we have gotten along tolerably well for all our differences."

"What does interest you, Elizabeth?" There was a calm seriousness in his tone that startled me.

"Music, books. And I do love flowers. Are there gardens at Dunwick?"

"Gardens you could get lost in.

"And a piano?"

"A fine grand piano from Germany."

"Books?"

"A library that is constantly updated. Do you think Dunwick will be to your liking now?" There was a hint of a smile on his lips.

"I shall adore it." I flashed a happy smile at him, wishing the wedding were the next day.

I tried to get Michael to tell me more about Dunwick, but he went on in great detail about Italy and the Greek Islands. We were back at St. Catherines Lodge before I realized two hours had passed, and my spirits sank when Michael left. Even tea and cream cakes couldn't raise them. Yet, once starting through the patterns at the dressmaker's, my enthusiasm returned as the head designer of the establishment showed me a number of sketches for wedding gowns, traveling suits, and other entirely new creations.

Once the designs were settled upon, the next priority was to decide on the material for the wedding dress. I regarded sample after sample until my eyes were bleary. Finally, the sheen and rich texture of one particular sample stood out above all the others. It was a silky, satin brocade imported from France. The designer applauded my choice, explaining how the material lent itself so well to tiny seed-pearl decoration. All my energies had been exhausted in material, and Mrs. Berrey agreed we should come back the following day to finish choosing the fabrics for the rest of the trousseau.

Arriving home, I barely had time to bathe and change for dinner. I had Mary lay out my dainty pink frock. I felt gay, frivolous, and extremely feminine. Whether I looked pretty or not, I felt pretty.

To my delight and joy, I learned from Mrs. Berrey that Michael would be having dinner with us. I lifted my skirts and dashed ahead of Mrs. Berrey to the stairs. Halfway down, I quickly halted when I saw Michael staring up at me from the foyer. I smiled, even though those dark eyes were appraising me grimly. I continued down the stairs at a more decorous pace and was rewarded with a slight upward curve of Michael's lips. I tingled when he pulled my hand through his arm and led me into dinner.

For a man in his mid-sixties, Papa was an engaging raconteur and could be quite witty at times. Between his stories and Mrs. Berrey's relating of our afternoon adventures at the dressmaker's, the evening passed swiftly and pleasantly. After we had coffee in the drawing room, Mrs. Berrey discreetly retired upstairs and Papa went to the library, leaving Michael and me alone to say good night.

Trembling with expectation, I walked with him into the foyer, dreaming of his arms around me, his lips on mine.

"My dear Elizabeth, I promise I shall endeavor to make the ensuing weeks most memorable for you," Michael said as he placed his hands on my shoulders.

"Just to be with you will be memorable enough," I replied, boldly lifting my head to receive the long-desired kiss.

"My dear, sweet Elizabeth," he murmured, taking my head between his large hands and placing a swift kiss on my forehead. "I'll see you tomorrow." He lifted his cape from the rack, swooped it over his shoulders, then vanished out the door into the night.

I stood there bewildered. Was that it? Was that all there was? There had to be something more! My mind and body wanted . . . no, demanded more. I sighed heavily, then slowly climbed the stairs to my bedchamber. Once in bed, I wondered if there was something wrong with me. Was I expecting more of a fiancé than I should? Was Papa forcing Michael to go through with a marriage he didn't want? Sleep soon enveloped me, soothing my new and curious desires and drowning my uneasy speculations.

In the weeks that followed, I felt as though I had been caught in the vortex of a swirling eddy. The mornings were consumed with preparations for the wedding, constant fittings, and visits with an ingratiating bootmaker. The afternoons sped along at Kensington Gardens, the British Museum, riding and the zoo in Regent's Park, along with all the usual tourist attractions in London which Michael had never had the time to see. He was most taken with Madame Tussard's exhibition of waxworks depicting famous and infamous characters. We even took a cruise up the Thames to Hampton Court Palace. All the sights and sounds that I had taken for granted became wondrous new delights as I saw them again with Michael.

The nights came from the tales of Scheherazade as we dined in London's finest restaurants, then viewed Shakespeare at Drury Lane or Haymarket, the ballet or opera at Covent Gardens.

During this time, Michael was considerate, courteous and most charming. I was falling deeply and irrevocably in love with him, even though—in moments when he wasn't aware of my adoring gaze—I sometimes noticed a dark, brooding look come over his face and haunt his eyes. Was he having second thoughts about the marriage? But then he would smile at me, banishing my doubts and fears.

It was less than two weeks before the wedding and, as Michael had business to attend to that afternoon, I contented myself playing some of Chopin's lighter pieces on the piano. Piano artistry was one of my better accomplishments. Perhaps because I enjoyed it so. I was completely engrossed in one etude until my fingers halted at a particularly difficult run of notes and I lost the tempo. I sat and rubbed my hands for a minute, studying the music before me and refingering the passage mentally.

"Don't stop, Elizabeth. It was lovely."

I spun around at the sound of his deep, resonant voice. "Michael! What a pleasant surprise! I didn't expect to see you this afternoon," I said happily, leaving the piano bench and walking toward him, my outstretched hands eager to be encased in his. He took them and led me to the divan, his countenance dark and troubled. "Anything wrong, Michael?"

"I'm afraid so," he replied somberly.

My heart stopped and I held my breath. The wedding was to be postponed indefinitely. I just knew it. All my dreams came crashing down like a stone castle without mortar.

"What happened, Michael?" I asked hesitantly, my voice quavering.

"Some disconcerting news has reached me from Dunwick. I hope you won't be too disappointed, Elizabeth, but I'm afraid I will have to cancel our holiday in Italy and Greece as we originally planned. I feel I should be close at hand if things take a turn for the worse and my presence is required there."

"Oh, Michael." I sighed with relief. "We can holiday any time. We can go directly to Dunwick after the wedding if it will ease your mind."

"I wouldn't dream of depriving you of a wedding holiday. Besides, I might not be called to Dunwick. To be on the safe side though, I have taken a cottage just outside of Keswick in the Lake District. I understand the area is breathtakingly lovely. Perhaps at a later time we can travel

41

abroad. Are you very disappointed, Elizabeth?"

"No . . . no. I hear the Lake District is enchanting," I said, thinking anywhere would be enchanting with Michael. "The poets have nothing but praise for the area."

"You're sure you don't mind?"

"Not in the least." His hands gripped mine tightly and his dark eyes searched mine with such intensity I was sure he was about to crush me in his arms and kiss me soundly on the lips. To my great dismay, he did neither. He released my hands to search for something in the pocket of his waistcoat.

He removed a small, black velvet case, flipped the lid open and showed it to me. "I had hoped to have this for you much sooner, but it took some time to find the right stones."

I gasped and my eyes grew wide at the sight of the gold ring set with a huge, multi-faceted, blood-red ruby surrounded by two rows of tiny diamonds. I was speechless as I looked from the ring to Michael in awe.

He took the exquisite ring from the box and held my hand while he slipped it on my finger. As he leaned down, I closed my eyes and raised my face to receive his kiss, my lips beginning to tremble at the thought. I felt his warm lips graze my cheek before he pulled away.

"There . . . now we are truly betrothed," he said calmly, although there was a turbulence in his eyes I couldn't comprehend. "Now . . . play some more Chopin for me."

A controlled madness embraced our house on the morning of my wedding day. Servants were skittering around with frantic expressions on their faces. Rumors filtered up from the kitchen that cook was on the verge of collapse, for after the church services there was to be a large reception in the ballroom of Whitter House, requiring an enormous amount of food. Only Charles remained unperturbed as he glided around giving calm, explicit instructions.

Mrs. Berrey flitted about my bedchamber checking the trunks while Mary fluttered about me making sure every auburn curl was in place before she placed the crown of veils on my head. Only Maude, in her peach-colored gown, was oblivious to the commotion around her as she sat, with feet up, on my chaise lounge.

"Really, Elizabeth, that is the most exquisite gown I have ever seen. That brocade . . . those seed pearls . . . and that design is so becoming on you. I must change dressmakers. Madame Saunders, you say?" Maude's fan stopped in mid-air for a moment.

"Yes," I replied studying myself in the mirror. The graceful puffed sleeves, the low-cut, tight bodice, tiny seed pearls glinting on shimmering, white silk brocade. It was far more beautiful than I had imagined it would be.

"I still can't get over Lord Tyrone being a Protestant. I thought all Irishmen were Catholic. But then, Ireland is a land full of eerie peculiarities. I'll bet you a new fur muff that you come back to London within a year. You'll never be able to stand Ireland. They are quite barbaric over there, you know," Maude said disdainfully.

"I'll take that bet," I replied with a laugh. Nothing was going to upset me today. Not even Maude's derogatory remarks. I was bursting with too much happiness.

"Here . . . here," clucked Mrs. Berrey. "Young ladies do not indulge in betting with each other." Her eyes narrowed and she waggled her finger admonishingly before she turned her attention to Mary. "Are Miss Elizabeth's traveling clothes ready?"

"Yes, mum. I'll lay them out during the reception," Mary replied.

"And are the trunks going to Keswick properly packed?" Mrs. Berrey pressed on.

"Yes, mum."

"And Miss Elizabeth's personal effects that she will retain, have they been set aside?"

"Yes, mum."

"Oh, Mrs. Berrey, please do stop worrying. I gave Mary a list of the items I wish to keep along with some winter clothes I have a fondness for. They shall be boxed and crated to be shipped to Dunwick while we're in the Lake District," I said, seeing Mary's anxiety increasing.

"Well, nevertheless, I shall go over it all before it is shipped. I wouldn't want anything left out," Mrs. Berrey stated with authority.

"It's a pity your tour of Italy and Greece had to be canceled. I fail to see what could be more important than your wedding holiday. I wouldn't let anything interfere with mine. Are you leaving for Keswick right after the reception?" Maude asked as she studied her slippers.

"No. Michael feels it would be too tiring for me to travel immediately after the reception and all the excitement and hubbub of the day. He thinks the scenery would be far more enjoyable in the daylight and after a good night's sleep," I replied.

Maude fell to giggling and I looked at her in wonder, then to Mrs. Berrey, whose face flushed as her hand went to her bosom. I was about to question Maude about her sudden mirth but was diverted when Mary placed the long veil on my head. With a sense of urgency, I excused Mary and asked Maude to tell my father I was ready and would be down shortly.

Alone with Mrs. Berrey, I found myself floundering for the words to ask the questions I desperately needed answers to. Taking a deep breath, I plunged in recklessly.

"Mrs. Berrey, why did Maude giggle when I mentioned the wedding night?"

"Miss Maude is a whimsical creature given to hysterical outbursts over nothing. Pay no attention to her," Mrs. Berrey replied, continuing to fuss about the room and avoiding my gaze.

44

"What happens on the wedding night? What am I supposed to do?" I decided there was only one approach, the direct one.

"Now, Liza, don't go worrying your head about it. Just do whatever Lord Tyrone asks of you, that's all. But do try to act pleased about it, even if you aren't."

"Pleased about what?" Rather than being solved, the mystery was deepening.

"Never mind. This is no time to discuss such things. Besides, I've told you all you need to know. We'd better get downstairs. There can't be a wedding without a bride, now can there?"

I sighed, knowing it was futile to pursue the subject. Mrs. Berrey had that set look about her that no amount of persuasion could alter. I followed her out the door along the hall to the staircase where Papa waited in the foyer for me. I held my head high, smiled and descended the stairs.

When I saw Michael turn to watch me walk down the long, carpeted aisle of the church on Papa's arm, my eyes locked with his in sheer joy. Nothing else existed but Michael as I automatically made my responses to the marriage ritual. My entire being floated to the heavens when Michael lifted my veil, his dark head slowly bending down to mine. The kiss was warm but fleeting, and when I opened my eyes, I saw that the same look in Michael's eyes I had seen before, an odd mixture of tenderness and anger. Again, the same unanswerable questions and uneasy sensations gnawed at me.

As we turned, my arm through his, to begin to leave the church, I glanced at Papa. He was beaming proudly, his happiness more than evident, and I knew my misgivings were nothing more than an overactive imagination. I had expected more from Michael's kiss, and when it wasn't there, I had foolishly read all sorts of dire implications in the eyes of the tall man who was now my husband.

The reception was lavish and extravagant. Everywhere in

the ballroom, happiness appeared to be contagious, even though Mrs. Berrey constantly looked on the verge of crying.

Though Papa radiated charm and conviviality, there was a floridness to his face I had never noticed before, and he was smoothing his mustache with a rare frequency. But his odd behavior soon vanished from my mind as Michael and I were assaulted from all sides with heartfelt congratulations.

With the food decimated, the cake cut, crumbs drifting down the tiered china cake-holder, and the musicians gone, the last of the guests found it prudent to leave. I changed into a simpler frock and joined Papa and Michael in the drawing room. As I seated myself on the divan, Papa poured me a glass of sherry, then replenished his and Michael's glasses of Scotch.

We were discussing some of the more humorous aspects of the wedding when Charles entered, carrying a silver salver with a letter on it.

"For you, Lord Tyrone," Charles said, making his way to the fireplace where Michael stood.

"Thank you, Charles." Michael put his glass on the mantel as he took the envelope from the tray and roughly tore it open. As his eyes moved back and forth over the letter, his face darkened into a satanic scowl, while the scar down his cheek appeared to have a life of its own as the gash became a livid red and the pulse at his temple throbbed. He absently traced a lean finger down the length of the scar, a gesture I had never seen him make before. He violently crumpled the paper in his large, powerful hand and glared at me strangely. For the first time I knew fear.

"Bad news, Michael?" Papa asked.

"I'm afraid so. I must leave for Dunwick at once."

"Michael!" I cried, jumping to my feet. "I'm coming with you."

"Elizabeth," he said gently as he came to me and put his

hands on my shoulders. "It would be foolish to change all our plans for some minor trouble that shouldn't take me more than a few days to clear up."

"But, Michael," I pleaded.

"No, Elizabeth. You will go on to Keswick and I will join you in a few days. And it isn't as if you'll be alone. I've engaged a housekeeper to look after things during our stay there. A few days, more or less, won't matter that much, will it? It'll give you time to rest up from your journey," Michael said in that magical, soothing voice of his.

"I suppose so, Michael," I said dejectedly as he tossed a beseeching look over my shoulder toward my father.

"Tell you what, Elizabeth," Papa said, "I have some business in Glasgow which I was going to take care of next week. There is no reason why I can't take care of it right away. I can ride with you as far as Penrith, where you get off the train, then continue on my way to Glasgow. It will give us another day together before I lose you to Ireland. How does that sound to you?"

"Fine, Papa, fine." I forced a smile and felt a little better. After all, two or three days wasn't a lifetime nor the end of the world. Only a minor delay.

"I must be off. The sooner I get there, the sooner I can have the situation resolved. I'll see you shortly in Keswick, Elizabeth." Michael lightly kissed my forehead as he dashed past me into the foyer, followed by my father.

I heard Michael's and Papa's muffled voices discussing something in a conspiratorial tone, but I couldn't quite make out the words. But the loud slam of the front door was something I could understand. Michael was gone.

I lay alone in bed on what was to have been my wedding night, trying to rationalize how it was all for the best. This way, on our first night together, we would be in the Lake District, making the holiday very special indeed.

It was June 28, 1869, and I was Lady Elizabeth Ellen Tyrone. I said the name over and over, savoring the sound of it. My dreams were sweet, picturing Michael rushing to the cottage in the Lake District, scooping me into his brawny arms after a loving kiss, then carrying me to our bedchamber. There was nothing in my dreams to portend my terrifying and inexorable destiny.

Three

Victoria Station was noisy and smoky as trains hissed and steamed a departure or arrival. Papa gripped my arm tightly as we made our way to our train through the horde of people on the platform.

As we settled ourselves into our compartment, I noticed that Papa looked exceptionally tired. So, although anxious to talk about Michael, I remained silent as I watched him doze to the hypnotic click-clack of iron wheels against iron rails. I indulged in fanciful daydreaming, occasionally brought back to reality by the impressive scenery.

The big engine coughed its way into Penrith Station, causing Papa to sit up abruptly, his eyes flying open in surprise.

"I must have nodded off. Sorry I wasn't much company for you, Elizabeth," Papa apologized, rising as the train came to a full stop.

"That's all right, Papa. I marveled at the scenery. And do sit down. I can manage by myself. After all, I'm a proper married lady now."

"I will see you to the platform and make sure your luggage is taken care of and that the carriage to Keswick is here. I will brook no argument, Elizabeth. Or should I say 'Lady Tyrone'?" He winked and grinned at me.

After making sure the luggage was safely secured to the coach that would take me to the hotel in Keswick, Papa kissed my cheek and looked at me with a grim expression. "You will write often, won't you Elizabeth?"

"Of course, Papa." I smiled and returned his farewell kiss.

"Are you happy, Elizabeth?"

"More than I thought possible."

He took a deep breath, then smiled. "Then I've done right. Take care of yourself, Elizabeth."

"Yes, Papa. And thank you."

"For what?"

"Michael."

"Good-bye, Liza," Papa said, then swiftly disappeared back into the train as the whistle blasted deafeningly.

I waved, tears welling in my eyes. Papa hadn't called me "Liza" since I was a little girl. Sadly, I climbed into the coach, then observed the countryside as we drove to the hotel in Keswick.

Michael had been thorough. A light tea was waiting for me at the hotel and a trap stood outside, ready to take me to the cottage after I had refreshed myself. It was a welcome respite after the long train ride.

Dust swirled from the wheels of the trap as it briskly rolled and bounced its way over the earthen lane. The sweet, fresh aromas of the country filled my lungs, and my eyes widened appreciatively at nature's fine greenery. I smiled absently at the beauty around me. London had its points and could stimulate the brain to heights unknown. But here, in this pastoral setting, I felt a new awareness of life, a completion of myself as a person. All I needed was Michael to bring that awareness to fruition.

I gazed eagerly as the driver brought the trap to a halt in front of a long, two-story, lime-washed, slate-roofed house. Stout chimneys, plastered and protected by slate ridges, stood gallantly at either end of the white cottage. A profusion of colorful flowers danced in carefree abandon around its base, lending it a fairy-tale quality. I instantly fell in love with the place. It exuded a homey warmth and friendliness I had never seen in London. As the driver helped me down from the trap, I wondered if Dunwick would have the same effect on me.

As I walked along the irregular, stone-slabbed path to the cottage, the sturdy door was opened by a large, robust woman who appeared to be in her late fifties. She curtsied only slightly as I approached, her corpulence preventing her from completing a full curtsy.

"Welcome to Amble Cottage, Lady Tyrone," she said, her open friendliness falling on me like a welcome spring rain. "I'm Mrs. Rydal, and I'll be keeping house during your stay here." She looked past me to the trap where the driver was unloading my baggage. "And Lord Tyrone, my lady?"

"Lord Tyrone was called away on urgent business in Ireland. He'll be arriving in a few days," I explained.

"I see," she said with a bright smile. "Dear me . . . here I am, standing and chatting away when you must be exhausted from your journey. I have a pot of tea on the stove and, after tea, I expect you'll be wanting a bit of a rest. I didn't prepare anything fancy for dinner as I didn't know the precise time you'd be arriving." She stepped to one side and waited for me to precede her into the cottage.

Even though I'd already had a light tea at the hotel, my throat was dust-dry from the ride in the trap. Another cup would be most welcome.

The interior of the cottage was not very bright due to an overabundance of dark wood paneling and the dark beams that braced the white ceiling. But the open casement windows coaxed clean, cooling breezes into the room. With the thick, humid air of summer beginning to make its presence known in London, this was a delight to my senses as Mrs. Rydal ushered me into the small, yet cozy, parlor. I removed my hat and gloves, placing them on a marble-topped table near the parlor's entry door, then sat on the horsehair divan, which was altogether more comfortable than sitting on a train, coach, or trap.

As Mrs. Rydal hurried away to the kitchen, I heard the trap driver struggle up the narrow wooden stairs with my baggage. I smiled to myself and wondered how the wiry man would have reacted had all the trunks and crates been shipped here instead of to Dunwick. Dunwick . . . How I wished Michael would have let me go with him. I did so want to see the place that would be my new home.

"Here we go, Lady Tyrone." Mrs. Rydal placed the tea things on the low table in front of the divan, then left the parlor once again.

I poured my tea, stirred in cream and sugar, then took a closer look at my surroundings. On entering the house, I had seen only one other principal room on the ground floor, the dining room, which was separated from the sitting parlor by the entryway and staircase. On the parlor side, a fireplace was recessed into the highly polished dark wood wall which was ornately carved and fitted with a bookcase above built-in cupboards. The friendliness of the room seemed to pervade the entire cottage.

I heard Mrs. Rydal say something to the departing trap driver as they met in the hallway. The driver departed as Mrs. Rydal lumbered up the stairs. I had leisurely finished two cups of tea before she came back down. By that time, I was most anxious to get out of my traveling clothes and into a fresh frock.

Upstairs, I found my unpacked baggage set down in a corner of one of the two bedchambers. With my traveling suit off, I decided to lie down on the invitingly soft bed for a moment or two, which ultimately turned into an hour. After washing and dressing in a more suitable frock, I went downstairs. My nostrils flared as they picked up the scent of freshly baked biscuits. With a growing appetite, I went

52

directly to the dining room.

"Ah . . . there you are, Lady Tyrone. I was just coming up to fetch you. I have your supper ready," Mrs. Rydal said, then went back into the kitchen located off the dining room.

I seated myself at the table, thinking how pleasant it would be when Michael sat across from me.

The table was graced with cold roast beef, freshly picked and cooked dandelion greens, a boiled, parslied potato — and the much anticipated hot biscuits with a bowl of fresh creamery butter. I devoured everything with zest, for I was far hungrier than I had imagined, a fact which seemed to please Mrs. Rydal.

"It warms my heart to see a young woman appreciate good, wholesome food," she remarked as she cleared the table.

"It was so delicious. I'm afraid that in the month we'll be here I shall puff up like a toad on your marvelous cooking." I laid a hand on my flat stomach and saw a smile of pride wash over her rotund face.

"Was everything satisfactory upstairs?" she asked.

"Yes."

"I've lit the lamps in the parlor. Perhaps you noticed the piano. Lord Tyrone had it shipped up from London some weeks ago, and a man from Penrith came to tune it."

"It was the first thing I noticed," I said laughingly.

The morning sun sliced through the double casement window to tease my eyes open with its undeniable warmth and glitter. I yawned and stretched lazily, then was jolted upright by the unfamiliar surroundings and the absence of Mary pulling the drapes aside. It took me a minute to realize where I was and who I'd become. Lady Tyrone. Alas! Without a Lord Tyrone.

It would have been easy to indulge in a little self-pity, but I was really too excited by the prospect of exploring the area without concern for anyone's wishes but my own. I remembered, from somewhere in my tutor's lessons, that the Lake District had been described by the poets as "the very Eden of English beauty." And I was most anxious to know that beauty, that Eden.

While I consumed an ample breakfast, Mrs. Rydal informed me that Michael had also leased two riding horses and had hired a stable boy to tend to them.

"The stable is in back of the cottage and off to one side, my lady," Mrs. Rydal said, bringing more tea. "If you like, I'll have Ned saddle a horse for you."

"That would be splendid," I exclaimed, thinking what a marvelously thoughtful man Michael was. "It's a lovely day and I do want to see the lakes."

"I think you'll find, my lady, that Derwent Water is only a short walk from the cottage. I think it is one of the prettiest lakes, even though most folks prefer Grasmere and Windermere Lakes."

"I shall see them all," I boasted. Then, on second thought, I asked, "Are they very far away?"

"No. If you stay on the main road, you shall certainly see most of them, my lady. The villages are fairly close together, so there is little chance of your getting lost, and there is always someone about to give you directions. This time of year we have a lot of visitors in the area."

"I'll go change while you have Ned saddle a horse for me."

The sun smiled down on me, the brim of my riding hat offering some respite from its glare as I kept the chestnut mare at a slow trot, my eyes drinking in the sights around me, my ears delighting in the warbling songs of the numerous thrushes. I felt a sense of freedom I had never felt in Regent's Park.

As I slowed the mare to a leisurely walk, I was lulled into distraction by the moody mountains rising in the distance like purplish-blue apparitions. Paying little attention to the sudden curve in the road, I was totally stunned when the mare reared in frenzy at the swiftly moving trap that had abruptly materialized. The high arching of the animal and my relaxed grip caused me to fall rather unceremoniously to the side of the roadway where I landed on the soft grass which the sun had not yet divested of morning dew.

With dazed eyes, I looked up to see a gentleman standing beside me, a highly distressed expression on his face. He dropped to his knees and extended a helping hand. "Are you all right, miss?"

"I believe so." I blinked my eyes to get them to focus more clearly. "Just a bit dazed, I expect."

"Do you hurt anywhere?"

I shook my head, which I shouldn't have done, for it only made it throb.

"It's all my fault. I shouldn't have been in such a hurry. Can you ever forgive me?" the well-dressed gentleman asked.

"There is nothing to forgive. I should have had better control of the horse and been watching where I was going," I answered as I started to rise.

"Here . . . let me help you." He rose and took my hands, giving me the leverage I needed to get to my feet.

As I stood brushing tufts of grass from my russet-colored riding skirt and readjusting my hat, I felt a twinge in my foot. I started toward the mare, who was patiently waiting by the side of the road, but when I went to put my full weight on my right foot it crumpled beneath me.

"Good Lord! You are hurt!" the gentleman cried, then quickly scooped me up in his arms before I sank to the ground. Despite my numerous protestations that the injury wasn't serious, he placed me on the seat of his trap and tied the mare to the rear of it. "Now miss, if you'd be so kind as to tell me where you live, I'll deliver you home and explain to your parents what happened."

His overly anxious expression and the reference to parents, as though I were a child, caused me to erupt in peals of laughter.

"I beg your pardon. Did I say something humorous?" He stared at me in wonder.

"No . . . no . . . not really," I choked out between spasms of mirth.

"Then, may I be so bold as to ask why the laughter?"

"It's nothing really. I'm staying at Amble Cottage," I replied a little more sedately.

"Where is that?"

"Stay on this road and we'll soon be there." I furtively glanced at this stranger who seemed to have a zealous need to be assured of my well-being. He seemed fairly young, and his hatless, unruly dark-brown hair framed a rather handsome face. The soft gentleness of his good looks was in sharp contrast to Michael's primitive, almost savage, handsomeness. A warm friendliness radiated from the stranger's hazel eyes, whereas Michael's dark eyes always seemed enigmatic and brooding.

"Does your foot hurt very much?"

"No. It only hurts when I put pressure on it," I replied quietly. The compassion in his voice and the concern in his eyes induced a cordial feeling in me. "You're not English, are you?"

"By birth, yes. But I've been in America for several years and I have a facility for picking up dialects," he answered.

"Oh."

"Forgive me. Let me introduce myself. I am David Cooke, twenty-eight years of age and a bachelor whose main objective is to get you home to your parents so they can get you proper medical attention." He glanced at me kindly and smiled before a dark frown creased his brow. "I just remembered. You said you were staying at Amble Cottage. Does that mean you don't live there?"

"I'm on holiday. Although I appreciate your solicitude, I don't believe I have need of a doctor."

"And now I've spoiled your holiday. I am sorry. I'm

afraid your parents will not think very highly of me."

"Mr. Cooke, I am here on holiday, waiting for my husband to join me."

"You look much too young to be a married woman of any standing."

"My wedding day was the day before yesterday," I explained as he turned and looked at me with utter amazement.

"This is your honeymoon?"

I nodded.

"You're toying with me, aren't you?" His hazel eyes sparkled with merry mischief. "No man would desert his new bride and leave her to honeymoon alone. At least not a man in his right mind."

"I resent that, sir!" His words were like cold daggers piercing my heart. I didn't need a perfect stranger telling me a bride shouldn't be left alone on her wedding night, never mind intimating that Michael might have mental problems. The man's shocked look halted my tongue from hurling more furious words at him.

"I am so very sorry. Please accept my apology. I truly thought you were teasing me," he said contritely, a red wave of embarrassment creeping to his cheeks.

"My husband, Lord Michael Tyrone, had a last-minute business crisis which kept him from accompanying me. He thoughtfully and generously insisted I leave London's heat and enjoy the lakes until such time as he could join me." I wondered why I was being so defensive. This David Cooke was a total stranger to whom I owed no explanation.

"Again, Lady Tyrone, I can only offer you my humblest apology and hope my rude and unthinking words will not turn you irrevocably against me," he said imploringly.

I don't know whether it was an ingrained weakness or my youth, but I could never be angry with anyone for any length of time. And David Cooke's heartfelt contrition undermined any resolve I might have harbored to dislike the man.

"There's my cottage," I said in a tone that signified my waning hostility.

He drew the trap to a halt and dashed to my side to help me down. When he saw me wince, he immediately lifted me in his arms and carried me to the door, which opened as if by magic.

"Oh, my goodness!" Mrs. Rydal exclaimed, her eyes wide as she wiped her hands on a spotless apron. "Why, Lady Tyrone, whatever happened?" She stood aside to let David Cooke carry me into the house.

"A slight mishap," I replied, signaling him to take me into the parlor as Mrs. Rydal followed. "The divan, please."

"I'll send young Ned into Keswick for the doctor," Mrs. Rydal said as Mr. Cooke gently lowered me onto the divan.

"I don't think that will be necessary, Mrs. Rydal. I've only twisted my ankle a little. Nothing's broken."

"It's best he have a look at it, anyway. I wouldn't want Lord Tyrone accusing me of not taking care of you properly." With that, she flounced out of the room. I didn't protest any further when I realized the position Mrs. Rydal might feel she was in.

"You'd better let me take your boot off, Lady Tyrone," Mr. Cooke said, bending on one knee at my feet.

"No. I'll wait for the doctor." I wasn't about to remove either my boot or my stocking before a man who was not my husband or a doctor. Maude would probably not think a thing of it, but my shyness caused me to seek the protection of the prevailing social ethic.

"Would you mind very much if I waited until I heard the doctor's prognosis?" Mr. Cooke asked.

"Not at all," I replied, somewhat glad for the company. "Do be seated, Mr. Cooke."

"I would like to make sure your foot is as uninjured as you claim it is." He smiled as he rose, then sat in an overstuffed wing chair.

"What brings you to the Lake District, Mr. Cooke?"

"I'm a writer, Lady Tyrone."

"A novelist?" My interest was stimulated.

He laughed quietly. "I'm afraid nothing so prestigious. I write travel articles for magazines. English and American magazines. I make a fair living at it, but nothing spectacular."

"It sounds fascinating. Are you doing a piece on the Lake District?"

"Yes. For an American magazine. And I think I might sell the piece to an English one also. Do you mind if I smoke?"

"No. I have no objection."

He pulled a pipe and tobacco pouch from the pocket of his tweed jacket and proceeded to fill the pipe, tamping the tobacco into the bowl with his finger before lighting it. "Tell me, Lady Tyrone, what are your impressions of the Lake District?"

"I'm afraid I can't be of much help to you there. This morning was to be my first sojourn in the area."

"Now I do feel like a positive cad. Perhaps you'll let me rectify my careless actions by allowing me to escort you in your explorations."

"Under the circumstances, I don't think that would be possible. My husband will be arriving in a day or two."

"Until he does, I would deem it a great privilege to discover the beauty of the Lake District with a genteel lady such as yourself," he persisted.

"We'll see." I had to admit the prospect of viewing the sights with a knowledgeable companion held a great deal of appeal for me. After all, it would only be for a day. "I've heard so much about America. Could you tell me about it, Mr. Cooke?"

"Not much to tell. During the years I was there, I never got much farther than New York City."

"What's it like? How does it compare to London?" I asked eagerly.

"London has a steady, sedate quality that can't be found in the frenzied activity of New York City," he began, then went on in great detail about the burgeoning city.

Fascinated by his descriptive discourse I was almost sorry when the doctor arrived. Mr. Cooke discreetly left the room.

After a thorough examination of my bared foot, the doctor pronounced it nothing more than a slight sprain. He wrapped it tightly with a bandage and put my stocking and boot back on. He suggested I remove the bandage in the evening and soak the foot in very warm water doused with salts. He predicted that by morning my foot would be back to normal.

When the doctor left, Mr. Cooke returned to the parlor and resumed his seat. He seemed genuinely pleased to learn of the doctor's findings.

"Will the gentleman be staying for tea?" Mrs. Rydal asked from the parlor doorway.

I shifted my gaze to Mr. Cookie. "Would you care to join me for tea?" I hoped he would accept. I wanted to hear more of the American city.

"I'd be delighted," he replied.

Our tea consisted of freshly baked pork pies and warm gingerbread topped with heavy whipped cream. Afterwards, we returned to the parlor where we remained until late afternoon when Mr. Cooke took his leave.

Over the next few days the rain came down in savage sheets, precluding any thought of riding about the countryside. The odors of sodden earth and wet vegetation permeated the cottage. I occupied my time reading, playing the piano, and writing letters.

In my letters to Papa, Mrs. Berrey, and Maude, I made no mention of Michael's absence. In fact, I avoided mentioning him at all and focused my letters on enthusiastic

60

descriptions of the scenery, which I hadn't really seen. I extolled Mrs. Rydal's cooking, dwelled on the lovely cottage, praised the gentleness of the chestnut mare—anything I could think of—except Michael.

Where was he? Why hadn't I heard from him? Why wasn't he with me in the Lake District? In desperation, I wrote to him and addressed it to Dunwick, praying it would reach him.

When the weather became conducive to outdoor activity, I found I had no heart for it. Without Michael, there seemed no purpose to it. I diligently rode the mare into Keswick every day to see if any mail had arrived from Dunwick. Empty-handed and gloomy, I would often return to the cottage to learn that Mr. Cooke had paid his respects in my absence. Several times he caught me at home, but on those occasions I politely, but firmly, declined his invitation to tour the countryside with him.

After two weeks with no contact from Michael, I wasn't fit company for anyone. I was frantic with worry that something terrible had befallen my husband. Yet, reason told me that if Michael had met with some tragic fate, I would have been notified. That thought kept me sane.

With only a week and a half left on the lease of the cottage, a humiliating gloom settled on me. None of my letters had been answered. No message received from Michael. I felt utterly abandoned and knew I would have to return to my father's house in London, an unwanted bride.

As I vented my shame and frustration in a fugue by Bach, pounding the piano keys with a vengeance, the persistent Mr. Cooke once again came to call. Burdened with the thought that Michael no longer wanted me, I welcomed Mr. Cooke's offer to show me the Lake District. I would not go back to London without having accomplished something. Besides, I felt a strong need to get away from the cottage and Mrs. Rydal's sad-eyed looks. My situation was bad enough without having to bear her doleful glances of pity. She happily served Mr. Cooke tea while I changed into a more suitable frock for the venture.

"May I say you're looking quite charming this morning, Lady Tyrone." He rose eagerly from his chair as I entered the parlor. "I'm delighted you changed your mind about exploring the countryside with me."

"I expect you have seen most of it by now," I said.

"Some . . . but not all. Shall we get started? I have the trap outside."

I nodded and led the way to the waiting trap. After helping me onto the seat, Mr. Cooke climbed up beside me.

"I see your foot has healed. Was it very painful?" he asked.

"It was back to normal the next day, just as the doctor predicted. Where had you planned to go first?" I asked, feeling a twinge of excitement.

"I thought we'd go straight down to Lake Windermere first, then stop at Grasmere for some refreshment and view the Lake there—unless you had something else in mind."

"It sounds fine to me." My skirts billowed as the trap picked up speed, and I had to tie my wide-brimmed bonnet securely under my chin. Mr. Cooke once again regaled me with tales of his days in New York City. It was going to be a delightful day and I relaxed, determined to enjoy my last days in the Lake District before I had to return home and face a myriad of embarassing questions.

When we reached Lake Windermere, Mr. Cooke assisted me in getting down from the trap, then tethered the horse to a tree on the side of the road. We casually strolled down the grassy bank to the water's edge. I looked out over the splendid lake that resembled a long, lean finger slightly bent at the first joint. My eyes swept up to the distant, pale mountains which stood like silent sentinels over the fragile lake. The white canvases of a sailboat or two skimmed across the water like footless ghosts. We stood quietly for some time, absorbing the beauty before us. Then Mr.

Cooke suggested we walk along the perimeter to capture another angle from which to view the lake. After some time, we came to an exceptionally lovely spot where the grass was spread like a velvet carpet. As we sat down, Mr. Cooke took a small notebook and pencil from his pocket.

"Notes for your article?" I asked as he flipped the notebook open and began to write.

"Yes. I find it helpful to put down my first impressions of a place. They seem to flee from my mind after a day or so."

"Then you haven't been here before?"

"No."

"I would have thought that by now you'd have seen most of the district, especially the lakes."

"There were many other things to occupy my time. Also, I was sure I could eventually convince you to accompany me so that I would benefit by having two points of view. What do you think of the lake?" His voice was serene and gentle, like the reedy grasses bending in the moving air.

I gazed at the lake, watching the sun kiss the fleeting ripples as a strong wind danced over the surface. "It's not something I can put into words. Only a poet could do it justice," I finally said, then added as an afterthought, "I think that the way it nestles in the mountains has a lot to do with its beauty. But then, with the exception of the Serpentine in Hyde Park, I don't recall seeing many lakes."

When I turned away, he concentrated on his notebook, his pencil moving swiftly over the pristine pages. I felt comfortable and at peace sitting there by the lake with Mr. Cooke. He did not rouse in me the turbulence, the uncertainty that Michael did. The silence that reigned between Mr. Cooke and me was restful and undemanding. Whenever a moment of quiet fell between Michael and me, there was a sense of stormy undercurrents that bordered on some unknown terror.

The trap rolled down the lane toward Grasmere. As we

approached the village of Rydal, the woods seemed to close in on us, casting ominous shadows over the road until we turned right at Penny Rock. Suddenly, the view opened with dramatic impact. A pleasant lake, green fields, and clusters of white-limed houses lay before us. Great fells loomed ahead like resting giants cloaked in a violet haze. The lush vale of Grasmere was ringed by the serrated fells. It was breathtaking!

Mr. Cooke slowed the horse to a walk. "That's Dove Cottage on your right where William Wordsworth and his sister, Dorothy, made their first home in Grasmere. When they left in 1808, Thomas DeQuincey became it's new resident."

I looked at the white structure topped with a greenish-gray slate roof that was almost obscured by syringa, rhododendrons, jasmine, lilies, and roses amongst a riotous display of other flowers. Not only did the colorful vegetation sparkle vivaciously, but the little diamond panes of the windows twinkled invitingly as the sun's rays skittered over them. "It looks so small," I commented.

"When Wordsworth married Mary Hutchinson, a family soon followed and they outgrew the house. They moved then to another one that became known as Allan Bank, also here in Grasmere. During his most affluent days they moved to Rydal Mount where he died in 1850. Rydal Mount is a fair-sized mansion," he explained.

"You are a very learned man, Mr. Cooke." I was duly impressed by the man's knowledge of the area.

"Literature is a passion with me." He smiled gently at me. "Are you hungry?"

"Yes," I replied eagerly, suddenly realizing that I was famished.

"We're almost at Town's End. We'll stop at the Prince of Wales. The food is quite good there."

Our meal was superb. Succulent slices of ham, newly picked peas, small, whole boiled potatoes, green chard, and biscuits were followed by a rich trifle.

"I'm afraid we won't have too much time to explore Grasmere and there is really so much to see here. For today, would you care to examine the churchyard and view the graves of William and Dorothy Wordsworth?" Mr. Cooke asked as we sipped our tea.

"Could we go back and have a closer look at Dove Cottage?" I asked hopefully.

He pulled his watch from his vest and studied it. "I'm afraid not. It's thirteen miles back to Keswick and it would be best if we returned before dusk."

"You're quite right." Though disappointed, I smiled.

"Tomorrow, if I may, I would like to take you boating on the lake. Then we can explore the village at a more leisurely pace," he suggested.

"I think that would be very nice of you," I replied, trying to mask my enthusiasm.

True to his word, Mr. Cooke called for me early in the morning and I found myself once more traveling the road to Grasmere. The road was lined with stone walls encrusted with moss, while various ferns warily poked their lacy shoots from uneven crevices.

Helping me into the rented boat, Mr. Cooke said, " 'Within its mountain urn, smiling so tranquilly and set so deep . . .' "

"Why, that's quite beautiful, Mr. Cooke. I didn't know you were a poet," I said sincerely.

"I'm not." He laughed, giving the boat a push and jumping in. "I was quoting Wordsworth. It seemed apropos."

"Have you ever written any poetry?"

"I can't afford the luxury. I have to work for a living, remember?" His hazel eyes smiled as flecks of green were highlighted by the brightening sun. "Why don't you call me 'David'? 'Mr. Cooke' sounds so impersonal."

"You've been in America too long, Mr. Cooke. Their manners and social customs are not as rigid as ours. We would have to be far better acquainted than we are now for me to use your given name."

"What a pity! And a great waste of time."

"Nonetheless, it is a custom I adhere to quite rigidly."

The day slipped by as did the ensuing days, and Michael slipped from my mind with the same ease. I had Mr. Cooke to dinner several times as a gesture of my gratitude for taking me out to dine so frequently.

On the day before I was to return to London husbandless, I promised myself I would not think about it as I enjoyed the last day of sightseeing with Mr. Cooke. He warned me to wear my sturdiest walking shoes, for he was taking me to see a wondrous marvel of nature. He had been saving it for the very last so that I would have a memorable vision to keep with me on my journey away from the Lake District.

Mr. Cooke left the trap at Rothay Hotel and we proceeded on foot northward to Easedale Tarn along a wellworn path. We crossed the Easedale Beck by a footbridge and continued up the valley where I got my first glimpse of Sour Milk Ghyll. I was awestruck.

Like liquid snow, the water cascaded from a dizzying height over tiered, lichen-covered rocks. It was more than enchanting; it was bewitching.

"Oh, Mr. Cooke," I shouted in wonder over the noise of the dashing water. He smiled and nodded. Then, taking my hand, he led me up the craggy stones for a closer view. I was exhilarated by the miraculous creation of nature as a misty spray caressed my face. I stood rapt in the glory of the sight, forgetting that Mr. Cooke still clung tightly to my hand.

I felt like a child again, one who had eluded the critical eye of a parent and had discovered the true meaning of freedom. We climbed ever upward on the slippery rocks, our laughter lost in the gushing water's din.

Though I was tired from the long walk and climb, it was

a weariness that left me oddly stimulated. After a light lunch of cheese sandwiches and tea at the hotel, I asked Mr. Cooke to take me back to Amble Cottage, for I had a lot of packing to do.

On the long journey back to Keswick, we discussed the haunting beauty of the Lake District for some time until we turned down the lane that led to Amble Cottage.

"Are you staying on in Keswick, Mr. Cooke?" I asked.

"No. It's time to move on."

"Where will you go next?"

"To Wales, I think. Some magazines have expressed an interest in an article on Caernarvon," he replied, reining the horse to a stop in front of the cottage. "Well, Lady Tyrone, this has been a day I shall always remember." He took my hand in his. Then, suddenly, his eyes slid past me, and a frozen expression of uncertainty swept his face as his hand abruptly dropped mine.

Bewildered by the stunned look on his face, I turned toward the cottage to behold a gaunt Michael stonily staring at us. "Michael!" I cried, my heart swelling with happiness. He had come back! He had come back for me!

"Well, Elizabeth, I'm glad to see you have found some divertissement during my absence," he said as he strode toward the trap, his dark eyes piercing mine relentlessly. His arms reached out for me and I went into them eagerly as he lifted me out of the trap. I sank into his strong arms with a longing I didn't know was possible.

"Oh, Michael," I repeated on the verge of tears, my head tilted back so I could gaze at him.

"You must introduce me to your escort, my dear," Michael said with a tight smile.

"Mr. Cooke, my husband, Lord Tyrone. Michael, this is Mr. David Cooke." My gaze never veered from Michael as his arm circled my shoulders.

"Lord Tyrone." Mr. Cooke nodded in acknowledgment. "I have been showing Lady Tyrone the glorious scenery of the Lake District."

"For which I am deeply in your debt, Mr. Cooke." Michael's lips were still set in a stiff smile, but his eyes brooded with distrust and malice.

"Perhaps you and Lady Tyrone would do me the honor of dining with me tomorrow," Mr. Cooke said.

I looked at Mr. Cooke quizzically. He knew the lease on the cottage was up the next day and we would be leaving. Why did he ask us to dinner? Maybe he forgot about the lease, I mused.

"I'm afraid that is quite impossible, Mr. Cooke. We shall be leaving for Ireland first thing in the morning," Michael said, his arm tightening around my shoulders possessively. His white silk shirt was carelessly tucked into his tight black breeches, the latter still dust-laden from hard riding. "Good day to you, Mr. Cooke and, again, thank you for your cordiality towards my wife." Michael looked down at me. "Come, Elizabeth. You must be quite weary from touring the countryside."

He led me into the cottage before I could say good-bye and thank Mr. Cooke myself.

As we stood in the entryway, I asked, "Michael, where have you been?"

His arm dropped from my shoulder abruptly. "Really, Elizabeth. Couldn't the interrogation wait until dinner? I have just arrived after a grueling ride. I would appreciate it if your questions could wait until I've cleaned up and taken a short rest." He bent over and lightly kissed my forehead.

I stood there mute as I watched him climb the stairs. Suddenly, his words to David Cooke came back to me. "We are leaving for Ireland first thing in the morning." He was not deserting me! I was going back to Ireland with him. I did not have to go back to London in a cloud of shame. I sighed and smiled to myself. After all, Michael was here and ready to take me to my new home in Ireland. Though my wedding holiday hadn't been all I'd hoped for, there would be thousands of days at Dunwick.

Untying my bonnet, I whipped it off and gaily tossed it on a table. I slumped in a chair, closed my eyes and let imagined visions of Dunwick play in my mind, each image becoming more grandiose than the last. I must have dozed off, for the next thing I knew, Mrs. Rydal was lighting the oil lamps. When she told me she had prepared a tub for me upstairs, I was quite thankful. I felt grimy and was still in a frock with a muddied hem from all the scrambling over the rocks at Sour Milk Ghyll.

The door to the bedchamber I was using stood open with no sign of Michael inside. I looked across the hall to see the door to the other bedchamber firmly shut. I closed my door, struggled out of my clothes and donned a robe. In the lavatory, the tub still steamed and I slipped into its fragrant warmth, letting the soothing water ease the weariness from my bones. Toweling myself dry, I put the robe back on and peeked down the hall. The other door was still closed.

I prepared myself for dinner, donning a pale blue silk gown that bared my shoulders and whose material displayed hints of green which the flickering light caught at the folds. The month without Mary had taught me to become fairly adept at dressing my own hair, and tonight I coaxed the long auburn tresses into a soft plait, coiled it atop my head like a tiara, then secured it with bone hairpins. The time spent outdoors had given my face a rosy glow. I looked in the mirror and thought that even though I was no beauty, I did look healthy.

Michael was already seated in the dining room, sipping a Scotch. He rose as I entered. In his black formal attire with a white ruffled shirt, he radiated the same compelling, masculine appeal he had at my birthday ball. I wanted to rush into his arms and have him kiss me with the same desire I felt for him. But my innate shyness prevented me from displaying such forward behavior.

69

"My dear Elizabeth, you look most charming this evening," he said as he came and kissed me on the cheek, then held my chair for me.

I was bubbling with questions, but pushed them down as Mrs. Rydal served the meal. I continued to smother my curiosity as I watched Michael attack his food as though he hadn't eaten for days. Finally, he leaned back in his chair, seemingly sated.

"Michael . . ." I began.

"I know, Elizabeth. My behavior has been abominable and you have my humblest apologies for leaving you to manage by yourself for so long. Believe me, if matters hadn't been beyond my control, I would have joined you in a day or so. I hope you can understand my position, Elizabeth, and find it in your heart to forgive me."

"Oh, Michael, there's nothing to forgive. I realize you have duties that demand your immediate attention, but I wrote so many letters. You never answered or sent a message to let me know you'd be detained so long." Suddenly I saw Michael's expression darken.

"I never received any letters, Elizabeth. Are you sure they were posted correctly?"

Of course they were. I went into Keswick and posted them myself."

He reached over and patted my hand. "Perhaps they were lost. They did have to cross the Irish Sea."

"Even if you didn't receive any of my letters, why didn't you send me word of your delay?"

He rose and went to the sideboard where he poured himself another Scotch before returning to his seat. "I meant to, Elizabeth. But the days just seemed to fly away, and before I knew it, the month was over." He stared at the whiskey as he slowly twirled the glass against the table.

"Well, you're here now and I suppose that's all that matters. But it is a pity you didn't get to see the scenery here. It is breathlessly beautiful."

He took a long pull of the Scotch. "Elizabeth . . . I forbid you ever to take up or associate with perfect strangers again. Do I make myself clear?"

I was stunned. My blue eyes gleamed with bewilderment and indignation at his harsh tone. I could almost feel the latent fury behind his words. "What do you mean, Michael?"

"This David Cooke. How well do you know him?"

"I met him the first day I was here. He was very kind to me," I protested.

"I don't care how kind or thoughtful the man is. I don't want you to have anything to do with anyone I haven't approved of in advance. Do you understand me, Elizabeth?" He downed the rest of the Scotch in one swallow.

"But why, Michael?"

"Elizabeth, you must learn not to question the judgment of your husband." He pulled his watch from the black vest and glanced at it. "It is later than I thought. You must be tired and longing to go to bed. Don't let me keep you."

"I'm not the least bit tired," I declared, which wasn't quite true. All the walking and climbing had taken its toll. "I would like to stay with you and talk. We've had so little time together and I would like to hear more of Dunwick."

"There'll be plenty of time for talk, Elizabeth. We have a long journey ahead of us tomorrow and you will need all the rest you can get tonight. And, quite frankly, I have a number of papers to go over, so I think you'll find me a bit of a bore this evening."

"I could sit in the parlor and read until you're finished," I said, almost pleading.

"I'd rather you wouldn't. It would please me greatly if you went to bed and got some rest," he said with finality. His chair scraped roughly against the wooden floor as he rose.

Hurt mingled with anger as, with all the pride I could command, I rose and said goodnight. Then, with shoulders

71

straight, I walked sedately up the stairs to my bedchamber.

As I undressed, I wanted to cry but no tears would come. I had cried myself out the first several days at Amble Cottage. I was beginning to wonder who was the greater stranger to me, Mr. Cooke or my husband, Michael.

After unplaiting my hair and getting into the delicate nightwear of my wedding finery, I slipped under the downy covers and closed my eyes. But they refused to stay closed. I stared into the inky darkness, waiting to hear the tread of Michael's step on the staircase, my pulse accelerating with expectation.

I never heard him come up the stairs as drowsiness fogged my senses and sleep claimed me. Yet in the midst of that sleep, some slight sound brought me to full consciousness. I opened my eyes, blinking them to focus. There in the open doorway, with the pale amber light of a candle behind him, stood the tall, powerful physique of Michael Tyrone.

"Elizabeth . . ." he murmured.

"Yes?" was my hoarse response.

"Have I wakened you?"

"Not really."

He stepped into the room and closed the door behind him. My eyes began to adjust to the shadowy moonlight filtering through the lace curtains of the bedchamber. He came to stand by the side of my bed. Untying his robe, he let it fall to the floor. He was naked and I stared at him in wonder and curiosity while wishing there was more light in the bedchamber. He lifted the covers and slipped into the bed beside me.

"Elizabeth," he whispered just before his lips found mine.

His mouth moved over mine in a most peculiar, yet delightful way. I was so enchanted by the novelty and passion of his kiss that I was unaware he was deftly unbuttoning my nightdress, and taking it off. His fingers played over my flesh like an experienced concertmaster. When his lips left mine to trail down my neck to my breasts, all shyness and inhibitions left me. I allowed myself the luxury of trailing my fingers over the hard sinews of his body. Glorious sensations consumed me. All conscious thought was subjugated to the demands of my body. I didn't even wince when Michael and I became one for the first time. He had brought me to an ecstatic splendor I had never known existed.

The day dawned gray and misty, but all I saw was sunshine. I rolled over in bed, reaching for Michael. I sat up abruptly and frantically looking around the room for him. When he was nowhere to be seen, I dressed hurriedly, then scurried downstairs, fearful he had once again left me.

"Well, Elizabeth. I'm glad to see you up early and ready to travel." His deep voice filled the room and the sound flowed sweetly to my ears.

"Michael!" I cried, all thoughts of shyness and propriety gone. I ran to him and threw my arms around his waist. As I pressed my head to his broad chest, tears misted my eyes.

"Here . . . here . . . what's all this about?" He stroked my head for a moment, then placed his lean forefinger under my chin and tilted my head back, his ebony eyes searching mine. "Tears, Elizabeth?"

"I'm so happy, Michael."

He smiled. "I'm glad, Elizabeth. I only want your happiness. I suggest we eat a hearty breakfast. We have an arduous trip before us. But we'll soon be home. I'm sure you'll love Dunwick."

Four

I really don't know what I expected Ireland to be like. Castles of pure fantasy. People who jabbered in some incomprehensible, ancient language. Barbarians roaming the countryside in animal pelts. An antithetical land of the sublime and the ridiculous, of high culture and savagery. But as we traveled from Belfast to Dunwick, I heard no gibberish, saw no savages, only an indescribably beautiful landscape where the greenery possessed a rich, lush color I had never seen before.

As the carriage kept a stead pace on the reddish, hard-packed earth of the road, I got my first glimpse of Dunwick. Bathed in bright sunlight, it stood in defiant majesty on a verdant plain, scornfully regarding the trees and shrubbery growing in homage about it.

The regal, pale-gold Georgian mansion rose three stories high, as if in mutiny against the sky. It glinted and shimmered like a huge, square, golden box dropped and planted in the midst of green velvet. The truncated pyramid roof was half-hidden behind a parapet ornamented with a bold white cornice. Flue pipes sprouted from tall, plastered chimneys which, in turn, rose symmetrically to face each other from the line of the roof.

After leaving the main road and gliding up the pebbled

driveway, the carriage came to a halt before a white balustraded set of stone steps which opened onto a front terrace. I drew a deep breath as Michael's hand reached up to help me from the carriage, my eyes fixed on the splendor of the Georgian manor. With his hand on my elbow, we climbed the stone-carved steps to the impressive door of my new home.

As we approached, the door opened and I felt a strange sense of foreboding. My feet moved forward, though my mind didn't want to enter. If Michael hadn't had a firm grip on my elbow, I might have bolted when we entered the marble foyer whose walls displayed the armament of another era. Shields emblazoned with coats of arms, maces, and crossed, double-edged swords made the foyer look like the entrance to a medieval castle whose history was steeped in violence.

A tall, thin pike of a woman, around fifty years old, approached me, her long-sleeved, high-necked, blackish-brown dress brushing the marble floor with a challenge. Her face was small and sallow, her chin peaked, her nose thinly aquiline. Her black hair, webbed with gray, was drawn tightly against the scalp, bunned and skewered at her nape. Her skeletal hands were crossed and resting on the folds of her dark skirt. Narrow ferret eyes of an indeterminate shade of gray stared at me critically with a lingering glow of malice.

Michael addressed her. "Mrs. Meehan, I would like you to meet my wife, Lady Elizabeth." Then, looking down at me, he said, "Mrs. Meehan is the housekeeper at Dunwick, Elizabeth."

"Welcome to Dunwick, my lady." Her voice had a sharp, metallic timbre as she gave a spare, almost reluctant, curtsy. There was something about her that alarmed me, an intangible dread.

"Mrs. Meehan." I nodded in acknowledgment as a chill shuddered through me at the sound of a raucous screech.

Running down the wide, semi-circular, marble staircase located to the right of the foyer, was a petite child of about ten years old, all bubbly and excited. Shouting, "Father! Father!" she jumped down the last few steps, raced across the floor and threw herself at Michael, wrapping her arms around his waist. She had a full, oval face; sparkling, deep green eyes; a short, upturned nose; a rosebud mouth, and fiery red hair which struggled to escape from the ribbon with which it was bound at the back of her neck. Michael quickly extricated himself from her possessive grasp.

"Callie, there is someone here I want you to meet." He turned the child by her shoulders to face me. "This is Elizabeth, my wife."

I smiled my warmest, friendliest smile and bent to greet her, even though I was in a numbed state of utter shock. I recoiled in horror when the child spat at me, her brilliant green eyes full of venomous hatred.

"Callie!" Michael shouted indignantly.

"I hate her! You promised not to bring her here! And she's not beautiful like Mama. She's a witch! An evil witch! Take her away from here, Father. Take the evil witch away!" cried the child in a high, shrill voice.

Michael quickly grabbed the child's arm, his dark eyes blazing angrily. "Callie, you apologize to Elizabeth this minute!"

"I won't! I won't!" She struggled futilely in her father's grasp, stomping her feet and shaking her head.

"Apologize at once!" Michael roared.

Callie stiffened, her eyes becoming green slits as she defiantly looked up at Michael. "I hate you and there is nothing you can do to make me apologize. And if you don't get rid of her, I will."

I saw Michael's grip loosen and a strange aloofness settle over his face. "Apologize, Callie." His voice was calm, low and menacing as the tension in the foyer mounted.

A peculiar smile widened those rosebud lips, but the

child's eyes remained hard. "I would like to go to my room, Father."

Michael's hand dropped and the young girl walked to the foot of the stairs where she turned, fixing me with those chilling green eyes. "You won't last long at Dunwick. The banshee will see to that." She turned and began to tramp up the stairs.

"Mrs. Meehan," Michael said authoritatively.

The gaunt woman nodded and left to follow the child. I could have sworn I detected a smug smile on those thin, pallid lips as she passed by me. Bewildered, I watched the woman and child ascend the staircase, my attention diverted by a frail-looking young woman who flattened herself against the wall as Mrs. Meehan and the child brushed by her on their climb to the top. My eyes frantically shifted from Mrs. Meehan to Michael, then to the young woman on the stairs before returning to gaze at Michael with glazed eyes. Michael . . . my husband . . . Michael . . . the father of a child about whom I had no prior knowledge. I stood there mute, the blood draining from my face. I felt like a player in a drama who had absolutely no idea of what the play was all about. Even when Michael took my hand between the two of his, I still felt as though I was a disembodied specter in some ghoulish nightmare.

"Elizabeth."

I heard my named called in a vacuum, an echo in a chamber where reality was fast slipping away. I couldn't speak.

"Elizabeth," Michael repeated. "I deeply regret Callie's behavior. Please don't let this incident force you into disliking Dunwick out of hand."

"Michael . . . a daughter?" My voice was alien to me as I looked at Michael, numbed by the knowledge and not noticing the young woman as she approached.

"I should have told you, Elizabeth. But with one thing and another, it slipped my mind," Michael replied.

"How could a daughter slip your mind?" I couldn't believe what was happening. I didn't even know what questions to ask or how to ask them. There was a whirring in my brain that precluded reason.

"It's a long story, Elizabeth. One which is best told after you've had a rest." He stared at me stonily before his attention was diverted by the young woman who had come to stand beside him. He dutifully kissed her on the cheek. "Ah . . . Rose. This is Elizabeth." Then to me, he said, "Elizabeth, this is my sister, Rose Kathleen Tyrone."

"Elizabeth . . . how nice to meet you at last." She embraced me, putting her cheek against mine and kissing the air next to it. "We've heard so much about you. I'm so glad Michael brought you home at last."

There was a defeated weariness about Rose Tyrone that wrung my heart. As she stepped back, I looked at her pale oval face, her lifeless amber eyes, her black, lackluster hair drawn into a severe bun at the back of her head. She was as tall as I, but her frailty made her appear smaller. Though she smiled warmly at me, there was a void in her eyes that made me wonder if she saw me at all.

"I'm very happy to meet you, Rose. Michael didn't tell me he had so young a sister," I said, returning her smile haltingly. Evidently, Michael hadn't told me anything.

"I'm twenty-five and no longer feel all that young," she replied with an air of melancholia. "But you must be exhausted. Why don't I show you to your room and help you get adjusted to your new surroundings?"

I quickly turned to Michael, my eyes burning with questions. His fine, strong hand rose to cradle my cheek gently.

"Do as Rose says," he said quietly, but with a distinct note of command in his voice.

Rose slipped her arm through mine and led me to the wide staircase. "I'm sorry we didn't get to the wedding, but my health wouldn't permit a trip across the Irish Sea and Uncle Jack had to remain here in Michael's absence. You must tell me all about it . . . every detail."

"Uncle Jack?" I queried as my comprehension grew murkier. I had indeed married a total stranger and was now thrust into a completely foreign household. Suddenly, I wanted to go home to London, to Papa, to Mrs. Berrey, to familiar faces and well-loved surroundings.

"Apparently, Michael has told you nothing of his family or Dunwick. Well, I'm not surprised. Isabel's death left him a quiet, brooding man, and Callie offers little in the way of consolation. By the way, I do apologize for Callie's behavior. She was perfectly horrid to you. But she's like that with strangers and, more often than not, with everyone in the house except Mrs. Meehan, of course. I'm afraid Mrs. Meehan is the only one who has any control over the child," Rose explained as we reached the landing and started down a twisting corridor.

"Isabel?"

"I am rattling on, aren't I? Isabel was Michael's first wife and Callie's mother. She died some time ago. I wouldn't advise questioning Michael about her. He doesn't like the topic brought up in his presence. And Uncle Jack is our mother's brother. You'll meet him at dinner tonight."

"Will your mother be there too?"

"No. She passed away five years ago."

"Oh, I am sorry."

"Here we are." Rose opened an ornate door and we stepped inside.

The room was pale green with gold leaf enhancing the elaborately carved moldings. The high-relief, plastered ceiling displayed an exquisite floral pattern in scrolls and swirls. A large, gold-veined marble fireplace was flanked by carved white panels which supported a deep mantel. The heavy drapes were of green sateen as were the trappings on the canopied four-poster bed. The rich patina of cherry-wood furniture gave a warmth to the room, as did a sumptuous Persian carpet. Running my finger over a delicate writing desk, I opened a drawer and beheld writing paper with the Tyrone crest just below my initials.

"It's beautiful, Rose," I said sincerely, although somewhat preoccupied.

"Michael's taste is exceptional for a man. He sent back specifications for the renovations shortly after he reached London. His room is adjacent to this one and connects by means of a lavatory." She waved her hand in the direction of a formidable door. "Well, I'll leave you to get some rest. If there is anything you require, pull the bell cord by the bed and one of the maids will attend to your needs."

"Thank you very much, Rose."

"I'll see you at dinner." She smiled, her hand on the knob of the open door. "By the way, dinner is at eight sharp," she added, then softly closed the door as she left.

I moved to the window to regard the vast, tree and shrub-studded lawn where the crescent driveway arched to the house. Unseeing, I stared at it, vaguely wondering if Papa had known that Michael had been married before and had a child from the marriage. But what did it matter now? What was done, was done, and it was a reality I had to face. I sighed and began to remove my traveling clothes. The month I had spent at Amble Cottage had imbued me with a certain amount of independence in doing for myself. I found I enjoyed the privacy as I wearily lay atop the wide bed needing a moment of physical and mental rest.

The tapping on the bedchamber door roused me slowly as it became more persistent. "Milady," a voice kept repeating.

"Come in," I called, struggling to prompt my senses from the effects of a deep sleep and to sit up. A young girl in her early teens entered and curtsied at the side of the bed. A white maid's cap sat precariously atop her unruly red curls.

"I came to see if I could assist you in dressing for dinner tonight," she said.

I stood and stretched my taut muscles. I really didn't need any help, but she had such an anxious-to-please look that I said, "You could lay out fresh clothes while I bathe."

"Yes, milady." She bobbed.

"What is your name?" I asked with a sleepy smile.

"Clara, milady. Clara McDoughall."

"Well, Clara, have my trunks arrived from London?"

"Yes, milady. Some time ago. Everything has been aired and properly put away."

"I think there was a gold-colored gown in one of the trunks. Did you happen to notice it, Clara?"

"Yes, milady. A beautiful golden gown with a full, billowy skirt and gold braid scalloping the hem." Her pale blue eyes shone as she recalled it.

"I think I'll wear that to dinner, Clara."

"Milady . . . if I'm not being too bold . . . I . . . well . . ." She hesitated, her face flushing with embarrassment.

"Yes, Clara, what is it?" I asked with a kindly smile. She looked as though she were afraid of me and I wanted to put her at her ease. I had the feeling I was going to need all the friends I could gather here at Dunwick.

"Well . . . I wouldn't leave my door unlocked if I were you, milady."

"Why not?"

"The banshee, milady, the banshee," she answered with an expression of genuine horror.

Mrs. Berrey had warned me of the Irish proclivity for fairies, leprechauns, banshees, and the like. She had told me to be indulgent, but not to take their dark manifestations of Celtic lore seriously.

"I don't think a locked door would stop banshees if they wanted to get in," I replied lightly.

Clara looked thoughtful for a moment, as if my words held a truth she hadn't thought of. Then, before laying out my evening wear, she went about picking up the travel clothes I had shed earlier.

Bathed, dressed, and putting the finishing touches to my hair at the ornate dressing table where some of my personal effects had been neatly laid out, I began to regret my dismissal of Clara as I struggled with the clasp of my heavy gold locket. Suddenly, I was jolted in my seat when warm fingers touched mine at my nape. I raised my head to look in the mirror. All I could see was the well-clad torso of Michael, whose broad shoulders were unmistakable.

"Let me help you, Elizabeth," he said, quickly securing the clasp, then laying his warm hands on my bare shoulders as he bent down to meet my gaze in the mirror.

"I didn't hear you come in, Michael," I said.

"The doors at Dunwick are kept well oiled, my dear. You look very lovely tonight, Elizabeth." His dark head dipped, and his lips sought and settled in the curve of my neck.

I closed my eyes as waves of a new delight rushed through me. My breath came faster, my heart pumped wildly, and when Michael's fingers dug into my shoulders, I felt nothing but his kiss searing its indelible mark on my neck. I crumpled inside when he stepped back.

"Shall we go down to dinner? Uncle Jack is most anxious to meet you." His voice was flat and toneless as I stood to face him, his countenance a marble mask of indifference, while I seethed with emotion.

As we entered the large, glittering dining room, I was relieved to see that Callie wasn't present. I had enough adjustments to make without having to deal with a child who obviously hated the sight of me. Rose, and a man I assumed to be Uncle Jack, were already seated. The portly man, whom I judged to be about sixty, rose from the table and came to greet us.

"So this is Elizabeth." He beamed, his florid face cherubic as merry dark eyes scanned my face. His stubby hands grasped mine and held them firmly. "You do have an eye for women, Michael. However did you persuade this lovely creature to marry the likes of you?" He kissed me soundly on both cheeks.

"As you've probably gathered, Elizabeth, this is Uncle Jack," Michael said with a doting fondness in his voice.

"Jack Donahue, at your service, my dear." He took my arm from Michael and led me to my place at the table, then held my chair. He quickly resumed his seat next to Rose who sat across from me. Naturally, Michael sat at the head of the table.

"Well, Michael, did you enjoy the Lake District in England?" Uncle Jack asked as one of the maids began to serve dinner.

"As they say, a poet's paradise," Michael replied, avoiding the deep questions in my eyes.

"Only those poets who haven't seen Ireland," retorted Uncle Jack. Then, with a wink at me, he asked, "Did you find it a paradise, Elizabeth?"

"Uncle Jack!" Rose cried, her pallid complexion trying to blush.

"Oh, Rose, I'm only sporting," Uncle Jack said with a devilish twinkle in his eyes.

I saw Uncle Jack as a basically merry man enjoying life to the fullest, the sort of man one took to on first meeting. He was tall, but not quite as tall as Michael. His body was heavy but compact, the kind of build that would soon turn to fat if it were left to idleness and inactivity. His face beamed friendliness and joviality, with ingenuous fawn-colored eyes deepened by bushy salt-and-pepper eyebrows that matched his full head of hair. His slightly bulbous nose and wide, full lips, strengthened by a firm, square jaw similar to Michael's, gave him an aura that was captivating.

"Seriously, Elizabeth, what was the Lake District like?" Rose asked.

I did my best to describe the scenery in the most glowing phrases I could think of, then concluded by saying, "Michael could probably do more justice to it than I." I looked directly at Michael with a dare in my eyes.

"Elizabeth has covered it quite nicely," he said, steadily returning my gaze and defying my challenge.

"Well, Elizabeth, wait until I show you Ireland. It will annihilate all thoughts of the Lake District or any other place for that matter," Uncle Jack said.

"I'll look forward to it," I replied.

When dinner was concluded, Michael suggested we take tea in the drawing room. I walked with Rose through the foyer with Michael and Uncle Jack behind us. The door was open and I found myself in a spacious room with an assortment of settees, Queen Anne and Louis XIV chairs, with occasional tables interspersed throughout the vast room. But the two dominant features were the massive marble fireplace over which hung a great, gilt-framed mirror, and at the far end of the room, in front of floor-to-ceiling windows, an impressive grand piano. My fingers longed to roam over the keyboard, but I sedately followed Rose and joined her on one of the settees before which was a low table with handsomely carved legs and a silver tea service. Michael slumped in a well-padded chair, his long legs stretched out before him, while Uncle Jack went to the sideboard and poured two glasses of Scotch. Returning, he handed one to Michael, then took a chair opposite him. They were soon lost in a discussion of crops and weather.

As Rose poured our tea, I endeavored to answer her many questions about London. We talked at great length about the theater, museums, and fashions. As the evening wore on, Rose was visibly and rapidly tiring. Relief flooded her face when I rose and announced my intention to retire, tossing a questioning look at Michael.

"You go ahead, Elizabeth. Uncle Jack and I haven't finished our discussion. I'll be up later," Michael said. He left his chair to plant a brotherly kiss on my cheek.

I walked up the stairs with Rose still talking of London as we reached the door to my bedchamber.

"I would like to show you through the house tomorrow, Elizabeth, that is, if you want me to," Rose said, a tremor in her voice, as if any rejection of the offer would send her into uncontrollable weeping.

"I'd like that very much, Rose."

"Right after breakfast, then," she said, brightening.

I smiled and nodded in agreement, then went in and closed the door. I pulled the bell cord, for the tiny hooks down the back of my gown were beyond the reach of my fingers. Clara came swiftly and, with her aid, I was ready to retire.

Before getting into the neatly turned down bed, I walked to the window and pulled the drapes aside to watch the waning moon race between darkened clouds, searching the night sky for an unknown companion to ease its lonely existence.

I turned from the window to stare at the closed door to Michael's bedchamber. I don't know how long I stood there, but even after climbing into bed, my eyes remained focused on the door, waiting for it to open as my mind recalled the tender and provocative kiss Michael had placed on my neck earlier in the evening.

After so exhausting a day, sleep blanketed me, but I thought I heard strange, maniacal screams emanating from a distant part of the house. The eerie sound merged with vague, tenuous dreams of a tall, dark man who stood close to me, but kept drifting away in murky, vaporous clouds.

As I descended the marble staircase to the foyer, the house seemed inordinately quiet for the morning hours. Entering the dining room, I found Uncle Jack reading a newspaper. He was the only one present.

"Good morning, Uncle Jack." Though disappointed by Michael's absence, I managed a smile.

"Good morning, my dear. I've been waiting for you." Uncle Jack folded his newspaper, laid it on one side, then joined me at the sideboard where we proceeded to fill our plates from a selection of porridge, fried eggs, sausages, rashers of thick-cut bacon, fried potatoes, and grilled tomatoes. A platter of crisp fried bread sprinkled with salt and pepper was already on the table along with pots of coffee and tea. Uncle Jack kept increasing the portions I had placed on my plate.

"I'll never be able to eat all this," I cried as I took my seat at the table.

"Keep washing it down with tea or coffee, my dear, and before you know it, the plate will be empty," Uncle Jack suggested as he sat down across from me.

"Where is Michael?" I asked, pouring tea into my cup.

"You'll find Michael is an incurable early riser. He left over an hour ago to inspect the estate, which is so vast he sometimes doesn't return for several days." Uncle Jack sliced through a plump, juicy sausage.

"And Rose?"

"I'm afraid the excitement of your arrival has exhausted her and she requested a breakfast tray be sent to her room. Ha! Breakfast! I'd hardly call a piece of dry toast and tea a breakfast. Even a hummingbird couldn't exist on that."

"I'm truly sorry. If I had known Rose was ill, I wouldn't have talked so long last night," I said. "What is the nature of her malady?"

"No one seems to know, at least not the doctors. I suspect the ailment is more in her mind than her body. The more she gives in to it, the weaker she becomes. But don't let it worry you, my dear. More often than not, Rose has a breakfast tray brought up to her."

"Doesn't Callie have breakfast with the family?"

"Callie is no longer allowed in the dining room. Her tantrums discouraged one's appetite, to say the least. And, after several episodes of throwing food-laden plates around the room, one of which destroyed a priceless Ming vase, it was decided she should have her meals in her rooms upstairs with Mrs. Meehan, much to everyone's relief, not to mention good digestion. I fear you'll have to make do with only my company at breakfast for the most part," Uncle Jack said with a hint of joviality.

"I couldn't wish for better company."

"Michael has told us a good deal about you, Elizabeth, when he dashed over for a couple of days from your holiday to straighten out a particularly unsavory matter with Callie. I understand you are the only child of one of the wealthiest men in London."

"Yes, I am. I suppose my father does have a good deal of money." A couple of days! Michael had been gone for a whole month! Why hadn't he returned to Amble Cottage immediately after clearing up the matter with Callie? Where had he gone? And what had Callie done to warrant Michael's personal attention? The questions were becoming more and more complex and the answers more elusive. Perhaps when I knew everyone better, I could be more forthright in making inquiries. Until then, I would wait and listen.

"It was quite a surprise to all of us when Michael went to London on what was to be a short business trip, then stayed on. He sent a message stating he was not returning to Dunwick until he had made you his bride. Love at first sight, I suspect." He chuckled and winked at me. "Anyway, knowing Michael to be a very stubborn, determined man, we knew there would be a new Lady Tyrone gracing Dunwick. Nothing had better stand in Michael's way when he decides he wants something, for he invariably gets it. Well . . . what do you think of Dunwick, Elizabeth?"

"I haven't really seen it yet."

"Of course, how stupid of me! Once you get your bearings and feel settled, I'll take you on a tour of our northern coast. Michael tells me you are an excellent horsewoman. It'll be a joy to have someone to ride with. The coast is most spectacular and there is no place more beautiful or fascinating than Ireland. And I'm going to do my best to convince you of that fact, my dear," Uncle Jack said. "Well . . . now . . . that's what I like to see, a lass who eats a real breakfast."

I looked down at my plate to find it empty. It astonished me that I had eaten all that food. I would have to be more circumspect in the future, or I would become enormous.

"Good morning, Uncle Jack. Good morning, Elizabeth. Have you finished your breakfast yet?" Rose asked timidly as she entered the dining room. "If not, I can wait."

I turned to look at her. Her day frock was drab as was everything about her. Some bright colors would do wonders for her, I thought, then smiled. "Good morning, Rose. Yes, I'm quite finished. In fact, I doubt if I'll be able to eat another thing for the rest of the week." As I left my chair, I glanced at Uncle Jack. "Excuse me."

"Of course, my dear," he replied. "Go along with you. And, Elizabeth . . ."

"Yes?"

"Wait until you taste the smoked salmon at dinner tonight." He winked, and my stomach lurched at the thought of food.

"Do you mind if we start with the upstairs and work our way down?" Rose asked like a frightened rabbit. "I do so want you to see my room."

"Whatever you wish, Rose. Are you sure you're not too tired? We did stay up rather late last night."

"You know, I feel quite energetic this morning. I even had a poached egg with my breakfast," she exclaimed, an ever so slight sparkle in her eyes.

When she opened the door to her bedchamber, my first impression was one of being bathed in a rosy mist. The walls were pale pink as was the marble fireplace. The drapes and bed trappings were of deep-red velvet, a hue which was echoed in the scrolls and floral designs of the predominantly pink Aubusson carpet.

"What do you think of it, Elizabeth?" she asked with

pride.

"It's lovely, Rose. So warm and inviting."

"Michael isn't fond of it. Too much pink and red for him. But I feel quite comfortable here."

"Then that's all that counts," I said, noticing how the room lent color to her otherwise pallid complexion.

"Now that you know where my bedchamber is, I hope you won't hesitate to visit me whenever you wish. I do so want us to be sisters."

She had such a doleful expression on her face I couldn't help but put my arms around her and hug her warmly. "Of course we shall be sisters. Legally, we are."

Arm in arm, we went through a myriad of bedchambers and sitting parlors until we came to the far wing of Dunwick Manor.

Rose stood before massive, solid mahogany doors that were closed. She glanced around the corridor furtively before placing her hands on the knobs. "If Mrs. Meehan were around, I wouldn't dream of showing you this section of the house. But she has taken Callie to the Talbots' for the child to select a new pony. They'll be gone a few hours. That is why I wanted to show you the upstairs first." Her hands turned the knobs and swung the two doors open to reveal a dark corridor that led to a completely separate part of the house. "These are Mrs. Meehan's and Callie's apartments. They have their own private rooms and staircase leading downstairs and to the kitchen," Rose explained further.

"Perhaps it would be best if we didn't go through those rooms." I felt like an intruder in a world I didn't want to know anything about.

"Nonsense. You are the mistress of this house and have every right to see all of it," Rose said with a firmness that startled me. "This used to be my brother's and Isabel's wing. When she died, Michael moved to the other side of the house where you are now. At the time, Callie insisted on moving into her father's room. At first Michael was against it, but Callie became hysterical, so Michael relented and had Mrs. Meehan move in with Callie, making the whole wing a private apartment for them."

"Does Callie always get her ways?" I asked.

"Always. This is Callie's room."

She turned the knob and led the way into a most peculiar room for a ten-year-old girl. It was uncommonly neat, almost sterile. No toys or clothes scattered about. It was totally lacking in youthful exuberance. It was like all the other vacant bedchambers, lacking that human, lived-in quality, bereft of warmth and life. Pity for the child stirred in me.

"Doesn't Callie have any toys?" I finally asked.

"Callie is a bit odd when it comes to toys."

"What do you mean?"

Rose shrugged. "It's hard to explain." She looked a bit flustered, then went to the connecting door and opened it, letting me precede her. "This was Isabel's room."

I gazed audibly in amazement. The room was done in heavy blues and greens augmented by vast amounts of gold leaf thickly applied to every cornice and molding, then spattered across the ceiling as if the sun had left rays behind in its hurry to leave. It was a large room and ornate to the point of being garish. I felt as though I would suffocate under its flamboyance.

I was ready to turn and quickly leave when, over the mantel of the fireplace, my eyes locked on a large painting of a woman whom I instinctively knew was Isabel. Her fiery red hair was piled high in curls atop her head, emphasizing her long, white, slender neck. She had the same general features as Callie, but maturity had given them an ethereal beauty that was hard to describe. There was an angelic guise to her face, but her eyes betrayed that seemingly innocent appearance. Like multifaceted emeralds, they glittered satanically with a life of their own. They held

90

me captive, hypnotizing me into a state of rigidity until Rose's voice broke the eerie spell.

"I guess you realize the portrait is of Isabel."

"Yes. I gathered as much," I replied, quickly diverting my eyes to view the rest of the room.

Toiletries were set out on the decorative dressing table as if someone would be using them at any minute. A sheer, lacy nightdress was draped across the foot of the bed, with slippers set out below as if waiting for their owner to step into them. Fresh flowers were in a vase on the table by the window. The entire room had an expectant look about it, posing eagerly for its prospective inhabitant. A chill ran through me. There was an unnatural aura to the room, a heinous cloying to the air. I had to get out of there, and turned to Rose. To my surprise, she was still standing in the doorway as if she could not bring herself to enter.

I felt more at ease when we closed the two great mahogany doors.

"If I didn't know Isabel was dead, I'd think she was still alive from the looks of that room," I remarked.

"Callie keeps it like that. She considers it her private shrine where she can be with her mother. On occasion, the servants have heard her talk to her mother for hours."

"That's not healthy for a young girl," I exclaimed.

"We know. But there seems little we can do about it, and Mrs. Meehan encourages it."

"I'm beginning to think Mrs. Meehan is at the root of the child's problems."

"Michael thought so too at one time and tried to send Mrs. Meehan away, but Callie put a stop to it."

"How?"

"Let's just say she has her way, and leave it at that."

We walked down the long, twisting corridor in silence for several moments until I said, "Isabel was certainly a beautiful woman."

"Yes. She was."

91

"Michael must have loved her a great deal," I said, hoping my voice didn't betray the sadness I felt.

"Elizabeth, please don't tell anyone I showed you those rooms," Rose pleaded.

"Why?"

"Callie would raise a storm for months, tearing the house apart, you too, I'm afraid. No one is allowed in her mother's shrine."

"Then why did you let me in there, Rose?" I asked as we began our descent down the marble staircase to the ground floor.

"I thought it was your right and that you might have wanted to see what Isabel looked like. It is the only portrait of her in the house. It was placed there the day the painting was completed and was never moved, not even after her death. Isabel loved the painting so much, she wanted it to be the first thing she saw in the morning and the last at night," Rose explained.

Reaching the entry foyer, Rose stopped before large sliding doors that stood between the entrance to the dining room on the left and the drawing room on the right. She easily slid the two doors apart to reveal a palatial room of glass and marble.

Pink travertine marble columns lined either side with floor-to-ceiling mirrors between them, giving the vast, oblong room a look of endlessness. At the far end of the room, facing us, were tall French doors, side by side, that spanned the entire wall in a great semi-circle. Our shoes clicked softly in rhythm on the mottled white-marble floor as we walked down the vast hall to the French doors. Rose opened one of them and we stepped out onto a wide, balustraded terrace whose steps stretched down to the earth below. I stood absolutely enchanted with the sight that met my eyes.

"Breathtaking, isn't it?" Rose mused wistfully.

"Oh, yes. And so beautiful!" I exclaimed, my enthusiasm

bubbling to the surface as my eyes widened at the landscape before me.

A white stone path led from the bottom step of the terrace to the edge of a large, artificial circular pool in the middle of which stood a Grecian goddess holding an up-ended urn that spouted a stream of crystal water. On either side of the path leading to the pool were colorful flower beds alternating with Greek statues and oversized urns. Dispersed over the spacious lawn, whose grass was like sheared green velvet, were hedges — conical, spiral, diamond-shaped — all trimmed with precision. I lifted my eyes, and off in the distance, half-hidden in the mist, solemn moors sat squat and foreboding.

"What are those?" I pointed toward the purplish haze.

"Those are the Sperrin Mountains. Bleak, lonely moors," Rose replied, a sadness in her eyes as though it were a description of her soul.

"Why don't we take a walk down to the pool?" I asked cheerily, wanting to chase the sorrow from her eyes.

"You go ahead, Elizabeth. I've had more than enough exercise for this morning. It's more than I've had in a long time. I think I'll tend to some needlepoint. In back of the pool there are some benches. It's quite nice."

"Will I see you later, Rose?"

"Of course, Elizabeth. By the way, when I was supervising the unpacking of your things, I noticed several boxes of books. I had them put on the shelf in the upstairs sitting parlor. Would you mind if I borrowed one sometime? I saw you had some of the newer novels."

"Feel free to take one any time you wish, Rose. Didn't you say we were sisters?"

"Thank you, Elizabeth." Rose gave me a warm hug, then disappeared back through the French doors.

As I strolled down the terraced slope, I was beginning to feel I had some friends at Dunwick, namely Rose and Uncle Jack. The white pebbles made crunching sounds beneath my feet as I walked along the path to the pool, stopping to inspect each statue, each urn, each flower bed. At the pool the water that had looked so blue from the terrace was actually crystal clear. I started on the path around the pool, which was bordered with thick hedges where bushes of fuchsia poked through here and there. Behind the hedges, lime and hawthorne trees were scattered over the grassy ground.

An eerie feeling came over me as I strolled along. A strong sensation that I was being watched. I even imagined I saw the shrubbery rustle. Once or twice I peered into the thicket but saw nothing. When I came to a small clearing, I sat down on the stone bench to contemplate the scenery around me. Looking before me, I had an excellent, unobstructed view of the pool, the terrace and the rear façade of the manor house. I sat there serenely, caught up in the beauty of my surroundings.

Without warning, a bloodcurdling scream shattered my eardrums as hands clamped down on my shoulders, fingers painfully digging into the soft flesh under my frock. My throat constricted as I sat there numb with terror for a fleeting second or two until my courage overcame the shock. As I was about to turn and face the demon, the hands left my shoulders and Callie came bounding over the bench to sit beside me.

"Scared you, didn't I?" she said with a haughty air.

"You most certainly did, young lady. Whatever possessed you to do a thing like that?" I was doing my best to be civil. I wanted to give the child a chance and refused to let the few tales I heard about her influence my opinion. I wanted to draw my own conclusions.

"Father said I should be nice to you. That was my way of being nice," she snickered, her brilliant green eyes shining demoniacally like Isabel's eyes in the portrait.

"I'm sure your father didn't have that kind of action in mind, Callie," I said calmly.

She shrugged indifferently. "When are you going back where you came from?"

"I'm not. This is my home now."

"This is not your home! Father will soon send you back. I'll make him," she declared, her eyes narrowing.

In the face of her constant irrational statements, I decided to change the subject. "Don't you go to school or have a tutor?" I smiled, trying to be pleasant.

"I have a tutor." She paused a minute, then giggled. "He can't stand me for more than a hour at a time. At least that's what he pretends. He really wants the free time to find Aunt Rose and moon over her. He's a stupid man. A stupid man." A look of pure hate filled her eyes, then left as suddenly as it came. "You're so plain-looking, I don't see why father brought you to Dunwick."

"I'm his wife and live where my husband lives," I replied patiently.

"My mother is beautiful, the most beautiful woman in the world," she stated unexpectedly. "Father still thinks so and loves her, not you. And you're being here won't change that."

"It was never my intention to change anything at Dunwick, Callie." Though I tried to remain objective, her words cut through me. It was strange that the child should talk of her mother as though she were still alive. Was Isabel alive?

"You'll never change anything at Dunwick. The banshee won't let you," she said with a frightening gleam in her eyes.

"The banshee?" At that, I had to smile broadly.

"I wouldn't laugh at the banshee if I were you. She's the harbinger of death and she'll take her revenge on you." An odd smile tugged at her rosebud lips as though the thought of harm coming to me delighted her.

"You're a big girl now, Callie. Surely you don't believe in banshees and fairies at your age," I said, trying to be rational.

"The banshee of Dunwick is real . . . very real." Her voice dropped and her face shone with an otherworldliness as she continued. "Years and years and years ago, the first Lady Tyrone of Dunwick discovered her husband was in love with a beautiful village girl. She sent her carriage to bring the girl to the castle so she could see for herself just how beautiful the girl was, for Lady Tyrone was very ugly . . ." Callie tilted her head toward me." Ugly . . . like you.

"Anyway, the girl was so beautiful that Lady Tyrone became enraged and sent the girl back alone and on foot, knowing the girl would have to make her way through the wild Sperrin Mountains. As dusk began to fall and Lady Tyrone was sure the girl would be entering the pass, she let loose her great mastiff dogs and willed them to tear the girl apart.

"They never found the girl's body and she was never seen in the village again. A month later, Lady Tyrone was found dead, her throat torn open. Everyone knew it was the village girl, who had become a banshee and was able to assume any form or being she wished. She became a great mastiff and destroyed the ugly old Lady Tyrone. She is still here to this day, destroying all the ugly Lady Tyrones. My mother is too beautiful for her to touch. But you . . . she'll gobble you up and spit you out in little pieces," Callie concluded, her voice quavering, her eyes glazed.

I couldn't contain my laughter. "Oh, Callie, who ever told you so fantastic a tale?"

Callie looked at me cold and hard, sending a chilling wave down my spine, choking all laughter from me.

"Isabel always tells the truth. She never lies and never tells fantastic tales. You'll see when the banshee comes for you." She almost hurled the words at me as her eyes sparkled in anticipation of the event.

"Well, I don't believe in banshees, and even if I did, I'm

sure your father wouldn't let one gobble me up and spit me out," I said, regaining my composure and feeling a bit of humor coming back.

It was the first time I heard Callie really laugh, a half-giggle yet devilishly throaty. "My father save you? Father wouldn't dream of saving you. He's waiting for the banshees to take you so he can have all your money. That's the only reason he brought you here. So he could watch your money." She paused, her breathing coming hard and fast, her face beginning to glow as if she had made a new discovery. "That's it! That's why he brought you here! He wants the banshees to get you."

"And who told you I had money?"

"Mrs. Meehan. She says you're rich and that's why Father married you."

I refused to let myself believe such a thing, and could only conclude that the child had been without the companionship of her peers and under the influence of Mrs. Meehan for far too long. Her mind had turned in on itself, making fairie tales a reality and reality nonexistent. I wondered if I had the strength and patience to bring the child back to a world where beauty and love existed in abundance. Or was it too late? I felt I had to try, regardless of her brutal words.

"Callie, I would like to be your friend. We could take walks together, read and play games if you like." I reached out and took her hands in mine.

"Don't you touch me! Don't you ever touch me!" she hissed, her green eyes flashing as she yanked her hands from mine as though they were scalding her. She spit at me, then raced back down the path to the terrace.

With sad confusion I watched her bright red hair bob up and down as she sped along, then saw Michael come out onto the terrace as the child bounded up the steps. She threw her arms around his waist and I could see she was talking to him hysterically. Michael drew her from him and, with his hands on her shoulders, said something which caused her to stamp her feet and shake her head violently before she dashed into the house. From the terrace, Michael scanned the area before descending the steps. I left the bench and, retracing my steps, went to meet him. We faced each other by the pool.

"Michael . . . I didn't expect you back so soon. Uncle Jack said when you inspect the estate you're usually gone for the day, if not several days," I said, my nerves still a little raw from the encounter with Callie.

"I went to have a word with the farm manager, not to make a general inspection," he said coolly. "Callie tells me you struck her several times. May I ask why?"

My jaw dropped, my eyes round with shock as I stared at Michael, totally dumbfounded.

"Well?" He gave me an imperious glance that, under different circumstances, would have caused my heart to lurch.

"Michael, you certainly don't believe me capable of striking a child, do you?" I touched his arm, wanting him to embrace me and tell me he knew I wouldn't—and couldn't—do such a thing. Instead, he stood there, unapproachable.

"I wouldn't blame you if you did. I know how Callie can push one's temper over the edge."

"But Michael, I never raised my hand to her. Never. Don't you believe me?"

"Let' say no more about it, Elizabeth. I came looking for you to see if you'd care to go riding with me after lunch. I thought you might like to have a look at the glens," he said, drawing my arm through his as he led me to the house.

The ensuing week was blissful. For the most part, our days were spent touring the glens and villages. Michael was courteous, attentive and informative as he acquainted me with the estate and general area. In the villages I detected a note of pride in his voice as he made the necessary introductions. He took me to Lough Foyle where we sailed and picnicked. In the evenings he taught me to play draughts, or I would entertain everyone by playing the piano, much to the delight of Uncle Jack and Rose.

But it was the nights, the glorious nights when Michael came to my bedchamber and made love to me. His hands moved over my flesh with an expertise that made me willing, if not eager, to be joined with him in physical bliss. My happiness knew no bounds. The words Callie flung at me in the garden that day had no meaning for me. Even the portrait of the beauteous Isabel couldn't make me doubt Michael loved me.

My letters to Papa, Mrs. Beerey, and Maude reflected the ethereal state of my emotions. At the time, there was no doubt in my mind that my joy was endless and would continue for eternity. I never dreamed that dark shadows of suspicion—and fear for my very life—would slowly gnaw away at my state of utter rapture.

Five

Ten whole days had passed since I had arrived at Dunwick and, since the encounter on the stone bench, I had not seen Callie. Even Mrs. Meehan was scarce. I had only an occasional glimpse of her, like some passing shadow. When she stopped me in the foyer as I was on my way to take breakfast, I couldn't hide my surprise. She stared at me with disdain while extending a silver salver toward me.

"I believe these are for you, Lady Tyrone. They were delivered early this morning," she said as though chipped ice coated her throat.

"Thank you, Mrs. Meehan." I took the two letters from the tray.

"I assume you are finding your stay at Dunwick acceptable, Lady Tyrone."

"Quite." I forced a smile while thinking what a peculiar way she had of phrasing her words. Like Callie, Mrs. Meehan gave me the distinct impression she didn't expect me to be at Dunwick for very long, that my presence here was not permanent. My eyes followed the woman, her back stiff, her head high as she ascended the stairs. I didn't like her condescending attitude and manner toward me. I didn't like it at all. Thoughtfully, I tapped the letters in the palm of my open hand as I continued toward the dining room.

"Good morning, my dear. I trust you slept well," Uncle Jack said as I bent to kiss his cheek.

"Yes. Very well," I answered, giving my usual reply to his usual question as I made for the sideboard.

"Letters from England?"

"Why, yes." I suddenly looked down at them. Trying to analyze Mrs. Meehan's attitude had erased their existence from my mind. One was from Papa, the other from Maude. I shoved them into the pocket of my skirt to be read later. I filled my plate with a substantial amount of food, knowing that if I didn't, Uncle Jack would vociferously object.

"I understand you and Rose are getting along famously," he commented.

"I don't see how anyone could help but get along with Rose. She is so good-natured," I replied, taking my seat at the table. My life at Dunwick was beginning to settle into a comfortable routine that somehow made me feel more at home.

"And frightfully timid," Uncle Jack added. "The poor soul totally lacks spunk. I daresay she quivers in terror when a lark sings. Ah . . . now that you are here, maybe some of your pluck and backbone will rub off on her. I heard how you stood your ground with Callie."

"What do you mean?"

"How you gave her what-for when she began to display her nastier traits."

"I take it the story that I slapped Callie has gotten around," I said testily. "Well, I hate to undo your high opinion of my mettle, but I never touched Callie. And I wouldn't dream of hitting a child."

"Somehow, I found the story hard to believe, especially from Mrs. Meehan's lips. I didn't think you would strike Callie, no matter how great the provocation. That child could tell Mrs. Meehan the Irish Sea was plum pudding and Mrs. Meehan would believe her," Uncle Jack stated.

"Well, I'm glad someone believes me."

"Tell me who doesn't, and I'll have a stomping good talk with the bounder."

"Michael," I replied.

"My dear Elizabeth, Michael will always believe you above Callie." There was a genuine solace in his warm brown eyes. "We all would."

"I hope so. By the way, where is Michael today?"

"Riding hard to the wind, I suspect. Some trouble or other with one of the tenants."

I looked down at my plate, not wanting Uncle Jack to notice the sparkle of love and physical satisfaction in my eyes. It was several minutes before I spoke again. "I haven't seen Callie about lately. Is she sick?"

"Callie is remarkable in that sense. I've never heard of her being ill. No. Her tutor has returned from Derry where he took a short holiday. Can't say that I blame him. The child is a terror and teases him unmercifully about Rose."

"Is he sweet on Rose?"

Uncle Jack shrugged. "Rose barely knows he's alive." He added thoughtfully, "A steady beau would make a different woman of her, I suspect. Maybe you can get her to be more socially inclined. Get her outside the walls of Dunwick. I'm sure you'll be a much better influence on her than Isabel."

"Didn't Rose and Isabel get along?" I blurted out, knowing I was opening doors that might have better remained shut.

"Isabel always gave the impression they did. But, with Isabel, one never quite knew the truth. She was a consummate actress and had the capability of charming anyone she desired. She had a sorcery about her that bewitched all who met her."

"Did she charm you, Uncle Jack?"

"Definitely. But I enjoy being charmed." He winked at me.

"Would you mind telling me more about Isabel?" My curiosity was plunging me headlong into dark waters where I might hear words that would be unpleasant, if not painful.

"Isabel? What can one say about her? She was an extraordinarily beautiful woman whose beauty could have a devastating effect on those about her. Rose was in complete awe of her and trusting, jumping to attendance if Isabel so much as crooked her finger. Mrs. Meehan doted on her to an unnatural extent, almost as if Isabel were some infallible goddess."

"And Michael?" I held my breath.

"Michael? Well . . . she had but to command and he obeyed."

"And Isabel, herself. Aside from her beauty, what was she like? As a person, I mean."

"Ah . . . the woman. She had a domineering personality, a mercurial temper and took particular delight in seeing others in pain, either physical or mental. She was like a player in a drama, playing all the roles herself or concentrating on one. But it was her drama. She wrote, directed and produced it. God help anyone who wanted to change the script, for then she would display just how vindictive her wrath could be. She had an enormous energy that kept her skittering about the countryside, a restlessness that kept her nervously pacing about the house if the weather was inclement. The servants constantly prayed for fair skies, for if she was confined to the house, her vexation usually fell on their heads."

"You sound as if you weren't too fond of Isabel, Uncle Jack."

"I'm always fond of lovely ladies, but that doesn't mean I trust them," he replied with a chuckle.

"How did she die?" I asked hesitantly.

"She drowned off Rathlin Island. Let me see . . . it must have been about four years ago. Yes, four years ago. A year after my sister's death and the day after Callie's sixth birthday. In fact, it will be five years when Callie is eleven."

"How tragic!" I exclaimed. "It must have upset Callie greatly to lose her mother at that tender age."

"Oddly enough, the child took the episode quite impassively. Never shed a tear. Went about as though nothing had happened. Had all of us baffled. But we were all in a state of shock and really didn't pay that much attention. Michael was beside himself with grief. He secluded himself on Rathlin Island for several weeks after the funeral, refusing to have anything to do with the outside world. It was a bad time for all. But it's over now. And you're here." He smiled at me, drained his cup, then pulled a pocket watch from his vest. He held it in an outstretched hand, regarding it through squinting eyes, then left his chair to come and kiss me on the cheek. "Well, my dear, I must be getting along. I have an appointment in Derry this morning and shall be late if I don't hurry." Then, as he reached the doorway, he said, "I haven't forgotten about our little ride to the coast."

I poured myself another cup of tea and sat at the table feeling slightly dispirited. Michael must have been deeply in love with Isabel. And there was no way I could compete with a beloved memory, especially one who had left in her daughter's image a constant reminder. No wonder Michael avoided Callie and constantly pushed her from him. She brought back memories that he couldn't bear to endure. The pressure of tears behind my eyes made me blink rapidly. I had to pull myself together and stop torturing myself by dwelling on the loving relationship between Michael and Isabel. I had to think about something else. Anything else. Then I remembered the letters from London. I quickly drained my cup, knowing I would find some divertisement in Maude's gay chatter and gossip. I went into the drawing room where I could read them in solitude. I opened Papa's first, saving Maude's as a treat.

"My dear Liza,

Do forgive your old father for being so remiss in answering your many letters. Your descriptions of the Lake District were impressive and I was glad you found it so beautiful. Am also happy that Dunwick exceeds your expectations.

I have taken care of your request which Michael passed on to me. Your monthly allowance will be deposited directly to Michael's account in Belfast. I am also transferring the trust fund of £50,000, left to you by your mother, into Michael's holdership.

I shall be leaving for Paris within the week on business for a few days. Mrs. Berrey and Mary send their regards.

Affectionately,
Your Father

What was Papa talking about? I didn't even know my mother had left me £50,000. Did Michael know? Was Callie right? Had he only married me for my money? If only I knew Michael better, I might be able to make a rational judgment. Though he was tender and attentive to me during the day and passionate at night, there seemed to be an impenetrable wall around him that prevented me from knowing him, knowing him as a man and as a human being. I could never tell what he was thinking, even though he appeared capable of reading my every thought. I couldn't think about it all now. Callie . . . Michael . . . Isabel . . . I would think about it later. Perhaps Maude's letter would erase the perplexing and troubling thoughts from my mind altogether.

"Dear, dear, dear Elizabeth, or should I address this to Lady Tyrone?

I am posting this at Dover. I'm on my way to Paris,

105

Vienna, then Venice. Imagine! Venice! The Bridge of Sighs . . . gondolas . . . those romantic Italian men. But more of that in a moment.

I've been so naughty not answering your letters, but things here have been mad. I haven't had a moment to myself. By the way, you never did give me the details of what went on in your Amble Cottage. Couldn't find the words? Or afraid the paper would burn if you wrote the words down. No mind. We'll get together soon and trade all the spicy details.

Edwina got herself into a bit of a scandal. Seems she had secretly been seeing (and you know what I mean) a certain MP from the House of Lords, and his wife found out about it. Anyway, there was quite a flurry of feathers, so Edwina flew . . . flew to the country and buried herself there. Then, to put nuts to the cake, the MP's wife ran off with an American, an actor, no less. It's been the talk of every salon in London. Of course the scandal sheets have reveled in the news, printing every new rumor no matter how silly. I should have sent you the clippings, I know, but really, Elizabeth, I have been in such a tizzy myself.

You remember Harold . . . Harold Payne-White? Well, sit down. Harold and I are married. What do you say to that? I would have asked you to the wedding, but you were in Ireland and everything happened so quickly. I'll admit I flirted with Harold quite outrageously when you left on holiday with your Lord Tyrone. The thought of your being married crushed me, and all I could think of was being a spinster left to wither on the vine, so to speak. Anyway, I had Harold teetering on the edge of losing his mind, so he proposed. I do believe he was shocked when I accepted.

So we are off for our holiday on the Continent. Mrs. Harold Payne-White! The very rich Mrs.

Harold Payne-White. I know what you are going to say, Elizabeth—my father is a rich man. But, Elizabeth, he is nowhere near as rich as the Payne-Whites. They have scads. Absolutely scads!

The boat will be here shortly and I do want to post this so you won't think I've forgotten you. I'll write again when we've returned to London if I'm not too exhausted. You know how men are! Don't expect any letters from the continent. I'll be much too busy taking care of Harold's needs, if you know what I mean, and I'm sure you do.

Lovingly,
Maude"

So Maude was now Mrs. Harold Payne-White, I thought to myself with a certain amount of amusement. I could picture Maude at her conquettish best in luring Harold into her web. My mind and heart went back to London and to what now seemed to be my childhood. I was lost in this reverie when a gentle voice dispersed it.

"Elizabeth?"

I turned to see Rose poised to take flight like a deer who had heard the ominous snap of a twig in the forest.

"Yes, Rose."

"Am I disturbing you? I can come back later if you wish."

"Oh, no, Rose. I was only reading some letters I had received from London and I'm quite finished," I replied.

"I was wondering if you'd care to take a walk with me. The weather is so lovely. But you don't have to if you don't want to." Her voice was tight, anxious.

"I'd be delighted, Rose. A good walk will do me a world of good after the breakfast I had." I smiled and took her arm.

"I do hope the news from London was cheery," Rose said as we made our way to the terrace.

"It was. In fact, my best friend, Maude Archer, has married and is on her way to the Continent for a holiday."

"How lovely!" Again that faraway look came into her fawnlike eyes. "I've never been to the Continent. Have you, Elizabeth?"

"Once. My father took me to Paris when I was quite young," I replied as we stepped onto the terrace. The crisp morning air was exhilarating.

"What was it like?"

"I was so young my memories of it are rather vague. Notre Dame, museums . . . so many buildings that, after a while, they all merged as one. My most vivid memories are of the crusty bread and buttery croissants. And how everything had a sauce of some kind on it. I used to scrape the sauce off to see what was underneath. Some of it wasn't all that tempting."

Rose looked at me and smiled. It was the first time I had seen a broad smile on her face. It gave her a whole new countenance, one that was quite pretty.

"Is your friend, Maude, going to Paris?"

"To Paris, Vienna, then Venice."

"Maybe she'll write and tell you all about those places or better yet, send picture cards."

"From what she said in her letter, I doubt it." I withdrew my arm from Rose's and dug in my pocket for the letter as we strolled down the steps to the pool. "Let me read it to you."

"Oh, no. I wouldn't want to pry into your private affairs," she protested.

"Sisters, remember?"

I read Maude's letter to Rose, trying to give visual and character sketches of the people involved and leaving out any references to Michael and me. I could see Rose was thrilled to be taken into my confidence and I enjoyed having someone to share my life with, for it seemed Michael was going to be occupied elsewhere, more and more, claiming he had been too neglectful of the Dunwick estate of late.

"Your friend sounds like a very enthusiastic person," Rose commented.

"She is. No one enjoys a party more than Maude."

"By the way, I've started reading one of the books from your sitting parlor upstairs. George Eliot's *Silas Marner*. It's wonderful and I find it hard to put down," Rose said with relish.

"She has a newer one out. I believe it's called *Romola*. I haven't read it yet."

"She? I thought George Eliot was a man."

"A lot of women writers use men's names," I said.

"I didn't know that. Oh, well, I'm trying to read it slowly so I won't run out of books to read."

I shrugged. "If we run out, we'll go to Derry or Belfast and buy more."

"I don't think Michael would approve, Elizabeth."

"Why wouldn't he?" Her comment startled me. What difference would it make to Michael if I made some purchases? After all, I still had my allowance from Papa, even though it was to be placed in Michael's account.

"Michael is a very frugal man. I don't think he'd consider buying a lot of books a justified expenditure."

"I never thought of Michael as being parsimonious. Why, in London, he spent money quite lavishly," I said, a little stunned by her statement.

"In London, he was wooing you. Here at Dunwick, I think you'll find things a little different."

I sighed. "I know so little about Michael, Rose. I do wish you'd help me to understand him."

Rose stood still and turned to face me, her eyes hazy as she put her hand on my arm. "I'm deeply moved by your trust in me, Elizabeth. No one has ever asked me to help them with their problems before. I appreciate your confidence in me. You're not at all like Isabel."

"Uncle Jack told me a little about Isabel this morning and her tragic death followed by Michael's seclusion on Rathlin Island."

"It was a blow to all of us. Of course, Michael took it much harder than the rest of us," began Rose, slipping her arm through mine once again. "Isabel was an overpowering woman, both in beauty and personality. I would have given anything to look like her. She was everything I wanted to be but wasn't, and I worshipped her blindly. She was charming, witty and totally at ease with people, men and women, but especially men. She could talk to them in such a manner they would stumble over themselves just to be near her. And there were the parties and the balls. The house was always full of merry people. But I never knew what to say to the young men who visited. I'd blush and stammer something ridiculous until I had to leave the room or die of shame. There was only one man I ever felt at ease with."

"Oh? Who was that?" I asked.

"When I was seventeen, a young man started calling on me here at Dunwick. He came for a number of years and I was sure he was going to ask for my hand in marriage. I was so happy and floated on air whenever he was near." That same glassy stare came into her eyes again, as if she had transported herself to another place and time.

"What happened?"

"I don't know. Suddenly he stopped coming. He seemed to have vanished off the face of the earth and I never saw him again." She fell silent as we walked step in step, her eyes downcast as though she were counting the pebbles on the path.

"I'm sorry, Rose."

"It was a long time ago, Elizabeth." She made a valiant stab at a smile but it never fully formed. She sighed deeply. "My, I am rambling on. Gracious! I haven't talked this much in years. I'm so glad you came to Dunwick, Elizabeth."

"So am I. Now tell me about Michael. What was he like as a child?"

"I'm afraid there is not much I can tell you. Michael is almost ten years older than I. He was away at school when I was born. I think I was about five years old when I really became aware of him as my brother. I remember him as a dark giant who was very strong yet gentle with me. I was always in awe of him. I really saw little of him until he married Isabel. And then it seemed too late to get to know him. He belonged to Isabel and was a total stranger to me. I wish I could help you more, tell you more, but . . ." Her voice trailed off.

"That's all right, Rose. I suppose, in time, I will come to know Michael for myself." I spoke the words with spirit and confidence, not wanting Rose to know that every now and then I sensed a distance in Michael. While my desire, need, and love for him grew deeper and deeper, Michael had moments of preoccupation. There were times when his attentiveness toward me sadly waned. He no longer came to my bedchamber with a fair amount of frequency as he did in the beginning. But when he did, his ardor was as fervent as ever. I chided myself for letting doubts creep into my mind. Yet there were times when Michael seemed like a stone colossus, completely impenetrable.

On those occasions when he was distant, as though lost in a world I knew nothing of, I wanted to reach out to him, to hold him and have him tell me what was troubling him. But when he looked at me with those dark, brooding eyes, my courage failed and I wrapped myself in a cocoon of pride.

"Elizabeth . . . "

"Yes, Rose?" I dragged myself back from thoughts of Michael.

"After lunch will you play for me? I love to listen to you play the piano."

"Of course. I'd be happy to."

After a pleasant lunch on the terrace, I went into the drawing room while Rose went to her room to retrieve her needlework to keep her hands busy while I played for her.

As I was about to sit at the piano, Mrs. Meehan entered. I remained standing and asked if Uncle Jack had returned from Derry.

"No. I expect he will be gone a few days, Lady Tyrone," she replied stonily with her usual scornful smile. "I have a message for you from Lord Tyrone. He will be meeting Mr. Donahue in Derry. He said not to expect him back for a few days."

"Thank you Mrs. Meehan, but Lord Tyrone has already informed me of his plans," I fibbed. But it was worth the fib to see the look of superiority slip from Mrs. Meehan's face. I might not have been as close to Michael as I would have liked, but I was not about to let anyone else in the household know that, especially Mrs. Meehan. It took every bit of self-control I had to keep the embarrassed anger from rushing to my face. Why hadn't Michael told me himself? Why did he have to speak to me through Mrs. Meehan, of all people?

As I watched the gaunt, rigid form glide from the room, I lost the desire to play the piano. Michael was slowly becoming an enigma to me. Leaving me alone at Amble Cottage for so long, when he actually had spent only a few days at Dunwick made me wonder where he'd been the rest of the time. And now having Mrs. Meehan tell me he would be away for several days was more than curious. It was downright secretive. If he wasn't so loving when we were together, I would have had grave suspicions about him.

I decided to tell Rose I was in no mood for the piano. But the radiant smile on her face when she entered the drawing room, needlework in hand, caused me to sit at the piano

112

and launch into one of Chopin's gay mazurkas.

Michael and Uncle Jack were not gone for a few days. They were gone for a whole week. As I was coming down the staircase Michael and Uncle Jack entered the foyer. My heart leapt at the sight of Michael's rugged, handsome face, and when his dark eyes caught mine he smiled. I could no longer contain myself. I lifted my skirts, raced down the stairs, two at a time, and threw myself into his arms.

His arms closed about me like a vise and he buried his head in my shoulder. I felt a rapture consume me as I cried, "Michael . . . Michael."

"Elizabeth. You're looking well," he said warmly.

"She's looking lovely," Uncle Jack interjected, kissing my cheek. "Well, I'm for a hot tub and a change of clothes before dinner."

"An excellent idea," Michael concurred. He kissed my forehead and was bounding up the stairs before I had a chance to catch my breath and collect my thoughts.

At dinner, Michael appeared more handsome than ever and it set me to wondering why he had chosen me for his wife. He could have had any beautiful woman he wanted. My eyes kept straying to him as Uncle Jack regaled Rose and me with descriptions of his adventures in Derry.

"What did you do in Derry, Michael?" I asked when Uncle Jack decided to pay more attention to his food.

"Took care of some unfinished business," he replied casually.

"Perhaps next time you go to Derry, Rose and I can go with you," I suggested.

"We'll see."

"Things are too unsettled in Derry. The Fenians are everywhere. They've infilrated all walks of life and the *Irish People* newspaper barely hits the streets and it's gone,"

Uncle Jack remarked.

"The Fenians?" My finely arched eyebrows rose quizzically.

"About seven years ago a group of men formed what came to be know as the Fenian Society. One of them, John O'Mahony, derived the name from the Gaelic *Fiann* or *Fianna,* as in *Fianna Eirionn,* translated—the champions of Erin. They were lengendary freebooters who fought all invaders of Erin. Today, Fenians swear allegiance to an Irish Republic and vow to shed blood to free Ireland from English rule, even if it means devastating revolution. They strongly oppose parlimentary reform, demanding a total break from England. Fenianism has been sweeping through Ireland like wildfire, with men like James Stephans, one of the founders of the society, demonstrating his persuasiveness and his rare gift for organizing men. The fine, virile writing of the *Irish People* quickly disseminates the Fenian view and many people are espousing it. I have a feeling it is going to be a force to contend with," Uncle Jack said, forking more ham onto his plate. "What say you, Michael?"

"Violence never solved any problem. Archbishop Cullen of Dublin condemns the society, and most of the churchmen are following his lead. They fear Ireland will be tossed into Marxism, with Fenianism being warmly embraced by the working man," Michael replied. "Their proposed terror and violence will not only tear Ireland apart, it will tear families apart, ripping out hearts and souls."

Uncle Jack looked around the table with a taut expression on his face which slowly melted into his usual cheeriness. "Michael, my lad, here we go on about dreary politics when we are graced with the presence of two lovely young ladies."

"You're quite right, Uncle Jack." Michael turned to me. His ebony eyes, which had been so alive moments ago, were now unreadable. "Have you been keeping yourself occupied and amused during my absence?"

"Yes, Michael. Rose and I found many things we enjoy doing together."

"Elizabeth plays the piano so beautifully I could listen to her forever," Rose stated.

"Then perhaps, Elizabeth, my dear, you will honor us with a recital after dinner," Uncle Jack said.

"I'd be delighted." I brightened at the prospect of spending the evening with Michael in the room.

It was one of the most pleasant evenings I had spent at Dunwick. Michael displayed the same endearing charm he had in London, and I was elated when he accompanied me to my bedchamber. Once the door was closed behind us, he put his hands on my shoulders and smiled down at me. My skin rippled as the fine hairs on my arms quivered in expectation.

"It was a lovely evening, Elizabeth. Rose was right. You do play the piano with exquisite grace," Michael said tenderly.

"Thank you, Michael." My voice was barely a whisper as I waited for the kiss I was so sure would come. As he bent his head to mine, my eyes closed in anticipation, then flew open in disappointed surprise as his lips barely brushed my mouth. As he stepped back, my eyes searched his questioningly.

"Michael . . . " I called as his hand grasped the knob on the door to his bedchamber.

"Yes, Elizabeth?"

"I'd like to talk to you. I have so many questions I need answers to."

"Please, Elizabeth. Couldn't it wait until tomorrow? I'm really not up to any lengthy discussions tonight."

There was a slump to his shoulders, and slightly darkening circles under his eyes that spoke of extreme fatigue. I didn't have the heart to press him further. Instead, I smiled fondly at him.

"Of course it can wait. Good night, Michael . . . . "

"Good night, Elizabeth. And do try and forgive my absenses. I'm afraid they are unavoidable right now."

The bright morning sun injected its summer warmth into the green earth. I wore a sky-blue cotton frock with a lace collar and tufts of lace peeking out of the long sleeves. The material was cool, and the tiny daisies that were scattered about the cloth gave the frock a very dainty appearance. I descended the marble staircase feeling fresh and alive only to have my heart sink at the sight of Michael and Callie standing in the foyer, dressed in their riding clothes and poised to leave.

"Are you leaving, Michael?" I asked, even though my throat was dry and closing up.

"Yes. I promised Callie I'd take her riding to the village. Would you care to come with us?"

"Yes, I would. It will only take me a moment to change," I replied enthusiastically. Being with Michael mattered more to me than any breakfast.

"Nooooo," Callie screeched, stamping her foot and shaking her head violently.

"Callie! Stop this instant or you'll stay home," Michael ordered in a tightly controlled voice.

The child calmed instantly. A cold, calculating glint hardened in her eyes as a soft, sweet smile settled on her bowlike lips. "But Father, you promised this would be our day alone. You wouldn't go back on your promise, would you?"

Michael looked at the child, then at me. "Elizabeth . . . do you mind?"

"Of course not." I smiled. It wasn't the truth, but I certainly wasn't going to argue, especially in front of Callie, who already deemed me her mortal enemy. Instinct told me the child was going to do everything in her power to

116

come between Michael and me and I couldn't let myself be drawn into the trap of playing the cruel stepmother. I was sure I could win her over in time. As I watched them depart through the great main door, there was an odd burning sensation at the back of my neck as though someone's eyes were radiating heat waves. I turned to look up the staircase to the landing and caught a glimpse of Mrs. Meehan before she disappeared down the corridor. The smug smile of triumph I noted on her stern face remained in my mind as I entered the dining room.

Uncle Jack and I exchanged our customary greetings and I sat at the table, my plate replete with the usual fare.

"Couldn't help but overhear the little scene in the foyer," Uncle Jack said. "A bit of advice for what it's worth, Elizabeth. Don't let Callie get the upper hand or she'll destroy you."

"Whatever do you mean, Uncle Jack?"

"She's a possessive child, unwilling to share anything or anybody to whom she has taken a fancy. And, because of you, she now sees Michael as her singular belonging."

"But Michael is her father. It's only natural for a daughter to resent what she feels is a threat to their relationship," I said.

"You don't know Callie. She will do her best to remove you from Dunwick and I mean that literally. She is a full-grown woman, a she-devil masquerading as a child. She's not normal, Elizabeth," Uncle Jack warned with a seriousness uncommon for him.

"I grant you, she may be spoiled and thirsting for attention, but that's not unnatural in a girl of her age who doesn't see her father that often," I countered, doing my best to rationalize Callie's behavior.

"Callie has no feeling for her father. In fact, she's incapable of loving anyone, with the exception of herself and perhaps Isabel. Before you came, she would have nothing to do with Michael. Went out of her way to avoid him. Take

117

my word for it, Elizabeth, Callie isn't at all the spoiled child you think she is. Her brain is twisted and warped. She's evil, Elizabeth, evil."

I had never seen Uncle Jack look and sound so adamant and forbidding. There was a hard glint in his usually merry brown eyes. I wanted to question his accusations against Callie further, but before I could, his face lightened and he spoke.

"I think now is the time for me to show you some of the northern coast of Ireland, my girl. What do you say?"

I managed to smile. "I'd like that."

"Then as soon as you've finished your breakfast, run upstairs and get into your riding habit."

Uncle Jack cut a fine figure of a man astride the large gelding, displaying an excellent knowledge of horsemanship as we trotted northward through the countryside.

Cattle, black and brown, dotted the landscape, munching contentedly on lush grasses as we cantered down lanes and sheep walks. Mossy stone walls latticed the undulating fields, while white stone cottages sat snugly clutching the earth as the sun turned gray-thatched roofs to gold that sparkled against the verdant sod.

As we approached the coast, the thundering roll of the Atlantic Ocean filled my ears along with the strident call of the gulls. My nostrils flared as the sweet, salty air assailed them. Ahead of us, in the distance, shadowy, irregular shapes were silhouetted against the blue sky where puffs of clouds danced in profusion as though urged along by a playful breeze. I shielded my eyes from the bright sun with my hand, but still couldn't discern the strange forms on the high headland whose rocky foundation rose imperiously from the sea.

"What's that up ahead, Uncle Jack?"

"Dunluce Castle."

"Is that where we are headed?"

"Not this time, my girl. We'll explore the old castle another day. Today I thought I'd show you the Giant's Causeway. It's a little further on," he explained.

"Dunluce Castle? Do people live there?"

"When we get closer, I think you'll see that human habitation of Dunluce Castle is quite impossible. It is a ruined relic of the early thirteenth century, built by the Anglo-Normans to defend the coast from invaders."

We reined in the horses just short of the castle grounds so I could get a glimpse of the eroded bastions and towers. The castle was a formidable sight, looking as though it had grown defiantly from the cliff itself. In spite of its awesome strength, the castle was incapable of defending itself against the slow, steady invasion of moss-covered stones. Gulls soared above and dove through the structure as though the castle had become their private abode.

"It must have been very grand at one time," I commented. "It's still quite impressive."

"Yes. But there are many admirable castles in Ireland. Some truly splendid. What you shall see this morning will astound you, I'm sure." He smiled and winked at me as he urged his horse into a trot. "Shall we have a bit of a race?"

"Definitely," I replied, eager to feel the salt-laden air whip over my face and have the ground rush by as my body moved in unison with the horse.

We raced along, not really caring who was ahead until Uncle Jack held up his hand while slowing his horse to a walk. I patterned my pace to his and followed him when he left the main road to turn down a lane. As we rode along, I noticed peculiar stone formations beginning to rise on either side of us like upended petrified logs. With my eyes rounded, my head swiveling in all directions, I felt as though I were being led down an enchanted pathway to a secret land of exotic creatures.

The rocks soon scattered, opening to reveal the sea's edge

and a bizarre causeway reaching out into the turbulent waters. Uncle Jack helped me to dismount and after we tethered the horses to a jutting rock, we proceeded to walk out onto the alien causeway.

"There it is, Elizabeth — the Giant's Causeway. Isn't it all I promised it would be?" His broad smile flaunted an unchallenged confidence.

"It's incredible!" I gasped, stunned and almost speechless with the impact of the view.

The massive rock formation marched out into the sea and polygonal columns of varying heights, shining red and gold as the sun flung its rays across the uneven surface of thousands of vertical pillars which were almost perfectly hexagonal. I had never seen anything like it. It gave the impression that man had deliberately thrust the shaftlike stones into the sea's bottom, arranging them in careful order with a definite purpose in mind.

"It's incredible!" I repeated, unable to find adequate words to describe the thoughts flashing through my mind. "Are they real?"

"We're standing on them, aren't we?"

I gingerly stepped up and down on the strange colonnaded stones that defiantly paraded out into the open sea like mismatched soldiers. "Whether I'm stepping on them or not, I still find it difficult to believe. How did they come to be here?"

"Well now, it seems there are those who firmly believe it was the giant Finn MacCool. He was fairly aching to have a brawl with the Scottish giant, Finn Gall, so he pounded these rocks into the sea to reach Scotland. When he completed the span, he decided to go home and have a bit of a rest before taking on Finn Gall. When Finn Gall saw the causeway, he thought he'd have a go at MacCool first. Mrs. MacCool was sweeping a bit of dust from the house as Finn Gall came up to her and peeked in the door.

" 'Be that your husband abed, now, Mrs. MacCool?' says

Finn Gall.

" 'Nay. Sure and that's me wee babe,' she answers.

"Now Finn Gall thought to himself, if that's the wee babe—how large is the father? He ran all the way back to Scotland, that frightened he was, tearing up the causeway behind him once he'd gotten out.

"And that, they say, my dear Elizabeth, is why the causeway goes out so far and abruptly ends. Mind you now, I, myself, have other thoughts about it. I tend to believe Mother Nature was sampling our Irish whiskey a bit too heavily and ran a bit amuck here."

"Oh, Uncle Jack." I laughed and had been so fascinated by his story, I hadn't realized we had reached the tip of the causeway. I scanned the vast empty ocean before me. A purplish haze off in the east caught my attention. "Is that Scotland?" I pointed toward the vague outline.

"No, my dear. That's Rathlin Island."

I narrowed my eyes, straining to discern the island where Michael had spent his days mourning for Isabel. But it was too elusive as low scudding clouds wiped the outline from the sea.

"I don't know about you, Elizabeth, but I could use a nice pork pie and glass of stout about now."

"The pork pie sounds tempting, but I'd prefer a cup of tea instead of stout."

"Good. I know an inn not too far from here where the pork pies are made to perfection."

We made our way back to the waiting horses and were soon off toward the inn. After a leisurely repast, we continued to explore the countryside, not returning to Dunwick until quite late in the afternoon.

To my surprise and joy, one of the maids informed me Michael was waiting in the library for me. I handed her my gloves, hat, and riding crop, lifted my skirts and dashed to the library. The door was open and I saw Michael's tall, powerful physique standing before the fireplace, his legs apart, his hands clasping and unclasping behind his back as he stared at the ashy grate.

"Michael," I called quietly.

"Sit down, Elizabeth," he said without turning around.

"How did your day with Callie go?" I asked politely, desperately wanting him to turn and look at me with love in his eyes. But when his dark eyes finally met mine, there was a hollow quality to them, a distant reserve I couldn't fathom.

"Elizabeth . . ." He came and hovered over me, his hands still clasped behind his back. "I don't know how to tell you this . . . ."

Oh, my God, I thought. Callie has convinced him I should no longer remain at Dunwick. I felt panic seeping into my blood and, at the same time, a lightheaded giddiness came over me. A child had convinced this dynamic, strong-willed man to abandon me, to dismiss me without ever really knowing me. My hands clutched the heavy padding of the large leather chair until my knuckles were white. I gripped the armrests as I started to rise, my only desire being to seek the seclusion of my bedchamber. I didn't want to hear the words of rejection from Michael's lips.

"I think you should remain seated, Elizabeth," he said while one hand gently but firmly pushed against my shoulder. He sat down in a leather chair nearby, leaned close to me and took my hand in his.

His dark eyes reflected a grim anguish that seemed to confirm my suspicions that he wanted me to leave Dunwick. The words that came were not the ones I had expected, yet they were words I did not want to hear.

Six

"Elizabeth," Michael began, his voice low, his hand tightening on mine. "While you were out riding with Uncle Jack, I received an urgent message from London. Your father has died."

I slumped in the chair, all emotion temporarily deadened as I tried to absorb the dire news. As Michael continued, his voice came to me as if it were in a hollow chamber and I stared into emptiness. All thoughts of questioning him regarding his spurts of odd behavior had vanished.

"I've made all the arrangements. We leave for London first thing in the morning. I sent Clara up to pack whatever articles you might need for our stay in London. Are you listening to me, Elizabeth?"

"What . . . what . . . happened?" I stammered.

"A fatal heart attack, I'm afraid." He studied me for a moment. "Shall I send for the doctor?"

"No . . . no. I'll be all right. It's just that . . . well . . . Papa was so alive . . . so vital. I can't believe . . ." My voice refused to function. The shock was beginning to wear off and leave a residue of sickening reality.

Michael released my hand and left the chair. He strode to the gleaming mahogany sideboard and poured two snifters of brandy. Returning to the chair by my side, he handed one to me.

"Drink it, Elizabeth. Then, perhaps, it would be best if you lie down for a while. I'll have a tray sent up for your supper," he suggested as I took the snifter and sipped at the liquid, which quickly scalded my throat. "Down it all at once, Elizabeth."

I complied, only to rewarded with a choking cough. My hand flew to my burning throat.

"Come . . . I'll take you to your room, then see that cook prepares a tray for you," Michael said.

I stood, my body trembling. Even Michael's strong arm around my shoulder couldn't banish the limpness creeping through me, nor the feeling of utter helplessness that was beginning to devour me. By the time we began to climb the marble staircase, tears were splashing from my eyes beyond control. As we entered my bedchamber, I saw Michael give a not to Clara and she left the room discreetly, a distraught look on her face as my crying reduced itself to erratic sobs.

"Will you be all right?" Michael withdrew a large hand-kerchief from his pocket and proceeded to wipe my tear-stained face, then sat down on the bed beside me. "Would you like me to leave?"

"No," I exclaimed in a clogged voice. He handed me the handkerchief, and his arm slipped about my shoulders once more, his other hand drawing my head against his deep chest, holding it there until all my sobbing and trembling had ceased. I lifted my head and looked up at him. "You'll be coming to London with me, won't you, Michael?"

"Of course, my dear. Aside from seeing you through the funeral, there will be the solicitors to deal with," he replied.

I took a deep breath and swallowed hard. "I'll come down for dinner, Michael. I feel a lot better now and I really don't want to be alone."

"Are you sure?"

"Yes. I'll get into a hot tub. It'll help me assimilate it all.

At least he didn't suffer."

"No, he didn't." Michael's finger slid under my chin and he tilted my head back. His lips came down on mine, sweet and soft, but all too fleeting. Yet, I smiled weakly.

"I'll send Clara to you."

The church service was impressive and majestic. The cortege and burial were solemn, yet conveyed a stately air. I knew Papa would have approved highly of the entire proceedings. Despite the hot, humid weather, which seemed even worse in the city, a large number of people turned out for the funeral; statesmen, dignitaries, nobility, and luminaries of industry. All came to pay homage, sincere and insincere, for Papa did have those who disagreed with him. Michael remained steadfastly by my side. I could almost feel his strength flowing into me.

I found much had changed at the London house when Michael and I arrived two days before the funeral. Mary had left to get married. Mrs. Berrey had gone to live with her widowed sister in Devon, supported by a generous annuity from Papa. The entire staff had been cut to a minimum. But Charles remained. It was as though he were part and parcel of the house.

A large number of mourners returned to the house, where an elaborate and sumptuous buffet had been laid out along with whisky and fine French wines, including champagne.

Whigs, Tories, Liberals, and Socialists intermingled and, occasionally, became quite vociferous as ideas and ideals clashed, especially when the topic of laissez faire poked its head into the conversation. I could hear the once adamant utilitarian, John Stuart Mill, now argue so convincingly for state intervention that he sounded like a Socialist, a radical departure for him. I remembered he had been a frequent visitor and how he and Papa would talk long into the night.

I recognized a number of people, quite notable, who used to visit Papa at the house when he was alive. But so many people were pressing their condolences on me, I was beginning to feel a bit smothered by it all. With relief I saw Maude's familiar face poking its way through the host of people.

"Oh, Maude, I'm so glad you could come," I greeted her warmly, taking her hands in mine.

"I was devastated to hear about your father, Elizabeth. Is there somewhere we can go to talk privately?" she asked.

I looked around the room for Michael, who was not difficult to find, for he towered above almost everyone, his blue-black hair like an ebony beacon. I recognized the two men with whom he was in deep conversation, Benjamin Disraeli and Lord John Russell. From the rapt look on Michael's face I knew he would be engaged for some time.

"I think my father's study is empty. We can go in there." I thrust my arm through Maude's and led her down the hall.

"I noticed you checked on your husband before leaving. I can't say that I blame you. If one ignores the scar, he is devilishly handsome. I heard a number of women talking about him and in most flattering tones. You have no idea how I envy you, Elizabeth. Your Lord Tyrone is all man." Maude's powder-blue eyes shone.

"Your Harry is a handsome man too," I stated, crimson flushing my cheeks. The study was deserted and I closed the door behind us before we settled ourselves in comfortable chairs.

"I'll tell you about Harry in a moment. But I must say you look positively radiant despite the circumstances. Marriage and Ireland must agree with you. I want to hear all about it. Every little detail."

I went into a long description of Dunwick, then moved on to Uncle Jack and Rose. Maude was stunned to learn Michael had been married before and was the father of a ten-year-old child. Hoping I had sated her curiosity to the point where no further personal questions would be asked, I concluded with, "Marriage must agree with you, too, Maude. You're as beautiful as ever."

"You have no idea how hard I have to work at keeping my appearance up. Lotions, creams, powders. All tedious, yet so necessary. I have a maid who does nothing but dress my hair. She's a gem and I'm constantly on guard lest someone steal her from me. Some women in London's social register can be quite insidious. One has to be watchful every moment," she declared.

"You never did tell me about your holiday on the Continent. Were Paris, Vienna, and Venice as exciting as they say?"

"The whole trip was an absolute horror. If it hadn't been for some other English tourists in those cities, all I would have seen were the walls of our hotel suites," she said with venom.

"Why Maude, whatever do you mean? Where was Harry?"

"Harry? Hmph! He spent more time with his dandy friends than he did with me. Oh, he did his husbandly duty the first night and in record time, I might add. I did everything I knew to make myself attractive to him, but it seemed he found it distasteful even to touch me. In short, Elizabeth, Harry prefers the company of young men or boys, if you know what I mean," she said disdainfully.

"How awful for you, Maude," I replied consolingly. Poor Maude, I thought. She did so like her men, and to have an unresponsive husband must have been a horrible shock for her. And Harry! He always appeared so manly and virile. Not for a moment would I have guessed he preferred his own gender. I wondered if I could ever look at Harry again without revealing a trace of aversion.

"Oh, in the beginning I was desolate, but now I've learned to compensate for Harry's lack of ardor," Maude said with a gleam of triumph in her eyes.

"Oh, Maude, you shouldn't say such things or even think them," I admonished. I couldn't conceive of a married woman seeking the company of other men, regardless of her husband's attitude. Too rigid an upbringing, I guess. And I certainly couldn't visualize myself in the arms of any man other than Michael.

"It's easy enough for you to fell righteous. You have that sublime, virile husband of yours to cling to. By the way, you'd better keep an eye on him. I hear Edwina is back in London looking for a new liaison, to put it mildly."

"I don't think I have to worry about Edwina here in London when we'll be in Ireland." I smiled, trying to exude a confidence I didn't really possess.

"The Irish Sea isn't all that wide. Besides, I've seen Lord Tyrone here in London since you've moved to Ireland," she announced with a sly glitter in here eyes and a smug smile curving her bow-shaped lips.

"His business requires a good deal of traveling," I answered, hoping I had hidden my shock at the information. I didn't know Michael had been near London since we had left England. When and where had Maude see him? She certainly wouldn't make up a story like that. Doubts, which I thought I had left behind at Dunwick, returned to plague me.

"Business! My dear Elizabeth, don't be so naive. Business is the excuse men use to do as they please. I know some of my married gentlemen friends drive that old alibi right into the ground."

"Maude!" I was appalled that Maude would speak of her flirtations so openly.

"You look positively stunned, Elizabeth." She laughed. "Don't be so prudish. You should be well aware of the relationship between a man and a woman by now. Of course I have gentlemen friends. A good number of them, I might add, and I'm always on the lookout for new faces. Did you think I would sit and pine away while Harry romped about with his male chums? Hardly, Elizabeth, hardly. And, as long as I am discreet, Harry is quite content with the arrangement."

The door opened sharply and male voices preceded the entry of a group of gentlemen with Michael.

"Oh, Elizabeth . . . I didn't know anyone was in here," said a surprised Michael in the company of Mr. Disraeli, Lord Russell, and two other gentlemen I didn't know. He turned to look at Maude. They stared hard at one another as though communicating unspoken messages. Small knots formed in the pit of my stomach. After listening to Maude's revelations, then seeing her and Michael study one another with such intensity, new fears began to envelope me. "And how are you, Mrs. Payne-White?" Michael asked politely, a little too politely, I thought.

"Never better, Lord Tyrone." Her long lashes fluttered like hummingbird wings.

"So I see." His eyes lazily appraised her before turning back to me. "Elizabeth, would you mind vacating this room? These gentlemen and I have some rather urgent business to discuss."

"Not at all, Michael," I said, a tremor rising in my throat.

Maude and I rejoined the throng, and I noticed a strange light come into Maude's eyes. She made an appointment with me to have tea the next day and do some shopping, then excused herself. I managed to play the gracious hostess until the last of the guests departed, though how I did it was beyond me. My head was spinning from the shocking conversation I'd had with Maude.

It was not until the early hours of the morning that I heard Michael enter the bedchamber next to mine.

Rising much later than usual, I was surprised to learn he was still abed. I had finished breakfast and was having another cup of tea when he entered the dining room looking gaunt and tired.

"Good morning, Elizabeth." His voice was deep and still thick with sleep as he took his seat at the table.

"Good morning, Michael. I take it the gentlemen were here quite late," I said, forcing down the impulse to rush to him and smooth the tired lines from his face.

"Yes, they were." He picked up the carefully folded newspaper at his place and began to scan it as Charles laid a platter of eggs, sausages, and fried tomatoes before him.

"Did you have anything planned for today, Michael?" I asked as he refolded the paper and laid it aside.

"Why?"

"I promised Maude I'd have tea with her and do some shopping this afternoon," I answered, looking for some telltale sign of emotion at the mention of Maude's name. There was none.

"The solicitors will be here this morning, but I expect we'll be through well before noon. The reading of the will shouldn't take too long."

"Did you have plans for us this afternoon?" I would have gladly canceled my appointment with Maude if Michael had wanted to be with me.

"No. In fact, I'm meeting with some gentlemen this afternoon, which will take up the greater part of the evening too. You'll have to dine without me tonight, I'm afraid." His tone was matter-of-fact.

"I see." I wanted to scream that there must be something more to life than business.

"By the way, this Maude Payne-White, are you very close friends with her?" His dark eyes studied me intently.

"Yes. Why do you ask, Michael?"

"I . . . never mind, Elizabeth. It's not important. Will you be glad to get back to Dunwick?"

"Yes. I miss Uncle Jack and Rose," I replied, disconcerted by his abrupt change of topic. What was he going to say about Maude? And did I really want to hear it?

"Your father's holdings should only take a few days to

straighten out. Then we can leave for Dunwick."

Later that morning, two thin, hawklike men dressed entirely in black, with the exception of a glimmer of white shirts, were shown into my father's study, where Michael and I, along with the staff, had been patiently waiting for them. They walked across the room like two crows strutting on hot grass. After brief introductions, one sat behind my father's desk while the other stood beside him, surveying the room with haughty indifference before handing the seated man a medium-sized portfolio. The man behind the desk—balding, yet with a profusion of whiskers sprouting wildly from his chin—cleared his throat and began to read off a number of minor bequests to the staff, the largest going to Charles.

When the staff left, the solicitor droned on, enumerating in great detail my father's vast holdings. I knew Papa had been a wealthy man, but I never realized the extent of that wealth nor how vast his business holdings were. I was overwhelmed by the enormous amounts of money involved and the staggering number of companies my father had an interest in, if not control of. I was relieved when the solicitor concluded and replaced the papers in the portfolio.

The man stood, his ferret eyes squinting at me as he cleared his throat again. "Well, Lady Tyrone, you are lucky indeed to have an able husband to handle your affairs. We'll say good day to you both, and it has been a pleasure to meet you. If we can be of further assistance, please do not hesitate to call on us."

I thanked them and waited while Michael saw them to the door. The wait seemed interminable. I couldn't imagine what was taking Michael so long. I rose from the chair to search for him, but he came into the study before I'd taken more than a few steps.

"Well, Elizabeth, though I will take care of the companies and stock, I feel it is you who must make the decision about this house," He motioned for me to sit down again while he went to sit at Papa's desk.

"What decision?"

"Whether to maintain it or sell it." His attention was focused on some papers he had pulled from the top middle drawer of the desk.

"Hadn't we better keep it so you'll have someplace to stay during your clandestine visits to London?" I asked bitterly, remembering the glance that passed between him and Maude, and her observations of Michael in London.

Suddenly, he looked up at me, his expression grim. "You sound cynical, Elizabeth. Something wrong?"

"No." My lower lip trembled. I was not a very good actress. I could feel the hurt and anger bubbling to the surface. "Why didn't you tell me you had made several trips to London when I thought you were in Ireland?" I finally blurted out.

"I didn't think they were of any consequence. Brief business trips. Does it bother you?" His face was an impenetrable mask.

"Yes, Michael," I replied truthfully. "I think you should have let me know. I could have gone with you and visited with Papa before he . . . before he . . ." My voice cracked and tears welled in my eyes.

Instantly, Michael was by my side, lifting me from the chair and holding me in his arms. "Oh, my dear, I never gave it a thought. And, if I'd had any idea of what was going to happen, I certainly would have brought you with me," he said quietly in that deep, soothing voice of his as he stroked my head.

His warmth and his calming words mollified me. He was right. He'd had no idea anything would happen to Papa. And he was on business trips! I was letting Maude's foolish accusations addle my brain.

"I'm sorry, Michael. I suppose I'm still feeling the shock of Papa's death and the strain of yesterday."

"That's all right, Elizabeth." He held me at arm's length

and stared deep into my eyes. "I think this afternoon of shopping with your friend will take your mind off everything for a while. Shouldn't you be getting ready?"

I nodded and started for the door.

"Elizabeth . . . don't make any plans for tomorrow afternoon and evening. I want to go over a few things with you in the afternoon, and I have tickets for the theater in the evening."

"All right, Michael," I replied, my spirits lifting.

Maude's frock was quite fashionable, the rose color exceptionally becoming to her. She was glowing with an anxious excitement that reminded me of the days when she was about to embark on one of her puerile escapades. We proceeded with our assault on the Regent and Bond Street shops. The newspapers were filled with the news of my father's funeral and the impressive inheritance that would be an addition to the Tyrone estate. I felt like a minor celebrity as clerks and shop girls scurried and fluttered about me like a cloud of butterflies. It was all highly embarrassing—especially when Maude hastened to remind them who they were dealing with.

Even though I didn't purchase many items, I felt in an extravagant mood and quickly acquiesced to Maude's suggestion we take tea in one of London's posh hotels. From past experience I knew Maude was in an extravagant mood. Sporadically, a few gentlemen would approach our table to pay their respects to Maude and, when she introduced them to me, they gave me a most peculiar smile and held my hand longer than was proper.

"Maude, I do wish you'd stop flaunting me like some prize hen at a county fair," I declared when we were at last by ourselves.

"Oh, Elizabeth! You're such a mouse! I don't know how you ever caught a man like Michael Tyrone. By the way, what's he doing with a conservative like Disraeli? I was a bit startled when they walked in to the study the other day. I

should have thought that being Irish he'd be backing Gladstone."

"I don't question Michael about his politics," I replied,
but thought maybe I should. It might help me to understand him better. I stored the idea in the back of my mind
where I could dredge it up when the right opportunity
presented itself.

"Well, perhaps you have something there. Men have a
habit of becoming so tedious and dull when they get started
on politics." Her brilliant smile flashed around the room,
her eyes searching the tables relentlessly.

"Are you expecting someone, Maude?"

"No. But I wouldn't want to miss anyone . . . anyone of
importance, that is. By the way, are you almost finished
with shopping?"

"I did want to get a few presents to take back with me,
especially something for Rose."

"Rose . . . Rose," she muttered, her angelic face briefly
creasing in a frown. "I remember now. Lord Tyrone's sister.
From the way you described her in your letters, she sounds
as though she is afraid of her own shadow."

"I didn't mean to make her sound like that. She's very shy
but very sweet," I replied, thinking how much I enjoyed
and genuinely liked Rose—far more than I ever had
Maude. I was beginning to realize that in my youthful
mind, I had never really seen Maude as a person, only as an
object of adoration. I had worshipped her glittering façade, the ease with which she dealt with people, the glam-
our she exuded, her reckless approach to life. Qualities I
did not possess, but as an impressionable young girl,
wished I had. By being near Maude, I had hoped those
exciting characteristics would extend themselves to me.
Now I knew they never would and, for some reason, that
no longer bothered me, for I detected a nervousness about
Maude that was hard to define and somewhat frightening.

"I do hope you won't be too long in deciding on gifts. I

134

have an engagement this evening and I must get some rest, for it promises to be a very strenuous night," She smiled slyly, like a conspirator plotting an intrigue.

"Why don't we call it a day after tea? I can finish my shopping tomorrow," I suggested. I had suddenly lost my taste for Maude's company. Her forthcoming strenuous evening and Michael's late business meeting clashed in my mind.

"When are you returning to Ireland?"

"The day after tomorrow."

"Perhaps we could meet tomorrow for tea. You haven't seen my townhouse in London," Maude said.

"I'm afraid I can't make it, Maude. Michael asked me not to make any plans for tomorrow afternoon."

"Oh." She pouted prettily. "Then I probably won't see you again before you leave. I have the theater tomorrow night. But we will write, won't we?"

"Yes."

"I have an idea. I'll come and visit with you next summer. You're near the northern coast, aren't you?"

"Yes."

"Good. Sea breezes are preferable to the heat of London. And Bath and Brighton have become so boring."

I waited up for Michael as long as I could. Even in bed, I tried to maintain my vigil by propping up the pillows. But sleep soon claimed me, a fitful, nightmarish sleep. By morning, the strange dreams still clinging to my hazed brain, I awoke more determined than ever to preserve my decorum and pride. Michael might have married me for my money, as Callie suggested, and he might prefer the company of other women to mine, but I was not about to give either him or the world the satisfaction of witnessing my distress. I would do my best to be as imperturbable as Michael.

"Will Lord Tyrone be coming down to breakfast, Charles?" I asked as I entered the dining room.

"His Lordship did not return last night, my lady."

"He's still not at home?"

"No, my lady."

"Then I'll breakfast alone. And, Charles, I'll require the carriage when I'm finished."

"Yes, my lady."

I shopped leisurely. Wasting time. Dawdling over every item. I was determined to make Michael wait for me this time. Anyway, he would probably have some excuse to cancel the theater this evening. More business.

At the drapers, I abandoned all prudence and indulged in a wild buying spree. I selected bolts of linens, moires, silks, cottons, velvets, light and heavy wools, satins—yards and yards of colorful and exotic materials along with a wide variety of trims and laces. I chose the latest patterns in fashion, ordering everything to be shipped directly to Dunwick. It was all so easy. The mere mention of the Tyrone name brought wide, eager-to-please smiles as the owner of each shop insisted on waiting on me personally. I bought bottles of the finest fragrances, bath salts, soaps, and powders from France. Rose and I would do justice to the grandeur of Dunwick. Only Uncle Jack presented a problem, which was quickly solved by a helpful proprietor from whom I purchased fine leather riding gloves, a finely woven woolen scarf and a strong gold chain for Uncle Jack's pocket watch.

I did not forget Callie, Mrs. Meehan, and Clara. For Mrs. Meehan, I selected a dozen fine linen handkerchiefs edged with exquisite Belgian lace: for Clara, a fancy beaded reticule; and for Callie, a china doll with movable arms and legs, eyes that opened and closed, and real lashes. The doll was made in Dresden, Germany and was dressed in the latest little-girl fashion with long golden curls. I adored it and could only hope that Callie would. I instructed the various merchants to have everything sent directly to Dunwick along with their bills.

It was midafternoon when I returned to the house, and I felt glorious. The shopping spree had cleansed me of any misgivings I might have had. I greeted Charles profusely, handing him my bonnet and gloves before heading for the staircase. A door slammed loudly. I heard the sure, steady click of Michael's feet on the marble floor coming toward me and I froze.

"Elizabeth!" he called. I turned to see a dark scowl on his face, his eyes ablaze with anger. "Where the devil have you been? You knew I requested your presence here this afternoon."

"When you weren't here this morning, I assumed you would be away on business for the day, so I went to do a bit of shopping," I explained, pleased with my little display of defiance. In fact, I felt quite brave as I smiled up at Michael's stony expression.

"Come into the study," he ordered gruffly, taking my elbow in his large hand and squeezing it a bit too tight.

I was astonished to find the two crowlike solicitors in the study. I looked at Michael, totally bewildered. "I thought we had finished with the will."

"At my direction, I had these gentlemen draw up some papers which I want you to sign after you've read them, Elizabeth. They will explain any portions you don't understand." He steered me to the chair behind the desk and pulled it out for me. On the desk was a pile of very legal-looking papers. "Read them thoroughly, Elizabeth."

"Couldn't you tell me what they say?"

"It's necessary for you to read them yourself, Lady Tyrone," said the same solicitor who had read the will. I could only infer that his partner lacked a larynx.

I sighed with resignation and began to read the technical paragraphs, at first lightly, then with studied intensity. They didn't make much sense to me. Whatever I possessed was surely already Michael's. Why did he want me to sign papers to that effect?

Having read the documents, I sat and stared at them, pretending I was still perusing the contents, until my mind could clear and I could make some sense of it all. But my mind was a jumble. I could see no reason for Michael resorting to these legal exercises. Finally, I looked up to see Michael standing behind the large leather chair in front of the desk, his hands gripping the back of the chair with such ferocity his knuckles were white. Our eyes locked in mutual tension for a split second, and I knew my entire life with Michael depended on signing the papers without question.

"Do you understand the import of the documents, Lady Tyrone?" asked the ferret-eyed solicitor, breaking the strange spell between Michael and me.

"Yes," I replied.

"Will you kindly give us your impression of the significance of the papers?" the lean solicitor asked.

"All my father's holdings and businesses would be controlled by my husband, along with any liquid assets," I replied tonelessly, thinking the whole procedure was superfluous and a waste of time. Everything I possessed was already Michael's.

"Correct, Lady Tyrone. It would be irrevocable."

Without looking at Michael, I quickly signed the documents. When I finished, a dark cloud drifted over the sun, shutting out the light from the window behind me like a portent of evil.

Pushing the papers aside and rising from the chair, I gazed directly at Michael. There was a softening, a warmth in his eyes as he returned the gaze. I smiled and he responded in kind. No inheritance in the world meant more to me than a smile from Michael.

I dressed with great care that evening. I wanted Michael to be proud of me. The cerulean-blue gown was of the finest French peau de soie. Silver embroidery graced the snug bodice and ran along the scalloped edge of the cascading full skirt where ruffled tulle of the same color danced in profusion from the satin scallops. A necklace and earrings of rich aquamarines sparked among glittering diamonds were my only jewelry besides my wedding rings. A cape of the same peau de soie was lined with a silver-threaded silk. I felt quite grand, especially with my freshly washed auburn hair piled high atop my head in the latest fashion, emphasizing my long, slender neck.

Drawing on elbow-length silver gloves, I descended the staircase. Michael waited below, resplendent in black formal wear with a ruffled, white silk shirt. He appeared so dynamic, powerful, and handsome, my heart gave a little jump and a new feeling stirred in me, a feeling I could only label as desire. On the bottom step I placed my hand in his outstretched one.

"You are quite beautiful, Elizabeth," he said without smiling.

I was too stunned to respond. No one had ever thought me beautiful, let alone used that word to describe me. "Lovely" was the usual word, and then used only as a social nicety having no real import. From the expression on Michael's face I could almost believe he meant it. Or had he said it to allay any uncertainties I might have had regarding the fact that I had turned my entire inheritance over to him? At that moment, I preferred to believe he meant it. I could think about the possibilities of other meanings later.

After taking our seats in one of the large, private boxes which formed a semi-circle around the theater, Michael studied the program while I scanned the orchestra and other boxes. It was a dazzling display of opulent gowns, precious gems, and intricate coiffures.

"Well now . . . fancy finding you here!"

Michael rose, and I turned in my seat, dumbfounded and dismayed to see Maude and her unknown but distinguished-looking escort seating themselves in the two empty chairs behind us.

"Maude!" I cried.

"Isn't this fortunate! I do get to see you after all before you leave London. By the way, this is Anthony Nutting. Tony, my dear, I'd like you to meet two close friends of mine, Lord and Lady Tyrone." Maude's eyes devoured Michael as he shook hands with her escort.

"How do you do, Mr. Nutting," I said, trying to maintain my composure as a hot wave of embarrassment coursed through me. Or was it jealousy?

"I had no idea you'd be at the theater tonight, Elizabeth. I was telling Tony all about you and how I planned to spend the summer in Ireland with you," Maude said, then gazed at Michael sweetly. "That is, if Lord Tyrone has no objection."

"Elizabeth's friends are always welcome at Dunwick," Michael replied, then tossed me a glance of perplexed irritation.

"Now that you will be living in Ireland, what are you going to do with the London house?" Maude's eyelashes fluttered as her gaze shifted between Michael and me.

"We'll be keeping the house for the time being, Mrs. Payne-White. Charles will remain to see that everything is kept in order," Michael said politely, but I could sense his annoyance.

"Will you be staying in London then, Lord Tyrone, to oversee Mr. Whitter's business affairs?"

"No. I'm having everything transferred to Belfast, where I can expedite matters more easily."

I had held my breath, waiting for his answer to Maude's question. If Michael had said he was remaining in London while sending me back to Dunwick alone, I don't think I could have remained in the theater another moment.

The buzzing murmur in the theater hushed as the lights dimmed and the curtain opened on the first act. At every intermission Maude fawned and fluttered at Michael, tapping him playfully with her fan while teasing him to tell her of Dunwick and Ireland. Several times during the play I noticed her white hand on Michael's shoulder as she whispered in his ear. I felt horrid. It was the first time I found the theater neither entertaining nor fascinating. In fact, I hardly knew what the play was about. It was like a dull drone in the background as my thoughts kept reverting to Maude's flirtation with Michael and how he did nothing to discourage it. No matter how hard I tried to concentrate on the actors and actresses emoting on the stage, I couldn't shrug off the small drama being played in our theater box. I longed to be back at Dunwick. Even Callie was easier to bear than this.

I forced a smile and applauded loudly when the cast took their final curtain call, even though my heart wasn't in it. The lights came up and everyone began to take their leave.

"Tony and I are going to the Savoy for a late evening repast. Why don't you and Elizabeth join us, Lord Tyrone?" Maude asked, flashing her brilliant white teeth.

"Thank you for the kind offer, Mrs. Payne-White, but I'm afraid it is impossible. Elizabeth and I are leaving early in the morning for Ireland and we must get our sleep," Michael answered, placing the cape around my shoulders and letting his hands linger there for a moment.

"What a pity! Surely you can sleep on the train," cajoled Maude.

"I'm sorry, Mrs. Payne-White," Michael said emphatically.

"Do call me 'Maude,' Lord Tyrone. After all, I am Elizabeth's oldest and dearest friend."

"Good night," Michael said curtly, his eyes fastening on Maude.

I said my good-byes to Maude and we hugged briefly before Michael ushered me from the theater. I was elated and relieved when Michael declined to join Maude and her companion at the Savoy. I couldn't have endured watching

Maude play the coquette and possibly see a spark of interest rise in Michael's eyes, if it hadn't already. Michael said very little on the drive home except for some cursory remarks about the play. His thoughts seemed to be elsewhere.

As I climbed the stairs I left Michael heading for the study, where he said he was going to have a nightcap before retiring. With the assistance of a maid, I removed the delicate gown and prepared for bed. As I lay in bed in the darkened room, I waited for the tread of Michael's footstep in the room next to mine. Instead, I heard the front door slam. I was stunned. I leapt from the bed and dashed to the window that overlooked the lamp-lit street. Michael's tall, cloaked figure was striding down the street into the darkness.

I don't know how long I stood there staring into the void. Perhaps minutes, perhaps hours. When I finally returned to bed, I was dazed. I dared not close my eyes, for if I did, I knew there would be images of Maude whispering to Michael, Maude in his arms. Had they been plotting a late night rendezvous in the theater? Was her escort only a ploy, and the invitation to join them at the Savoy actually a signal to Michael that she would be waiting for him there after he had made sure I was in bed?

The more I thought about it, the more I wondered if Maude's appearance in our box at the theater was planned and not a coincidence. I resolved to question Michael about it in the morning. But, on second thought, did I want to hear the answer? Slow tears made a path down my cheeks. As I furiously tried to wipe them away, the flow increased. I didn't know this night was only a minor discomfort compared to what awaited me at Dunwick.

Seven

The trip back to Dunwick was a delight. Michael was effusive with compliments and general conversation. It was as if a great burden had been lifted from him. I never mentioned his leaving the house the night before for fear it would spoil his rare festive mood. It seemed we were home in no time. Yes. I had come to think of Dunwick as home. There was nothing in London for me anymore. Michael's family was now the only family I had.

I almost bounded up the steps to the great Georgian mansion and, before taking off my bonnet and gloves, I ran across the marble foyer and hugged a waiting Rose with warm enthusiasm.

"I've missed you, Elizabeth," she said with deep affection.

"And I you, Rose." I embraced her again.

"I'll be highly offended if I don't get one of those big hugs, young lady," Uncle Jack boomed.

I threw myself at the bearlike man with abandon, my head almost crushed against his barrel chest as his arms squeezed me tightly.

"By George, Michael, it's a good thing you're her husband or I'd steal her away from you. And don't think I couldn't my lad. I can still cut a fine figure with the ladies," Uncle Jack boasted good-naturedly. "What do you say, Elizabeth? Want to leave that rascal nephew of mine and come away with me?"

"Tomorrow, Uncle Jack," I replied with a half laugh as I extricated myself from his burly arms. "Right now all I want is a little rest and a hot bath before dinner."

"Tomorrow then. We'll flee to America." Uncle Jack chuckled.

"It's a good thing I didn't meet you before Michael. He might not have won me so easily," I teased, then turned a smiling face to Michael. The smile slipped from my face when I saw the old somber expression returning to his eyes, a dark brooding I couldn't understand.

"I'll go up with you, Elizabeth," Rose said, her plain-cut dark maroon frock emphasizing her pallid complexion.

As we climbed the stairs arm in arm, I was tempted to tell Rose all about the purchases I had made in London and how they would be arriving any day. But I checked myself, wanting the gifts to be a surprise. I was anxious to see the expression on her face when the bolts of beautiful cloth were unpacked. I told Rose of the funeral and the reception as I shed my traveling clothes and Clara went about preparing a hot tub for me.

Cook had outdone herself in fixing a welcome home dinner of Michael's favorite foods. Hot scallop soup followed by roast goose with potato and sausage stuffing, brussels sprouts in a cheese sauce, and a turnip bake. Mounds of hot soda bread and fresh whipped butter were on the table at all times. For dessert, a rich jam cake.

When we retired to the drawing room, Michael and Uncle Jack settled into an animated discussion of politics while I regaled Rose with tales of London. She asked about Maude, and I kept my comments brief lest I inadvertently blurt out how Maude had behaved toward Michael. As the evening drew to a close, Rose and I went upstairs and said our good nights to one another. I stood, fully dressed, in my bedchamber and stared out into the darkness, completely unmindful of time. My earlier nap had taken the edge off sleep. My thoughts spun in my head with unceasing rapidity as questions tumbled into my brain begging for answers. I knew I'd have no rest until I confronted Michael. I went out into the empty hall, closing the door quietly behind me, then went down to the main floor. No one was in the drawing room and I knew Michael was not in his bedchamber upstairs.

I tiptoed to the open library door and looked in. Michael was alone, sitting behind the large mahogany desk, his jacket, vest, and tie carelessly tossed over a leather chair. His white silk shirt was open almost to his waist, revealing the dark hair that covered his deep chest. His jet-black hair gleamed with sparks of gold in the light of the oil lamp. The scratch of his pen was shattering in the silence of the room, and he was so engrossed in his writing he didn't notice me entering.

"Michael," I called quietly.

His head jerked up in astonishment and he quickly slid the paper he was writing on into the middle desk drawer. "Why . . . Elizabeth. I thought you had gone to bed. Something wrong?"

"Yes," I said quickly before my courage failed. His dark eyes smoldered with flecks of amber in the yellowish light of the lamp.

He leaned back in the chair and folded his hands over his hard, lean stomach. "Sit down, Elizabeth, and tell me what is troubling you."

I practically dropped into the Queen Anne chair di-

145

rectly in front of the desk. My legs were trembling. How does a wife tell her husband she wants him to come to bed with her? It isn't done. I groped for words that wouldn't come and felt like a complete idiot for placing myself in so ridiculous a position.

"Well, I'm waiting, Elizabeth."

"I'd like some money of my own, Michael." I was a coward. He was so masculine, so handsome, so formidable sitting there, my courage wilted like a cut flower without water.

"Don't you have everything you want? Have I denied you anything?"

"No . . . but I would like my own account so I could make purchases without having to disturb you with the bills." So far, so good, I thought to myself, for someone who was making up dialogue as she went along.

"That's what a husband is for. To take care of the bills." Michael looked half amused, half irritated.

I wanted to retort, is that all? But I didn't, even though the notion was gnawing at my bones. "I'd feel ever so much better if I had my own money. There is enough, isn't there, Michael?"

With a wry smile he rose, came to the front of the desk and leaned against it, his arms folded over his chest as he looked down at me. "What's this all about, Elizabeth? You didn't come down here in the middle of the night to discuss having your own account.

Michael always seemed to have the knack of seeing through me. I felt his dark eyes piercing mine, searing through to my brain, and I couldn't stand it. I left the chair and went to the book shelves, letting my finger trace over the titles absently.

"Elizabeth . . . you must trust me. I'm your husband."

I spun around. My emotions, so long bottled, suddenly burst forth. "Are you, Michael? Are you?" I cried.

146

He pushed his tall, rugged frame erect. "What's gotten into you, Elizabeth?" His handsome face clouded and his eyes narrowed. "What has Maude been filling your head with?"

"Nothing!" I exclaimed rather loudly. "I do have a mind of my own, Michael."

"Why don't we talk about this in the morning? We've both had a long and tiring day."

"Don't patronize me, Michael! I'm not a child!"

"No one knows that better than I, my dear. You're every inch a woman. And a very tempting one at that."

"Then why haven't you bedded me for many a week? Am I so plain and dull in comparison to the beautiful Maude Payne-White? Do you find being in her bed and arms preferable to mine?"

"Elizabeth! What has brought all this on? Surely you can't be jealous of a woman I hardly know. You must stop thinking and talking such nonsense."

"Is it really nonsense Michael?" A horrid thought struck me, a thought that I inadvertently voiced aloud. "Perhaps it isn't Maude you fancy, but her husband, Harry Payne-White." The moment the cruel words slipped off my tongue, I knew I had made a grave mistake.

All color drained from Michael's face, turning his scar a livid reddish-purple. Sheer hostility etched itself deeply in his sharp features and his hands clenched into tight fists at his side, his large knuckles white with tension. There was a frightening glow in his eyes as he strode toward me, and my anger and bravado turned to fear.

Towering over me, he pressed my head between his strong hands. I was helpless as those hooded ebony eyes bore deeply into mine.

"Michael . . . I . . ." I never finished my apology. His mouth covered mine in a kiss I had never known possible. My senses quivered. I marveled at the wonder of his heated kiss. He raised his face, and my eyes opened to find those dark eyes searching mine. I smiled up at him with parted lips, yearning to relive the sensation.

Swiftly, his sinewy arms went around me, almost lifting me off the floor as his mouth moved over mine in a deeper, slower kiss. Instinctively my hands went around his neck and I held his head to mine as I boldly kissed him back, caught up in the flame of my own desires. His embrace tightened, searing my body with the heat of his as the kiss intensified with a ravenous passion. Suddenly, he broke off, shoving me away and turning his back to me. I reached up and placed my hands on those broad shoulders, laying my head on his well-muscled back.

"Oh, Michael," I whispered, then felt those great shoulders heave before he walked back to the desk.

"Don't press me, Elizabeth. I beg of you, don't press me."

There was a painful sadness in his eyes which he quickly masked, his expression marbleizing into carved ice. "Go to bed, Elizabeth. You, of all people, should know better than to question my manhood." His voice was low and menacing. He started for the seat behind the desk.

"Will your work always take precedence over our marriage?"

He turned, and in rapid strides came to stand before me. After gathering me into his arms, he said, "My dear Elizabeth. I never realized you would take it amiss if I did not come to your bed. You must excuse my negligence. Pressing matters have consumed my time. I must ask your patience and indulgence. I hope to have everything rectified soon. Again, be patient with me, Elizabeth."

"What is so pressing that you hardly get any sleep and

are drawn away from Dunwick so frequently?"

"I cannot discuss it with you." He released me and went to sit behind the desk.

"Why not?" I persisted. "I am your wife, Michael."

"And I am your husband. You will take my word for whatever I do or say. I don't have to answer to you. Now, that's the end of it, Elizabeth."

I caught the tone of raw anger creeping into his voice. I thought it prudent not to prod that anger into rage. "Good night, Michael."

"Good night, Elizabeth."

With a heavy tread, I mounted the staircase, then went down the hall to my bedchamber. Having dismissed Clara, I sat at my dressing table and brushed my hair, my nightdress already on. Maybe Michael was right and I should learn to practice some patience. My father had always indulged me, perhaps too much so.

I had no right to expect that same instant gratification from Michael. He was my husband, not my father. And he did have the extra burden of my father's vast holdings. I loved Michael so much, perhaps too much. Was I smothering him with my concern for his welfare, my desire and love for him? I decided to be more circumspect in the future, to restrain any jealous impulses I might feel about Maude before my emotions got out of hand again. As my new resolves took a firm hold on me, sleep came — a deep, sound sleep.

Several days later all the packages arrived from London, sending a wave of excitement through the house. I was overcome with guilt about not having thought of purchasing gifts for the entire staff. After all, I was mistress of Dunwick. While exercising that prerogative, I should also be showing the servants that I recognized them as human beings. When all the packages had been piled in the upstairs parlor, Rose and I began to sort

149

them out.

"I've never see such exquisite material. And those patterns! Is this what they're wearing in London?" Rose exclaimed, a light kindling in her pale amber eyes.

"Yes. And you should see the new bonnets they are wearing. Quite saucy," I replied, catching her enthusiasm.

"You'll be a grand lady, Elizabeth."

"And so will you."

"Oh, I couldn't take any of your pretty cloth," she replied, fingering a pink moire with affection.

"Well, I certainly didn't buy all this for me. Some of the fabrics were chosen with your coloring in mind, especially that pink moire you have there."

"Well . . . maybe just one frock," she said, continuing to gaze lovingly at the moire.

"We'll get a dressmaker, a milliner, and a bootmaker from Derry to fit us. But first, I would like your help with something."

"Anything, Elizabeth, anything. I'd be so delighted." Rose was positively radiant.

"I would like you to help me select soaps, powders or perfume for the female members of the staff and tell me which you think they'd prefer. I have tins of tobacco for the men." I had originally purchased the tobacco for Uncle Jack, but I was sure he wouldn't miss it. Besides, I had the scarf, gloves, and chain for him.

It took the entire morning and half the afternoon to sort everything out. After presenting Clara with the delicately beaded reticule, which she stared at with unbelieving eyes and unending thank you's, I instructed her to tell Mrs. Meehan to have the entire staff assemble in the foyer. Rose and I put all the gaily wrapped gifts in a basket and toted them downstairs, waiting in the drawing room like gleeful children until Mrs. Meehan came in with a resentful and imperious air to inform me that

150

everyone was present in the foyer.

I distributed the small gifts amidst multiple curtsies and thank you's, explaining how they were a small token of my appreciation for kindness towards me. When I handed Mrs. Meehan her boxed gift of lacy handkerchiefs, she looked at me coldly. Her hatred of me was almost palpable.

"I also have a present for Callie. Do you think you could bring her to the drawing room, Mrs. Meehan?" I asked when the other servants had returned to their duties.

"Now?"

"Please," I said tightly, a little annoyed by her lack of propriety. She should have added 'Lady Tyrone' or 'my lady.' She stalked off toward the staircase as I joined Rose in the drawing room.

"Was everyone surprised, Elizabeth?" Rose asked.

"I think so. And I think they were pleased to have a little gift from London." We went on to talk of material and patterns, but in the back of my mind I was wondering what was taking Mrs. Meehan so long in bringing Callie to the drawing room. I was about to give up on Callie when Mrs. Meehan entered with the young girl in tow. I rose, put on my warmest smile and went to Callie, whom Mrs. Meehan had thrust in front of her.

"Well, Callie, wait until you see the present I bought for you in London," I said, taking her hands in mine, which she roughly withdrew.

"I don't want any presents from you. I want you to go away," she spewed at me, then strutted past me toward the piano. She hoisted herself onto the piano bench, then banged on the keys loudly, producing horrid, discordant sounds that reverberated throughout the house. Rose fled, her hands clasped tightly over her ears.

Calmly, quietly, I tried to get Callie to stop, but my

151

pleas only increased her frenzy. I looked to Mrs. Meehan, who stood there with her hands folded over her dark skirt, a smug smile curling her lips. I was about to physically remove Callie from the piano when a deep, masculine voice stopped me.

"What the devil is going on in here?"

I spun around and saw Michael standing in the doorway, his riding crop slapping against his mud-splattered black boots. Tight black breeches clung to his muscled thighs, and his white shirt was smudged with dirt. His black hair raged about his head like a swirling dark cloud and his sharp features were drawn taut with controlled anger.

"Callie! Callie! Stop that din this instant!" he ordered, to no avail as Callie added screeching to her atonal thunderings on the piano. He turned to Mrs. Meehan. "What's the child doing down here?"

"It was at her ladyship's request." Mrs. Meehan tossed a self-satisfied glance at me.

"Elizabeth?" Michael's eyes locked with mine.

"I purchased a gift for Callie in London and I wanted to give it to her," I explained.

"Give it to Mrs. Meehan. And, Mrs. Meehan, take that child back upstairs," Michael said, his gaze following me as I retrieved the boxed doll.

Mrs. Meehan's eyes narrowed in triumph as she took the box from me, then went to the piano. She touched Callie on the shoulder. The child stopped immediately, then skipped from the room as though nothing had happened. Mrs. Meehan followed. I stared at Michael in bewilderment while he glared at me stonily, his crop slapping at his boot with increasing speed. For a minute I thought he was going to speak, but he abruptly turned on his heel and left.

Ever since that night in the library, Michael and I had

been polite to one another, but a cool reserve lay between us like an invisible barrier, which he seemed to reinforce at every opportunity. Michael faded from my mind as Callie's peculiar behavior took precedence in my thoughts. And what I found even more amazing was how the touch of Mrs. Meehan's hand radically altered the child's raucous actions. Not only did I find it hard to comprehend, but it frightened me a little.

After dinner, when Uncle Jack, Rose, and Michael settled in their usual places, I took the presents from atop the piano bench with the sudden realization that I had bought nothing for Michael. I chewed at my lower lip, trying to think of a plausible excuse for not doing so. I forced a smile, then went to Uncle Jack, handed him his gifts and bent to kiss his cheek before taking a seat beside Rose.

"Well . . . well. Presents, Elizabeth?" Uncle Jack chuckled, laying his pipe aside before he began to unwrap them.

"A few mementos from London," I replied, gratified to see the pleasure on his face.

He pulled the scarf around his neck, tried on the gloves, which were a perfect fit, then fondled the gold chain. "My dear, they are marvelous and I shall treasure them." He carefully put the items back in their respective boxes. "And Rose, what did our Elizabeth bring you from London?"

"More than she should have," Rose replied, taking my hand in hers. "Beautiful fabrics for gowns and frocks to be made into the latest fashions."

"Those newfangled things with the bustle in back? On you and Elizabeth, they'll be appealing, but there are some females who have no need of any extra protruberances in the back," Uncle Jack said with an impish grin.

"I feel a bit neglected," Michael said, smiling. His dark eyes gleamed with rare humor.

"What? No presents for your husband? That's not like you, Elizabeth," Uncle Jack exclaimed jovially.

My mind was agile and I smiled. "Michael received his present in London."

"You must refresh my memory, Elizabeth," Michael said, retaining his humor.

"In my father's study, the afternoon before we left for the theater. Remember?"

"Ah . . . yes. A most gracious present," Michael said. The smile remained on his lips, but vanished from his eyes, leaving them hard, black coals.

"What was it, Michael?" Rose asked innocently.

"That is between Elizabeth and me," Michael replied, causing Rose to blush.

"Uncle Jack, why don't we take a ride to Dunluce tomorrow?" I asked quickly, wanting to change the subject.

"Can't, my dear. Would like to but I have pressing duties elsewhere," Uncle Jack replied.

"Rose? Would care to ride with me?" I asked.

"I don't ride, Elizabeth."

"When she was a young girl, she was thrown from a horse and has been afraid of them ever since," Michael explained.

"You must try again, Rose," I urged. But she shook her head, leaving no doubt that she never would venture to mount a horse again. "Well . . . I shall go alone, then."

"Take a groom with you, Elizabeth," Michael commanded.

"I think I shall retire now so I can get an early start." I rose from the divan ignoring Michael's words. I said my good nights and, once in the foyer, was taken aback to see the shadowy form of Mrs. Meehan slipping down a corridor as though she had been listening to the conversation in the drawing room. I had honestly tried to like the woman, but there was something about her that put me off. Her singular control of Callie, which verged on the bizarre, and her obvious hatred and resentment of me were attributes I could neither understand nor deal with.

I slipped into bed, sensing that sleep would come soon. As my legs slid along the cool sheets, I was unnerved to feel my skin being scratched and cut as though the bed were implanted with a thousand sharp needles. I drew my legs up swiftly, leapt from the bed and lit the oil lamp on the night table. I drew the covers back cautiously, fearful I might find some grotesque insect or animal inhabiting the bed. I was shocked and mystified by what I saw. The beautiful porcelain doll I had given Callie lay smashed and scattered across the bottom half of the bed.

My first instinct was to seek out Mrs. Meehan and ask for an explanation after showing her the senseless destruction of the doll along with the sadistic sprinkling of the shards in my bed. But on reflection, I thought it best to ignore the incident. To make an issue of it might only increase Callie's penchant for cruel practical jokes, for I was sure it was the child's idea of an amusing way to cause me distress.

I cleaned it up as best I could, wrapping all the fragments in a piece of the fancy paper I had used to wrap gifts. When I returned to the bed I could still feel tiny slivers of the fragile porcelain embedded in the linens. In the morning I would have Clara change the linens. I slept, but not without nightmares of ugly gnomes whipping at my legs with miniature rapiers.

The next morning after breakfast, I went to the stables, thankful I had worn my velvet riding habit. There was a definite nip in the air, a portent of summer giving way to fall. I refused the groom's offer to accompany me, for I wanted to explore on my own without a pair of eyes watching my every move.

The air was brisk and clean upon my face as I cantered down the same lane I'd traveled with Uncle Jack when we went to the Giant's Causeway. The glen still presented its plush carpet of green grasses running toward the sea's edge. I saw a leaf or two fall from a hawthorn tree nestled along the hedgerows. Thrushes, hidden among the leaves, sang joyously.

Being alone, my senses were keen and I observed the wonders of nature. There was an awesome beauty about the change of seasons that never failed to stir my emotions. But here in the Irish countryside, it overpowered me far more than it ever had in London.

Once again, my eyes caught the impressive outline of Dunluce Castle erratically groping toward the sky. My curiosity increased as an excitement swelled within me. I nudged the horse to proceed to the ruins of the ancient castle where I dismounted and lightly tethered the horse to a jutting rock.

I entered the decaying structure whose skeletal shape and half-formed walls were slowly giving way to lichen encrustations. I walked over the grass-covered floor like one being lured on and on, exploring every passage, every hidden nook. I peered through gaps that might have once been windows in the gray-green stone edifice. Five circular towers—two intact, three just remnants now—lay like weary, hollow eyes that suggested a long-lost splendor. The crumbling structure hinted at a fabulous power now eroded by the stronger force of nature to which it had been abandoned. Touching the sea-damp-

156

ened stones, one could almost feel the centuries slip back to a nobler yet harsher time. I was overwhelmed with the strange beauty of the place and let my fancies drift to knights and damsels playing out their human destinies perhaps not too different from my own.

Finally shaking myself from the indulgent reverie, I continued my explorations. Drawn by a stone-framed open door through which a clear blue sky hung like an unworked tapestry, I walked through and found myself on a narrow, grassy knoll that jutted out high above the swirling sea lapping at the jagged rocks far below me. I stared down at the frothy, angry sea that sent burly waves to challenge the formidable cliff. The hypnotic surge and pounding of the maddened waters caught me in its rhythms, compelling me to inch closer and closer to the edge to absorb every nuance of the cresting waters whose force was reduced to lacy foam by the craggy rocks they assailed so mightily.

My state of enchantment was abruptly shattered when a rough rock clouted me under the shoulder blade. I spun around to locate the source of the missile, but my sudden movement, coupled with the impact of the hurled rock threw me off balance, causing my foot to slip on the slimy, moss-covered rock. Without warning, I began to slide helplessly down the sloping promontory to the sheer, straight drop of the cliff.

I clutched at projecting crags of stone, but my fingers could not find a hold on the slippery, sea-misted rocks. The sharp, unyielding stones tore at the heavy cloth of my riding habit, scraping my legs and arms. Just as I thought all was lost and my body would be stilled by the rocks and consumed by the sea, my fingers held fast to a prominent ridge. I clutched at it with all the strength at my command. As I turned my head to seek some purchase for my dangling feet, I watched my loosened riding hat tumble down, bounding off the ridge of the cliff to the sharp-toothed rocks and beckoning sea below. I clung to the ridge with fierce determination while my feet doggedly searched for support. I cried for help, but soon realized that even if someone were up there, the roaring sea would drown out my feeble cries. Panic was starting to overtake me and I knew if I didn't get a foothold soon, my strength would give out. Suddenly, my foot lodged on something solid and unyielding. Soon, my other foot found a purchase and I pushed myself to a position where my hand found a solidly wedged protruberance.

Slowly and painfully, I inched my way back up to the grassy knoll, my hands and legs bruised and bleeding. My entire body throbbed as though it had been totally and thoroughly lacerated. Reaching the safety of the knoll, I lay flat, letting the terror drain out of me and taking deep breaths to stop the quivering of my body. I looked at the innocent blue sky and tried to sort things out in my mind. Was that rock deliberately hurled to knock me over the edge? Or had some time-worn stone loosened in the ancient walls to drop by chance at that moment? I would have liked to believe that, but reason told me the rock had struck at an angle no falling stone could have. It had to have been hurled.

I lay immobile for some time, wondering if the unknown, unseen assailant was still lurking somewhere in Dunluce Castle, waiting for another opportunity to attack me. Even though a new wave of fear filled me, I knew I had to get to my horse and back to Dunwick. Staying at Dunluce Castle any longer would only imperil me further. Although, if someone had been watching me, they would have seen me go down the embankment toward the cliff and, thinking me dead, might have left.

With that thought in mind, I summoned my tattered

courage, got to my feet and then limped my way through the ancient labyrinth to where I was positive I had tethered the horse. But my horse was nowhere in sight. I narrowed my eyes, scanning the area for the animal, but without results. In despair, I hobbled toward the road with the fervent hope I might happened upon a farmer or traveler who could take me back to Dunwick, or at least summon help, for I wasn't sure my legs could carry me the distance.

I hadn't trudged too far when the sweet sound of carriage wheels reached my ears. I watched the open, one-horse buggy approach me, the driver reining in the horse as he came alongside.

Astonished, I stared open-mouthed into the handsome face of David Cooke. Hatless, his brown hair played in wild confusion about his head while his wide hazel eyes surveyed me with alarm.

"Lady Tyrone! Whatever happened?" He curled the reins about a knob on the front of the buggy and leapt down.

"I had a mishap and I'm afraid my horse deserted me." My hand pushed at my disheveled hair unconsciously as if one pass could set it straight. I was suddenly highly aware of my appearance as I saw Mr. Cooke's eyes go to my hands.

"Good grief! Your hands, Lady Tyrone!" he exclaimed, taking both my hands in his and turning them palms up. Genuine alarm clouded his face. "Your gloves are torn and there is blood seeping through. Let me take you to a doctor."

"I appreciate the offer, but I don't really need a doctor. However, I would consider it a great service if you would give me a ride back to Dunwick." I was quite sure he would not refuse me.

"Of course. Here . . . let me give you a hand up." His

159

strong but gentle hands felt reassuring around my waist. He went around to the other side of the buggy and hoisted himself onto the seat close beside me. "Do you care to tell me what happened, Lady Tyrone? Did your horse throw you again?"

"No," I replied sharply, a little miffed at the insinuation I was a poor horsewoman constantly being thrown by her horse. But the warmth and friendliness of his expression softened my initial reaction. "I was exploring the old castle and got a little too close to the edge of the cliff and lost my footing. I was clumsy and slid down the slope for quite a distance."

"Good Lord! You might have been killed."

"I have to admit there were several moments when I thought I would perish in the sea like my riding hat," I concurred, then directed him on the proper route to Dunwick.

"Whatever were you thinking of, riding about the countryside alone? You seem to make a habit of it, and it always proves to be disastrous, although last time the fault was mine." His words were filled with such deep concern, I could not take offense.

"Every one at the house had duties to attend to. Besides, I really wanted the freedom to explore without a groom watching over me," I answered honestly.

"It was provident I came along when I did. If only I hadn't tarried along the way, I might have been able to prevent your mishap altogether."

"Perhaps. But I'm most grateful you came at all. I doubt if I could have made the walk back to Dunwick. By the way, what brings you to Ireland, Mr. Cooke?"

"My articles on the Lake District were so well received, I was requested to cover the scenic sights of Northern Ireland. A magazine publisher in New York is exceptionally enthusiastic and wants to make a series of it. So I'll be here for a while. He's paying all my expenses and I think he wants to make sure he gets his money's worth." He smile wryly. "I've already sent a few pieces to London and New York on Belfast and the northeast coast of Ireland. Antrim holds some truly astonishing scenery. Such headlands and imposing castles."

"Did you stop at the Giant's Causeway?"

"Yes."

"Did you walk out on it?"

"No. I wanted to reach Portrush before dinner and secure lodgings for the night there. I hear the beach under the cliffs is strikingly beautiful."

"You must stop and have dinner with us at Dunwick," I urged as the bumpy ride in the buggy kept reminding me of my bruised body.

"I wouldn't want to impose."

"We'd all be delighted, I'm sure," I said, thinking how Rose could do with the company of a nice young man. I was so taken with the idea, I added, "In fact, why look for lodgings when Dunwick has so many empty rooms? I insist you stay with us while you are in Northern Ireland. We are centrally located and you could make daily sojourns to whatever part interested you. After two gallant rescues and your kindness in the Lake District, I feel it is the least I can do."

"It is most hospitable of you, Lady Tyrone. And, since you insist, I shall be most happy to accept. Quite frankly, I was getting a bit weary of lonely inns and their fare. A well-cooked meal about now would do wonders for my appetite. And do call me 'David.' I feel as though we are old friends by now."

"Dunwick isn't too much further . . . David." I felt a little bold using his given name, yet oddly enough, I felt I knew him better than I did my husband.

"Are you sure your husband won't mind, Lady Tyrone?"

"If I am to call you 'David,' then you must call me 'Elizabeth.' And, as for Michael, I don't see how he could object to extending hospitality to a man who has been so courteous to his wife. Besides, Michael isn't around the manor house too often."

"If I had a wife as lovely and charming as you, I would never leave home."

I turned my head to look off in the distance. I didn't want David to see my flaming cheeks. "Look! There's Dunwick!"

He guided the horse into the crescent driveway, saying, "Impressive, very impressive."

As we entered the foyer, an agitated Michael was pacing up and down, his riding boots slapping hard against the marble floor. He stopped and his eyes flashed to David and me, shock registering in those dark eyes as they swept over me.

"Elizabeth! What happened to you? Where the devil have you been?" He strode toward me and gripped my arms with his powerful hands. I winced as they tightened on my bruised arms. His dark gaze swirled down into mine. "Who did this to you, Elizabeth? And I want the truth."

"Why . . . no one, Michael, no one. I did it to myself."

"I had just returned home when they told me your horse had come back riderless. They were saddling a fresh horse for me when you were seen coming up the driveway. I was about to search for you. What possessed you to go off alone like that? Didn't I tell you to take a groom with you?" He stopped to take a deep breath. "I'll have someone go for the doctor."

"I don't need a doctor, Michael. I only have a few cuts and bruises." I was indignant at his castigating me before

162

a guest, but then felt my anger melt as I discovered the genuine anxiety in his eyes. Then, as his gaze slid past me to David Cooke, who was patiently waiting in the background, Michael's look of concern was instantly replaced by a fierce, satanic expression. His hands gripped my arms with increasing pressure. "Michael, you remember David Cooke. He was kind enough to show me the Lake District during your absence. Fortunately, he was coming down the road as I was trying to get home. I don't think I would have made it without him."

"It seems our Mr. Cooke is determined to become your guardian angel, Elizabeth," Michael said with a sardonic smile on his face and sarcasm dripping from his words. "Thank you, Mr. Cooke."

"It was my pleasure," David replied.

"Michael, I've invited David to have dinner with us and be a guest at Dunwick until he has completed his series of articles on Northern Ireland for his magazine." As I spoke, I watched Michael's expression harden.

"I hope I'm not imposing," David said.

"If my wife extended an invitation, then you are most welcome. You must excuse us now. My wife needs attention." Michael swopped me up into his strong arms before adding, "I'll send one of the servants to show you to your room."

He carried me up the stairs as though I was no more than a young babe. At the top of the stairs he told one of the maids to see that David and his luggage were shown to one of the guest rooms, then she was to have Clara come to my bedchamber.

Michael sat me on my bed, then knelt down and removed my riding boots while I slipped off my tattered velvet jacket. Finding my shirtwaist stained, I removed that, too, so that only my chemise covered the upper portion of my body.

"Stand up and take off that shredded skirt," Michael ordered. As I did, his finger lightly traced the bruises on one of my arms. "How did this happen, Elizabeth?"

"I was at Dunluce and went too close to the edge, lost my balance and slid down a slope," I explained, my skin quivering under his touch. I purposely left out the incident of the rock being thrown at me. It sounded rather far-fetched. The work of an overactive imagination. Feeling no shame or embarrassment, I let my riding skirt fall to the floor. Was it because I hoped against hope that I would fire Michael's ardor? But when he ordered me to lie on the bed, then rudely shoved my petticoats up to my thighs, I felt highly vulnerable. At the same time, a tremor of excitement dashed along my veins.

He scrutinized my legs where my torn cotton stockings clung to my skin, dried blood welding material to flesh. He tried to roll the blood-encrusted stockings down, but stopped when he saw my face grimace in pain.

"Where the devil is that maid of yours?" he roared. "Don't move, Elizabeth. I'll be right back."

Mesmerized, I watched the tall, powerful man enter my water closet to return with towels and a large bowl of tepid water. With great tenderness, Michael soaked my legs with wet towels until the dried blood softened and released its hold on the cotton. When his fingers touched my thighs to roll the stockings down, a singular sensation flashed through me and my flesh shivered. But Michael was too engrossed to notice my reaction to his touch. Once the stockings were removed, he carefully washed off my legs with a clean cloth.

"Your knees are badly bruised, Elizabeth," he observed as Clara entered the room. "Clara, prepare a warm tub for your mistress."

Looking distressed at the sight of me, she bobbed a curtsy and disappeared into the lavatory as Michael pulled my petticoats down. He rose from the bed and looked at me with a studied expression, then bent over and placed his large, fine-boned hand alongside my cheek.

"I have some salve which I'll give to Clara. It will help to heal the cuts and scrapes. Have a bath now, then I'll have a light tea sent up. Stay in bed for the rest of the day. I'll see to it you have a dinner tray." He kissed me lightly on the forehead.

"I'm perfectly able to come down to dinner, Michael. I don't have any broken bones. Besides, I invited David to dine with us and it would be ungracious of me not to put in an appearance."

"David?" His dark eyebrows arched high.

"Yes. David." I lifted my chin with a touch of defiance.

"I wasn't aware that you and he were on a first-name basis," he said coldly.

"I don't feel it necessary to continue with formalities since he had come to my rescue on two occasions and is to be our guest for a while."

"As you wish, Elizabeth." He glared at me stonily, then abruptly left through the connecting door.

I came to the conclusion that Michael would forever be an enigma to me. Minutes ago, he was caring for me as though I were the most precious object on earth. Now he had suddenly wrapped himself in a curtain of icy indifference.

Between the warm tub, the slave, a cup of bouillon, and soda bread heaped with creamery butter, I fell into a sound sleep. Clara woke me in plenty of time to get dressed for dinner.

Clara hooked the back of my russet-colored gown, then put the finishing touches to my hair as I sat at the dressing table. Astonishment flashed in my blue eyes

165

when I saw Michael's reflection in the mirror as he entered through the connecting door. He looked exceptionally handsome as he came toward me. That was the second time in one day he had used the connecting door to my bedchamber, and I wondered, with some excitement, if it was a portent of things to come.

"Are you ready to go down to dinner, Elizabeth?" he asked.

His entrance and question startled me. Of late, Michael was not in the habit of escorting me to dinner. I rose and took his proffered hand. "Yes, Michael."

"Uncle Jack and Mr. Cooke are waiting for us in the drawing room."

"Where is Rose?"

"She'll be down shortly," he replied, drawing my hand through his arm as he led me out into the corridor.

When we entered the drawing room a beaming Uncle Jack kissed me soundly on the cheek.

"My dear Elizabeth. What a harrowing morning you must have had. By George, those are nasty bruises on your arms. How fortunate Mr. Cooke came along when he did. I should have canceled my appointment and gone with you this morning. I shall never forgive myself," Uncle Jack said.

"It was my own fault for being so clumsy, not yours. The bumps and bruises will soon fade, Uncle Jack." I smiled warmly before I went over to David, who took my hand and kissed the air over it. "I see you have met our Uncle Jack."

"Yes. Mr. Donahue has been regaling me with stories about Ireland. I'll have a wealth of material for my articles before I leave here."

"We have a lot in common, Mr. Cooke and I. Both semi-world travelers, you know," Uncle Jack said. "Ah! Here's Rose!" He went to the open doorway, slipped his arm about Rose's waist and drew her into the room toward David. "Mr. Cooke, my niece, Rose Tyrone. Rose, this young man is David Cooke, a writer of travel articles for magazine. He's spent several years in that metropolis, New York City."

"How do you do, Mr. Cooke." Rose shyly extended her hand, which David took and attended to in the same manner as mine.

"Miss Tyrone," David said with his usual captivating smile. "Meeting you forces me to believe people are telling the truth when they speak of the great beauty of the Irish rose."

Uncle Jack laughed heartily. "I do believe Mr. Cooke kissed the Blarney Stone before venturing into Northern Ireland."

"Now that Rose is here, I think we can go in to dinner. Elizabeth," Michael said, offering me his arm.

I thought his behavior exceedingly formal. Nevertheless, I decided to enjoy his sudden attentiveness.

The cream of potato soup was followed by poached salmon with egg sauce. The venison, which had been carved in the kitchen, was served with carrots, parslied potatoes, cauliflower, and thick slabs of bread.

"This had been an unexpected treat," David remarked as he finished his dessert. "Everything was absolutely delicious. My compliments to your cook. She has an exceptional way with salmon."

"You'll find we have excellent fishing around here, Mr. Cooke. Trout . . . salmon . . . the streams abound in them. I do hope I can persuade you to do a bit of fishing with me during your stay here," Uncle Jack suggested.

"I'd be honored." David raised his wineglass in a salute to Uncle Jack.

"How long do you intend to be in this part of the

country, Mr. Cooke?" Michael asked.

"Difficult to say, Lord Tyrone. The magazine in New York is going to run a series of my articles. I'm not sure just how many they want," David replied.

"Are you an American?" Rose asked quietly.

"I spent a number of years in America, and I'm afraid I've picked up their accent. Actually I'm English, born and schooled in England. However, I still have a number of literary contacts in America."

"How fascinating!" Rose exclaimed.

"Care for a brandy, Mr. Cooke?" Michael asked, pushing back his chair and rising.

"Yes, I would, Lord Tyrone," David replied.

"We adjourned to the drawing room, where David and Uncle Jack dominated the conversation with tales of New York City, each trying to outdo the other in friendly competition. I watched Michael stare moodily into his brandy as he swirled it. I wondered if he disapproved of my inviting David Cooke to be our guest. Was he jealous? Laughter simmered in me. Michael jealous of David? I could really dream up idiotic notions.

"Elizabeth . . . why don't you play for us? Some Chopin, I think," Michael said. It was more a command than a request.

I declined, saying that my hands were still quite sore from my ordeal. So we all settled into a quiet, companionable silence. I was gratified to see David had sat next to Rose.

Uncle Jack puffed on his pipe and Michael refilled his brandy snifter, languidly relaxing in his chair. As the hour grew late, I excused myself. I was amazed when Michael followed suit and escorted me to my bedchamber. Following a quick good night at the door, he went down the corridor to his own room.

As I lay on my bed, my eyes never left the connecting

door. Noises began to emanate from Michael's room. A chair scraped against the floor as though he had risen from it in haste. The steady thud of pacing feet was barely muffled by the carpet. The tread of footsteps would approach the connecting door, only to stop and echo away. I watched the door and waited . . . and waited . . . and waited . . . .

Suddenly, the door was thrust open with such force that it bounced back against the wall. A naked Michael strode toward my bed, then climbed in beside me with a determined glint in his eyes. He extinguished the oil lamp beside the bed. Willingly, I went into his arms, overjoyed by his presence. But this was a Michael I did not know. There was no gentle unbuttoning of my nightdress. It was practically torn from my body.

Michael's kisses were urgent, tinged with uncontrolled passion as they covered my face and body. His lovemaking bordered on a sweet savagery that sparked a feral, primordial instinct in me, and I matched his ferocity with complete abandonment. Our mutual passions sated, he rolled to one side. Both of us panted for air as our damp bodies glistened with sweat.

As I lay there staring into the dim room, I thought I'd never sleep again, such was my rapture. I gazed over at Michael, whose breathing had steadied and indicated he was asleep. I ran my hand over his thick black hair, kissed his cheek, then turned on my side. I do believe I fell asleep with a smile on my face.

Eight

Breakfast looked like a gala affair with Uncle Jack, David, and Rose seated around the table when I entered the dining room. I was delighted to see Rose at the breakfast table, her face radiant as David captured her imagination, recounting his travels with descriptive embellishments.

"I've persuaded our young friend to do a bit of fishing with me this morning, Elizabeth," Uncle Jack announced as I placed my laden plate on the table and took my seat.

"Oh? Is Michael going with you?" I asked with a smile.

"Good Lord! Michael go fishing?" Uncle Jack chuckled. "I'm afraid he doesn't have the patience for it. No. Michael left for Rathlin Island quite early this morning."

"Oh." My heart sank. In my mind, Rathlin island and Isabel were one and the same. Would Michael ever forget her?

"What do you ladies have planned for today?" David asked.

"It's time Rose and I went to Derry to see about hiring a seamstress, don't you think so, Rose?"

"Oh, I don't know, Elizabeth. Derry?" Her voice was

tinged with a certain amount of stress.

"I don't think Rose has ventured too far from Dunwick since her young man disappeared," Uncle Jack said.

I looked anxiously at Rose, who had lowered her head as a red flush covered her cheeks. Uncle Jack was a dear, but seldom measured his words. "Then it will be a refreshing experience for both of us."

A few hours after Uncle Jack and David headed out on their fishing expedition, Rose and I left for Derry with a driver and footman in attendance. Dreary row houses, two and three stories high, sat with an air of despair in the cobbled streets outside the seventeenth-century wall that guarded the town of Derry. Leaden smoke, puffing from flues embraced by bricked chimneys, added to an atmosphere of quiet, hopeless anguish. Even the tall, narrow windows and doors emitted an air of dejection, like forlorn faces screaming their despondency in silence. Rose informed me it was Bogside, where the Catholics lived. The aura of despair evinced by Bogside sent a shudder through me.

Excitement was clearly etched on Rose's pallid face as we passed through the entrance of the thick stone walls into the city of Derry. We tended to our main business first, securing a seamstress and making arrangements for her to come to Dunwick, then proceeded to the bootmaker's and the milliner's, both of whom were more than willing to service us in any way they could.

"I could do with a bit of lunch. How about you, Elizabeth?" Rose asked as we walked along the crowded street, her face now rosy from the nip in the fall air.

"A hot cup of tea would taste good about now," I concurred.

We found a small teashop that wasn't too crowded and ordered cheese sandwiches to go with our tea.

"What do you think of David Cooke, Rose?" I asked

before biting into my sandwich.

"He's so interesting and knowledgeable. Imagine! Having traveled to all those places."

"And good-looking too."

"Yes. And good-looking too." Rose smiled shyly. "You seem to know him quite well, Elizabeth."

"I feel I do," I replied, then went on to tell her how we had met in the Lake District and how he had showed me some of the more interesting sights there.

"Where was Michael?" she asked.

I had put my foot in it this time. I couldn't tell her he had been at Dunwick, for she knew he had spent only a day or so there. "As you know, he had to make that trip home, then urgent business in London claimed him for a time." The explanation seemed to satisfy her, but I changed the subject anyway. "Callie tells me her tutor is quite fond of you."

"Mr. Duffy?" She gave a tinkling laugh. "You shouldn't believe anything Callie tells you, Elizabeth. She's a great one for making up stories. Mr. Duffy hardly knows I'm alive. I doubt if two or three sentences have ever passed between us since he's been tutoring Callie. He has his hands full with that one."

"Perhaps Callie needs to be in a girls school where she would have the company of other girls her own age," I suggested. "It isn't healthy for the child to have only the company of Mrs. Meehan."

"Michael has tried several times to place her in school, but after a week or two she is always sent home."

"Surely they could have tried to discipline her. That's what she needs," I persisted.

"Callie doesn't take kindly to discipline. One of the teachers who tried was rewarded with a broken arm."

"Oh, Rose. You must be joking," I exclaimed.

"No. Callie tied a string across the school's staircase shortly before she knew the teacher would be descending.

172

Fortunately, the teacher only broke her arm in the fall," Rose explained.

"That's serious! The woman could have broken her neck," I said, shocked by the incident.

"Callie performed tricks like that at all the schools Michael put her in — all except one. At Miss Wyngate's school for young girls, they made a concerted effort to control Callie, and Callie retaliated by setting fire to the place."

"Good Lord!" I gasped. Rose was not one to tell untrue stories, nor one to color tales with half-truths.

"So you see why Michael had to resort to a private tutor and keep her at Dunwick."

"What about local playmates? Perhaps some village children?"

Rose shook her head. "That didn't work out either. The village children will have nothing to do with her anymore."

"Why?"

"Oh, they tried at first. But if she didn't get her way or win the game they were playing, she'd go off screaming and tell Michael all sorts of lies. After a while, Michael would no longer listen to her fabricated complaints and that's when Callie really became persona no grata in the village . . ." Rose hesitated.

"Go on, Rose. Don't leave me wondering what happened," I urged.

"Well . . . there was one particular little girl who always stood up to Callie, refusing to be bullied or intimidated by her. Callie hated her. The girl had a pet dog who followed her everywhere, and it was no secret she adored her dog. The girl beat Callie at a game, and the next morning the dog was found on the doorstep of the girl's cottage with its head bashed in. Though no one could prove anything, the entire village blamed Callie, and that ended Callie's going into the village and playing with the children there."

"No child could do such a thing," I defended, horrified by the deed. "Perhaps the poor animal had been run over by a carriage."

Rose shrugged. "Callie is very strong for her age and highly unpredictable."

"Mrs. Meehan appears to have absolute control over her, though."

"That's why Michael kept her on after Isabel's death."

"Oh? Wasn't she hired to take care of Callie when Isabel passed away?" I asked as a three-tiered platter of creamy cakes and sweets was placed on our table.

"Mrs. Meehan was Isabel's governess as a child. When Michael married Isabel, Mrs. Meehan came with her to Dunwick as her companion. Eventually, she became housekeeper since Isabel hated to have anything to do with the running of the house."

"Then Isabel wasn't from around here?"

"No. Her family has vast land holdings south of Dublin."

"Then Isabel was wealthy?" I was becoming more and more intrigued.

"Exceptionally so. She was the only child of one of the richest families in Ireland. I understand her dowry was enormous and her family had settled in large annuity on her, which, of course, became Michael's when she died," Rose replied, nibbling on an eclair.

"Uncle Jack said she drowned off Rathlin Island. Did they ever find her body?"

"Yes. Some days after the accident, her body was washed up on the rocks. Michael and Uncle Jack immediately went to Rathlin to identify the body, but it was so grotesque, having been picked at by the gulls, they decided to bury her on Rathlin. We had a memorial service here for her and interred an empty casket in the Tyrone vault."

174

"Is the vault on the grounds?"

"Yes. But it's about a mile or so from the manor house. The Tyrone cemetery is midway between the manor house and the ruins of the ancient Tyrone Castle," Rose replied.

"I'm surprised Uncle Jack didn't show me that straight-away," I said.

"Well . . . the history behind the old castle isn't very savory and there is hardly anything there now. A few old stones. Not even the outline of the castle is visible any more."

"Now you've quickened my curiosity," I said, laughing.

"Some old story about an ancestor who put to death a village girl out of jealousy. It all happened so long ago, I think the tale has become exaggerated over the years. Well, I've had more than enough lunch. Shall we head back to Dunwick?"

"As long as we're here, why don't we window-shop a bit?" I suggested while somewhere in the recesses of my brain I heard Callie telling the story of the banshee.

"All right. I could use some embroidery thread and linen."

"And we can see if there are any new books out."

Like children set loose in a vast candy store, we wandered the through the streets of Derry, gleefully making little purchases we could take with us. We returned to Dunwick in time for afternoon tea.

At dinner, I seemed to be the only one upset by Michael's absence, and it showed.

"You look a bit down, Elizabeth. Couldn't you find what you were looking for in Derry?" Uncle Jack asked.

"I'm worried about Michael," I replied.

"Don't go concerning yourself about Michael. With this fog and rough sea, he has enough sense to stay on Rathlin and not attempt to cross," Uncle Jack replied soothingly.

"Uncle Jack is right, Elizabeth," Rose agreed. "There's a large farm cottage on the island that serves as an inn. He can stay there when the weather turns. He's done it many times before."

"Sometimes for two or three days," Uncle Jack added.

When the four of us retired to the drawing room, Uncle Jack lit his pipe, then entertained us with several tales of Irish folklore. I had heard some of them before, but it was always a joy to listen and watch him, for he never told the stories the same way twice. His animated renderings were like watching a play in which all the characters were played by the same actor.

I thought sleep would come quickly after the busy day in Derry, but as I lay abed Rathlin pounded in my brain. Rathlin . . . Isabel's true resting place, where Michael paid frequent homage. Isabel . . . Rathlin . . . The names echoed louder and louder in my head like the steady ringing of bells. Callie was right about one thing. There was a banshee at Dunwick. And for me, that banshee was Isabel. A specter I didn't know . . . couldn't see . . . couldn't fight . . . couldn't conquer, for she lived on in Michael's brain and heart.

As drowsiness clouded my brain, my thoughts took a new twist. A strange, frightening one. Isabel was as wealthy as I. And, like me, she was an only child. She had met with a fatal accident, as I had almost done at Dunluce Castle. Was it all coincidence? Or was there a pattern to it? Was Michael . . . ? I refused to let myself think it. Never . . . never. Yet a seed of doubt was planted. I could only pray it wouldn't take root and grow. Real sleep never came. A hazy mist enveloped me and eerie apparitions floated in and out of my fogged mind.

Several days had passed and still Michael did not appear. I felt as though I had been in a battle and lost, even though Rose and I had been kept quite busy by the seamstress. Rose fluttered about as if she had found a new world. The only moment of real joy I had was seeing the expression on Clara's face when I ordered two new frocks and some undergarments to be made in the latest fashion for her.

And it was during Michael's absence that I had my first confrontation with Mrs. Meehan. I had summoned her to the library. It seemed the most appropriate place to talk business, and the room had an authority about it that I hoped would cast its aura on me.

"You wanted to see me, Lady Tyrone." Her voice was sharp, clipped, and decidedly chilly as she stood rigidly erect before the desk where I was seated. Her hands were folded over her dark skirt as she peered down at me disdainfully.

"Yes, Mrs. Meehan. Do sit down."

"I prefer to stand, Lady Tyrone," she replied.

"As you wish." I didn't press the issue, even though I disliked having to look up at her. Perhaps that was her intention. "As Dunwick now has a mistress who prefers to run her own household, you'll no longer be obliged to continue in that capacity. From now on, I shall see to the menus and household matters. I would appreciate your turning the household ledgers over to me as soon as possible."

"I assure you they are in perfect order," Mrs. Meehan said, her gray eyes stabbing at me like steel blades.

"I am quite sure they are, Mrs. Meehan. From what I gather, you have been doing an excellent job. But taking care of Callie is a full-time occupation in itself."

"Callie is no trouble if you know how to handle her."

"I'm sure. All the same, I feel it is my duty as mistress to run the house," I said with a finality which I hoped conveyed my determination to Mrs. Meehan in the strongest possible terms. I couldn't go on spending all my days playing the piano or reading. I needed a concrete occupation to make me feel useful.

She stared at me stonily for a few seconds, then said, "I'll get the account ledgers for you straight-away, Lady Tyrone, but I don't think his lordship is going to approve."

"By the way, Mrs. Meehan, I've had a shipment of material sent from London and would like to have some frocks made for Callie. Would you be so kind as to take her measurements so I can pass them along to the seamstress," I said as the darkly clothed woman began to leave.

"That won't be necessary, Lady Tyrone. I see to all Callie's clothing and I make sure she lacks for nothing."

"I see. Well, that will be all, Mrs. Meehan." I wasn't about to let her walk out on me. I wanted to be the one who decided when the interview was over.

After she left, I sat at the desk feeling quite pleased with myself. I had established myself as mistress of Dunwick. Still, Mrs. Meehan's warning that Michael wouldn't approve cast a shadow over my elation. I poked through the unlocked drawers of the desk and found everything neatly in order. I would have to ask Michael if there was another desk that could be placed in the upstairs sitting parlor for my use. I knew I couldn't use Michael's desk and the library to pursue my new duties.

True to her word, Mrs. Meehan returned with the ledgers within twenty minutes. After she left, I poured through the books for the rest of the day. I had a good mind for figures and readily concluded that Mrs. Meehan had done an excellent job of recording all items purchased and amounts paid out.

I took the ledgers up to my bedchamber, deciding to use my small cherrywood escritoire until a larger desk could be located. I was concentrating on the current week's menu when I heard the unusual sound of Callie running up and down the corridor of the wing I was in.

She seldom, if ever, came to this section of the house unless it was for mischief. Her raised voice was so shrill, I could hardly make out the words she was screeching at the top of her lungs.

When I flung open my door and went into the corridor, she spun around, her face was a red as her hair, her green eyes glinting maniacally. When she saw me, her screaming changed to a high, hollow laugh.

"Callie! What's wrong?" I headed toward her, only to have her keep backing away.

"Father's come home . . . Father's come home . . . and he knows what you've done . . . he knows . . . "

"What are you talking about, Callie?" The way the child looked at me gave me the chills. There was a mad look in her eyes that frightened me.

"He knows what you've done . . . Mrs. Meehan told him . . . Mrs. Meehan told him . . . " she continued in a singsong voice. "He's waiting for you in the library. Bad woman . . . bad woman . . . " She darted down the corridor toward the other wing of the house, her red hair bouncing behind her like a fiery demon.

I found it hard to believe Michael would send a child to tell me he was waiting to see me in the library. But it would only take a minute to check, and if he was home, I wanted to greet him in private, in the hopes he might exhibit some affection.

I picked up my skirts and briskly walked down the corridor to the wide marble steps. As I thrust my foot forward to start the descent, my ankle struck a tautly strung cord. My hand flailed at the banister without ever finding it before a scream escaped my lips and I hurtled into oblivion.

When my eyes began to open like leaden drapes, I beheld the fuzzy image of a strange man whose mustache, pointed goatee and gaunt face gave him a satanic appearance.

179

"Lady Tyrone," said the stranger as though calling through a long tunnel.

"Is she coming around, Doctor?" It was Michael's voice.

"I believe so," replied the man hovering over me.

I closed my eyes. The pain in my head was so strong it dimmed the pain in the rest of my body. The stairs . . . the marble staircase . . . I had tripped and fallen. Was I dying? I thought I heard Michael's voice again. It was muffled and indistinct. I raised a feeble hand and blinked my eyes before hoarsely whispering, "Michael . . . "

"Yes, Elizabeth . . . I'm here," he said gently, taking my extended hand and sitting on the bed alongside me.

"I fell."

"We know, Elizabeth, we know." He patted my hand reassuringly.

"Am I dying?"

"Lord Tyrone. If I may . . . " the doctor said. Michael released my hand and rose from the bed, stepping to one side as the doctor bent over me. "Lady Tyrone, if you can, please let me know if you feel anything when I press down."

I nodded, then audibly gasped when he pressed on my ribs. When he probed the rest of my body i winced several times, but it was nothing like the pain around my ribs. I was now able to focus more clearly, and I saw Michael at the foot of the bed, his hands clasped behind his back as he solemnly stared down at me. The doctor straightened up, stood back, and drew a deep breath.

"Well . . . as I said before, Lord Tyrone, it's a miracle she has no broken bones, and I don't believe there are any internal injuries. Her ribs and head have been badly bruised, possibly a few fractures in the ribs, and she'll have numerous black and blue welts on her legs and arms. It would be best to keep an eye on her." He picked up his black bag from a chair and snapped it shut. "Send for me if she sees spots before her eyes or has any dizziness or vomiting. Otherwise, rest and time will be the best medicines I can prescribe for now." He headed for the door, Michael swiftly following him. "No . . . no," the doctor protested with a raised hand. "Stay with Lady Tyrone. I can find my way out."

"Good night, Doctor. And thank you," Michael said, quietly closing the door, then coming to sit on the bed once again.

"Then I'm not going to die, Michael?" I asked, thinking at the moment it might be less painful if I did.

"No. You're not going to die." Michael smiled as his hand smoothed my unpinned hair. "I imagine you'll hurt for a while, though. Do you feel sick or dizzy?"

"No. I just seem to hurt all over."

"Tell me, if you can, Elizabeth, what happened? You're not usually clumsy and you've been up and down those stairs a hundred times."

"Didn't you hear Callie screaming?"

"Yes. But I had just returned from Rathlin and was taking a bath before dinner," Michael replied.

"I went out to see what all the fuss was about and she told me you were home and waiting in the library to see me. When I reached the landing there was a cord stretched across the top step, which I didn't see, and it caught my ankle, throwing me off balance. The next thing I knew, I was here with the doctor standing over me."

"There must be some mistake, Elizabeth. All of us came dashing to the landing when we heard you scream, and there was no cord across the stairs, for I was the first one who rushed down the stairs." Michael's eyes clouded and his expression was grim.

"I tell you, Michael, there *was* a cord and that's why I fell," I insisted.

181

"Why don't we say you thought there was a cord?"

"But there really was, Michael. Why won't you believe me?"

His large, well-shaped hand stroked my head lightly. "Whatever you say, Elizabeth." He smiled in a most peculiar manner.

"Didn't anyone else hear Callie screaming?"

"I imagine everyone was getting ready for dinner. Then, Rose and Uncle Jack are used to Callie's antics and wouldn't pay any attention. I can't speak for your friend Mr. Cooke."

"How long have I been in bed?" I couldn't think straight. My head was pounding and every time I took a breath my rib cage felt as though it would crumble.

"A little over five hours. It's eleven in the evening," Michael informed me. "Do you think you'd like some tea?"

I nodded, which was a grave error, for it greatly increased the pain in my head.

"Toast?" Michael added.

"Yes."

Michael pulled the bell cord and Clara appeared in minutes. "A tea tray with toast and some broth for your mistress."

She bobbed and fled to do his bidding.

Michael gently raised me to a sitting position, propping several pillows behind my back. "The doctor left some powders on the night stand that will help ease the pain. You can put them in your tea."

The act of sitting up shot pain from my head to my toes again and again. I was thankful when Clara brought the tea so I could take the powders. Michael went to the window and gazed out into the inky night while I tore open a packet, letting the white grains trickle into my tea. I drank the brew quickly, then proceeded to spoon the hot broth down my throat. It all tasted exceptionally good.

"Are you finished, Elizabeth?" Michael asked, coming back to the bed.

"Yes."

"Feeling any better?" He removed the bed tray and resumed his seat on the bed.

"A little. Although I think I'd like to lie back down."

After assisting me, he turned the oil lamp low. "I'll leave the door to my room open in case you need me."

"Thank you, Michael."

He bent and kissed me on the forehead before going into his bedchamber.

The next two days passed quickly as my youthful body set about healing itself. Michael was most attentive, easing the extra burden placed on Clara. Rose spent part of both morning and afternoon with me, explaining that Uncle Jack's absence was due to his playing host to David Cooke.

On those occasions when I was alone, trying to read, I couldn't stop my mind from struggling to sort out recent events. The near accident at Dunluce and now the staircase. Accidents? No. I could no longer think either occurance was accidental. Someone wanted me out of the way permanently. I would have to master my rising fear and be extremely cautious in the future. Was the cord across the staircase a replay of the way in which Callie had dealt with a teacher she didn't like? Throwing things in a tantrum was Callie's style. Had she thrown the stone at Dunluce? Yes, Callie could be cruel and vicious, yet I found it difficult to believe a ten-year-old child could be a calculating murderer. The battered dog came to mind, but I pushed it away. Now, Mrs. Meehan was another story. Her hatred of me was no secret, at least not to me. And I firmly believed that woman capable of murder if she thought it necessary.

Uncle Jack and Rose were above suspicion. Michael

. . . well, my heart refused even to consider the possibility.

The third day saw me up and about, spending a good deal of time in the upstairs sitting parlor. The black and blue marks had taken on a hideous ocher shade, and if I coughed or took too deep a breath, my rib cage would remind me how tender it was.

I held onto Michael's arm tightly as we went down the staircase to dinner, my first time since the accident.

"Elizabeth, my dear, how good to see you up and about again. Nasty business falling down the stairs like that," Uncle Jack said as we entered. He took my hands in his and lightly kissed my forehead.

"Indeed it was, Elizabeth," David agreed with a warm, gentle smile.

Throughout the meal, conversation was light, the brunt of it being borne by Uncle Jack. The incident of my falling down the stairs was not mentioned again. Indeed, it seemed as though everyone found it better to pretend it never happened.

We took our usual places in the drawing room while Michael poured brandy for the men. Rose picked up her petit point and pretended to be working diligently on it, but I saw her gaze wander furtively every now and then to David. Uncle Jack sipped his brandy and puffed on his pipe with all the appearance of a contented man. Michael, slouched in a chair, his long legs stretched out before him, glumly studied the contents of his brandy snifter.

"Michael . . . you seem unusually pensive tonight. Troubles with the tenants?" Uncle Jack asked before taking a long pull on his brandy.

"You should know by now, Uncle Jack, I'm not the chatty sort," Michael replied.

"I guess not. You and Rose are cut from the same cloth, I suspect." Uncle Jack puffed on his pipe rhythmi-

184

cally for several moments. "Elizabeth . . . we've missed your delightful renditions on the piano. Do honor us by playing something."

"It would be my pleasure," I replied, most anxious to have my fingers race across the keyboard. Three days seemed like an eternity away from the soothing comforts of the piano. I played some melodic and poignant pieces of Schumann. Then, during an interval, I noticed David looked penetratingly at Michael. I felt a strong undercurrent of emnity travel across the room as Michael, seeming to sense David's look, turned to glare at him.

"I trust you enjoy my wife's musical efforts, Mr. Cooke," Michael said, a challenge in his dark eyes.

"Her playing is the music of the gods," David replied lightly, rising and coming toward the piano, then taking a seat beside me on the bench.

I glanced at Michael to see cold fury set on the sharp, angular planes of his face, the corners of his wide mouth turned down as his square jaw thrust itself forward with prideful arrogance. I indulged myself in the fancy he might be jealous. I was almost happy to have fallen down the stairs, for the mishap had apparently turned Michael's attitude into that of a devoted husband.

"Do you mind, Elizabeth?" David asked as his hands skimmed an arpeggio over the keyboard.

"Not at all. Do you play?" I asked, looking into his smiling face.

"A bit. Nothing classical. Just some tunes of the day. I'm not a pianist like you, more of a pub player." He commenced to play one of the more popular songs of a few year ago with unpracticed skill.

"Rose . . . you know that song. Sing for us," Uncle Jack insisted.

"Oh, no . . . I couldn't." She lowered her eyes shyly.

"Of course you can. Why, you have a beautiful voice," declared Uncle Jack.

"Please, Miss Tyrone," David urged. "If you don't, you'll have me believing my playing is so poor no human voice could follow it."

Demurely, Rose came over to the piano and began to sing in a clear bell-like soprano. With the exception of Michael, who had gone to the sideboard for another brandy, we applauded gaily when she had finished. As David launched into another song, I left the bench to stand beside Rose and encourage her to sing again. She did so with more east this time, and when she reached the chorus, Uncle Jack came over and joined in, his tenor voice surprisingly mellow. Caught up in the spirit of camaraderie, I found myself wanting to join their song fest as David went from one tune to another, but my ribs were still too tender and instead I listened to their happy voices. Michael remained remote, keeping to his chair, but I could feel his eyes burning into me, studying me carefully as though trying to come to some decision. It unsettled me, like the deadly calm before a storm.

"That was jolly good," Uncle Jack exclaimed when David declined to continue. "Haven't sung like that in ages."

"You have a truly lovely voice, Miss Tyrone," David complimented Rose, causing her to blush.

"You do, Rose," I concurred. "I'll have to get some sheet music of the new songs so we can have a sing when David isn't here to play for us."

"Which I'm afraid will be quite soon," David said.

"What do you mean, my boy?" Uncle Jack inquired.

"I shall be leaving Dunwick early tomorrow morning. I must return to London. My editor there seems to be having a problem with some of my articles and wants to go over them with me," David explained.

"We shall miss you, David," Uncle Jack said sincerely.

"The hospitality here has been greatly appreciated,"

David said.

"Have you finished your work on Northern Ireland?" I asked, noticing the light fade from Rose's eyes and a dull sadness take its place.

"Hardly. Why, Jack here, has opened up vistas I never would have found on my own. And that is another reason I must see my London editor. I would like to do an extended article on the history of Londonderry. If he buys the idea, I'll be spending a good deal of time in this area," David said.

"We shall look forward to it," Uncle Jack said, slipping an arm around David's shoulders and leading him to the sideboard. "We'll have to have a drink on that."

"Elizabeth . . . I believe you've had enough excitement on your first day up. Come, I'll see you to your bedchamber," Michael said. As usual, it was a command not a request.

Rather than risk a scene on David's last night with us, I went dutifully to Michael, saying my goodnights to all with a warm smile. I hoped that Uncle Jack would see the light in Rose's eyes and also retire so that she could be alone with David.

When we reached my bedchamber, I said, "Michael, I have relieved Mrs. Meehan of the household ledgers and other duties concerning the house." I held my breath, waiting for him to explode with anger.

"I know," he said quietly.

"You don't object?" I asked, amazed at his quiet acceptance.

"Why should I? This is your home to run as you see fit."

Rashly, I threw my arms about his neck and smiled up into his face. "Oh, thank you, Michael." A peculiar sheen flickered over his ebony eyes and it frightened me.

"You don't have to thank me, Elizabeth." He reached up and removed my hands from his neck. "It is your right."

I stepped back, masking my embarrassment with feigned aloofness. "I shall need a writing desk in the upstairs parlor. A fairly large one."

"There is my mother's desk in the attic of the east wing. She used it for household duties, and I think you'll find it satisfactory. I shall have it brought down tomorrow. Good night, Elizabeth." He quickly turned and headed for the door to his own bedchamber, then stopped, his decidedly masculine physique framed in the doorway. He turned his head to look at me. "By the way, Elizabeth, I don't want you encouraging Mr. Cooke to become a permanent resident here whenever he is in the area." He closed the door with a bang and I heard a key turn in the lock.

Michael was nowhere to be seen when we said our good-byes to David. Rose appeared despondent, but cheered visibly when David said he would write to her. The day promised to be a dreary one as a misting rain noiselessly settled in. I returned to the upstairs sitting parlor where I began to plan a small party for Callie's birthday which was the following day. I had already given instructions to the cook to prepare a cake for the event.

It was Callie's eleventh birthday. All of us, including Michael, sat in the dining room waiting from Mrs. Meehan to bring the young girl down. Michael was restless and irritable as if the entire affair were loathsome to him. Even Uncle Jack and Rose wore looks of apprehension.

When Mrs. Meehan finally led her in, Callie was quite sedate dressed in a beautiful, fancy pink frock. Michael rose from his chair and went to kiss his daughter on the forehead, which she accepted with total indifference.

"Where are my presents?" she asked petulantly with a light stamp of her foot.

"Remember what I told you, Callie," Mrs. Meehan warned, standing off to the side.

Callie narrowed her brilliant green eyes at Mrs. Meehan, then flounced to the table and took a seat.

"Well, Callie, would you care to make the first slice in the cake?" I asked. "Michael . . . you'll help her, won't you?"

"Take the candles off!" she demanded, causing Rose to jump from her seat and comply with the demand. "Where's the knife?"

Michael picked up the large knife in front of him and handed it to Callie. I glanced at Uncle Jack and thought I saw genuine fear in his eyes. I passed it off quickly, thinking my imagination was getting the better of me again. Michael placed his large hand over Callie's, steadying the knife in her hand as it sliced through the rich, sweet cake. Then he signaled a serving maid to complete the cutting and serving of the cake.

"Now can I have my presents?" Callie asked.

"Please may I," corrected Mrs. Meehan.

"Please may I have my presents," Callie reiterated slowly, emphasizing each word with stinging sarcasm.

"Of course, Callie." I smiled and tried desperately to inject a little gaiety into the supposed festivities. I went to the side buffet and picked up the four brightly wrapped packages and brought them to her. Michael had relinquished his place at the head of the table to let Callie sit there, and he sat next to me across from Uncle Jack.

She opened each package impassively. There was the water color set from me, artist's paper from Rose, and a brightly painted wooden soldier from Uncle Jack. Michael had given her a gold locket. She pushed the gifts aside without another glance, then attacked her cake ravenously. With her plate empty but her mouth puffed out with cake, Callie gathered up her presents and raced out of the room, Mrs. Meehan trailing rapidly behind her.

"Well . . . this certainly wasn't the gala party I had in mind," I said lightly, even though I felt crushed by the somber fiasco.

"Excuse me." Michael pushed his chair back violently, and leaving his cake untouched, he stalked from the room.

"Michael," I called. The distress in my voice was evident, but if he heard, he paid no heed.

"Don't feel badly, my dear," Uncle Jack said, finishing one piece of cake, then helping himself to another from the side buffet. After resuming his seat, he continued. "We stopped having birthday parties for Callie some time ago."

"Why?" I asked in all innocence.

"Michael's scar . . . " he began.

"Uncle Jack!" Rose interrupted with a shocked expression.

"Good Lord, Rose! Elizabeth is a member of this family and Michael's wife. If anyone is entitled to know, she is," Uncle Jack sputtered.

"Know what?" I asked anxiously.

"On Callie's fourth birthday, Isabel had a large party for Callie. When it came to the cutting of the cake, Isabel insisted Michael help Callie with the chore. Michael finally relented and as he approached the child, who was standing on a chair to reach the cake, he bent over and placed the knife in her hand. Before anyone knew what happened, the knife flashed in her hand and Michael jolted upright, his hand over his cheek, blood pouring through his fingers as he stared at the child in astonishment. Callie was mute and motionless, the bloodied knife still in her hand. Then Isabel's laughter echoed through the room, causing Callie to squeal with delight as she lunged at Michael again with the upraised knife. But this time, he caught her wrist and twisted it until the sharp instrument fell to the floor. Callie cried. Isabel slapped Michael and ran to Callie's defense. Michael stalked from the room, forbidding any more birthday parties," Uncle Jack concluded.

"Oh, dear Lord! What have I done?" I was frantic with remorse at having made Michael relive what must have been a horrible ordeal for him.

"Don't go blaming yourself, my dear," Uncle Jack soothed. "You didn't know. That scoundrel nephew of mine should have told you."

"Uncle Jack, you know Michael hasn't mentioned the incident since the day it happened. He can't bear to talk about it," Rose said.

"Well . . . he should have told Elizabeth," Uncle Jack grunted.

"How horrible for everyone," I cried, visualizing the unsavory scene and stemming the tears that were forming behind my eyes. My poor Michael! To have his own daughter do such a thing, and then to have his wife react so abominaly. And here I had put him in the precarious position of having it happen all over again. I felt a deep sense of shame and guilt.

"Oh, Elizabeth . . . I should have told you," Rose moaned, coming to sit beside me.

I patted her hand. "It's my own fault. From the beginning, you tried to discourage me. But I blithely persisted. In the future I will consult you or Uncle Jack when a notion like that comes into my head again."

"Ladies . . . I do believe a glass of sherry is in order. Shall we go into the drawing room and indulge ourselves?"

I forced a smile. "Uncle Jack, I think I'd like a whiskey."

His brown eyes widened in astonishment, then filled with loving amusement. "Now, there's a lass after my own heart. What say you, Rose?"

Rose looked at Uncle Jack with blinking eyes, then at me. Suddenly, the tension seemed to flow out of her. "I've never had a whiskey," she exclaimed.

"Neither have I," I retorted with a tight smile.

"Ladies, I shall treat you to one of Uncle Jack's finest whiskies. Then, as Elizabeth's clever fingers seek out the proper chords, we'll sing to the glory of Ireland. For Ireland is all that truly matters."

We all stood at once and a grinning Uncle Jack gathered Rose and me in his burly arms and led us into the drawing room.

Days melted into months without incident and winter plodded in with its dreary rain and persistent fog as chilling blasts skipped over the land. Rose and I had our new outfits and would make excursions into Derry or Belfast to commence our Christmas shopping. Occasionally, screams of anger or frustration would filter down from the east wing of the house. But, like Uncle Jack and Rose, I soon learned to ignore them. Michael was hardly ever at home, and when he was, his demeanor toward me was cold and distant, which made my growing love for him all the more painful. On the other hand, Rose was glowing with a new-found radiance as letters from David came from London fairly regularly. She would read them to me with great tenderness, then immediately sit down to answer them in carefully worded and lengthy epistles.

Christmas was at hand, and after a flurry of last-minute shopping, Rose and I, with the admirable help of Uncle Jack, set about decorating the manor house and the great fir tree that had been set up in the marbled hall between the dining and drawing rooms.

I had sumptuous meals planned for both Christmas Eve and Christmas Day and ordered the same food to be served to the staff, which surprised and delighted cook, not to mention the staff.

192

Christmas Eve, after a highly praised dinner, we did not go into the drawing room as usual, but paraded into the marble hall to admire the tree. In accordance with long established custom, the staff soon filed in, with the exception of Mrs. Meehan. Holiday greetings were exchanged as Michael passed out packets of money to the staff. When the traditional ceremony was over and the staff had left, Michael took a deep breath and turned to me.

"Well, Elizabeth, shall we open our presents now?"

"We always open them on Christmas Day," I replied.

"I spend Christmas Day on Rathlin Island. So for the last five years we have opened our gifts in the evening," he explained stiffly.

"I see." My heart sank with the knowledge that Michael wanted to be at Isabel's true grave on the sacred holiday. I surpressed my growing melancholy, determined not to spoil the occasion. We passed around the elaborately wrapped gifts with a merry spirit. I was enchanted with the necklace that Michael gave me—a single, large black opal dangling form a gold chain—and he seemed genuinely pleased with the hand-carved jade chessmen I had chosen for him.

With thank you's and expressions of appreciation given and received, we retired to the drawing room where I played Christmas songs and old carols. To my surprise, Michael joined in the singing, blending his deep baritone with Uncle Jack's tenor and the soprano voices of the women. It was one of the happiest Christmas Eves of my life. I would have been ecstatic if Michael had come to my bedchamber. But he didn't.

"We must be present when Callie opens her gifts this morning," said Rose, who was now a familiar face at the breakfast table.

"I don't know if I can tolerate that dour face of Mrs. Meehan so early in the morning." Uncle Jack grimaced.

193

"Did Michael get off all right?" I asked.

"I expect so," Uncle Jack replied. "He's always up and about before any of us. Such a restless fellow! I had hoped his marriage to you, Elizabeth, would have made him settle down a bit more. But he appears more driven than ever."

Michael has always been active," Rose added.

Concluding our breakfast, we adjourned to the marble hall to await Callie. I sat in one of the many Louis XV chairs that randomly lined the mirrored and marbled walls of the great hall.

Callie blithely skipped into the room without acknowledging anyone's presence while Mrs. Meehan discreetly paused at the entrance. Callie circled the huge tree several times, then carefully scrutinized the brightly wrapped boxes beneath it. She sat down, legs sprawled out before her, and began to open them. When she had finished, it seemed every imaginable toy was scattered around her, none holding her interest for very long. An hour or so passed and Uncle Jack seemed far more intrigued by the toys than Callie, who yawned with more and more frequency. Finally, she rose from the floor, stared at the tree, then plucked one of the delicate ornaments from a branch and hurled it onto the marble floor where it smashed in myriad glass splinters.

"I want to go back upstairs," she announced peevishly, causing Mrs. Meehan to glide into the room.

"Aren't you forgetting something, Callie?" Mrs. Meehan asked as she took the child's hand.

"What?"

"Your gifts for everyone." Mrs. Meehan led Callie from the hall, then brought her back several moments later.

Callie handed a small package to Uncle Jack, one to Rose and one to me, saying, "It's a barm brack. Cook helped me." She put the gift in my hand.

"Thank you, Callie," I said, repressing a laugh when she stuck her tongue out at me.

Rose shook her head and sighed when Mrs. Meehan and Callie left. "That child will never change, I fear."

"Some of these toys are quite ingenious," Uncle Jack said, holding a wooden puzzle in his hand.

"Do you think Michael will be home this evening?" I asked.

"I had hoped so, but from the looks of the fast-changing weather, I doubt it. The wind is beginning to come up and the waters between Rathlin and the coast can be quite treacherous," Uncle Jack replied. "With the exception of a rising wind, the day isn't too bad. How about a brisk morning ride, Elizabeth, before the day deteriorates?"

"Excellent idea, Uncle Jack. You don't mind, do you Rose?" I asked, thinking a good ride over the fields was just what I needed.

"Not at all, Elizabeth. I'm anxious to start one of the books you gave me."

Rose and I went upstairs, she to the parlor, I to my bedchamber to change into my riding habit. I placed Callie's barm brack, or fruit cake as we call it in London, on my dressing table.

The horses were waiting for Uncle Jack and me. The damp chill in the air was a harbinger of impending snow. As this might be the last opportunity for a while, Uncle Jack and I rode the horses hard and far, racing over meadow and heath. Though the cold air whipped over my face, I felt elated and utterly free. By the time we returned to the house our cheeks and noses were cherry red.

By late afternoon, the winds had whipped into a fury and I knew Michael would remain on Rathlin Island and would not be at home to enjoy the lavish Christmas dinner I had planned.

195

Boiled cod with oyster sauce was served directly after the cream of potato and leek soup. Escalloped oysters, a salmi of wild goose, a saddle of mutton, boiled potatoes, parsnips, and carrots made up the main course. For dessert there was a sponge cake topped with lemon sauce and beaten cream.

They were Michael's favorites, and I was deeply disappointed he was not there to share the meal. Uncle Jack's unceasing praise for the dinner did nothing to assuage my frustration at Michael's absence.

As I prepared for bed, my eyes landed on the unwrapped bram brack Callie had given me. I took it to the small marble-topped table by the chaise lounge. I broke it in half, only to hear sharp clinks hit the marble top. The sound had a strange timbre to it. I put the cake down and went to fetch a brighter oil lamp from the night stand next to my bed. As I held the light close to the small table, miniature diamondlike fragments reflected prismatically in the yellowish light. I broke the cake into more bits, scattering the glittering pieces over the table.

I picked one up gingerly, and to my sudden horror, realized that the cake was lethal, embedded throughout with tiny shards of glass. Perplexed, I wondered if the child comprehended the dangers of ingesting broken glass. Surely an eleven-year-old girl was fully aware of the dire consequences slivers of glass would have on the human stomach. The glass in the cake was neither an accident nor a practical joke. It had been put there deliberately. Dunluce, the stairs, now this . . .

I couldn't bring myself to believe a child was capable of such terrible acts. But one thing I was sure of, someone wanted me dead.

Nine

When Michael had returned from Rathlin Island looking gaunt, I had longed to take him in my arms and comfort him, but he seemed in a distant, unreachable mood.

As the months passed his days were consumed by estate affairs, trips to Belfast, and visiting the tenant farmers. Such weariness kept him from my bedchamber. At least I assumed it was weariness. And then he was gone again.

One slate-gray, rainy March day, I was engrossed in the new sheet music I had received from London. They were the more popular songs of the day and I was having some difficulty in reaching the correct rhythm when Rose burst into the drawing room, high animation lighting her face.

"David's coming back to Dunwick," she cried, waving a letter in her hand. "He's really coming back!"

I left the piano and went to hug her. "I'm glad for your sake, Rose."

She flushed as we separated. "His editor has approved an in-depth article on the history of Derry."

"When will he be here?"

"I don't know. All he said was that he was on his way,"

197

she replied, excitement shining in her brown eyes before a more pensive attitude took hold of her. "Do you think Michael will disapprove? I know he doesn't particularly like David."

"It's three against one. Certainly you, I, and Uncle Jack approve, and that's all that matters," I said with a soothing smile, happy with the thought that Rose had become a new person since meeting David. She was vital, alive with a new sense of purpose in life, and regardless of Michael's admonition, I fully intended to extend our hospitality to David if only for Rose's sake. "Rose, do come and listen to the new music and see if I have the correct tempo."

We went over several of the songs, and as Rose concluded a particularly lilting tune in her fine soprano voice, the sound of applause reached our ears. We turned our heads simultaneously toward the open door of the drawing room.

"Splendid! Perfectly splendid!" David beamed, looking handsome and elegant in a well-tailored traveling suit.

"David!" Rose cried as we both went to greet him. "I only received your letter today saying you were coming."

"I travel faster than the post," he said, taking Rose's hand and raising it to his lips. Then, kissing my hand in similar fashion, he asked, "And how have you been, Elizabeth? No more accidents, I hope."

"No. I've been holding up quite well, thank you," I replied with a wide smile.

"And where is Mr. Donahue? I haven't seen the old boy in some time."

"He's down in the gardens checking the soil conditions," Rose replied. "Would you like to go see him or go up to your room first?"

"I'd rather take a stroll and look for Mr. Donahue first. You will join me, won't you, Rose?"

"I'd love to. I must have a cloak though." Her eyes

shining, Rose went to the bell cord and pulled it.

"What about you, Elizabeth? Care to come with us?" David asked.

"No. I want to refinger some passages on the new sheet music." I had a feeling they would like to be alone to renew their acquaintance.

When a maid appeared, Rose requested her gray merino cloak. While we waited David told us about his trip to London. They soon left, and I returned to the piano, happy for Rose yet feeling my own loneliness intensify. I forced myself to concentrate on the music before me. The piece was going quite nicely when a strident cry cut through the melody issuing from the piano.

"Why do you always play the piano?"

I was startled to see Callie standing alone in the middle of the drawing room, her hands over her ears. "Why . . . hello, Callie."

"I asked you a question." She took her hands from her ears and half skipped to the piano.

"Because I enjoy it and find it relaxing."

She cocked her head to one side, studying me, then began to hop in a circle around the piano and me. Her prancing round and round was annoying, but I held my tongue, knowing any protest on my part would only serve to make her continue her annoying antics. Finally, she stopped and came to sit on the piano bench next to me.

"Would you like to learn how to play the piano?" I asked, a little surprised that she would sit next to me.

"I already know how," she announced haughtily. "Want me to show you?"

"If you wish."

She pounded the piano with her fists, creating a horrid, discordant clamor. "See . . . isn't that pretty?" she asked, her hands poised above the keys, ready to resume the atonal onslaught.

Seeing she was in a mood to be fairly amiable toward me and desperately wanting to divert her attention from the piano, I asked, "Would you like me to play a game with you?"

"What game?" Her clear green eyes narrowed in suspicion.

"You choose the game," I replied, hoping it would have nothing to do with the piano.

She sat thoughtfully for a moment, one finger touching her lips, then announced, "Hide and seek."

"All right. But the library, dining room, and upstairs are off limits. Promise?"

"I promise," she said quickly, then slipped off the bench. "I'll hide first. You close your eyes and count to twenty."

Aloud, I slowly counted to twenty with eyes shut, thankful for the momentary peace. When the numerical goal had been reached, I opened my eyes and methodically searched the drawing room. I went into the marble hall, knowing full well there would be no place to hide there, for the mirrored walls made hiding virtually impossible. Back in the foyer, I peeked down the corridor that led to the kitchen and servants quarters below stairs. I smiled to myself. I hadn't added the downstairs to my list of out-of-bounds territories. I headed down the corridor and was about to descend the steps when I noticed a door ajar at the end of the corridor.

I had never paid much attention to that door, thinking it was some sort of closet, for it was always closed. I hurried to it and pulled it open to see a flight of steps going down to an inky, unknown interior. This would be Callie's idea of fun, luring me down in the dark, gleeful if I should trip or fall.

"Callie," I called from the doorway, then vaguely heard some movement down in the unlit chamber. I was onto her ways and wouldn't attempt to go down in the dark.

I went back to the foyer and lit one of the many lamps that sat sentinel on a long narrow table. Holding it firmly, I went back to the open door.

Warily, I placed one foot on the stone staircase, then cautiously made my way down to the bottom, holding the lamp high and almost at arm's length. A dank, musty odor emanated from the ancient stones and dirt floor. I slowly swung the lamp from side to side, finding the long, rectangular chamber empty of human life—at least from what I could see in the dim light. Some old casks rested wearily on half-rotted wooden stands. As my eyes adjusted to the murky light, I made out a dark form huddled on the floor off to the side.

"Callie?" I whispered.

I lifted the lamp higher and peered with strained eyes into the sunless room, trying to discern the shadowy form on the floor. I moved closer and the thing rose. It was the largest black mastiff I had ever seen. It stood to face me, pulling its upper lip back to bare white, menacing teeth. A growl started somewhere deep within its bowels, exiting from its mouth in a frothy snarl. It crouched, hair bristling as if ready to lunge at my throat.

"Good boy . . . good boy . . ." I kept saying as I began to shake with terror and slowly moved backward toward the staircase. I held my breath as my heel hit the stone riser of the first step, but I managed to back up the staircase, my eyes never leaving the glaring animal's coal-like eyes.

In what appeared to be one leap, the huge beast was at the foot of the stairs. I hastened my backward ascent. He placed one paw on the first step, then began a stealthy climb in pursuit of me. Ears back, his glistening fanged teeth flashed in the amber light of the oil lamp while a low, dreadful growl deepened in his throat. I turned to make a desperate run for the door which, to my horror, suddenly slammed shut. In vain I pushed it, jiggling the latch and pounding on it with my fist. I glanced over my shoulder to see the mastiff halfway up the steps. Panic gripped me, and I screamed. Magically, the door opened and I slipped through, slamming it shut with my free hand. Breathing hard, I leaned against the door, the oil lamp shaking in my hand.

"Lady Tyrone . . . whatever were you doing down there?" Mrs. Meehan's voice was as chilling as the sight of the black mastiff, and her stony gray eyes shone with a peculiar self-satisfaction.

"A . . . monstrous dog . . . down there . . . it came after me," I gasped.

"You must have been imagining things, Lady Tyrone. There is nothing down there," she said imperiously.

"There is! I am not imagining things! I saw it!" Anger was swelling within me.

"I'll go down myself." She took the lamp from my trembling hand. When she flung open the door I involuntarily cringed against the wall, expecting the black beast to bound out savagely.

She entered. I could hear the martial click of her heels on the stone steps as she descended into the dark chamber. My breathing had returned to normal when she reappeared.

"You must have been mistaken. There is nothing down there, Lady Tyrone," she declared, shutting the door and blowing out the lamp.

"I know what I saw, Mrs. Meehan. I did not imagine it," I said firmly, then marched back to the foyer.

"Whatever you say, Lady Tyrone," she replied, placing the lamp back on the table.

Her patronizing attitude was beginning to infuriate me. As I was about to respond with a few terse words of my own, a maniacal screech reverberated through the foyer and Callie came bounding out from behind the marble staircase.

"Couldn't find me . . . couldn't find me! But the banshee found you. I heard you scream." She squealed with insane laughter, clapping her hands and dancing about the foyer.

"Good Lord! Whatever is going on here?" Uncle Jack came from the marble hall into the foyer with Rose and David behind him.

"Lady Tyrone was playing tricks on Callie, sir," Mrs. Meehan said with a superior, smug expression.

Stunned by her twisting of the facts, I stared at the woman in mute astonishment while Rose and David stood totally bewildered.

"Do take the child upstairs, Mrs. Meehan. I'm too old to tolerate her antics," Uncle Jack demanded.

"Yes, Mr. Donahue." With a look of triumph, Mrs. Meehan took Callie's hand and led the still laughing child upstairs.

"I was not playing tricks on Callie," I said defensively.

"I know . . . I know. That woman galls me. I do wish Michael would do something about her." Uncle Jack sighed heavily. "But you look shaken to the core, Elizabeth. You're as white as a ghost. What happened?"

"Nothing of importance. I was playing hide-and-seek with Callie and I entered an unfamiliar room," I said for the benefit of Rose and David. Rose looked so radiant, I didn't want to inflict my troubles on her. "May I see you in the library, Uncle Jack?"

"Certainly, my dear," he replied, drawing my hand through his arm. "You should know by now, Elizabeth, that one doesn't play games with Callie."

"That room at the end of the corridor . . . what is it?" I asked, pointing in the direction of the dark chamber.

"It's empty. Michael had plans to make it into another wine cellar but never got around to it," Uncle Jack explained.

"Does it have another entrance?" I asked.

"Why . . . yes. An outside entrance that would enable the wine merchant to deliver his wares without coming into the house. Why do you ask, Elizabeth?"

"I went down to look for Callie and a huge black mastiff came at me. I was not imagining it as Mrs. Meehan suggested. She went down there and the animal was gone."

"Perhaps the dog inadvertently wandered in and you frightened it," he suggested as we entered the library and seated ourselves.

"I'll concede it might have been an accidental encounter. But the fine shards of glass scattered throughout the barm brack were certainly not an accident. And though no one seems to believe me, my fall was caused by a cord stretched across the staircase." The words came in a rush and I went on to relate my experiences with the rock at Dunluce and the smashed china doll in my bed. "Uncle Jack, I believe someone is trying to do me grievous harm."

He stared at me thoughtfully for some time before he spoke. "Glass in the barm brack?" He shook his head ruefully. "It certainly seems to me that someone is out do you a serious mischief. There are some people who have a decidedly warped sense of humor."

"Then you believe me?"

"Of course I do, my dear. Why should you make up such tales? The doll, the barm brack, and perhaps the cord, sound like Callie's hand might have been involved. But whatever happened at Dunluce, Callie couldn't have done it. She's not allowed off the grounds unless Michael is with her."

I stood and started to pace. Uncle Jack rose and came to put his arm around my shoulders. "There . . . there, Elizabeth. There's no one here who wishes you any harm. We all love you. Granted, Callie is an obstreperous child and given to cruel pranks. I'll have a talk with Mrs.

Meehan. Perhaps she'll listen to me and try to curb the child's deviltry. Have you told Michael of all this?"

"Michael's absences seem to becoming more frequent. When he is at home he seems so preoccupied I hesitate to disturb him. When I do try and tell him about the events, he dismisses the tales as either imagination or overreaction on my part."

"I'm afraid Michael has a lot on his mind."

"What disturbs him so, Uncle Jack? He won't tell me."

"Oh, the running of the estate, for one. And he does have an inordinate amount of business to tend to. Be patient, Elizabeth. Give him time to adjust to the burden of your father's varied interests. I promise to keep a closer eye on you from now on. If anything troubles or worries you, come to me. Right now, I'm famished. Why don't we join the others and have our lunch now?"

I sighed, then nodded. With his arm still about my shoulders, we went into the dining room.

After lunch, I went to my bedchamber, thinking how much I missed Michael. He was in London on business and I wondered how he would react when he came home to find David once again a guest at Dunwick. He should be grateful to David for the way he had brought Rose back to life, not to mention the services he had rendered me, I thought. Yet the appearance of David was not the uppermost thought in my mind. Running through the back of my mind were Maude's urbane words of wisdom. "Business is the excuse men use to do as they please." I felt an odd heat course through my blood. Was Michael doing as he pleased in the company of Maude? Or Edwina? Doubts came to haunt me anew, doubts which could only be swept away by Michael himself.

As days passed into weeks and March into April, Michael's prolonged absence only served to increase my suspicions. Not even the merry company of Uncle Jack, Rose, and David could assuage my growing melancholia. I did my best to display outwardly a gaiety that matched theirs. But it was a hollow spirit that smiled and chatted as though totally carefree.

It was late morning as I sat on the terrace, an open book in my lap. I had tried to read, but found the words blurring as my attention strayed. Lost in a world of conflicting emotions, I jumped slightly when a cool hand touched my arm.

"I didn't mean to startle you, Elizabeth," Rose said, taking a chair beside me.

"I didn't hear you come onto the terrace. I guess my mind was elsewhere." I looked around. "Where's David?"

"He and Uncle Jack went to Portrush."

"I thought David had seen the beaches there."

"Uncle Jack wanted to introduce him to a pub or two."

We both smiled, knowing that Uncle Jack's penchant for Irish whiskey had overcome his better judgment many times. But he enjoyed the company of others when he tippled and liked to be where he could relate his innumerable tales and perhaps hear a new one or two to add to his repertoire.

"How do you feel about David?"

"I don't really know, Elizabeth. He is most pleasant to be with and decidedly charming. He reminds me a good deal of James MacGregor."

"James MacGregor?" I queried.

"The young man who used to come and see me so many years ago."

"Now I remember. You thought you might marry him one day."

She sighed. "It all seems so long ago. I sometimes believe it was all a dream."

"What happened to him, Rose?"

"I don't rightly know. I guess I'll never know." She fell quiet as if remembering a time when life held a promise of true happiness. "We had known each other since childhood. As we grew into young adulthood, our childhood friendship took on a new aspect. A love grew between us that I thought was eternal. But, a few months before his disappearance, his visits became more and more infrequent until one day he stopped coming altogether. Then he seemed to vanish from the face of the earth. No one has seen him since. His family never talks of him and considers him dead." Her eyes glazed but no tears came forth.

"How long ago was it?"

"It was just before Isabel died. Almost six years now." Rose stared wistfully over the grounds at some unknown point in the distance.

We remained silent for some time.

"Why don't we plan a picnic over by the River Bann for the four of us if it's a pleasant day tomorrow?" I suggested.

Rose seemed to shake herself from a deep reverie and brightened a bit. "That would be nice. It's been quite a while since I've been on a picnic."

"I'll go talk to cook now." I rose from the chair and tossed the book onto the empty seat.

"I think I'll go upstairs and decide on a suitable frock for tomorrow. It used to be so easy when my wardrobe was limited." She laughed.

The next day Uncle Jack felt poorly, and not even the favorable weather boosted his spirits. His feet were swollen, which he blamed on the gout, and his head ached resoundingly. He begged to be excused, promising to join us at another time.

Cook had packed a generous basket of jellied pig's feet, salmon cakes, pork pasties, and soda bread with crocks of butter and jams. Strong black tea laced with milk was poured into tightly covered jars and placed in cozies.

David, Rose, and I set out for the River Bann in a lighthearted mood with David driving the trap and the three of us squeezed onto the seat. I had never seen Rose happier. Instead of her usual spinsterish air, she displayed all the curiosity, excitement, and cheerfulness of a very young woman. Her carefree attitude was contagious and I forgot my doubts about Michael for the moment.

Reaching the Bann River valley, we searched for a suitable spot to enjoy our picnic. David found a lovely, grassy knoll not too far from the river's edge where some leafy elm and lime trees filtered out the rays of the sun.

"This is beautiful, David," Rose said as he tethered the horse before helping us down from the trap.

"Isn't it? Too bad Jack couldn't join us. I'll wager he has a good many stories about the river," David said, lifting the large picnic basket from the rear of the trap.

"Uncle Jack would delight in anything that has to do with food." Rose laughed.

The three of us laid out the cloth and placed the picnic basket on it. We sat for a while, enjoying the sun and David's colorful description of Canterbury Cathedral. The undulating river before us finally cast its spell and we wandered down to its banks. We stood in silence, mesmerized by the flowing waters until I noticed strange movements in the water.

"Look there! Can you see them?" I cried.

"What?" David edged closer to me.

"Those things there." I pointed to a horde of writhing wormlike creatures swimming up river, casting ribbony shadows in the crystal waters.

"Good Lord!" David exclaimed. "Shiny-looking little devils, aren't they? What are they?"

"I don't know. Rose . . . can you see them?"

She peered at the river. "Yes. They're elvers."

"Elvers?" David asked.

"Baby eels. Well, not really babies. They are about three years old and on their way to Lough Neagh. They'll stay there for eight years or so to mature, then head back to the open sea," Rose explained.

"Eels! There must be millions of them. They stay in the Lough for eight years, you say? Hmmm . . . that might make an interesting story. I'll have to make some notes on it when we get back. Will you help me, Rose?" David asked.

"Uncle Jack would be far more knowledgeable than I. But I'll do what I can," Rose said.

"I'd much rather talk to you about it. You're far prettier than Jack Donahue." David took Rose's hand in his, causing her to blush profusely.

We returned to the little knoll and began to empty the picnic basket. David continued to flatter Rose as we devoured the excellent food, stuffing ourselves a little more than we should have.

I watched David smile tenderly at Rose, yet something disturbed me; that tenderness was not reflected in his eyes. I had the nagging feeling he was giving a studied performance that belied his true feelings. I quickly chided myself for cloaking someone else with my own muddled emotions. Perhaps Mrs. Meehan was right. In my loneliness for Michael, I was letting my imagination run rampant. Could I be jealous that Rose had found an attractive man who was very attentive to her? Did I resent that attention because Michael's display of devotion toward me was waning? I sipped at my tea, which had become cold.

David lay down, his head in the grass, his hands spread over his lean stomach. Rose stood and stretched her hands to the sky.

"There's a place not too far from here where wild irises grow by the hundreds. Why don't we all go and pick

209

some for the house?"

"Rose, you are a very enchanting creature, but right now, nothing could move me from this spot. My stomach is crying out for a rest," David said, closing his eyes.

"I don't think I could move right now either, Rose. Why don't you wait a while and then we'll all go," I proposed, pulling up my knees, making sure my voluminous skirt was properly draped before putting my arms around them.

"I feel like picking them now. You stay here. I don't mind going alone."

"Don't go too far, Rose," I warned.

"I won't. It's over that small mound back there. I'll be within shouting distance."

I watched her tread happily over the soft, green grass. There was a silence in the air that matched the serene surroundings. It was some time before David spoke.

"I do believe I could spend the rest of my life right here in Northern Ireland."

"It is beautiful," I agreed quietly.

"But it must be very lonely for you with Lord Tyrone away so often." His eyes remained closed as he spoke.

"He has a great many duties to attend to, especially now, with the added responsibilities of my father's business affairs." My voice was calm, though resentment was simmering in me. I guess I didn't like to be reminded of Michael's frequent absences, especially by a young bachelor.

"If I were Lord Tyrone, I wouldn't leave a lovely young wife alone all the time. If I had to go away on business, I'd take her with me." His eyes opened and he sat up. A wry smile widened his full lips as he gazed at me. "I wish we were back in the Lake District, Elizabeth."

He began to lean toward me, a lustrous, bizarre gleam in his hazel eyes. Suddenly, his eyes slid past me as the sound of racing hooves echoed in the distance. David's back stiffened as I turned to see Michael approaching us astride his huge black stallion. The horse whinnied and pawed at the air as Michael sharply reined him in beside the trap. For a large man, he dismounted with graceful ease, then tethered the horse to the trap. His face was taut with controlled anger as he strode toward us, his long, powerful legs encased in tight fawn breeches and polished, knee-high black boots. His white cotton shirt was open at the neck and the full sleeves billowed behind him with the quickness of his step.

"I hope I'm not intruding on anyone's privacy." His dark eyes sliced suspiciously to me, then to David before returning to rest on me.

"Of course not, Michael." Every time I saw him my heart leapt a little. I couldn't help it. "I didn't know you were returning home today."

"Evidently," he remarked coolly.

"What do you mean, Michael?" I was a bit miffed by the intonation in his voice.

"At the house they told me Rose was with you." Michael's eyes burned into mine as though searching for an answer to a question I had no knowledge of.

"Rose is over the rise, collecting irises," David interjected, easing the mounting tension between Michael and me. "She should be returning shortly."

I swallowed hard and forced a smile as I gazed up into Michael's face. "Would you like a pork pastie or a salmon cake, Michael? I believe there are a few left."

"I would appreciate something to eat about now. I fear I've been neglecting my stomach of late."

He sat down close to me, placing his hand firmly on my shoulder in a gesture that was more possessive than affectionate. But the warmth of his hand pulsed through my linen bodice, sending a delightful shiver dancing through my veins. I passed him a pork pastie. After taking it from me, he took my hand and kissed it lightly.

Sadly, I came to the conclusion that the display of affection was for David's benefit. He wanted to make sure David realized I was *his* wife, *his* property.

"Have you seen the River Shannon yet, Mr. Cooke?" Michael asked.

"Not yet, sorry to say," David replied.

"Now is the time to see it, Mr. Cooke, while it is bursting with life. Farther south are the Rings of Kerry, the highest mountains in Ireland. There are sights in the south of Ireland that would almost write their own descriptions," he said.

"Sounds enchanting. However, I have to get permission from my editor to make any change in plan. He foots the bills, you know," David replied with a slow smile, yet there was a challenge in his tone of voice.

"I wouldn't delay too long if I were you, Mr. Cooke. There is much to see and a lot of ground to cover." Michael returned David's smile sardonically.

"I still have to consider my commission to do an indepth history of Londonderry. I'm committed to it for the time being. Then, perhaps, the south of Ireland would be a worthwhile pursuit." David's smile was tight and brittle while his hazel eyes glinted metallically.

"There are a number of books in our library that recount the history of Derry. You'd be more than welcome to take one or two to read as you travel," Michael rejoined.

"Very generous of you, Lord Tyrone. I shall take it under consideration," David said.

"I suggest you do, Mr. Cooke," Michael emphasized.

There was an edge to their voices that caused me to believe their words were superficial pleasantries shielding an intangible battle raging between the two men. I could almost feel Michael's hatred of the man sitting across from me. Nevertheless, his rude insinuations that David leave Dunwick seemed inexcusable to me. Before anything more could be said, Rose returned, her arms laden with white and purple wild irises.

"Michael!" she exclaimed. "How nice you could join us. When did you get back?"

"A while ago. Uncle Jack told me where to find all of you."

"Look, Elizabeth. Didn't I tell you there were hundreds of them? Aren't they beautiful?" Rose gave me a handful.

"They're lovely, Rose." I sniffed the flowers she'd given me and was surprised to find they had no distinctive fragrance.

"Well . . . I do think it is time we packed up and returned to Dunwick. I believe Mr. Cooke has a great deal to do," Michael said slowly and pointedly.

"What do you mean, Michael?" Rose asked.

"He means, my dear Rose, I am contemplating leaving Dunwick to see some of the sights of southern Ireland," David replied in a lighthearted manner.

"Whatever for?" Rose looked from David to Michael, then back to David, unable to hide her astonishment at the announcement. "Don't you have some research to do on Derry?"

"Your brother has been kind enough to offer me the loan of a few books on Londonderry's history. I can read on my travels through the south, then swing back to return them and have a brief stay in the city itself to fill in anything I think might be lacking in the previously written histories," David explained.

"Oh dear," Rose sighed. "I had hoped you would be spending all your time at Dunwick."

"Alas, my dear Rose, I'm afraid that is not to be. But you shall be in my thoughts until I see you again. And we can always write," David said gently.

Michael swallowed the last of the tea and, with my assistance, began to repack those items scattered on the

213

blanket into the picnic hamper. Picking up the basket in one hand, he extended his other hand to me and pulled me to my feet.

"Shall we go now?" Michael asked.

With some reluctance David rose then carefully folded the blanket and the four of us walked back to the waiting trap and black stallion. Michael tossed the hamper in back, then lifted me into the seat before untying his horse from the rear while David assisted Rose. I felt oddly uncomfortable on the drive back to Dunwick, for everyone was deathly quiet in sharp contrast to our merry ride out to the river earlier in the day. Occasionally, I could sense Michael's dark eyes staring at me as he rode his horse alongside the trap, but when I turned to look at him, he averted his gaze.

It was with relief that I saw the square Georgian lines of Dunwick loom on the horizon. As we rode up the graveled crescent driveway leading to the manor house, I saw an unfamiliar carriage at the main entrance. Michael's face froze in horror and he urged his horse forward in a wild sprint. I watched him bring the steed to an abrupt halt, leap off, toss the reins to a groom, then bound up the steps.

"Whose carriage is that, Rose?" I asked.

"It's the doctor's. Something must have happened," she replied with anxiety.

"I hope Uncle Jack hasn't taken a turn for the worse," I said, my brow creasing with concern.

Reaching the main entrance, the three of us quickly left the trap in the groom's care and, with hurried steps, made our way into the foyer. There, we saw a white-faced Michael holding onto Callie, who was screaming loudly as Michael tried to talk to the doctor. An agitated Uncle Jack stood by.

"I didn't do it! I didn't do it!" Callie kept crying stridently, trying to free herself from Michael's grasp.

214

"Rose . . . take Mr. Cooke into the drawing room. And Elizabeth . . . go to the library. I'll join you shortly," Michael ordered, his deep voice rising above the child's screams.

Rose quickly obeyed, taking a startled David with her while I hesitantly ventured closer to Michael and the group of distraught people in the middle of the foyer. I stopped short when Michael boomed, "Elizabeth!" The look in his eyes demanded obedience. Not wanting to add to the disturbance, I went into the library, my curiosity mounting to unbearable proportions. My anxiety grew as an ominous silence enveloped the house. I stared at the door, my hands tightly clutching the back of a leather chair. The door finally opened and Michael stepped in, closing the door softly behind him. His eyes bored into me as he stalked across the room to the desk.

"Sit down, Elizabeth," he said wearily as he took the chair behind the desk.

I sat down rigidly in the chair across from him. "What happened, Michael?" I asked in a whisper, half afraid to hear his reply.

"Mr. Duffy, Callie's tutor, has met with a serious accident. They have taken him to the hospital in Derry." He leaned back in the chair and gently tapped his lips with steepled forefingers.

"How seriously is he hurt?"

"Oh, I'm quite sure he'll live, but he does have an ugly wound."

"Wound? Was he shot?" My eyes widened in bewilderment as I wondered who would harm Mr. Duffy. He was so timid and unimposing.

"No. He was stabbed with a pair of scissors," Michael replied grimly.

"Who would do such a thing?" I asked, then remembered Callie's cry of "I didn't do it!." While I found it difficult to believe an eleven-year-old girl could actually stab someone, I fearfully recalled Dunluce, the staircase, and the glass-filled fruit cake. My voice was low, tentative as I murmured, "Callie?"

"Yes . . . and that is what I want to talk to you about, Elizabeth." He leaned forward and paused as his eyes searched mine. "As you have probably gathered by now, there is something decidedly wrong with the child. I've had her to every kind of specialist, here and in Europe, and the general consensus seems to be that she has the mentality of a three or four-year-old. They hold little hope that the condition will ever change. I hired the best tutors available, but they've had little success in teaching her anything. Her attention span is extremely short, her memory limited. She has absolutely no conception of right or wrong, good or bad. She's totally amoral. Unfortunately, her condition worsens as time passes and her spells of violence become more frequent. As you can see, she is quite big for her age and her strength is abnormal for a child her age."

"Why didn't you tell me this before, Michael?" A shudder ran through me as the full meaning of his words slowly seeped into my brain.

I sprang to my feet as anger rose in me like a tidal wave. Rage caused my hands to tighten into fists. "I should have been told about Callie's true condition, Michael." I swiftly told him of the china doll and barm brack, and reminded him about the fall down the staircase. The other incidents I attributed to accidents. "Now that I know Callie is capable of inflicting serious injury, I believe I have reason to fear for my life. It is an established fact that the child hates me. Why didn't you tell me right away? I'm your wife. Have you no sense of responsibility toward me? It was your duty to tell me of Callie's mental state. Do you realize I was putting my life in jeopardy every time I tried to be friendly with her? If I had known, I would have been on my guard in her presence. Do you think so little of me that you could subject me to the mischief of a mentally deranged child?"

He came and took me in his arms. "Oh, my dear, I'm truly sorry. Please forgive me. At the time, I thought it best you didn't know. I wanted to see how things would work out if you thought her a perfectly normal child. I was curious to see how Callie would react to someone who didn't shun and fear her. I was wrong to undertake such an ill-fated experiment. All I can do now is request your forgiveness and understanding."

His mellifluous voice had a calming effect on me. My anger began to wane as he continued to hold me. I could never stay angry with Michael. My love for him wouldn't allow it. I knew, in the end, I would always forgive him. I sighed. "Why did Callie harm Mr. Duffy?"

"I initially hired the man for his infinite patience and understanding of Callie's problem. Evidently his patience wore a little thin. He was attempting to teach her how to tell time when she snatched his prized gold watch and smashed it beyond repair. He rebuked her sharply and she retaliated with a pair of scissors," he explained, then released me. There was a sadness in his eyes, which he tried to prevent me from seeing. Compassion smothered all anger in me.

But other thoughts tumbled in my brain like a kaleidoscope. Three accidents which might have been fatal for me, and Isabel had accidentally drowned at sea. Was it all coincidental? Or was there a tenuous thread that connected the events? Impulsively, I asked, "Michael, how did your mother die?"

Michael's face clouded and a deep frown furrowed his brow. "What makes you ask a question like that, Elizabeth?"

"Curiosity, I suppose. I thought I should know about all the family while I have you in an expansive mood." I gave him a quick, tight smile.

"My mother was a splendid horsewoman. Liked nothing better than to gallop through the dales at daredevil speeds. One day the cinch gave way and she fell as the horse went to take a low stone wall. Her neck was broken and she died before Uncle Jack could reach her."

"How tragic!"

"Dunwick was a sad place then. Uncle Jack took it exceptionally hard. He and mother were quite close, especially after my father's slow, lingering death. And, of course, Rose missed her terribly. Then, to have Isabel die the following year . . ." His voice trailed off and he released me. "I think we've had enough of family matters for today. Why don't you go up to your room, Elizabeth? A rest before dinner might be beneficial."

"Yes, Michael. If there is anything I can do, you will let me know, won't you?"

He nodded, and I left the library.

Upstairs, as I started down the corridor to the west wing, I was startled to see Callie sitting on the carpeted floor, chin down and arms clasped about her updrawn knees.

"Callie . . . what are you doing sitting there?" I asked gently.

"I didn't do it, you know. It was the banshee. You can't stop the banshee. She always has her way."

"Where is Mrs. Meehan?" After recent events, I couldn't understand why Callie was being left unattended to.

She stood up suddenly, her green eyes blazing with an eerie light as they stared directly into mine. "Sooner or later the banshee will get you too. You'll see. She'll never stop until she has destroyed you."

She gave me a twisted smile, then laughed before running down the corridor to the east wing, her maniacal laughter echoing down the hall.

I went into the sitting parlor to work on the household accounts. As I carefully entered some numbers, I realized what it was about Callie I found so disturbing. Her eyes . . . those emerald-green eyes. If what Michael had said was true and she did have the mind of a three-year-old, it wasn't evident in her eyes. They were the eyes of a grown woman, lacking all innocence and filled with a world weariness that found compensation in hatred, in sheer evil. A quiver raced over my skin as the notion impressed itself deep within my brain. The picture of Isabel. Those haunting, terrifying green eyes in the painting were identical to Callie's. A premonition seized me. A premonition of my own death. Against all common sense, I felt driven to see Isabel's grave. Rathlin . . . I had to go to Rathlin.

Dinner was not a gala event, even though Rose wore one of her new gowns, a pale green moire trimmed with dark green velvet. Her sorrow at David's imminent departure rippled across her face like moonglow on a lake. Michael was distant and I knew his thoughts were elsewhere. David tactfully avoided any mention of the incident involving Mr. Duffy. Only Uncle Jack was as effusive as ever. Hearing David was about to sojourn to the south of Ireland, his dinner conversation revolved around Dublin and the River Shannon. The evening concluded on a brighter note as David played the piano and we gathered around to sing. Michael, as usual, did not join us. He sat broodingly in a chair, contemplating his brandy.

Rose and I stood on the front portico in the morning's gray light to offer our good-byes to David.

"Well, ladies, it looks as though we'll be parted for a while. I can never express my gratitude for your generous hospitality," David said.

"It's been a pleasure to have you here, David," I replied with a smile.

"Oh, yes," Rose added with a slight reddening of her cheeks.

"Do give my regards to Lord Tyrone and Jack Donahue. With luck, I shall see you again soon." He took my hand and kissed it warmly, then did the same with Rose. "I'd better make haste or I shall miss my train at Londonderry. I won't say good-bye. It sounds so final. So we'll leave it at adieu." He turned quickly and descended the stairs to the waiting carriage. Once seated, he waved a farewell which we returned in kind.

I glanced at Rose, whose eyes followed the carriage until it was out of sight. "He'll be back, Rose," I said, laying my hand on her arm.

"I wonder," she sighed.

I looked up at the sky where the sun was valiantly trying to pierce the morning mist. "I think it is going to be a nice day, after all," I said cheerily, trying to dispel Rose's gloomy mood.

She gave an indifferent shrug, picked up her skirts and went back into the house without a word. I watched her climb the marble staircase, her shoulders hunched in despair.

Before her depression became contagious, I quickly walked through the great mirrored hall and out the French doors to find Uncle Jack, who I thought might be in the rose garden. I could not shake the desire to see Rathlin Island. Peculiar ideas were starting to form in my imagination, and aberrant notion that Isabel might still be alive and living on Rathlin.

Ten

The sinking sun gilded the green foliage of hawthorn and wild ash trees, tracing its golden fingers over the furze and fern as I stood on the terrace before dinner. There was a wildness about the meadows and glens that lay beyond the formal gardens of Dunwick, a wildness that was at once savagely foreboding and singularly beautiful. The sweet song of the thrush and the mellow whistle of the blackbird rose in the stillness of the evening air.

"What are you doing out here all by yourself, Elizabeth?" Michael's resonant voice sounded as sweet and mellow to me as the songs of the birds.

"Taking a look at the land before the night hides it," I replied, looking up into his face with a broad smile.

"Elizabeth," he said quietly as his hands clasped my head and cradled it gently.

"Yes, Michael?" My desire to feel his lips on mine was making me lightheaded, and my heart pounded furiously. It was a short-lived excitement, for his hands dropped to his side and he walked to the stone balustrade.

"I'm leaving for London first thing in the morning. I don't know how long I'll be gone," he said, staring out at the evening's haze.

"I'll go with you."

"No. Not this time, Elizabeth." His tone was hard and flat.

"Why not?"

"I'll be traveling light and don't want to be burdened with trunks of female attire. And, as I said, I don't know how long my stay will be. Perhaps a day, perhaps a week. Some other time, Elizabeth, when my schedule is more settled."

I knew it was useless to argue with him. When Michael's mind was set, he was not the sort of man to reconsider. Besides, it would afford me the opportunity to go to Rathlin without the possibility of Michael's raising objections.

"I believe dinner is about to be served. Shall we go in?" he asked.

I nodded and took his arm.

As soon as he finished his brandy, Michael left the drawing room, explaining that he had to get some papers together for his journey to London.

"Uncle Jack," I began after Michael had left the room. "I've been thinking, what with Michael away, it would be nice if the three of us took a little trip to Rathlin Island. I'm quite anxious to see it."

"What a splendid idea, Elizabeth!" Uncle Jack exclaimed, then puffed on his pipe for a moment. "Why, I haven't been there in years. It'll be good to see it again, although there isn't all that much to see. What a treat for an old rogue like me to squire two lovely young ladies about."

"You'll only be squiring one lady about, Uncle Jack," Rose said, her eyes never leaving her embroidery.

"What do you mean, Rose?" I asked with a sinking feeling. Rose had been brooding ever since David had left, and I had hoped a trip would bring her out of it.

"I mean I shan't be going with you." She looked up

from her needlework.

"A change of scenery would do you good, Rose," I said.

"I'd prefer to stay at home."

"But Rose . . . " I persisted.

"You're wasting your time, Elizabeth. She can be as stubborn as Michael when she wants to be," Uncle Jack said with a rueful smile. "Well, if Rose isn't coming with us, what say we take the horses to Ballycastle instead of the carriage or trap?"

"The horses are fine with me, but maybe Rose will feel differently in the morning," I said.

"I won't, Elizabeth. Now, why don't you play for us? I enjoy your playing far more than I would any trip to Rathlin." She smiled faintly and returned to her needlework while I went to the piano.

Morning came. Michael had gone and Rose hadn't changed her mind about going to Rathlin. As the day promised to be clear and sunny, I wore my sepia-colored, poplin riding habit with a lacy, frilly ecru blouse. The hat was smallish, with ecru veiling and two diminutive plumes. I joined Uncle Jack in eating a very hearty breakfast, which he suggested as being in order for the strenuous ride to Ballycastle. Outside, we mounted the sleek horses and began our journey in high spirits after deciding to ride the coastal route to enjoy the scenery.

Along the coastline, the high craggy cliffs and rocks, worn by time and sea, thrust themselves out into the frothy, turbulent waters in majestic defiance. In the blue-misted distance, erratic shapes and forms lunged toward the sky like ancient, formidable castles. I eagerly anticipated a closer view, only to find they were not citadels at all, but huge, weather-worn rocks that had been carved and eroded by a capricious and vicious ocean.

As we rode through the quiet, unpretentious village of Bushmills, a knowing sparkle flamed in Uncle Jack's

223

eyes.

"My favorite village . . . Bushmills!" he exclaimed.

"Why is that?" I asked with humor.

"Not only is the fishing excellent, but they have one of the finest whiskey distilleries in Northern Ireland. Superb quality! On our way back we shall order a case. Or two. Michael will like that."

And so would you, I thought as I smiled warmly at him. I looked once again at the sea on our left. "If we didn't have a definite goal in mind, I'd be tempted to race on the sand by the water's edge."

"You'll have plenty of time for that, my dear. I expect the water is still cold. Even in the middle of summer it can be chilly, especially for an old codger like me."

Arriving at the bay of Ballycastle, we stabled the horses and went down to the quay in search of a boat that would take us to Rathlin Island. While Uncle Jack made arrangements with a boatman, I gazed out over the bay at the island, which was only six miles distant. My heart pounded. Would I find a living, breathing Isabel on that island? Or her grave? Reason told me she couldn't be alive or Michael couldn't have married me. But, considering my substantial inheritance, Michael might have feinged her death to marry me and secure my father's vast holdings and wealth. Then, when the opportunity presented itself, he would dispose of me, and after that, Isabel would be miraculously found alive on Rathlin Island and be restored as mistress of Dunwick. Men have been known to have no conscience or scruples where money is concerned, and Michael was a man, very much a man. Nonsense! I berated myself. My imagination was becoming as wild and distorted as Callie's.

A small, white-haired man doffed his cap, then assisted me into the large boat. His face, ravaged by the elements, was like the topography of Ireland itself, furrowed with deep, lowering glens lodged between rounded

224

hills and rugged mountains. His narrow, deep-set eyes were as blue as the sky he stared at.

"Don't like the look of 'er." His raspy voice was loud, as if he'd had to talk against the roar of the sea all his life.

"It's a beautiful day," Uncle Jack asserted.

The boatman shook his head sorrowfully, then headed out to sea. Although it was a calm day, the uneasy swells of the sea seemed abnormally high to me. I dreaded to think what this short, treacherous stretch of water would be like in a gale. After being tumbled about on the cresting waves, I was glad to see a small bay nestled in the craggy cliffs. Relief flooded over me as we pulled alongside a sturdy pier and Uncle Jack helped me out of the boat.

"There's a large farmhouse not too far from here that serves as an inn when necessary. I think it best we go directly there and have tea. I'm famished and could do with a pint or two after that boat trip." Uncle Jack took my arm.

"Tea would be most welcome and I could do with a glass of sherry myself," I confessed, my legs a little wobbly on the solid ground.

After an ample tea, I was ready to pursue my quest for Isabel's grave. When I announced my intention of having a walk around the small island, Uncle Jack begged to be excused from any walking tours saying he preferred to play a game of cards with some of the locals who had come in for a pint or two.

I decided the most likely place to find a grave would be near a church, where the gravesites were commonly located. The smell of the sea and the strident cries of gulls enveloped me as I trod the packed-dirt lanes. It was not difficult to find the church and the small cemetery which lay to one side of it. Back and forth I went, reading every word and name on the time-worn tombstones. Gnawing fear and panic inched its way inside me as I failed to detect an "Isabel Tyrone" on the gray, chiseled stones. There were only two left for me to inspect, and my throat went dry as I approached them. No Isabel Tyrone. Perhaps in my anxiety I had been careless and missed it. I retraced my steps and scrutinized each tombstone with studied intent. It was useless. There wasn't a "Tyrone" anywhere in the small graveyard. Not even an unmarked stone that might lead me to believe it was Isabel's resting place.

Without a grave, I was hard pressed to believe Isabel was truly dead. Dear God, let there be a grave, I silently prayed. My concentration was so intense as I went over the stones again, I wasn't aware that I was reading the inscriptions aloud.

"Is this a fancy of yours, my child?"

My hand flew to my breast as I spun around, startled to see a black-frocked man smiling at me. A tasseled, crownlike black hat was perched atop his head.

"Forgive my intrusion. I was looking for someone," I blurted out, feeling a bit sheepish.

"A beloved?"

"No. Only a name."

"Surely someone as young as yourself has better things to do than spend such a lovely day wandering about a graveyard. 'Tis a gloomy place for youth. Perhaps I can help you, then you can quit this place of the dead and find pleasanter pursuits on our fair island."

"I was looking for the grave of Isabel Tyrone," I explained, feeling a little more at ease.

His laugh was hearty and strangely out of place. "Well now, I'll just have to think on that one. A Tyrone here!" Again he laughed, but this time there was a hint of mischief in his voice and eyes. "If there was a Tyrone here, my child, I'm afraid everyone else would pick up their coffins and leave with great indignation. No. Lady

226

Tyrone would not be here." The laughter disappeared from his face and eyes. "Sad. Sad and tragic. So young and beautiful. Well, the good Lord has His ways and reasons."

"I don't understand. Why wouldn't Lady Tyrone be buried here? Wouldn't the people of the island permit it?" I was puzzled.

"It has nothing to do with the people of the island, my child. This is a Catholic cemetery. I think you would do best to look in the Protestant cemetery. Come . . . I'll walk with you a way. I don't often have a Protestant trespassing on my grounds. And such a delightful one at that."

"I'm sorry, Father. I didn't know there was more than one church on the island. Rathlin must be larger than I thought."

"I don't think so. If you have the stamina, you could walk the length and breadth of it in a day. It is only about one mile wide and seven miles in length. Admittedly, our respective parishes are not large, but with people of both persuasions on the island, each faith must be served. And I have learned to live with the fact that Protestants do exist." He smiled at me with warmth and affection. "Why do you seek the grave of Lady Tyrone, may I ask?"

"Curiosity, I suppose. You see, I am Lord Michael Tyrone's second wife," I replied truthfully. He stared hard at me with quizzical, appraising eyes. "Is there something wrong?" I asked.

"No . . . No . . . it's . . . well, you're nothing at all like the first Lady Tyrone. I can't imagine his lordship . . . " His voice trailed off in embarrassment.

"Would marry someone like me," I said, finishing his thought. "I'm aware that Isabel Tyrone was a great beauty and I am quite plain and ordinary."

"I meant no offense, my child."

227

"I know you didn't." I smiled and laid my hand on his arm. He covered my hand with his own as I asked, "Did you know the first Lady Tyrone?"

"No. I knew who she was, but never met or spoke to her. I saw her several times here on the island. A striking woman, though a mite mysterious. Ah . . . here we are. You'll forgive me if I do not continue on with you."

"Of course. And I do appreciate your kindness to me."

"Any time, my child, any time. Do not hesitate to call on me if you think I can be of assistance to you."

"Thank you. But we shan't be staying here for any time. Only for today," I informed him.

"Well, it was a pleasure meeting you, Lady Tyrone. Will you be able to find your way back?"

"I think so. If not, I know I can find my way to your church. Thank you again, Father."

He waved a good-bye, thrust his hands in his sleeves like a monk, and trudged back the way we had come.

I went on and was soon in the square cemetery. As before, I began a meticulous search among the stone markers, this time reading the chiseled letters to myself. I almost missed the unobtrusive marble slab lying flat in the ground, the grass unclipped around it. I knelt down and pushed the coarse grass from the marker to read:

Isabel Tyrone
1833 - 1864

The simplicity of the marker and its apparent neglect perplexed me. It made no mention of the fact she was the wife of Lord Tyrone or that she was a woman of title. Surely a noblewoman would have had a tombstone more elaborate than this, and surely it would have been tended with care. At least a remnant or two or floral tokens. If this gravesite was the reason for Michael's frequent trips to Rathlin, there were certainly no visible signs of his having visited here. The grasses about it were fresh and springy, with no evidence of any matting from the trodding of feet. Totally baffled, I felt my trip to Rathlin Island had stirred up more questions than answers. It struck me that Michael might have been using his trips to Rathlin to conceal trips made elsewhere.

Clouds raced across the sky, casting ominous shadows over the quiet graveyard. Trees and shrubs rustled as the wind rushed to keep pace with the puffy clouds that were beginning to darken. Light and shade no longer vied with each other as a general haziness laid a mantle over the ground. I thought it prudent to return to the inn.

I was within steps of the large farmhouse when a sudden squall unleashed slicing sheets of rain obscuring my vision. Soaked, I was made much of by the innkeeper's wife, who quickly led me to a large airy room and told me to disrobe while she fetched one of her daughter's frocks she was sure would fit me. Uncle Jack didn't have to tell me we wouldn't be going back to Ballycastle any time soon, for I could see the force of the wind bending all in its soggy path.

Even though the next day dawned with bright sunshine and blue skies dotted with feathery cirrus clouds, the wind still rode with semi-gale gusts, and I knew the waters between the mainland and the island would be turbulent, whipping mercilessly at any craft that dared to make the crossing.

With Uncle Jack absorbed in amiable company, where new faces presented new stories along with a pint here and there, I borrowed a simple linen frock from the innkeeper's daughter and embarked on an exploration of the island.

It seemed I had walked for hours over the green, hilly terrain when, abruptly, I reached land's end on a promontory high above the coast near the crumbling ruins of an ancient castle. I moved closer to the edge, but not too close, recalling the experience at Dunluce. I peered down at the swelling, turbulent sea, then raised my eyes to the veiled purple hills of Scotland which lay beyond the waters.

"That's the Mull of Kintyre. Have you ever been to Scotland?"

Alarmed at the sound of a voice when I had presumed I was alone, I spun around to behold a young man seated in a well-built wheelchair. Across his lap was a large pad, while on either side of the wheelchair, attached to the arms, was an assortment of paints, brushes, rags, and several tins of water. His sand-colored hair blew in soft curls about his impish, attractive face. There was an engaging boyishness about him that was immediately disarming. On closer inspection, however, I observed deep lines of pain and sorrow etched into that handsome face.

"No," I replied to his question in a clipped, tense voice.

"I can see that I've startled you. I do apologize. It is seldom we have visitors on the island. I'm afraid my enthusiasm for a new face overcame my better judgment."

"I thought I was alone. I didn't expect to find anyone out here this time of morning," I said, my composure returning.

"It is the best time of day for me. The light is strong, yet has a mellowness I find intriguing. Besides, I tend to get lazy in the afternoons and find my thoughts straying to other things." His smile was appealing as he gazed up at me.

"I didn't see you when I walked up here."

"Ah . . . but I saw you and that's the important thing."

"From your equipment, I take it you are an artist."

"I try to be."

"Have you ever sold any of your paintings?"

"Yes. A number of them."

"How do you get them shown?" I asked, surprised to find a professional artist in so desolate a place.

"I have an agent who displays them in London and other cities for me. I must say he does quite well for me."

"What is your name? Perhaps I have seen some of your work in London."

"I doubt it. I'm not that well known. Nothing in the Tate or National Gallery, I'm afraid." He laughed and it was a soft pleasant sound. "Call me 'Sean.' That's what everyone here calls me, and I fear it would make me most uncomfortable to be called anything else. And you?"

"Elizabeth," I replied, seeing no need to be formal and having some misgivings that he might become withdrawn if he knew I was the wife of Lord Tyrone. Besides, in the humble linen frock I felt like a plain Elizabeth.

"Elizabeth," he repeated. "A queen's name for a queen. And why have the wee folk brought you here to grace our tiny realm of isolation? A visit? Or permanent residence? I certainly hope the latter."

"I'm only here on a visit with my uncle. In fact, we would have left yesterday if it hadn't been for the storm," I replied.

"Now I know why I have always found storms so interesting and exciting. They can bring forth wondrous new things to the earth. And, for me, you are one of them."

I blushed. "May I see some of your paintings? That is, if you have some with you."

"I finished one this morning. A watercolor. I do my oils at home. Follow me, Elizabeth." He began to wheel himself along a well-worn path between ancient stones that appeared to be the last vestiges of a once remarkable wall.

"Can I assist you in any way?" I felt helpless as I watched him maneuver over the uneven path.

"I'm quite used to traveling over this ground. It's a challenge that I relish, for I always manage to conquer it." He smiled as he turned the wheels with powerful hands.

It seemed a tortuous route to me, but we finally reached a spot where a portfolio and basket lay on the ground. The view was panoramic! I could see why I'd been unaware of his presence. He had ensconced himself in the skeletal remains of an old castle that presented a visual barrier to the land side, but was free of any obstruction to the ocean vista.

"Was this place really a castle?" I asked as we halted.

"Yes. Very much a castle. You'll find that Ireland abounds in ancient castles. Unfortunately, like Ireland herself, they have fallen into a ruinous state. But you probably know that already. This particular one is where King Robert Bruce of Scotland is said to have taken shelter from the English when they drove him from his throne sometime in the early fourteenth century. But history is not my strong point." He took a deep breath and pointed. "There is my portfolio. This morning's work is in it."

I stood the porfolio on edge and undid the string ties, then gingerly opened it, taking care not to let the wind scatter the precious pieces of paper. I took out a marvelous watercolor rendition of the sea, executed exactly as one could see it from this vantage point.

"It's quite good. I get the feeling the spirits left the sea to dwell in your painting," I exclaimed with genuine admiration. He possessed an unmistakable talent.

"You are too kind, Elizabeth. But I adore being flattered. The painting is yours."

"Oh, no . . . no. I couldn't."

"I insist."

"Then I must pay you for it."

"And so you shall. I want you to sit over there . . . on that rock, so I can do a sketch or two of you," he ordered in a kindly way.

"I wouldn't want you to waste your time doing a picture of me."

"Waste time? It is a treat to have a new face to sketch. Everyone on the island is a mite weary of posing for me. You will be doing me an enormous favor for which I will gladly give you ten watercolors." Arranging the pad in his lap, he plucked a piece of charcoal from one of the tins attached to the arm of the chair. "Would it be too much of an imposition if I asked you to unpin your hair? It's quite a lovely shade of auburn, and I would like to have the full effect."

I hesitated for a moment. It wouldn't be very ladylike to have my hair flying about in front of a perfect stranger. But, right now, I was plain Elizabeth to this young man, not Lady Tyrone of Dunwick Manor.

"If you wish," I replied unabashedly. Plucking the bone pins from my chignon, I shook my long auburn tresses free and walked to the rock he had indicated.

It was satisfying to sit in silence and absorb the beauty of the scene around me while he concentrated raptly on the paper before him, his hand guiding the charcoal with practical strokes. With the wind in my hair and the warm rays of the sun upon my face, I was unconscious of the passage of time. A new sense of freedom engulfed me, a freedom of mind and spirit. I seemed to have entered the secret world of nature itself. Only when he spoke did I drift back to reality.

"My Lord, it's way past tea time," Sean declared, gazing at the pocket watch he pulled from his vest.

"Oh dear, Uncle Jack will be wondering what happened to me," I cried and made ready to take my leave.

"Don't go. I would like to make another sketch of you

233

before you disappear from my life forever," Sean pleaded.

"I must. Uncle Jack will think I've met with some horrible fate if I'm not there for tea. Besides, all this walking and fresh air has made me quite hungry."

"Bold, shining knight to fair lady's rescue. See that basket there? Well, it contains a goodly amount of food that will delight and tempt your palate. I would be honored — no, delighted — if you would stay and share it with me."

"If it weren't for Uncle Jack, I'd accept your offer." The thought of the long walk back on an empty stomach wasn't very appealing.

"Then, give in to your desires and set your mind at rest. This is a small island. One can't do a thing without someone knowing about it. I'm sure you've been seen here with me and your Uncle knows exactly where you are and that you are in good hands."

"Do you really think so, Sean?" I prayed he would say yes. My taste buds were awakened, wondering what the hamper held.

"I'm quite sure. Someone is always keeping an eye on me, and though I don't always see them, I know they are there. The people here seem to have an inordinate fear that I shall wheel myself off a cliff into the sea. And they always keep an eye on any strangers wandering about. So you see, I'm sure your uncle knows where you are by now and who you're with. Now, do say you'll stay and have a bite to eat with me."

"To tell the truth, my hunger overcame my better judgment some time ago," I said, laughing.

"Marvelous!" He tilted his head and grinned at me. "You're quite pretty when you laugh."

I lowered my eyes. Compliments unnerved me. As I opened the hamper, my mouth watered at the sight of small ham sandwiches, cold chicken, jellied pig's feet,

234

and a large jar of iced tea. I distributed the food and poured a mug of tea for each of us.

"Tell me about yourself, Elizabeth," Sean said as he munched on a piece of cold chicken.

"There isn't much to tell." I didn't want him to know who I really was. There was a rapport between us which I felt might vanish if he knew my true identity.

"Surely there must be something of note about your life," he urged, amusement tugging at the corners of his mouth.

"It's quite dull, I assure you." The ham sandwiches tasted like manna from heaven to me.

"Try me. I find dull stories fascinating."

"I was born and raised in London. Married an Irishman and moved to Ireland. See? Simple and dull." I took a deep swallow of tea.

"Simple, but certainly not dull. I'd never take you for a married woman though," he commented.

"And why not?"

"You're much too young. You can't be more than sixteen or seventeen."

"I'll be nineteen in a month or so. And you? Tell me about yourself."

"Born and raised in Ireland. Had an accident which paralyzed me from the waist down. Moved to Rathlin to paint. See? Simple and dull," he said and we both laughed.

We emptied the basket of food and drained the jar of tea. After putting our refuse in the hamper, I resumed posing for Sean, who kept me moving from place to place, standing and sitting. The entire afternoon slipped away before I insisted on heading back. I accompanied Sean back to his small cottage, which was on the same road and not too far from the inn where Uncle Jack and I were staying.

The next day proved to be inclement with gusty winds

235

and sporadic rain. Though I was restless and steeped in boredom with no piano, and no books, Uncle Jack seemed oblivious to our predicament. He had found new cronies, an endless supply of whiskey, and—best of all— an excellent player of draughts.

As I stared absently out the window at the gray day, images of Maude in Michael's arms danced before my eyes. Michael couldn't spend all his time steeped in business while in London, and I had seen the glances that passed between them at my father's funeral. My blood ran cold. I had to find some diversion before my imagination got the better of me. Hoping it wouldn't be too brash or impertinent of me, I decided to visit Sean. Even if I was turned away, the short walk would pass a little of the time. I borrowed a cloak to keep the misty drizzle from dampening my borrowed frock, and told Uncle Jack where I was headed. Then, in measured steps, I set out for Sean's small cottage.

I was greeted effusively at the door by a buxom woman in her fifties. She introduced herself as Mrs. O'Donnell, Sean's housekeeper. She gleefully ushered me into a fairly large parlor, large for a cottage, that is. Sean was at his easel, near a window.

"Elizabeth!" he exclaimed, his face brightening with a broad smile.

"I hope I'm not intruding."

"Intruding? Why, Elizabeth, you have banished the rain clouds from hovering over this cottage."

"The weather has again prevented us from returning to Ballycastle. I hope you don't think me too bold in coming here. Quite frankly, I was so horribly bored at the inn I thought I'd go mad if I stayed there a moment longer," I babbled like a schoolgirl making excuses to the headmistress.

"I revel in having you here. A gloomy day has turned to sunshine for me," he said, wheeling toward me to take

236

my hands in his. "Mrs. O'Donnell, some tea for our honored guest."

As the portly woman scurried off to do his bidding, I smiled at Sean, then let my gaze wander around the cozy, low-ceilinged room. My eyes immediately fell on the small piano by the window at the other end of the room.

"Ah . . . you've noticed my prize. I must say it took some doing to get it here."

"Do you play?" I walked to the benchless piano.

"After a fashion. Strictly self-taught, though. Time is one element I have in abundance. I'm prouder of my abilities on the violin."

"Would you play for me?"

"I was hoping you'd ask," he said with a grin. "What audiences I do have are bored to death with my limited repertoire. It will be an interesting and pleasurable experience to play for someone new. But you must give me a truthful opinion of my artistry. Promise?"

"I promise."

He wheeled himself over the carpeted floor to a table on which a wooden violin case rested. Opening it, he removed the violin and bow from its red velvet bed. Then, after a good rosining of the bow and some minor tuning adjustments, he commenced to play a piece which I recognized as an air by Johann Bach. Sean played with great emotional depth, yet quite sweetly. I was stirred. When he completed the air, I applauded enthusiastically.

"Well?" he queried, gazing at me intently.

"Beautiful. I congratulate you. You're quite an accomplished musician for one who is self-taught," I replied honestly.

"Do you happen to play a musical instrument?"

"Yes. The piano."

"How opportune! Why don't we play a piece together? I've never played a duet before," he said, nodding toward the piano. "The bench is to the side of the window."

I drew the bench to the piano and sat. With the exception of a short respite for tea, we spent the rest of the day amusing ourselves by testing each other's musical knowledge.

The days flowed one into the other as the sea remained tempestuous, and I spent every one of them with Sean. We'd play Bach, Handel, Beethoven, and the music of many other composers. Occasionally, I would read a book from his vast library while he painted. Sometimes, we would just sit and talk. When there was a break in the rain, we'd go to the cliffs, each time seeking out a different spot. I found myself wishing I never had to leave the island, for I had found a peace, a gentleness, and serene contentment. In Sean, I discovered the brother I never had, and an easy rapport swiftly developed as if he had known me all his life. Sean had the uncanny knack of knowing what I was thinking on any given occasion. He never asked about Michael and I never volunteered any information.

On the morning of the eleventh day of our stay on Rathlin Island, there was a sunny calmness to the sky, air, and sea. Uncle Jack informed me the boat had come to take us back to Ballycastle and we had to hurry if we were to reach Dunwick before nightfall. I should have been elated, but found myself reluctant to leave. My only consolation was the proximity of the small island to Dunwick, and I vowed to return.

I ran to my room at the inn and changed into my poplin riding habit, which had been cleaned and pressed. I laid the borrowed frocks on a chair. Outside the inn, I excused myself to Uncle Jack as he sauntered down the pier. I lifted my skirts and ran down the lane. I couldn't leave without saying good-bye to Sean.

"Elizabeth! What a pleasant early morning surprise," Sean exclaimed, opening the door himself. "Do come in and sit down. You are all out of breath."

"I can't," I replied. "We're leaving. I came to say good-bye."

"Don't you have a few minutes to spare?"

"No. Uncle Jack is waiting at the pier for me." I bent my head and kissed him on the cheek. "Knowing you is one of the nicest parts of my life. I shall always treasure the days on Rathlin Island." I started to leave, then stopped and turned to see Sean framed in the doorway. He waved and smiled.

"What is your last name, so I can write to you?" I called.

"Just address it to 'Sean, Rathlin Island.' I'll get it without any trouble," he shouted back.

I dashed down to Church Bay where Uncle Jack and the boat were patiently waiting. The crossing was smooth and swift, a sharp contrast to what we'd experienced on the day we'd come to Rathlin. Our horses had been well tended to in Ballycastle, and we began the trek home to Dunwick Manor in silence. I think Uncle Jack had talked himself out on Rathlin. We stopped at Bushmills, where we took tea and Uncle Jack ordered some cases of whiskey to be sent to Dunwick.

"Where the devil have you been?" Michael demanded, black rage in his eyes as he stormed out of the drawing room and into the foyer. "Rose tells me you have been gone for well over a week."

"Now . . . now . . . Michael," Uncle Jack soothed. "Our intentions had been to spend only a day on Rathlin Island, but you know how unpredictable and treacherous that stretch of sea can be. We found ourselves prisoners of the elements."

Michael's square jaw fell momentarily, then sternly clamped shut in consternation as his dark eyes warily searched mine. "What were you doing on Rathlin, Eliza-

239

beth?"

"I was curious about it. You spend a good deal of time there, so I wanted to see the island for myself," I replied.

"Did you now? And what did you expect to find there?" His ebony eyes were cold and forbidding. A vein throbbed at his temple as his jagged scar seemed to pulse in rhythm.

I lifted my chin defiantly, refusing to be cowed by his overpowering demeanor and physical presence. "I found a very nice young man whom I had a lot in common with."

"You seem to have a knack for finding companionable young men when I'm not around, Elizabeth," he hurled at me icily.

Resenting the implication, I glared at him, then turned on my heel and headed for the staircase.

"Elizabeth!" he called in a voice that sent both shivers of fear and delight through me. "We have a guest. A friend of yours, I believe. Mrs. Harold Payne-White."

"Maude? Maude is here?" I cried in disbelief. I spun around, stunned by his announcement.

"Yes. She is in the drawing room with Rose," Michael replied.

"When? How?" I was rooted to the spot in a state of semi-shock. I certainly wasn't very pleased about having Maude at Dunwick.

"Three days ago."

"Three days ago?" I parroted.

"Yes. She came back with me from London. As your birthday is fairly soon, I thought you might like to have Maude share it with you. Aren't you going to greet your guest before you change for dinner?" Michael asked, his eyes glowing like black coals.

I was numb. It was the first time I had ever heard Michael use Maude's first name. They might have spent a good deal of time together in London, I thought bitterly. And they had traveled all the way to Dunwick alone in each other's company. I swallowed hard as Michael cupped my elbow and steered me into the drawing room, Uncle Jack trailing behind.

"Elizabeth . . . how good to see you again," A radiant Maude rose from the divan and came to kiss the air by my cheek as she clasped my hands in hers. "We were all so worried about you. Rose said you went to some island."

"Yes. A little holiday," I replied, shrugging away from Michael and linking my arm through Uncle Jack's. "I'd like you to meet Mr. Jack Donahue, our uncle. Uncle Jack, this is my friend from London, Mrs. Maude Payne-White."

"A pleasure, madam," Uncle Jack said, bowing to kiss her proffered hand.

"I have been anxious to meet you, Mr. Donahue. Elizabeth spoke of you often in her letters," Maude said.

"Well, I hope. And do call me 'Jack.' "

"Always, Jack. And in glowing terms. You are indeed fortunate, Elizabeth, to be surrounded by such gallant, handsome men." Maude's words were addressed to me, but her eyes were on Michael.

"We have much to talk about, Maude, but our journey has been extremely rigorous and I am in dire need of a bath," I said, then went to greet Rose with a sisterly kiss as she rose from the divan.

"Of course, my dear Elizabeth. It won't be long before dinner, and I, too, must change. We'll have plenty of time to catch up on the news. I'll be here a whole month, so take all the time you want for your bath. Besides, Michael promised to show me the grounds before dinner, didn't you, Michael dear?" She fluttered her eyelashes as she went to his side and slid her hand through his arm.

"If you say so, Maude," he said, smiling down at her.

"If you'll excuse me," I said, then left the room. I lifted my riding skirt and raced up the stairs to my bedchamber. I shut the door and leaned against it as if it would stop the world from entering. Then I pulled the bell cord, and when Clara appeared I requested a bath.

Why did Michael have to bring Maude to Dunwick? He certainly wasn't doing me any great favor. My childish admiration for Maude, and my devotion to her, had vanished some time ago. When Michael and I had last been in London I had finally seen Maude for the flirtatious, frivolous, self-centered creature she really was, and I wanted no part of her. I was angry with Michael for bringing her, and even more furious at Maude for her obvious coquetry directed at him. Did she think me so unsophisticated or our friendship so strong that I wouldn't be aware of her provocative dalliance with my husband? Well, she would soon learn I was no longer a naive and docile sixteen-year-old. I knew what she was after — Michael. I was not about to step aside without a fight, if it came to that.

After the tub arrived full of steamy, scented water, I slid down until the water was up to my chin. In the soothing warmth, my gloomy mood evaporated and I became determined not to let my jealousy obliterate my better judgment and good manners.

Clara brushed my freshly washed hair until it shone, then with deft fingers, arranged a most becoming coiffure. I chose a simple, dark-blue silk gown whose small sleeves rested slightly off my bare shoulders. Thinking I looked quite grand, I went down to dinner, highly conscious of the fact that Michael had not appeared to escort me.

Rose and Uncle Jack were already seated at the table and Michael rose when I entered. As he assisted me into the chair, his hand brushed over my shoulder, sending rippling tremors over the surface of my skin. I never

242

failed to react sharply to his touch. It was as if my body had a mind of its own. The four of us waited patiently for Maude to make her appearance.

"Your friend, Maude Payne-White, is a most charming and attractive woman, Elizabeth," Uncle Jack observed.

"And she knows everyone and everything in London. The tales she has told me . . . Oh, Elizabeth . . . they make my ears burn," Rose added with high animation.

"Maude has a tendency to view social life with a religious fervor," I commented, noticing Michael smile wryly.

"Well, she . . . "

Rose never finished her sentence. Her eyes widened as they swung to the dining room door. I looked up to behold Maude in a dazzling, ultra stylish, bright-red satin gown. Diamonds glittered around her throat, wrists, and fingers, flashing their prismatic light around the room as she moved. Her hair was intricately and elaborately dressed with diamond-edged combs holding her golden curls.

"I do hope I haven't kept everyone waiting too long. My wretched maid couldn't tell her right hand from her left this evening," Maude complained as Michael and Uncle Jack rose from their seats.

Uncle Jack assisted in seating her. As dinner was served, I glanced around the table to note everyone's reaction to Maude's flamboyancy. At one time, I thought her exaggerated, almost theatrical finery glamorous. Now I found it a bit embarrassing, even though I saw a hint of envy in Rose's eyes and glowing admiration on Uncle Jack's face. As Michael's glance raked over her, an aloof and slightly satirical expression graced his handsome, sharp-boned face.

"Well, Mrs. Payne-White, how was your journey to Ireland?" Uncle Jack asked.

"Marvelous! One couldn't have a better escort than

Michael. Sooo attentive," Maude purred.

"What made you decide to come to Ireland, Maude?" I asked.

"You did invite me, remember? And when I told Michael how I wanted to be with you on your birthday, he insisted I come back with him. He said you could do with a bit of divertissement. I positively leapt at the chance. You know how I detest traveling alone, and London is so tedious in the summer."

"And Harry? Where is he?" Maybe it was petty of me, but I did want to remind her she was a married woman, at least in the eyes of the world.

"Oh . . . Harry. He took off with his *friends* for the south of France, or Italy, or Lord knows where," she answered contemptuously.

"Rose has been telling us about your fascinating stories of the social life in London. I, for one, would certainly like to hear the latest from London," Uncle Jack declared.

Speaking in a conspiratorial tone as she picked at her food, Maude began to relate some of the spicier gossip that was making the rounds of London society. While Rose's eyes bulged and Uncle Jack chuckled softly, Michael devoured his food with concentrated gusto as if he had heard it all before.

After dinner, we retired to the drawing room as usual and Uncle Jack insisted I play the piano. I knew everyone expected some light, frivolous Chopin, but when I saw Maude draw Michael onto the divan next to her and rudely begin to whisper in his ear, I launched into Beethoven's "Allegro Appassionata" with a ferocity that laid bare all my pent-up emotions.

Though I was mentally and emotionally agitated, the ocean voyage and the hard ride to Dunwick had taken their toll on me. Once in bed, I quickly drifted into sleep, not a deep, restful one, but more of a gauzy numbness. Somewhere in the tunnels of my brain I heard footsteps trodding back and forth like the pounding of a snare drum.

Suddenly, I sensed the connecting door had opened, and through half-lidded, sleep-misted eyes I saw Michael's dark shape framed in the doorway, the light from his room behind him outlining his powerful physique. Though I couldn't see his face, a vague terror gripped me as I ached for him to come to me, yet feared that he might. I was caught in a struggle between a desire to gain full consciousness and an urgency to surrender to the ignorant bliss of sleep. Sleep won the battle.

Eleven

I rose exceptionally early as sleep became more and more elusive. I had a tenuous recollection of a fearsome Michael glaring down at me in bed during the night, but eventually brushed it aside as the remnant of a dream.

The servants were laying out breakfast on the buffet when I entered the dining room. I had expected to see Michael, for he was an early riser, but was informed that no one had come down for breakfast yet. I was helping myself to eggs, rashers of bacon, and fried tomatoes when Rose joined me at the buffet, dabbing some eggs and one sausage on her empty plate.

"You're quite early this morning, Elizabeth," she remarked.

"It was easier to get up than to try to sleep any longer."

"I know what you mean. I've been so stimulated since your friend Maude came, I've been waking earlier than usual. Were you surprised to find her here?"

"In a way. When I hadn't heard from her in a while, I assumed she had forgotten about coming to Dunwick and had gone to one of her usual haunts at Brighton or Torquay." I took my seat at the table, followed by Rose.

"I've heard of Brighton. In the south of England, isn't it?"

"Yes."

"Quite a beach resort, I understand. I once read about the Royal Pavilion. Have you ever seen it?"

"Yes. When I was quite young. I remember it as a bizarre, Oriental structure. Very elaborate and ornate. We rode by it, but I never did get to go inside," I replied.

"Maude seems to have been everywhere. Scotland. The Continent. And her clothes! She says she has most of them made in Paris. And her jewels! Her husband must be a very wealthy man," Rose said breathlessly.

"He is. And he is very generous with her."

"Michael is so conservative," she muttered.

"Now Rose, you can't say we lack for anything. Michael never said a word when he got all those bills from my shopping spree in London, and you know he wouldn't deny us anything if we really wanted it."

She gave a short sigh. "I know. But when I see all those luxurious gowns and beautiful gems, I get a craving to possess some of my own. Though goodness knows what for."

"It's not like you to be envious, Rose." We fell silent for several minutes. Then, I had an idea. "When Maude returns to London, why don't you go with her? Michael has kept my father's house open and you could stay there."

"I couldn't!" she gasped.

"Why not?"

"Well . . . I just couldn't!"

"You can at least think about it," I suggested.

Rose's brow creased in a frown as though it might be something to consider. "Imagine my going to London and seeing the sights with someone like Maude. It would be one mad whirl of excitement—parties, theater, dancing." She drew in a deep breath. "Maude reminds me so much of Isabel."

My heart lurched. Isabel . . . Maude . . . Of course, that was the attraction for Michael. In Maude, he had found his beloved Isabel. My dour thoughts were brought to an abrupt halt when Uncle Jack and Michael entered the room. They expressed their good morning, Uncle Jack giving both Rose and me a kiss on the cheek, while Michael was remote. With plates full, they took their seats. I glared at Michael with wounded anger, but from the worried look on his face, I knew his mind was elsewhere and he hardly knew I was there.

"Where is Mrs. Payne-White this morning, Elizabeth?" Uncle Jack asked, his fork chasing an elusive bit of sausage around his plate.

"Maude is notorious for being late," I responded.

"Since she has been here she has had a tray in her room about mid-morning each day. She doesn't come downstairs until well after noontime," Rose informed us.

"That sounds like Maude," I said. "I suppose it's become a habit with her. In London, she attended every social function and they usually lasted into the early morning hours."

"Well, I'm afraid she'll find it quite dull and stuffy here at Dunwick," Uncle Jack stated languidly.

Out of the corner of my eye, I saw Michael's grim visage give way to a wisp of a crooked smile. An aching rage filled the pit of my stomach and I couldn't continue eating. Was Michael's smile one of pleasant remembrances of the late nights in London? Or for new activities right here in Dunwick? I sickened at the thought. Suddenly, the room seemed to be closing in on me.

"Rose, why don't we go for an early morning drive? Everything is so fresh-looking in the morning." There was a note of pleading in my voice.

"Go with Michael. I'm really not up to it." Rose said.

"Nonsense, Rose! The fresh air will do you good. You're as pale as a sheet." Michael's deep voice held a note of command. "Besides, I have business to tend to right after breakfast. I'll be quite busy for the rest of the

248

day."

"Michael's right, Rose," Uncle Jack joined in. "If it weren't for Elizabeth, you'd never leave the house."

"It's settled!" I declared, rising from my chair.

The drive did us both a world of good. It cleared my head of unfounded suspicions and brought a glow to Rose's cheeks. We returned to the house chatting gaily.

"I was beginning to think I had been deserted," Maude pouted from the middle of the marble staircase.

"Have you been up long, Maude?" I asked with a smile.

"Not really. I came down minutes ago, but couldn't find anyone. I was on my way back to my room when you came in."

"We'll have tea on the terrace," I said to the maid as she took our hats, jackets, and gloves.

"We had an excellent morning drive. You should have come with us, Maude," a flushed Rose exclaimed.

"What a horrible notion!" Maude cried with a grimace as she slowly descended the stairs. "Mucking about outside in the morning would destroy my digestion to say nothing of my complexion. Did Michael go with you?"

"No. He'll be busy with business all day." I watched Maude's face cloud with visible disappointment. For once, I was grateful for Michael's ardent attention to business. When Maude reached us, I linked one arm through hers and the other through Rose's. "Let's go out on the terrace and wait for our tea."

Throughout tea, Maude regaled us with tales of her many male admirers and their amorous attentions, causing Rose to blush and squirm in her seat. But Maude was undaunted. She pressed on with racy, intimate details concerning some of the more promiscuous women in her social circle, delighting in the gasps of shock that came from the lips of a thoroughly embarrassed Rose. While even I felt a bit awkward listening to Maude's scandalous revelations, I must confess a part of me was quite intrigued. I was aware that unbounded passion, once unleashed, could be overpowering. Deep in Michael's magnificent black eyes there constantly trembled a portent of that passion. But of late he kept that passion under tight control.

Relief filled Rose's eyes when Uncle Jack joined us on the terrace and asked Maude if she would care to go for a ride with him in the carriage. She quickly accepted, her lashes fluttering coquettishly.

"Oh, dear Lord," Rose exclaimed when they left, her hand splayed on her bosom. "Never in my life have I heard such things. Can she be making them up?"

I laughed. "Maude doesn't make things up, although she might embellish them a bit."

"I'm glad she wasn't here when David was staying with us. With Maude around, he wouldn't have even noticed me, let alone talk to me."

"You were rather taken with him, weren't you, Rose?"

"I don't know, Elizabeth. Whether he stirred up memories of James McGregor, or I was attracted to him for himself, I'm hard pressed to decide." Rose sat staring into space for a few minutes, then added with a smile, "I don't think it's a problem I'll ever have to solve."

"David said he'd be back, Rose. And, somehow, I don't think he would care for Maude's personality. She can be quite overpowering at times and David is the quiet type."

"We'll see," she said absently. "How did you like Rathlin Island?"

"I've been meaning to tell you about the trip, but with Maude's sudden and unexpected arrival I completely forgot."

"What a shame you were stranded there so long. It must have been horrid for you," Rose lamented.

"On the contrary. I had a delightful time. I met an

250

artist who was also a musician. He plays the violin and piano. Oh, Rose, we played duets; he did a number of sketches of me; I watched him paint in oils and he had a fine library of books. It was all so peaceful and serene there. He is a very kind and soft-spoken man. I do wish you could meet him. I know you'd like him immediately."

I was a bit breathless with growing excitement at the thought of going back to Rathlin.

"Why . . . Elizabeth, you're a married woman. What would Michael say?" She was genuinely shocked.

I laughed. "Oh, Rose, don't be silly! It was nothing like that. You've been listening to Maude too much. I feel sisterly to him, that's all."

"Oh," she murmured, then sighed. "I guess you're right. Maude has made me think in different terms about men and women. But tell me about him. What does he paint? Does he sell his paintings?"

"He paints everything. Landscapes. People. Still lifes. Everything. And he is quite marvelous at it. He told me he has an agent who sells his paintings in London. He even gave me one in return for posing for him. It's in my room. I have to get it framed. Remind me to show it to you when we go upstairs."

"What's his name?"

"Sean."

"Sean what?"

"I don't know. Just Sean. You know how artists are," I replied.

"I'd love to watch an artist paint. Why don't you invite him here for a visit?"

"I shall. But I doubt very much if he'd come. He's in a wheelchair and said he hasn't left the island since an accident left him paralyzed from the waist down."

"How tragic!" Rose exclaimed. "Is he an older man?"

"No. I'd say he's in his late twenties."

"How sad to be confined to a wheelchair at so young

251

an age." She sighed again. Her healthy glow from the morning's drive was slowly giving way to a paleness which was intensified by her raven hair. "Can we go upstairs now and have a look at the painting?"

"By all means," I replied.

A grand dinner was served on my birthday, cook elaborating on my original menu for the occasion. In the drawing room, Michael opened a bottle of champagne and everyone toasted my health. Callie's absence was not noted nor did anyone seem to care. The presents were lovely. A cameo brooch from Uncle Jack, a book of Lord Byron's poems from Rose, and a musical jewel box from France, given to me by Maude. From Michael there was a most unusual, but welcome gift—my own account in one of Derry's banks, on which I could draw at will and without his permission. But the best gift of all was Michael's devoted attentiveness, bestowed with a charm only he could radiate in so beguiling a manner when he wished. I was overwhelmed with happiness when he escorted me to my bedchamber and kissed me lightly on the lips, then made soft, gentle love to me.

The weeks passed with Michael seldom in attendance, which I could plainly see was most irritating to Maude. The staid routine at Dunwick made her increasingly fidgety. When Michael received a message late one afternoon, he angrily dashed off and told us not to expect him for dinner. In fact, he wasn't sure when he'd be back, and Maude's annoyance was more than evident at the dinner table. It wouldn't have surprised me if she'd announced her departure then and there.

That night as I prepared for bed I felt quite at ease and fell asleep the moment my head nestled in the downy pillows.

I don't know how long I had been asleep when unfamiliar and disturbing sounds echoes in my tranquil brain. Distorted noises . . . scraping . . . thuds . . . furniture moving and falling. But it was the loud crash of shattering glass in the hush of the night that brought me bolting upright in bed with eyes opened wide. The din was coming from Michael's room. Alarmed, I lit the oil lamp on my night stand and, holding it in one hand, tiptoed to the connecting door. All was quiet. My hand hesitated on the knob. If Michael had drunk too much he certainly wouldn't want me in there. Yet if something was amiss . . . I turned the knob slowly, then quietly opened the door to the well-lighted room.

My had flew to my mouth, stifling a scream. Michael was sprawled on the floor. I put the oil lamp down on a table and went to him as he stumbled to his feet, trying to drag himself upright by clutching at one of the bedposts.

"Michael!" I gasped. "What is wrong?"

"Get out, Elizabeth! Leave me be!"

Instinctively, I knew it was not alcohol that had reduced him to that state. I placed my hand on his shoulder, only to see him wince in pain. As I quickly withdrew my hand, I felt a sticky moistness clinging to it. I stared at my hand and realized it was blood. Michael's blood.

"Please leave, Elizabeth," he moaned, hauling himself onto the edge of the bed by means of the bedpost.

"I won't leave you like this, Michael." I went to him and moved his jacket aside, noting his extreme discomfort as I did so. Red blood was flowing freely against his white shirt by his left shoulder. "What happened, Michael?"

Ignoring my question, he nodded his head in the direction of the bureau. "Whiskey," he said hoarsely, his knuckles turning white from his grip on the post.

Silently, I filled a glass with the clear amber liquid and brought it to him. His hand shook as he took the glass from me. He drained the whiskey in one swallow, then handed me the empty glass. With painful effort, he began to remove his jacket. I quickly went to assist him after putting the glass down on a table. With the bloodstained jacket tossed on the floor, I unbuttoned his shirt and very gently removed it, revealing a large gaping wound in his shoulder.

"Oh, dear God, Michael. I'll send someone for the doctor right away," I cried and turned to leave.

"No! No one must know!" his deep voice boomed as his good hand caught my wrist and pulled me to him.

"I must, Michael. I can't leave you like this."

"Don't you understand what I said? No one . . . no one must know about this." His voice was low and taut. "I want your promise on that."

"I'll only promise if you'll let me help you," I countered.

"There's a bullet lodged in my shoulder. Do you think you can get it out without fainting?"

I looked into his dark, glazed eyes and nodded. For once, Michael needed me and I was determined not to let him down.

"In the top drawer of the bureau there . . ." He gave a directional sweep of his hand, then shut his eyes tightly as though willing himself to remain upright. "Some long tweezers . . . use them. And bring the whiskey decanter over here."

I followed his instructions quickly and poured him another glass of whiskey at his order. I knelt and removed his mud-spattered boots, waited for him to finish his whiskey, then made sure he could lie on the bed without my assistance before I went into the lavatory. There, I washed my hands and gathered up all the clean linens and towels I could find.

"Light a candle and pass the tweezers through the flame several times," Michael instructed as I came back to the bed and put a few layers of towels under his shoulder.

I turned the oil lamp up, passed the tweezers through the flame, then sat down beside him on the bed. Michael never uttered a word, nor did a single groan of pain escape his lips as I clumsily probed his shoulder. I was beginning to despair of ever finding the bullet as I poked with the large tweezers, feeling the pain that showed in Michael's eyes. Suddenly, there was a click of metal against metal. Hoping I had the instrument correctly placed, I squeezed the prongs tightly and gave a good tug. A spasm quivered through Michael's body as I withdrew the ugly object from his flesh.

"I've got it, Michael," I said, triumph in my eyes.

"Pour some whiskey over the wound, then sew it up."

Quickly, I retrieved needle and thread from my bed-chamber, poured whiskey over the wound, then sewed the jagged flesh together. Each jab of the needle seemed to pierce my own flesh. I washed his shoulder gently, then bandaged it as best I could with linen strips which I had cut from towels. I was gratified to see that the flow of blood had ceased.

"Pour me another glass of whiskey." With his good elbow, he pushed himself into a half-sitting position.

I handed him the whiskey, then fluffed the pillows behind him. He nodded for a refill, and I complied. After once more draining the glass, he fell back on the bed, his eyes closed. He offered no resistance when I removed his riding breeches, leaving him clad only in his long cotton underpants. My hungry eyes lingered on the well-muscled form stretched out on the bed. The thick dark hair on his heaving chest filled me with a longing to run my fingers through it. I could feel a peculiar heat course through my body as I blatantly stared at the figure of my husband lying before me with such latent potency.

"Elizabeth . . . "

"Yes, Michael," I answered quietly, raising my hand to feel his brow. "Michael, you have a fever. Please let me get a doctor," I pleaded.

"You promised."

"I know but . . . "

He opened his eyes. "No doctor."

I stood up from the bed to get a chair so I could sit by his side for the night. He grabbed my wrist and held it fast with an uncanny strength as he twisted my arm until I was forced to sit back on the bed.

"Where did you think you were going?"

"To get a chair so I could stay with you."

"Stay right here close to me, Elizabeth," he whispered. There was a pleading look in his watery, bloodshot eyes. His scar was livid, and I couldn't help but trace my finger over it lovingly.

"I won't leave you, Michael," I reassured him quietly. "But do let me get some cool cloths for your head."

"I'll be fine. But promise me you'll let no one in here. Do you understand?" he mumbled, his words beginning to slur.

"Yes, Michael. I promise."

He seemed to drift off into a hazy sleep as he slid down in the bed and his grip on my wrist relaxed. I repositioned the pillows to make him more comfortable. I don't know how long I sat there, but when my eyelids started to droop I thought I'd better get a chair. I tried to slide off the bed unobtrusively, but his eyes flew open and his right hand quickly cupped my neck. The muscles of his arm bulged as he drew my head down to his.

"Liza," he murmured groggily before his mouth covered mine in a way I never thought possible.

A fire licked at my skin as his feverish lips singed a path along my neck, then slowly returned to my mouth with a demanding probe I couldn't resist. As I threaded my fingers into his thick raven hair, he pushed me from him abruptly.

'Take that nightgown off," he ordered thickly and unevenly.

I stood and let the filmy gown fall to my feet, watching his eyes explore my exposed flesh with slow deliberation.

"Come to be with me," he said as he began to remove his remaining clothing.

With a pounding heart, I slid alongside him on the bed, any mental reservation, any sense of embarrassment, any inhibition vanishing as the heat of his hard, athletic body rendered me impervious to anything except pure sensation. As our lips met in raging urgency, my hands went around him, delighting in the feel of his sinewy back while his hands awakened the surface of my skin to new wonders. I was lost. No longer myself, but an instrument for Michael to fine tune and play at will, with adagio giving way to allegro as his special music reached stronger and stronger crescendos, causing a tympanic zenith to burst forth in both of us. The blood drained from my brain, and I felt on the verge of unconsciousness as my body was bathed with a wondrous awareness that hovered between reality and the mystical. My very soul seemed to have merged with Michael's in celestial agony and rapture.

As he lay back, his uninjured arm closed about me, pulling me close beside him. This time our lovemaking had been more than passion, desire, and need on Michael's part. I sensed there was a love in his caresses and kisses. I could only pray that the great amounts of whiskey he'd consumed hadn't deluded him into thinking I was someone else.

The rising sun threw long shafts of golden light across the bed. I roused slowly to find Michael's sinewy arm still locked about my naked body. I raised my head, supporting it with my hand, my elbow resting on a pillow. Michael's breathing was labored and his handsome face would occasionally grimace in discomfort. I lowered my face to his and kissed his lips to find them hot and dry. My makeshift bandages were now encrusted with dried blood.

I would have liked to remain exactly where I was for eternity, but reason and concern told me I must tend to my wounded husband.

I stole out of bed as Michael's sleep became fitful, and tiptoed into my own room where I quickly washed and dressed without ringing for Clara.

Slipping down to the kitchen, I told cook I had accidentally cut myself and wondered if she might have something to help heal the wound. She gave me a jar of herbal salve, which she claimed had exceptional curative powers. I declined her offer to tend to my cut, explaining that it wasn't serious.

I scurried back to Michael's bedchamber where I busily cut more bandages from a clean sheet I had retrieved from one of the linen closets. With Michael still in a feverish sleep, I snipped away at the makeshift bandage I had put on the night before. When I carefully pulled it away, I was pleased to see my stitches had held. I bathed the reddened area with great delicacy, then gingerly applied the salve before rebinding the wound with a more precise and proper bandage.

I sponged Michael's feverish body with loving tenderness, memorizing each sinew, each swell and hollow of his decidedly masculine form. Each movement of sponge and towel stirred my passion for him. I'll never know how I managed to get the bed cleaned and Michael under the covers. I suppose his tossing and turning made it easier for me. As I went to lock his door against unwanted intruders, I heard him cry out, then mumble something. I spun around, thinking he needed me, only to find him sound asleep. I went down to a belated breakfast.

"Something wrong, Elizabeth?" Uncle Jack asked. "It's not like you to be late for breakfast."

"Michael has a slight cold. I was doing what I could for him," I replied, feeling very wifely.

"Perhaps a tray should be sent up," Rose suggested.

"He doesn't want anything right now. I'll take one up about noontime."

"Well, I should go up and see how the old boy is," Uncle Jack said.

"Oh, no, Uncle Jack. He's sleeping right now," I quickly protested.

After breakfast I excused myself, saying I had promised Michael I would be there when he woke up. Neither Uncle Jack nor Rose seemed to doubt me and I breathed easier. Michael slept soundly through the morning while I sat in a chair by the bed and read a book.

Declining anyone's help, I carried a tray of tea and beef broth up to Michael's room at noon. He was sleeping fitfully and mumbling with a little more clarity than before, yet the words made very little sense to me.

"The drawer . . . must keep it locked . . . must destroy . . . can't let Elizabeth know . . . " His head moved from side to side on the pillow.

"Michael . . . " I called, gently touching him on his good shoulder. His eyes flew open and he stared at me, bewildered. "I've brought you some tea and broth. Can you sit up?"

"Yes." He winced as he pulled himself up in the bed.

"Do you want me to feed you, or can you do it yourself?" I asked as I arranged the pillows behind him.

"I can do it myself," he replied gruffly. "What happened?"

"You were shot," I replied, handing him the mug of beef broth.

"I know that! How long have I been in bed?"

"Since I found you on the floor last night."

"Who took the bullet out and bandaged my shoulder?" His eyes narrowed as he scrutinized me warily.

"I did. You forbade me to get a doctor. You were quite insistent that no one know you had been shot. What happened, Michael? Who shot you?" I asked anxiously.

"It's not your affair, Elizabeth. Have you been downstairs?"

"Yes."

"What did you tell them?"

"I said you had a slight cold." Taking the empty mug from him, I then handed him the cup of tea I had prepared. When he took the cup from my hand, I put my hand to his forehead and was gratified to find it fairly cool. "How do you feel, Michael?"

"Aside from a slightly painful shoulder, not too bad. You didn't have any of the servants help you get me into bed, did you?" There was a flicker of apprehension in his eyes.

"No. No one except me has been in this room since last night," I replied with a sinking feeling. He had no memory of the events that had occurred during the night. He held out the empty teacup, which I promptly refilled and he promptly emptied once again. "Would you like me to read to you, Michael?"

"Go downstairs, Elizabeth. And make sure the doors are locked behind you. I'm going to get some more sleep. I have to be on my feet by tomorrow."

He had become the same indifferent, aloof Michael. Silently, I picked up the tray and went downstairs where everyone was taking their seats for lunch.

"How is the old boy doing?" Uncle Jack asked.

"Something wrong with Michael?" Maude asked, looking a bit stunned.

260

"A slight cold. But he's feeling a little better," I replied.

"Then he won't be down this afternoon?" she asked.

"No."

"Oh dear. He was going to show me Londonderry today." A petulant anger coated her words.

"It's best he rests today," I said with a certain amount of glee. For once, things hadn't gone Maude's way.

"Elizabeth is right, Maude. Michael should rest," Rose interjected.

"My dear Maude, I would be delighted to show you around Derry if I may," Uncle Jack offered.

"I suppose that would be better than sitting around here. I don't know how you manage to survive, Elizabeth. Are things always so dull and boring?" Maude whined.

"The life here is to my liking," I replied, placing my knife across my empty plate.

"Well, I'll get my bonnet and parasol," Maude said, rising from her chair with Uncle Jack coming to her assistance.

I accompanied Maude upstairs to make sure she made no unecessary detours, even though the doors were locked and the keys in my pocket.

A translucent dusk was creeping through the glen. I crept into Michael's room to see if he would like a tray for dinner, only to find him wide awake, half-dressed and sitting up.

"Does your shoulder hurt much?" I asked.

"No," he replied curtly.

I was about to ask him about dinner when several loud raps sounded at the door to my bedchamber and Rose called my name. Closing the connecting door behind me, I went to see what had Rose so excited.

"David is here," she said breathlessly when I opened the door.

"David?"

"Yes. David Cooke. Isn't that wonderful? He came with Uncle Jack and Maude. He had just arrived in Derry and ran into them. Uncle Jack invited him to come back to Dunwick with them. Come down with me, Elizabeth, and help greet him."

"It's almost time for dinner. I'll greet him then. You go ahead."

"I'll go down briefly before changing for dinner." Her eyes glowed with elation as though life had given her a reprieve.

I went back to Michael and told him the news. His face darkened in a scowl. "I suppose you're anxious to see him," he sneered.

"Not particularly. I'll see him at dinner unless you'd like to have a tray sent up, in which case I'll have dinner with you."

"That won't be necessary, Elizabeth. Besides, I want everything to appear perfectly normal. Understand me?"

"No, I don't, Michael. Why all this . . ."

"Hadn't you better get ready for dinner, Elizabeth?" His tone of dismissal was final as one dark eyebrow arched imperiously at me.

I looked at him and sighed inwardly. His desire and need of me had disappeared with his fever. Cold, calculating reason now ruled his emotions. I wanted to tell him how much I loved him, how I wanted to regain the passion we had once shared, how last night had given me more rapture than I had ever known, and how I wanted to be in his arms, his body fused with mine, every night for as long as I lived. Instead, I left the room without a word.

For once, Maude was on time for dinner, dressed to rival the crowned heads of Europe. Even though Rose looked at Maude with admiration, her eyes betrayed a slowly ebbing excitement. David was his usual gallant and charming self to everyone, trying to give equal attention to all the ladies present. But Maude's wily charm could be devastating, and she soon had David's exclusive attention while Rose and I drifted into conversation with Uncle Jack.

Suddenly, the only sound in the room was the clatter of soup dishes being removed by the servants. All eyes were on the doorway, where Michael stood tall and erect, strikingly handsome in his formal black dinner attire. He smiled, his face giving no hint of the pain I knew he must be feeling.

"I must apologize for my tardiness. Please continue. Don't let me interrupt." He took his seat at the head of the table.

"I'm glad to see your cold is better, Michael," Maude said, looking a trifle perplexed as though she wasn't quite sure which man deserved her total attention.

"My wife is much too considerate of my reputation. Quite frankly, I imbibed much more than I should have the other night and was in no condition this morning to face the day," Michael explained, reaching for my hand and giving it a quick squeeze.

After dinner, David asked me to play the piano, saying how he had missed the quiet evenings with us at Dunwick. To Maude's dismay, Michael purposely sat alone in a large arm chair and David sat next to Rose on the divan, forcing Maude to sit alone in a Queen Anne chair.

I played a few pieces, but could see the pain in Michael's eyes, which his expression masked with the ease of one well-practiced in cloaking his emotions and feelings. Knowing he was in pain, I could not continue playing. My hands halted over the keyboard.

"Forgive me. I'm not feeling too well this evening.

263

David, why don't you play some popular songs for every-one?" I rose and went to Michael. "Would you please take me upstairs, Michael? I feel a little dizzy."

"Of course, Elizabeth." He lifted himself from the chair, then said to the others, "Do excuse us."

As we walked up the staircase, Michael whispered, "Thank you."

In the privacy of his bedchamber, I quickly removed his jacket and shirt, then re-dressed the wound, spreading more salve on it. I removed his shoes, but Michael declined any further assistance.

With hope blazing in my heart, I dashed into my bed-chamber and prepared for bed. After swiftly brushing out my long hair, I returned to Michael's room, only to find him in a sound sleep, completely oblivious to my presence. I stood staring at him, drinking in his virile good looks as my mind's eye relived the previous night in his bed. I was about to return to my room when the words he had spoken in his delirium came back to me. "Can't let Elizabeth know." And then something about a drawer. What shouldn't I know? What was it Michael didn't want me to find out?

With the dim light of the oil lamp to aid me, I quietly searched through his bureau drawers, but couldn't find anything out of the ordinary. My glance fastened on his small personal desk, and I tried the three drawers. All were locked. I stood there in total frustration as my curiosity now overpowered me.

I explored every place where I thought Michael might have hidden a key, to no avail. The only place I hadn't looked was his clothing. As my shaking hand probed the pockets of his pants, I had the disheartening feeling that the key was locked away somewhere in the library, which would end my search for the night. But when I rummaged through his jacket, my fingers touched the cold metal of a small key. Triumphantly, I went back to the desk and silently unlocked one drawer at a time.

To my disappointment, the drawers appeared to contain nothing but bills of lading; items purchased in America and shipped to Liverpool or Glasgow. With a shrug and an inaudible sigh, I closed and relocked two of the drawers. As I was about to close the middle one, I noticed it seemed to be deeper than the other two. Pulling it out as far as it would go, I noticed a plain envelope with no writing on it. I opened it and found another envelope inside, addressed to Michael at Dunwick. I was stunned to see that the address was written in my father's script. With trembling hands, I removed the letter and began to read it:

"My dear Michael,

I trust you are well aware of my financial and other assistance to the Tyrone family. Your father once said he would do all in his power to come to my aid if I needed assistance. Knowing you for the gentleman you are, I firmly believe that since your father has now passed away, you will fulfill his obligations.

My health has not been what it should of late and I fear for my daughter. I could never rest in peace knowing she is at the mercy of every dandy in London. She is quite plain, and clearly any suitor would only be after my wealth. I would consider any debt the Tyrone family owes me completely erased if you would take her for your wife, Michael. It would lift an enormous burden from my shoulders. Elizabeth is a docile child and will not give you any trouble.

Please come to London and have a look at her. If you can tolerate her plainness of face, I would happily welcome you as a son-in-law. I am sure that upon my passing my wealth and holdings will make for more than adequate recompense. I would like the issue of Elizabeth settled within the next week or so, for I fear my time is short. I will trust in your honor as a gentleman to do the right and proper thing.

Sincerely,
John Whitter"

I had been bought and sold in the market like some prize cow that no longer gave milk. Anger, blind savage anger, clouded my vision and throbbed in my veins like a raging sea. I had been cheated of a real husband, lied to, degraded and possessed by a man who had married me out of a sense of duty. I was only an obligation to fulfill with the promise of great financial reward. I slid the letter back in its envelope, then in the plain envelope, placing it in the exact position I had found it. Closing the drawer, I locked it, then returned the key to the pocket of Michael's jacket. Never would he know I had discovered his secret. My pride, or what was left of it, precluded such a disclosure.

I tiptoed back to my bedchamber, softly closing the connecting door behind me. *Plain . . . docile . . .* the words plunged into my heart like daggers of hot steel. There wasn't much I could do about my plain features, but I could certainly alter any docile traits. I felt totally betrayed, but didn't know how to avenge myself, and raw anger kept self-pitying tears from reaching my eyes. In my dreams Michael became a dark prince intent on destroying me.

I dressed without aid as the vague haze of an incipient dawn spread through the sky. The stablemaster was surprised to see me at so early an hour, but quickly obliged me by saddling a horse. Docile am I! I thought as I raced down the roads and lanes, through gorse and bracken, at a full gallop, heading for the sea, where I hoped the crashing sound of the breakers against the craggy rocks would drive the bitter resentment from my soul.

The strident screeching of the gulls increased as I encroached upon their hunting grounds where they were seeking their early morning meal. The grotesque, lichen-encrusted rock formations stood stolidly on the sandy beach, defying the assault by the sea. I sat on my horse, staring out over the expanse of sun-kissed ocean while I tried to bring some order to my tumultuous emotions. It was futile. The web of hate, love, and rage were intertwined like fine mail, each emotion interlocking with the other, too strong, too interdependent to be torn asunder and examined individually.

I slid down from the horse and tethered him to a jutting rock. Then, removing my stockings and shoes, I walked with riding skirt lifted down to the edge of the sea. The water lapped over my feet, drawing the sand from underneath as it ebbed and flowed, giving me the sensation of drifting. I closed my eyes and surrendered to its calming affect.

On my way back to the horse, sand clung to my ankles and feet. Stuffing my cotton stockings into my shoes, I laced my shoes together and flung them over the horn of the saddle. Then, I remounted the patient animal and headed back to Dunwick, imbued with a new resolve and strength.

I was startled to see Michael at the stables, his fury evident as he stood with arms folded and feet apart, watching me enter the courtyard and rein in the horse which a groom ran to attend to.

"And just what the devil did you hope to achieve by taking off at dawn, telling no one of your destination?" Michael stormed.

"What I do is my own affair," I replied calmly.

He reached up and eased me down from the horse, his

eyes ablaze with satanic wrath. "What are you doing without your shoes and stockings on?" he asked, looking down at my feet, his hands firmly about my waist.

"I didn't think wading in the ocean was the thing to do with my shoes on," I said flippantly.

"I don't ever want you to go out riding alone again. Do you understand me, Elizabeth?"

"I understand you perfectly well, Michael. But I shall do as I please," I flung at him.

"You will, will you? Well, we'll see about that!" He swooped me up in his arms and stalked toward the house. I could see the strain on his face and knew the pain in his shoulder was monumental.

We passed an astonished Rose and David, who were entering the foyer from the dining room as Michael carried me up the marble staircase. Once in my bedchamber, he rudely dumped me on my bed.

"Now, clean yourself up and be quick about it before breakfast is completely cold." He turned on his heel and left, slamming the door behind him.

After a wash, I put on a frock of pale yellow lawn trimmed with lace, then brushed my sea-dampened hair until it gleamed. I tied my long auburn hair back with a matching ribbon, not bothering with any elaborate coiffure. No longer would I try to compete with either Maude or Isabel. Michael had purchased me plain . . . and plain I'd be.

As I went down the corridor, I glimpsed Callie far down at the other end, sitting on the floor, her eyes shut tight, her hands pressed hard over her ears. As I was about to go see what was wrong with the child, Mrs. Meehan's erect figure appeared. She stood Callie on her feet and led her down toward the east wing. I shrugged and went on my way, but before descending the marble staircase, I checked for any lethal cord across the landing. More than ever, I was alert to my precarious position at Dunwick.

"What a strange thing to do, Elizabeth! Go riding before breakfast," Rose said. She had been waiting for me in the foyer.

"It was invigorating. I think I shall make a habit of it when the weather permits. Right now, I'm famished. Have you eaten, Rose?"

"Yes. But I'll join you. I can always use another cup of tea," she said as we linked arms. "Well, the ride must have done something. You look positively radiant."

"I feel radiant," I claimed as we entered the dining room.

Michael sat before his half-eaten breakfast, looking at me through narrow eyes, studying every aspect as if seeing me for the first time. I lifted my chin and maintained an air of haughty indifference.

"Everything looks delicious," I remarked as I heaped my plate and then took my place at the table. "Did you have any particular plans for today, Rose?"

"No. Nothing special." Sitting opposite me, next to Michael, she poured herself some tea.

"Let's go into Derry. We'll poke through the shops, then treat ourselves to lunch."

"I don't know." Rose looked furtively at Michael as though expecting his disapproval, but he never looked up from his plate. "Shouldn't we ask Maude and David?"

"That's a splendid idea." I continued to talk to Rose as though Michael wasn't present. He finished his breakfast and left without uttering a word.

David accepted our invitation readily, saying there was a building in Derry he wanted to examine more closely. But Maude declined, claiming she had just been to Derry and found it boring. There was a mischievous gleam in her eye as she seemed to weigh the thought of being alone in the house with Michael.

I felt a fleeting pang of jealousy, but my father's letter

to Michael had put things in a totally different perspective for me.

When we entered the house, arms laden with packages, the latest magazines, and several new novels, we heard low moans coming from the drawing room. Thinking Michael's wound had opened, I threw my packages on the foyer table and dashed to the drawing room.

A dazed Maude sat on the divan, her hair in disarray, tendrils springing out in every direction. She had the appearance of a wild woman and her eyes had a vacant stare.

"Maude . . . Maude . . . what happened?" I dashed to her side and gripped her shoulders, then tried to shake her out of her stupor as Rose and David came rushing over.

"Horrible! Horrible!" Maude groaned.

"What, Maude? What?" I pleaded.

"She's a devil!"

"Who?"

"That child . . . that red-headed she-monster!" Maude wailed.

"What the devil is going on in here?" Michael bellowed, tracking in dirt with his muddy boots.

"Maude's had a shock of some sort. Something to do with Callie," I explained.

"Oh, Michael!" Maude cried, jumping to her feet and throwing her arms around his neck. "If you hadn't left me here alone, this never would have happened."

"Calm yourself, Maude," Michael ordered, reaching up to remove her clinging arms. I could see him wince as the effort shot pain into his wounded shoulder.

"She's a horrid child. Jumping at me like that with a ghoulish scream. She half scared me to death!" Maude exclaimed, trying to restore her once elegant coiffure.

270

"Do sit down and be calm, Maude. Callie will be dealt with accordingly," Michael said. "I've brought you a letter from the village. It came from London and I thought it might be important."

Maude whipped the envelope from Michael's hands, glaring angrily at him, her traumatic experience all but forgotten. Rose sat down on the divan as Maude tore open the envelope and read the contents. She stared at the paper in her hand for several seconds before a high-pitched, gleeful laugh filled her throat.

"He's dead! Can you imagine? He's dead." Maude threw back her head, closed her eyes and visibly relaxed as she clutched the letter. "At last I'm free . . . and all that lovely money is mine."

"What are you saying, Maude?" I asked with a frown of concern.

"Harry. Dear old Harry. In a fit of temper one of his friends fatally stabbed him. He's dead!" Her laughter became gutteral.

Rose gasped. David sat down. Michael looked disgusted.

Calming down, Maude explained further. "His solicitors want to know if I would like to accompany the body home from Venice. Oh, it's so ironic! Just like our return from our wedding holiday." She laughed again.

"I'm so sorry, Maude," I said. "What are you going to do?"

"That's one journey I wouldn't miss for the world," she replied, smoothing her blond hair back.

Michael cleared his throat. "Mr. Cooke, I don't think Mrs. Payne-White should journey back to London alone in view of the circumstances. It would be most gallant if you accompanied her."

I looked at Michael in consternation, embarrassed by his audacity.

"You're quite right, Lord Tyrone. I will be honored to

accompany Mrs. Payne-White back to London. I will do my best to relieve her of any undue stress," David replied, strolling to the divan.

"It would make matters simpler for me if there was a man about." Maude smiled as she rose and took David's arm, her predilection for coquetry coming to the fore. "We shall leave first thing in morning. Is that convenient for you, David?"

He nodded and escorted her from the room.

Rose looked stricken as she excused herself. I was furious. Michael had no right to presume on David like that.

"Michael!" I called as he, too, started to leave the drawing room.

"Well?" His regal face was imperiously complacent, which increased my anger.

"Why do you persist in being so rude to David Cooke? This is the second time you have practically ordered him from the house."

"It bothers you?"

"Yes. It does. He was very kind to me when I was left on my own in the Lake District, and I consider him a good friend," I said with conviction.

"A friend? That's all?"

"Yes! That's all!" I cried.

"If that is the case, I would suggest you acquire no more friends, Elizabeth," he said coldly and bitterly.

"And just what is that supposed to mean?"

"My dear wife, I have every reason to believe it was your 'friend' who shot me." He wheeled around and stalked from the room.

Twelve

Trunks were piled on the marble floor of the foyer, ready for loading into the carriage as Uncle Jack came down the staircase with David, both in conversation. In light of Michael's revelation, I stared blatantly at David. I couldn't bring myself to believe he was the sort of man who could, or would, use a gun on another human being. His handsome face with its look of boyish innocence belied any tendency toward violence. His soft hazel eyes bespoke a gentleness that made me doubt Michael's veracity. I could only conclude that Michael was manipulating me, trying to destroy any friendships I might form, especially with men. David smiled when he noticed me standing by the doorway to the dining room

"Good morning, Elizabeth," Uncle Jack boomed. "Did you have your early morning ride?"

"Yes, I did." Michael hadn't tried to stop me from riding, but now there was always a groom present at a discreet distance.

"Good morning, Elizabeth." David took my hand and placed a warm kiss on it.

"Good morning, David. I do hope you'll take breakfast before you leave," I said.

"Of course he will, won't you, my boy." Uncle Jack gave David a hearty slap on the back.

Michael and Rose were already at the table, their plates replete with breakfast fare.

"Good morning, Rose. And how are you this fair morning?" David asked after a quick nod to Michael.

"I am well, but disappointed you must leave. It seems you no sooner arrive, than you depart," Rose replied.

"The hazards of being a writer. Harold Payne-White has always been grist for the writer's pen. His wealth and social position make him a newsworthy item and I am indeed fortunate to be able to cover the events first-hand," David said.

Michael glared at me with such force I couldn't mistake the warning in his eyes. Clearly, he didn't want me to mention anything about the shooting or that he had named his would-be assassin. We were all seated and enjoying our breakfast when an imperious Maude entered the dining room.

"What a ghastly hour for people to be up and about," she exclaimed. "But then, Harry never was very considerate of other people." She cast a dazzling smile at everyone in the room before bringing it to rest on David. "David . . . why don't you come all the way with me? To Venice, I mean. You might find it quite rewarding."

"It does sound promising. I'll have to see what my editor says. He does advance the funds, you know," David replied as he held Maude's seat for her.

"Money is no problem. Don't even bother your editor about it," Maude said.

"I couldn't possibly impose on you like that," David objected.

"I insist! Your company and services would far surpass any expense," Maude claimed.

David was silent as I watched Michael study him and Maude closely. Was Michael jealous? I wondered. A question and a disturbing notion seemed to rest deep in his dark eyes. I was at a loss to understand his shifting moods as Maude's incessant chatter began to rasp on my nerves. I was starting to wish they would soon leave. But, in an apparent attempt to delay their departure, she picked at her food slowly.

"Will you be coming to the funeral, Michael?" she cooed.

"At this point I really couldn't say," he replied.

"I promise you it will be quite an affair." Her blue eyes sparkled with excitement. "Harry always reveled in pomp. A large, splendid funeral would make Harry truly feel at rest. It's the least I can do for him. The trip to Venice will give me plenty of time to plan all the elaborate details which I know he would enjoy. A gilded hearse pulled by white horses with red and yellow plumes would be a nice touch, don't you think?"

"It would certainly attract attention," Uncle Jack commented.

"I think Harry would like it. And red satin to line the hearse. Oh, the prospects are unlimited," Maude declared mirthfully.

"Wouldn't it be a bit gaudy for a funeral, Maude?" I asked.

"For Harry? Never. He always liked to be daring and attract as much attention as possible. The only real problem is my having to wear black. So unflattering and old-womanish!"

"You'd grace and give light to anything you wore," Uncle Jack complimented her.

"You are an old rascal," Maude gushed, giving him a quick flutter of eyelashes.

"I'm so sorry about your husband, Maude. You have my deepest sympathy," Rose said quietly.

Poor Rose, I thought. After all that had been said, she didn't seem to realize Maude needed no sympathy. In fact, I do believe Maude would have preferred congratulations.

"Thank you, Rose." Maude smiled graciously.

"Well . . ." David began. "I think we'd best get started, Mrs. Payne-White. I'm sure the carriage has been loaded by now."

Uncle Jack jumped up and held Maude's chair back. Then he, David, and Rose went out into the foyer. Maude paused by Michael, who rose at her approach.

"You've been most hospitable, Michael. I do hope you can make it to London for the funeral," she said, then added, as an afterthought, "Of course, you too, Elizabeth." She extended her hand, which Michael took, kissing the air above it.

I had come around the table to join her, but as I passed Michael, he roughly gripped my arm and held me close until Maude had drifted out into the foyer.

"When you have finished your good-byes, Elizabeth, come up to my bedchamber." His eyes were warm and tender. I would have thrown myself into his arms had it not been for my father's letter, which had caused a stoniness in my heart. Without a word I wrenched my arm free and joined the group waiting outside.

"Elizabeth," Maude said to me, "I was telling Rose that when this dreary business is over, you'll both have to come to London and we'll do the town. Perhaps we can find a husband for you, Rose," she added rather tactlessly.

Much fuss was made over good-byes with Rose looking mournful and distressed. With its passengers settled safely inside, the carriage rolled down the crescent driveway. Rose and I stood watching until it faded into the distance, while Uncle Jack entered the house the minute it began to move away.

As we turned, arm in arm, toward the main door, I noticed a tear in the corner of Rose's eye.

"Why, Rose . . . I had no idea you had grown so fond of David. Will you really miss him that much?"

"It isn't all because of David's leaving," she replied as she brushed at her eyes.

"Then what is it? Don't tell me you were so taken with Maude that her leaving has saddened you?"

"I feel so sorry for her losing her husband at so early an age. Oh, I know she says she is happy he is gone, but the whole thing started me thinking about James McGregor."

"You'll never forget him, will you?"

"I've tried. Truly I have, Elizabeth. Only, every now and then, I see or hear something that brings him to mind. Sometimes I even imagine I see him walking along the road to Dunwick," she said wistfully.

"Maybe it's an omen, Rose. A good omen," I said, trying to console her.

"I can't wait forever, Elizabeth. Uncle Jack keeps telling me I'm not getting any younger and had better get a husband while I still can."

"He's teasing you, Rose. You're lovely. Far prettier than I am. And I don't blame you for waiting for the man you really want. You really don't meet enough men your age, Rose. I think we'll take Maude up on her suggestion and go to London," I announced with confidence.

277

"You're getting to sound more and more like Uncle Jack," she said with winsome smile.

"Just think, Rose. The theater, the opera, the ballet, the races. And Maude always receives invitations to every social function in London. A whirl of elegant people, posh places, French cuisine . . . a whole different world will open up for you," I said.

"You make it sound like a panacea for all the ills of the world. Do you miss London awfully, Elizabeth?"

I gave a small laugh. "Miss London? Oh, Rose, I've been happier here than I ever was in London."

"Then why are you so anxious for me to go to London?"

"Because I've been there and you haven't. And I think the trip would give you a whole new outlook. Introduce you to sights and sounds you've never been exposed to."

"Oh, Elizabeth." She blushed and squeezed my arm. "Let's go for a walk in the garden."

"Yes. That would be nice." We were halfway down the great hall when I remembered that Michael wanted to see me. "Oh, Rose, I'm sorry. I can't go just now. Michael wanted to see me about something."

I knocked lightly on the connecting door, then went in without waiting for an acknowledgment. Bootless and shirtless, Michael lay on his bed clad only in his black riding breeches.

"Well, Elizabeth . . . I was beginning to think you'd gone to London with your friends," he said as he brought his well-built frame into a sitting position. "Was it a very tearful and emotional parting for you?" he asked snidely.

"No." His derisive manner constricted my heart and a

cold emptiness engulfed me. "What is it you want of me, Michael?"

"Do I detect a note of sarcasm in your voice?"

"Did you ask me here to mock me?"

"On the contrary, my dear. You did such an excellent job on my shoulder, I was wondering if I could prevail upon you to rebandage it."

"Is it bothering you?" I tried to mask the deep concern I felt.

"A little stiff and sore but otherwise quite serviceable."

"I'll be back in a minute. The scissors and bandages are in my room."

"Elizabeth . . . was it you who undressed and bathed me last night?"

"Yes," I murmured. "Why?" I asked with my back toward him.

"I only wanted to make sure no one else knew of the wound," he replied casually.

I quickly went into my bedchamber to obtain what I needed to tend to his shoulder. I returned in seconds.

As I cut the front bandages on his dark-haired chest, I could feel his warm breath brushing against my cheek. My heart was thudding erratically as I moved up to snip the bandages at the top of his shoulder and our cheeks almost touched.

"Elizabeth . . " He whispered in my ear, causing my blood to drain to my toes, pushing me to the edge of vertigo.

"Yes, Michael?" I could scarcely say the words. He took a deep breath and I could feel his chest rise against my bodice. A warmth rushed through me and I could feel my cheeks grow red.

"Nothing. Let's get on with it."

I cleared away the bandages and examined the crescent-shaped scar. The area was a reddish-brown but seemed to be healing nicely.

"How does it look?" he asked, wincing a bit as I gently bathed the area.

"The wound appears to be clean. I don't see any signs of infection."

"Good. That salve helps to draw out the soreness. Do you have any more?"

"Yes. I'll go get it." I rose from the edge of the bed, got the salve and returned to apply it before rebandaging the wound. I sat on the bed beside him once again and asked, "Michael, what makes you so sure it as David Cooke who shot you?"

"Although it was late at night and moonless, I'm quite sure it was Cooke by the way he held himself."

"Then you're not absolutely sure."

"I wouldn't swear to it in a court of law, but I've learned to trust my instincts."

"I believe your instincts are wrong this time, Michael. David isn't the kind of man who would go about shooting people. And, of all people, why should he shoot you?" I was relieved to learn Michael had only thought it was David. It made no sense for David to be shooting at Michael. Unless Maude was somehow involved. No! I wasn't going to think like that. Besides, Maude and David didn't know each other that well.

"Let the incident be, Elizabeth. It's over with."

"If he did shoot at you, I find it curious that you never confronted him with the fact while he was here at Dunwick," I persisted.

"I have my reasons, Elizabeth. Drop the subject and never, understand me, never mention it again. Have you so little faith in me?"

I thought of the letter and couldn't answer him.

Clutching the jar of salve in my hand, I rose from the bed. He swiftly gripped my free hand with viselike strength.

"Elizabeth . . . you didn't answer me."

"I have no answer to give, Michael." I stared into his dark eyes, searching for a glimpse of tenderness, of warmth, of caring. But there was none. He let go of my wrist and I left the room without another word. After putting my nursing implements away, I went down to the drawing room.

All my frustrations, hopes, desires, and anger I took out on the piano, purging myself by pouring my soul into Bach's "Toccata and Fugue in G Minor."

An insidious change in behavior and mood was altering Michael. It was something I sensed rather than saw as factual with outward manifestations. There were subtle changes going on in his nature, which caused me to harbor an unknown fear. I could only hope it was a temporary state or that my imagination was overactive.

The days passed and, for the most part, Michael stayed at Dunwick, which greatly surprised me. I was even more astonished when he offered to join me in my early morning rides. He was attentive and courteous, yet maintained a quality of remoteness I couldn't penetrate. The evenings were routine: Michael and Uncle Jack immersed in a game of draughts or political conversation, Rose at her needlework and I at the piano.

Then something happened to alter the course of the apparent serenity at Dunwick and disrupt my life with a haunting, unknown terror.

Along with Rose, I retired early one night. When I entered my bedchamber I discovered a well-executed drawing of a stone building propped against the mirror of my dressing table. The square, one-story, windowless structure was drawn in great detail, while the shrubbery and general landscape were scribbled in wild, restless pencil scrawling. There seemed to be a calculated madness in the drawing that repelled and attracted me at the same time. My body stiffened as I made out some of the letters on the lintel over the stone door. *A* . . . *B* . . . *E* . . . *I*. There were some strange scratch marks preceding the letters and a pencil smudge by the *I,* making it difficult to determine whether it was meant to be an *L* or a *T.*

Slowly the letters came together in my mind. Depending on the smudged letter, the word intended would either be *Isabel* or *Elizabeth*. How silly of me, I thought. They are only arbitrary letters put there to give an air of authenticity to the building. But who would put this strange, almost eerie drawing in my bedchamber? to what purpose?

Callie! Of course! She was playing one of her pranks again. Or maybe she was having a change of heart toward me and the drawing was her idea of a gift. With a shake of my head and a sigh, I placed the drawing in my desk drawer and prepared for bed.

Evidently the drawing had left a deep, unconscious impression on me, for in my dreams the stone building pulsed, expanding and contracting, with a life all its own. Its doors were flung open and I approached through the tangled vegetation. From within came a whirlwind that sucked me deep into the building's black, cavernous interior as a screeching wail—something between a cry of pain and a derisive howling—assailed my ears. The door slammed shut and I was left in that inky emptiness while the din circled around me and icy, bony fingers prodded me from every side. I screamed and screamed in soundless horror until consciousness seized me and I awoke.

There was cold sweat on my forehead and the palms of my hands. I lit the lamp on the night stand, then went to the lavatory to splash cool water on my face as if it would wash away the nightmare. On impulse, I took the lamp and went to the desk. Pulling out the drawer, I peered inside. The stone house looked larger than before but what was even more ominous, the door of the edifice was standing open. I was sure it had been closed when I first viewed the drawing. I gripped the desk and closed my eyes quickly as my head spun and my breath came in short, rapid gasps. I swallowed hard and slammed the drawer shut. A cold breeze touched my nape and I quickly blew the lamp out and dashed back to bed.

I had grown accustomed to seeing Michael waiting for me at the stables in the morning. When he wasn't there, I waited a short time before deciding to go on without him. I told the stablemaster where I would be heading in case Michael came along later.

Returning to Dunwick, I made straight for the dining room. Breakfast and hot tea were foremost in my mind. The dining room was unexpectedly empty. Usually Rose and Uncle Jack would be taking breakfast by now. Michael I was never sure of. As I consumed my meal with a hearty appetite, I became uneasy about the abnormal silence in the house. I quickly finished my tea in order to seek someone out and learn why I was the only one at breakfast.

My steps echoed on the marble floor of the foyer as I headed for the staircase. I had taken only two or three steps when I realized something was amiss.

I went back down to find the doors of the drawing

room wide open. Normally they were closed during the early morning hours. I stepped in and was immediately aware of an unfamiliar quality to the room, a peculiar aspect I couldn't put my finger on. I was about to leave when it dawned on me what was wrong with the drawing room. The piano top was down. The large kidney-shaped top wasn't silhouetted against the light from the huge windows behind it. The top was always kept up, and I shook my head with a smile at my own inability to see the obvious. I went to prop the shiny mahogany lid back up, thinking one of the maids must have forgotten to do it when she had finished polishing. I lifted the lid and put the holding post in place.

"No! Oh, good Lord, no!" I cried aloud as I stood there physically frozen in horror and dismay. The strings were coiled like writhing snakes around the sound board. Someone had cut every piano string on the instrument.

High-pitched laughter suddenly filled the drawing room, erratically rising and falling. I spun around to see Callie crawling out from under a high settee which stood against the wall.

"Callie . . . did you do this?" I asked, controlling the anger I felt. I had to remember I was dealing with a four-year-old mentality, even though the young girl before me was almost my size.

"Me?" Her finger pointed to her chest and her emerald eyes glistened with childish innocence.

"Now tell me the truth, Callie. No one is going to hurt you. You cut the piano strings, didn't you?" Considering the situation, my voice was quite calm.

"The truth? You know the truth."

"The only truth I know is that you're not as innocent as you pretend. How could you do such a thing?"

"*I* didn't do a thing!" she protested loudly.

284

"Callie . . ." I moved closer to the child and tried to touch her shoulder, but she jumped back.

"I warn you. Stay away from me," she hissed, her green eyes glittering with intense hatred.

"Callie, I only want to be friends. I want to know why you cut the piano strings. Then, perhaps I can understand you a little better." I stood perfectly still as I spoke lest she take flight.

"I told you I didn't do it," she growled. "It was the banshee. She was looking for you and when she couldn't find you she became angry."

"Banshees do not cut piano strings, Callie."

"She doesn't like you here. You make her very angry, so she drew her long fingers over the strings and they parted at her touch."

"I told you before, Callie. I don't believe in banshees. A human being cut those strings on purpose," I said, summoning up every bit of patience I had.

She shook her head and stamped her foot. "There are too banshees! My mother knows all about them. She put it all in her diaries and I've read them. But then you're nothing like my mother, are you?" The contempt in her voice had a vehemence that belied her youth.

"Your mother kept diaries?" The information surprised me. From what little I had learned of Isabel, she didn't appear to be the type of woman who would keep diaries. I could feel my curiosity rising.

"I'll bet you'd love to read them, wouldn't you?" Callie asked as though reading my thoughts. Her bowlike lips curled in a twisted smile. "Maybe I'll let you. But you really won't have the time. The banshees will take you away any day now."

I could see it was useless to try and carry on any sort of sensible conversation with the child and I started to

285

leave the room.

"Did you like the present I left in your bedchamber?" she called.

"The drawing?" I turned to face her.

"Not many people see their tomb before they die. The banshee described it to me."

"Callie, I don't think your father would care to hear you talk like that."

"My father?" Her laughter pierced the air and she wrapped her arms around her stomach, doubling over with mirth. As the laughter ebbed, she continued, "My father is the one who invoked the banshee, calling her up to rid him of his homely wife. He neither needs nor wants you. He still worships my mother. You're nothing to him. Nothing! I can hear him at night pleading with the banshee to deliver him from you. You'll never take my mother's place. Never . . ."

"I never had any intention of taking your mother's place, Callie," I said dully knowing my words never reached her brain. Though her bitter diatribe could hardly be taken seriously, somewhere in the back of my mind I wondered if there wasn't a speck of truth in what she said. "I think we ought to find Mrs. Meehan." Once again, I started to leave.

"Don't you turn your back on me!" she cried, running to me, her hand viciously grabbing my arm, her fingernails biting into my flesh.

"Callie, let go of my arm." I looked directly at her. Her face was contorted in delicious agony as if she had reached a plateau of diabolical ecstasy. My dread increased, for this was no little child displaying infantile jealousy. This was a creature who had evolved from a murky timelessness and had come to dwell in the body of a child. Her grip tightened and her eyes dilated until they were only black orbs haloed by rings of bright green. Instinctively, I wrenched my arm free and stepped back away from her. She began to stalk me as I continued to move backward, her face screwing up with irreverent triumph. Suddenly, her eyes slid past me and she threw herself on the floor, wailing.

"Lady Tyrone . . . what have you done to the child?" The frigid, controlled voice of Mrs. Meehan penetrated my dazed mind as I watched the older woman glide to the aid of the frenzied child.

"She hit me! She was cruel to me!" Callie screamed with all the melodramatics at her command.

"Now, now, Callie . . . we must be brave." Mrs. Meehan lifted the child to her feet and then turned to me. "Lady Tyrone, Callie is a very sensitive young girl and you shouldn't do or say things that might upset her."

The situation was incredible, but I refused to succumb to anger. "I did nothing to the child except question her regarding the wanton destruction of the piano," I stated quite calmly.

"Callie knows better than to destroy anything, don't you, my dear?" She smiled down at Callie.

Callie nodded. Then, with the instincts of a trapped animal, she fled the drawing room.

"Look for yourself, Mrs. Meehan." I pointed to the piano.

She walked to the piano slowly and gave it a cursory glance. "I'm sure Callie had nothing to do with it. She can be difficult at times, but only when she is severely provoked. You must have been quite sharp with her, Lady Tyrone, for her to be on the floor and wailing so. You should have informed someone she was here. We have been searching for her since early this morning."

"Mrs. Meehan, I am not the one who needs chastising," I said, struggling to keep my temper in check as my hands balled into fists at my side.

"In the future I suggest you keep your frustrations confined to adults and not vent them on a child. You are supposed to be older and wiser, Lady Tyrone," she said imperiously.

"I am not accustomed to being spoken to in that manner, Mrs. Meehan. In the future *you* control yourself and make sure Callie doesn't turn *her* frustrations to the destruction of property."

"I'm sure you are mistaken to believe Callie would do any damage to the piano."

"I suppose you believe it was the doing of a banshee as Callie claims." The woman was pushing me to my limits.

"There are mysteries in life which mortals have difficulty understanding. Now, if I may be excused, I have to tend to my charge before she disappears again."

"You're excused, Mrs. Meehan," I replied, seething with anger. The woman was as insufferable, unapproachable, and disquieting as Callie herself. Feeling in need of a hot cup of tea, I returned to the dining room. A vague smile flickered over my face as I poured the tea, thinking of Maude trying to cope with both Callie and Mrs. Meehan. As I envisioned the scene, my smile widened.

"Good morning, Elizabeth. Been for your ride, I see," Uncle Jack said, kissing me on the cheek before going to the buffet. "At last, some food. Thank goodness, they found the little rascal. I don't function properly until I've had a decent breakfast in me."

"Good morning, Elizabeth. How fortunate that you were off riding this morning. You missed all the commotion around here," Rose said, trailing in behind Uncle Jack.

"What happened?" I took a sip of the still-scalding

288

tea.

"It seems our precious Callie took it in her head to disappear very early this morning. Michael had everyone searching the grounds for her when Mrs. Meehan vowed she wasn't in the house. And before breakfast!" Uncle Jack declared, seating himself at the table with a full plate in hand.

"I spoke with her in the drawing room not too long ago. I wasn't aware she was considered missing," I informed them.

"It seems Mrs. Meehan woke shortly before dawn and went to check on Callie, only to find the child's bed empty. She searched the house, but couldn't find her anywhere. She caught Michael as he was about to leave for the stables and told him of Callie's disappearance. When Uncle Jack and I came down for breakfast, he enlisted our aid and, along with the servants, we searched the grounds for her. You had already gone riding, Elizabeth," Rose said.

"Where is Michael now?" I asked.

"He's probably giving Callie a good talking to," Rose replied.

"That child needs more than a talking to. When I was growing up, our father never hesitated to use his belt on us if the occasion warranted it," Uncle Jack asserted.

"You're quite right, Uncle Jack. She has been quite destructive this morning," I said.

"Oh? What did she do?" he asked.

"She deliberately cut all the strings of the piano. It is quite useless now."

"Good Lord!" Uncle Jack cried.

"What a horrid thing for her to do!" Rose exclaimed. "Whatever possessed her, do you think?"

"It's obvious she detests me. Knowing I enjoy playing

the instrument, it was probably her way of bedeviling me."

"Does Michael know?" Uncle Jack asked.

"I haven't seen him yet, but he shall certainly hear of it."

"He really should confine the child to her own section of the house," Rose said.

The three of us fell silent, Uncle Jack and Rose seemingly out of sorts from their early morning hunt as they concentrated on their breakfast. The verbal confrontation with Callie and Mrs. Meehan had left me drained. I finished my tea, excused myself and left to change out of my riding habit.

Michael almost knocked me down as he came plunging down the staircase as I was going up.

"I want to have a talk with you, Elizabeth." His manner was brusque and his tone harsh as he took my arm and ushered me into the drawing room, shutting the doors firmly behind him. "Why did you go out of your way to upset Callie and Mrs. Meehan?"

"Me? Upset them? I think you have it backward, Michael. It was Callie who upset me. Then, Mrs. Meehan, standing in this very room, found it necessary to upbraid me as though I were some scullery maid caught with her hand in the jam jar," I replied hotly.

"Callie said you struck her and called her vile names," Michael accused.

I gritted my teeth and clenched my fists. "And you believe her?"

"I would never take Callie's word alone for anything, but Mrs. Meehan backed her up and told me she was witness to it," he said stonily.

"And I wouldn't trust Mrs. Meehan's word on anything. Can't you see she despises me, Michael?"

"Nonsense, Elizabeth. It's your imagination."

I stalked over to the piano, fury swelling in my veins. "And I suppose this is my imagination?"

Michael came to my side and stared down into the piano with an austere expression, his angular features taut as a vein throbbed at his temple. "I'll have a man from Belfast come immediately to repair the instrument."

"Is that all you have to say?"

"What more is there to say?" he asked indifferently.

"I should think you would realize Callie may becoming too difficult for even Mrs. Meehan to control."

"What would you have me do, Elizabeth? Have the child locked away somewhere in an asylum?" he asked with deep bitterness.

Shocked by his suggestion, my hand flew to my bosom. "I never would let you put her away like that Michael. I never meant even to hint at such a thing. I only thought a professional nurse might have a better influence on Callie than Mrs. Meehan, who seems to foment and encourage Callie's erratic behavior."

"Callie is not your concern, Elizabeth. I would appreciate it if you would avoid interfering with either Callie or Mrs. Meehan," he said with finality. He went and stared out the window, his back toward me, feet spread, one hand pounding into the other behind his back.

I felt defeated and utterly deflated as I gazed at his broad shoulders. I wanted to be of help in his struggle to raise Callie and was sure a professional nurse would be far better for the child than the austere and enigmatic Mrs. Meehan. But I could see that whatever I had to say on the subject only fell on deaf ears. I gnawed at my lower lip as I started to leave the room.

"Elizabeth . . . " Michael began abruptly. "I shall be leaving for Belfast this afternoon. I don't know when I shall be returning."

"It doesn't matter," I murmured as I left the drawing room. Instead of heading up the stairs to change my clothes, I went back to the stables and had them saddle up my horse again.

On the sandy beach serene solitude was my companion and the sea was my music. I watched the gulls and envied their uninhibited freedom as they dove and swirled, their only concern a quest for food. The notion of riding to Ballycastle and taking the boat to Rathlin was a tempting thought, but I knew I wasn't bold enough to go alone. If I were a gull, there would be nothing to hold me back, I thought with a delicious, but silly longing. The quiet comfort and warm cordiality I had found in that white cottage with Sean for a companion taunted me with its alluring charm and peace. I closed my eyes and lazily recaptured those splendid days on Rathlin.

After dinner, Rose, Uncle Jack, and I made our usual trek into the drawing room. For once, I was glad Michael wasn't around. His presence only served to tangle my emotions with love, yearning, and despair.

"That scamp's mischief has gone too far this time," Uncle Jack grumbled. "I had come to depend on our after-dinner musicale. It improved my digestion one hundred per cent."

"Then you believe Callie did cut the piano strings and not some half-crazed, mysterious banshee?" I asked, forcing a lightheartedness to my words.

"Of course. Why . . . everyone in the house knows she did it, with the exception of the old dragon. Mrs. Meehan likes to perpetuate that old myth about the Dunwick banshee. I do believe the woman firmly believes in the existence of fairies and leprechauns. Michael should have dismissed her when Isabel died," Uncle Jack grunted.

"Why didn't he?" I asked.

"Lord knows. I haven't the foggiest notion," Uncle Jack replied. "How about a game of draughts, Elizabeth?"

"It would be my pleasure."

The next day, as if in answer to an unsaid prayer, Clara brought me a letter from Rathlin Island as I was working on the household accounts in the upstairs parlor. I pushed the ledgers aside and hastily opened the letter. It had been some time since I posted my letter to Sean.

"Dear Elizabeth,

   I received your letter with much happiness. I was delighted to find you had not forgotten me nor the lovely hours we spent together. I am determined to improve my musical abilities in an attempt to match your dexterity and perfection. However, I will concentrate on the violin, for I could never come up to your virtuosity on the piano. Your offer to send me some sheet music was deeply appreciated but not necessary. My agent ships everything I need or desire from London.

   Your sister-in-law, Rose, sounds like a charming and gracious young woman. How fortunate for you and her to be such close companions. News of your family at Dunwick doesn't bore me at all. In fact, I welcome it. It makes me feel part of your family.

   The painting and drawing are coming along quite well. I am presently working on a large canvas, which I consider to be my masterpiece. But then, every new painting I commence, I consider my masterpiece—until it is finished. Then, I feel I could have done better and tackle another one. I suppose that is what keeps me at the easel. Always searching for the true masterpiece.

I sincerely hope you will find the time and inclination to visit our small island again. And soon.

Ever yours,
Sean"

I found Rose on the terrace, her eyes closed, her hands resting on an open book in her lap.

"Rose . . . " I whispered.

"I'm not asleep, Elizabeth. Only resting my eyes and absorbing some of the sunshine," she replied.

"I received a letter from the artist I told you about, the one who lives on Rathlin Island. I thought you might like me to read it to you."

"I'd love to hear what he says if it isn't too personal," she replied, sitting up with a new alertness.

"Of course it's not too personal," I said with a wry smile, then read the letter to her. When I had finished she sighed.

"He sounds like a nice young man," she commented.

"He is," I said emphatically.

"Elizabeth . . . you sound as if you care a great deal for this man."

"I do."

"Don't let Michael know," she warned, a flicker of fear in her eyes.

"Why not? I have nothing to hide and I have every intention of inviting Sean to Dunwick if he can manage it."

Her smooth white brow crinkled in a frown. "My brother doesn't take kindly to having younger men about. You must have noticed that from the way he behaved with David."

"Oh, Rose. You certainly can't mean that Michael is jealous."

She thought for a moment. "No . . . I don't think it's jealousy. Ever since Isabel died, Michael has become an enigma to all of us. His entire personality seems to have changed. There is something ominous about him now. Something dreadful in his nature, waiting to explode. I wouldn't press or antagonize him if I were you, Elizabeth."

Waiting to explode . . . the words dove into my brain with meaning. I sensed that explosion would be my demise.

Thirteen

True to his word, Michael sent a man from Belfast to repair the piano. One of the servants helped him carry his paraphernalia into the drawing room, where an inquisitive Uncle Jack hovered over him, watching his every move with wide-eyed curiosity.

"My, my . . . never have I seen anything quite like this," the repairman observed as he set about removing the damaged strings.

I had no desire to stand around and watch him. It was like viewing major surgery on one's dearest friend. I went out onto the terrace and gazed down the wide stone steps, the white-pebbled path, then on toward the pool. Raising my glance, I could see the glen beyond. I had always limited my walks to a confined area around the pool, never really exploring the small glen whose sleeping valleys played host to hazel trees and brushwood.

My investigations of Dunwick's landscape had always been conducted from the seat of a horse on a specific pathway. It would be a novelty, I thought, to explore the hidden and informal parts, using the narrow footpaths that laced the estate. With Uncle Jack and Rose both occupied elsewhere, it would be an interesting, perhaps enlightening way to pass an hour or two.

I walked down to the pool and sat on the bench, peering about for a possible route to the glen. There seemed to be an ancient walkway that was barely discernible, overgrown with centuries of vegetation. But the footpath was in clear evidence. With a true spirit of adventure rising in me, I decided that was the path I would take and quickly left the bench to proceed on my journey into the unknown.

Now and then, a startled thrush would flap its wings noisily as it took flight from its perch on a great flowering whitethorn tree. Stray thistles caught at my skirt as if to halt or delay my progress. But I was too immersed in my new venture to mind their tugging burrs. I had been on a downhill course for some time when the shade of a rowan tree surrounded by a mantle of spongy moss lured me to take respite from the arduous walk.

The earth was warm from the sun as I sat down, and the soothing serenity of the glade put me in a reflective mood. I thought about my life in London, comparing it to my life at Dunwick and concluded that I preferred Dunwick, even though I knew my husband was becoming more and more of an enigma to me. But Uncle Jack and Rose were more family than I had ever known in London. I wouldn't trade that for all of London's galas and social whirl. I wished that I could feel the same way about Callie and Mrs. Meehan, but they didn't truly seem part of the Tyrone family. Both of them seemed to have a distinctly different aura, detached and distant.

I made a desperate mental effort to try and understand Michael, but there was no consistency, no rationale to his personality that would help me to understand him. If his love for Isabel was so strong, why wasn't he more deferential and loving toward her child, regardless of Callie's mental capacities? If he had married me merely for money and without love, why did he object to my friendship with David? I should have thought he would be indifferent, not jealous. But was it jealousy? Were there deeper and darker motivations which drove Michael? Everything about him seemed to be one large contradiction.

I looked up at the sun-drenched, shimmering leaves of the rowan tree and gave a long, audible sigh. To try and ask Michael about himself would be like talking to the rowan tree — words drifting on the wind to dissolve in empty echoes.

Off in the distance, the song of a lark reached my ears at the same moment I thought about Callie's revelations that Isabel had kept diaries. Knowing Callie couldn't read and had a great penchant for making up stories, I couldn't be sure that such diaries actually existed. But if they did exist, it might explain a lot of things and open up way to help me understand Michael. If Callie wasn't lying, the diaries were undoubtedly concealed somewhere in Isabel's bedchamber. To enter that shrine, however, would be an invasion of Callie's privacy, which she would bitterly resent and vociferously protest. I had no wish to subject myself to the horrid abuse that Callie could dispense, especially if she found me in her mother's room going through her personal things. Yet, the thought of finding the perhaps mythical diaries was beginning to obsess me. If I bided my time, waited for the right moment, getting into Isabel's room might not be all that difficult. I rose to my feet, consumed with the idea.

Looking for the path that had led me to the rowan tree, I was disoriented by a maze of beeches, hawthorn, and lime trees surrounding the glade. Unnerved, I realized I no longer had the advantage of height to view the landscape and get my bearings. I was deep in the glade and suddenly nothing looked familiar. There seemed to be several paths leading out of the glade and I wasn't sure which one would take me back to the formal gardens and pool. Hoping I had found the correct one, I trod the slightly uphill path for some distance until I began pushing aside branches and brush I hadn't remembered on my way to the glade. I stubbornly refused to believe I might be lost, even though the brush was becoming thicker and almost obscuring the path. I stood still and looked around, greatly alarmed to find myself hemmed in on all sides by thick growth which made it impossible to find the path back to the glade where I might start afresh.

Damp, mossy rocks beneath my feet made for a slow and treacherous headway, even though I was moving as rapidly as possible, my arms flailing at the shrubbery like a woman gone mad. Almost imperceptibly, the trees and brush began to thin out and I spied a clearing ahead, a meadow dotted about with whitethorns.

Finally stepping from the brush, my eyes widened in disbelief and I was struck with a fear that bordered on panic. Before me was a gray stone mausoleum covered with lichen, moss extending from the ground and partially creeping up the foundation, giving the building the appearance of being suspended in air. Though the soft stone had been gnawed at by the elements, I managed to discern the name Isabel Tyrone over the door's stone lintel. It was Callie's drawing come to life! The most frightening aspect, as in my dream, was seeing the door standing ajar. I trembled as my eyes fastened on the inky darkness inside. When the initial shock wore off, I cautiously made my way across the spongy ground toward the ominous structure. Warily circling around it, I could find no windows that would allow me to have a look inside. Thorn bushes, clawing at the rear, made any closer inspection impossible.

Circling back to the front, I stood before the open door. An icy draft emanated from the dim confines of the tomb, rousing my curiosity beyond endurance. My apprehension was smothered by an overwhelming desire to know what was inside the stone building. Was it really Isabel's tomb? Was she here, and not on Rathlin Island? I stood on the threshold, my hands braced against the stone frame of the door, and peered in. It took several minutes before my vision adjusted to the murky interior.

When my eyes finally did adjust, my whole body tensed and I gasped aloud at what I saw. Resting on a carved stone pedestal was an elaborately decorated stone coffin. To my horror, the lid was raised. The coffin stood open! Without conscious thought, I moved to the coffin's edge. I had to see . . . had to know. As if under a spell, I gazed down to look at whatever grisly contents the coffin might hold.

Startled and perplexed, I stared into the oblong casket. Reposing on a white satin lining was a doll with its head grotesquely twisted to one side, its glass eyes gouged out to leave two black holes gaping into the darkness. Its dress had been shredded beyond recognition and the hands, snapped off at the wrists, were lying at the feet of the doll. As my eyes grew more accustomed to the shadowy light, I detected deep scratches on the doll's porcelain face — erratic, jagged cuts etched in a wild frenzy.

Suddenly, the stone tomb began to darken, and I thought some clouds were scudding over the sun, until the dimness rapidly increased. A sudden squeal of a rusted hinge broke the spell the battered doll held over me, and I spun around to see the thick door closing. I ran to stop it, but was too late. I heard a bolt click in place, and I was locked in the black hole of the tomb.

I pushed against the door with all my strength, but it was useless. My first reaction was sheer anger and, to vent my rage, I kicked at the door and loudly called to be let out. My efforts accomplished nothing except for bruised toes and a hoarse throat.

It wasn't long before my anger gave way to frustration and deep concern. My eyes couldn't adjust to the absolute absence of light. I was totally blind and stumbled about the stone room, looking for a place to sit and think. I knew this was one of Callie's pranks, and when she tired of her little joke she'd open the door and run away laughing. But as minutes, and then what seemed to be hours dragged by, I began to wonder if her short attention span had caused her to forget all about me.

I tried the door again, pushing on it with my shoulder, then frantically pounding on the stone walls while screaming for someone to let me out. Deep down, I feared no one would ever hear me, for it was an isolated spot. On the verge of tears, I groped my way back to the stone bench I had stumbled across earlier. In the darkness time had no meaning as it swiftly moved along. The air was becoming fetid and clammy in my stone prison. I tried to lift my failing spirits by convincing myself that by now someone at the house would surely miss me and a search would be started. How would they know to look in the tomb? Pounding the walls with my bare fists made no distinguishable sound, and to scream for hours might render my voice useless at the crucial time. I had to find some object with which I could make a substantial noise upon the wall.

Kneeling down, I explored the dirt floor with my hand. Something furry skittered over my hand and I jumped up with a scream. More than likely, I told myself, it was a poor field mouse who was probably more frightened than I. Nonetheless, I decided to use my booted foot to probe the floor and finally kicked loose a stone. Picking it up, I began to pound at the wall until I could no longer raise my arm. With hot tears trickling slowly over my cheeks, I rested for some time before continuing to hammer against the wall with a steady beat.

Feeling utterly defeated, I let the stone drop from my hand, then whirled about as a slowly widening shaft of light filtered into my stone prison.

"Elizabeth?"

"Oh, thank God! Uncle Jack!" I ran to him, threw my arms around the burly man and held fast as my entire body trembled with relief.

"There . . . there . . . dear girl. We're here now. You're safe, and everything is going to be all right," he soothed, stroking my hair. "It's a good thing you thought to rap and let us know you were in there. We were about to leave," he said, gesturing to the servant who had accompanied him.

"Thank God you didn't leave. I was beginning to give up hope of ever getting out of there," I admitted as my tears ceased.

"Whatever possessed you to wander down here, Elizabeth?"

"I had silly notion I wanted to explore the grounds, lost my way, then accidentally came across the tomb and my curiosity got the better of me." I was feeling considerably calmer as we headed back toward the house.

"How did you get that old door open? That door has been closed for more than five years, and the hinges have rusted so badly I can't imagine how you ever managed," Uncle Jack declared.

"I didn't open it. It was open when I came upon it."

"That's odd," he mused.

"It's Isabel's tomb, isn't it, Uncle Jack?" I put my hand through his arm.

"Yes. It was built as a memorial. As you know, her real grave is on Rathlin Island. If you had told me you wanted to see it, I would have been happy to show it to you."

"I never really thought about it until I saw it today."

"Why did you close the door behind you?"

"I didn't. Someone shut me in there. I hate to say this, but I believe it was Callie. She seems bent on bedeviling

302

me." I went on to describe what I had found in the open coffin.

"Strange . . . a mutilated doll in Isabel's coffin."

"The piano . . . now this. I don't know what to do, Uncle Jack."

"Don't you worry your lovely head about it. I'll have a talk with Michael when he comes back. Callie seems to have grown quite a bit wilder lately. You should see her on that pony of hers. Like a wild young thing riding to the wind, defying the very laws of nature. She exhausts the poor animal."

"Perhaps if she had the supervision of a professional nurse . . . if only Michael were home more often . . ."

"Michael is a very intense man and particularly rigid where business is concerned. And, remember, as I've said to you before, he now has the added obligations of your father's holdings. From what I understand, that in itself is extremely time consuming," Uncle Jack said, patting my hand fondly as we walked along. "You must be famished, Elizabeth."

"Now that you mention it, I am."

"Well, by the time you change, dinner will be ready."

We proceeded along a path that was much clearer and more easily traversed than the one I had taken. The sun was low in the sky when we reached the formal gardens and the pool.

"What made you think to look for me down by the tomb?" I asked suddenly.

"One of the stable boys saw you taking the path from the pool and, in general, most of the footpaths lead to either the tomb or the ancient ruins of old Dunwick Castle. I was surprised when you didn't show up for tea, but became engrossed in the operations of the repairman and time flew by. By the way, you'll be happy to know that the piano has been completely restored. Anyway, as the sun coursed lower and you still hadn't returned to the house, I thought it best we look for you before the daylight vanished. I feared you might have stumbled and hurt yourself. Didn't you hear us calling you?"

"No. Evidently, the tomb is quite soundproof," I replied as we reached the terrace and went through the French doors.

Refreshed and in a clean frock, I sat down to dinner with a ravenous appetite. Never had the smoked salmon, ham, potatoes, and peas tasted so good. Rose listened with astonished horror to the tale of my entrapment, and even Uncle Jack appeared disturbed when I once again described the condition of the doll and where it had been placed.

After dinner, the evening took on an air of normalcy as I played the piano, with Rose embroidering and Uncle Jack sipping brandy and puffing on his pipe. One would have thought the entire day had been quite routine.

The possibility of Isabel's having kept diaries constantly floated in my mind, and when Mrs. Meehan was to take Callie into Derry to see the dentist, then enjoy a full day of shopping, I became obsessed with the notion.

After watching their carriage pull away down the long driveway at mid-morning, I slipped down the deserted corridor to the east wing. I prayed the door to Isabel's bedchamber wasn't locked. My luck held, for the knob turned easily in my hand. With some trepidation I entered the ornate room, feeling the icy green eyes of Isabel's portrait boring into my back. I turned to gaze at the majestic painting and couldn't tell whether she was smiling or laughing at me as those eyes seemed to follow my every move. I felt intimidated, an intruder in someone else's fantasy.

I looked about the slightly garish room, my eyes constantly diverted by a shimmer from the heavy gold leaf liberally applied around the room. As before, there were fresh flowers in a vase by the window, the nightdress flung across the bed as though someone had arisen only moments before.

My glance strayed to the dressing table, and there, in plain sight, was a smallish book bound in red velour with "diary" stamped in gold on the cover. Feeling triumphant, I eagerly picked it up and opened it to the first page, then skimmed through the entire book. Every page was filled with an illegible, childish scrawl. Callie had bested me. She had made up the diary and scribbled what she thought were words throughout it. I replaced the book exactly where I'd found it, feeling utterly foolish for having been duped into playing the snoop.

I was about to leave when the notion struck me that perhaps Isabel *had* kept some sort of journal, hidden elsewhere in the room. I was alone and it would be hours before anyone would be in the east wing, the maids having made their rounds early on. Why not take a look around the room and see what I could find?

I began my quest with the delicacy of a surgeon cutting into a patient for the first time. Everything had to be left exactly as I had found it. What I thought would be a fairly easy task was becoming a monumental hunt. I searched for an hour and found nothing of interest. I even examined the water closet.

About to admit defeat and leave, I glanced at the portrait and received the distinct impression it was jeering at me, the flashing green eyes mocking me. The portrait! That was the only place I hadn't searched. If nothing was there, I would leave and wipe the notion of a journal or diary completely from my mind.

I placed a small footstool under the portrait, stood on it, then lifted a corner of the heavily framed painting. Twisting my head to peer underneath, I saw a small green notebook stuck between the back of the frame and the wooden canvas stretcher. I leaned against the mantel to maintain my balance as my free hand slipped the notebook from its hiding place and shoved it into my skirt pocket. I put the footstool back where I had found it, carefully matching the round flat spots in the carpet to the carved legs of the stool.

The room seemed to close in on me as my hand slid into my pocket and clutched my newly found treasure. I opened the door and scanned the corridor. Finding it empty, I stole out, closing the door softly behind me.

Back in my bedchamber I settled on the chaise and slipped my hand into my pocket. Before I could extract the notebook, a knock at my door caused me to withdraw my hand quickly.

"Elizabeth? Are you in there?"

"Yes, Rose. Do come in," I replied, rising from the chaise.

"I've been looking all over for you," Rose exclaimed as she entered the pale green room. "I was beginning to worry you had gone and gotten yourself locked away somewhere again."

"I don't think I'll be making that mistake again." I laughed a bit nervously.

"I had to show you what came in today's post. Picture cards of Venice! And Paris!" she announced exuberantly.

"Maude?"

"No. David sent them. Here . . . have a look."

I took the picture cards from her with interest, happy to see her face aglow. There was no personal message, only the words "To the Tyrone family — David Cooke."

"How thoughtful of him," I remarked.

"Imagine, Elizabeth . . . Venice . . . Paris. It seems like another world. And so romantic." Her eyes had a dreamy quality to them, which wasn't unusual for Rose. But this time they appeared to reflect hope instead of despair. "Let's go somewhere, Elizabeth. I feel much too lighthearted to sit around the house today."

"By the sea?"

"Oh, yes. Portrush or Ballycastle."

"I'd rather go to Portrush. The beaches there are lovely and the village has a nice tearoom where the barm brack is delicious," I replied.

"I know the place. They also have a cream and raspberry jam gateau that is exceptional. I'll go tell them to get the trap ready. Then I'll get my bonnet and meet you downstairs." She was out the door in a flurry.

My curiosity would have to wait, I told myself as I tucked the small journal under some papers in my writing desk. I could savor the contents at a more leisurely pace in the evening. Besides, Rose was right; it was far too nice a day to spend in the house.

The crisp salty air sharpened our senses as the trap rumbled over the road. I had become quite adept at handling the reins of the trap, finding it not too much different from guiding a horse. We commented on the scenery, nodded and smiled to friendly and familiar faces. By the time we reached Portrush, our appetites had blossomed and we made directly for the tearoom, where the variety of sweets surpassed our expectations.

"They are delicious. I'm so tempted to have more," Rose said.

"Go ahead. We don't often indulge ourselves."

"No. I'd better not. I think I'll go next door to the tobacconist and get Uncle Jack some tobacco. Are you coming?"

"I'll wait here for you. I could do with another cup of tea. The salt air has made me extremely thirsty."

"Then, when I come back maybe I'll have one more cream and jam tart," she said with a sparkle of anticipation in her eyes.

When Rose and I had first entered the tearoom, there were two men seated at the table behind us. Neither

307

working-class nor gentry, they were fairly well-dressed and neat in appearance. Businessmen, I thought. Sitting alone without Rose to chat with, I became acutely aware of their conversation, for though they spoke quietly the timbre of their voices made their words quite clear to my ears.

"I have it on the highest authority," said one of the men in a deep, smooth voice.

"I didn't think his lordship would try it again." The other man's voice was raspy and gutteral.

"He's a divil of a man, his lordship is. Nerves like iron as if he had no conscience at all."

"Aye. How he does it stymies me. When is it coming about?"

"He can't wait much longer."

"No. I guess not. Will it be at sea like last time?"

"It's the easiest way. Make it look like an accident. No telltale signs. That way there's not too much fuss about it."

"Aye."

My brain spun; my pulse raced. His lordship. Were they talking about Michael? No . . . no . . . they were many lords in Northern Ireland. I tried to ignore them by sipping my tea and turning my thoughts to the serenity of the sea. But my ears kept funneling their words to my brain.

"Tyrone is not a man to be dissuaded when he's set his mind on it. No one ever questioned him the last time. Why, that man has a God-given power to convince anyone he is totally innocent of any wrongdoing while all the time being as guilty as they come. Mind you, Paddy, he'll do it again and get away with it again."

The blood froze in my veins and drained from my face. I had to put my cup down, for my hand could no longer hold it steady as the import of their words slowly dawned on me. Isabel's death was not an accident as

Michael had claimed. He had done away with her himself. And if I were to believe my ears, he was about to do murder again. Instinctively, I knew who his intended victim was. Me! Suddenly, it seemed imperative to get home. More than ever, I needed to read Isabel's journal. I had to know the truth about Michael.

"He'll be a bit more clever this time though," the raspy voice continued. "I hear say this new one is wily and sharp. It'll take every ounce of skill Tyrone has to pull this one off."

"That it will, Paddy, that it will. Well, time's a moving and I best get back before questions are asked."

I heard their chairs scrape the floor as they rose to leave. I bent my head down and stared at my teacup as the two men passed by me.

I sat lost in unwelcome thoughts, a grim smile on my lips after hearing myself described as wily and sharp. I was about as sharp as eiderdown and as wily as the daisies in the field. What did Michael hope to gain by my death? As it was, he had complete control of my inheritance. He came and went freely, unreproved by me. But deep down, I knew the answer before I had asked the question. Now that he had my fortune, my death would leave him free to marry a woman of his own choosing, not a plain, unsophisticated girl thrust upon him by an over-zealous father.

"Why, Elizabeth . . . you look as if you've seen a ghost. Did something happen while I was at the tobacconist?" Rose asked, giving me a start.

"No . . . no." I swallowed hard to rid my voice of a choking sound. "Are you going to have your tart?"

"I don't think so. The sky is beginning to darken and it might be best if we headed back immediately to Dunwick," Rose suggested.

Once home, Rose claimed that fatigue and an overindulgence of sweets made her in need of some rest before dinner. I used the same excuse, as I was most anxious to peruse what I believed to be Isabel's diary.

Wanting no sudden interruptions, I quietly locked the door to my bedchamber, then went to the writing desk. The journal was precisely where I had left it. Stretching out on the chaise and opening the book as though it contained the secrets of the world, I began to read Isabel's flowery script.

"I never would have had the need for committing my thoughts to paper if there was someone here interesting enough to talk to. Imagine! Me! Writing in a diary! Boredom can drive people to the most ridiculous extremes. As Lady Tyrone, I had expected a full social life in Belfast or Dublin. Theaters, balls, evening soirees, and musicals in the most noble houses in Ireland. Gowns to dazzle emperors and kings. And what do I have? Dull, dreary, dour Dunwick! With dull, dreary, dour people around me. A child I never wanted. Thank God, I didn't lose my figure. Then, Michael outrageous enough to suggest having another child. And now . . . now he wants me to ease up on my spending. The gall of the man! Most of it was my money to begin with. I'll spend as much as I like. I'll get even with that man one way or another."

It stopped. I turned the page to find it blank, as was the next one and the one after that. I flipped over a number of pages before my eyes fastened once again on the florid script.

"Michael totally ignores me now and I find it quite gratifying, although I tend to miss him in my bed. He had a way of making love . . . well, I don't need him. I rather like the idea of our going our separate ways, living our lives as we each see fit. A perfect arrangement! Now if only I could rid myself of that cow-eyed lecher, Jack Donahue, and that simpering, self-effacing sister of Michael's, life might be tolerable here. I hate the way they report my activities to Michael. Always someone spying on me. Thank God, I had the good sense to bring Mrs. Meehan with me. She keeps Callie from underfoot. I can't stand screaming children, and that child does nothing but scream.

Tomorrow I'm leaving to visit Dublin. Oh, how I delight in watching Michael's expression of raw anger whenever I go to Belfast or Dublin. The fool! What does he expect? But I'm far too clever and discreet for him ever to build a case of divorce against me. He'll never get rid of me until I've drained every pence from his pocket."

I was appalled at the bitter venom and hatred that dripped from her pen. In a strange way I could empathize with her feelings in regard to one aspect of Michael's character. He had the uncanny knack of shutting out those who didn't meet his criteria. I failed to understand her vehement antipathy toward the rest of the family. I had grown to love Rose and Uncle Jack, and bitterly resented Isabel's cruel and callous description of them. And, though I didn't like to admit it, I deeply loved Michael, regardless of his peculiar and perhaps dangerous attitude toward me. I had to get back to the diary before the words I had overheard in the tearoom destroyed my ability to think.

"Michael has limited me to only one party a month at Dunwick. Dunwick . . . how I loathe this place. But I must say, someone interesting has caught my fancy. Perhaps a bit young, nonetheless

I find him fascinating. Odd that I never really noticed him before. Rose may be a withering, fragile blossom, but she has attracted a certain male to her side whom I find quite intriguing. I'll have James McGregor eating out of the palm of my hand in no time. He's already started to nibble. The young ones are so easy to manipulate, it hardly puts one's charms to the test. It'll make everything quite handy and a pleasant divertissement during the wretched winter months when traveling can be beastly. Even now, it amuses me. My own private lover right here at Dunwick! How divine! I shall train him well to suit my every fancy. Eventually, we will have to find a more private trysting place, a place well hidden from village and household eyes. Once James submits to me completely, I shall give him the honor of selecting our private abode.

Rose is so laughable. She hasn't the vaguest notion of what is going on. She is so delighted that James and I are friends, it blinds her. The little idiot thought it quite sweet when she came upon the two of us holding hands in the garden. It's incredible that one human being could be so guileless and trusting. She could never believe her James would do anything sinful. It has become an enchanting game to see how far I can go with James while she is with us, even though I know it makes James highly uncomfortable. He has even gone so far as to threaten never to come to Dunwick again if I persist in such flagrant behavior. He may stop coming to Dunwick, but he'll never stop wanting me or seeing me."

My heart went out to Rose. She *was* too trusting, too good. It would crush her to hurt any living soul or creature. I could easily see she was no match for the likes of

.Isabel. I wondered if I would have been. I was certainly aware of Maude's attentions toward Michael, yet I was as powerless as Rose to intervene. Now I understood the dramatic disappearance of James McGregor. He probably couldn't face Rose, knowing he was the paramour of her brother's wife. I wondered if Rose had ever learned the truth. No . . . I was sure she would have told me and she wouldn't become so dreamy-eyed when she spoke of him. No . . . Rose never knew of Isabel and James McGregor. The following page of the journal consisted of only a few sentences. But they were telling ones.

"James is mine! Utterly! No longer have I need to place my thoughts in a journal. I shall be too busy living."

Thinking that was the end of the journal, I was about to put it down when I decided to riffle through the last few pages, even though I expected them to be blank like so many others. To my surprise, there was another entry covering the last two pages. But the script was not flowery like the rest. It was a jagged scrawl as if the hand that held the pen was trembling.

"Michael has found out about James and me and his anger has a vengeful rage about it. For the first time, I do believe Michael would actually do me physical harm. In fact, I fear for my very life. I know Michael has no feeling left for me and doesn't care if I have a lover. It is his love and concern for his sister that has turned him into a demon. I feel his eyes on me, stalking me as though I were prey, waiting for the right moment to strike me down. He has thrown a terror into me that is with me day and night. I must get away, but Michael keeps a tight hold on all monies and I would

313

need a substantial sum if James and I are to flee to America beyond Michael's reach.

The Tyrone jewels! They are worth a fortune and easily transported. By right, they are mine anyway. But how to get into the safe in Michael's study? Mrs. Meehan! She's clever at that sort of thing. But I will need some ready cash, too. Jack Donahue! That old simpleton might be of use yet. I'm sure he could lay his hands on several hundred pounds which, with the right approach, could trickle right into my hands. If I can implement the plan before Michael does something fatal, I will be free of all of them forever. I'm sure James will be more than anxious to go along with me in this. I can always get rid of him once I am established in New York or Boston, where I understand there are many men of great wealth. I must start immediately and, bit by bit, bring my clothes, jewels, and other personal items to our abode at . . . "

The journal ended abruptly, as if someone had intruded unexpectedly. But I did not have time to read more, for those few private thoughts had revealed a woman whom I knew I could never like, much less admire. She was a passionate woman who knew nothing of compassion. She barely mentioned her own daughter and when she did, it was with a contemptuous dislike. How ironic that Callie worshipped her mother.

As I closed the journal, an icy shudder ran through me and I quickly put it back in my desk drawer under some papers, knowing it was far too late to attempt to return it to the portrait. Callie and Mrs. Meehan would surely be back in the east wing by now.

I went back to the chaise and lay back, my eyes closed, my mind drifting. From Uncle Jack and Rose, I had gleaned the impression that Isabel was always gay

314

and frivolous, never morbid or gloomy. Yet her writings portrayed a bored, unhappy woman who eventually came to fear for her life—from the man who was now my husband. Did Michael actually do away with Isabel? Did his vengeance extend to James McGregor? It would explain his disappearance. And did I hear the plotting of my own demise in the tearoom at Ballycastle? They were questions I didn't want to think about, much less know the answers to.

Fourteen

It was late morning by the time I'd finished the household accounts and had a talk with cook about the following week's menus. I had developed a rapport with the servants that was on a healthy and agreeable basis. If only I could have had the same relationship with Mrs. Meehan and Callie, I would have been at peace with myself. But I knew it was impossible.

Shortly after I joined Rose on the terrace for tea, a maid brought me a letter on a silver salver. At once, I recognized Maude's distinctive handwriting on the envelope. I tore it open as Rose tossed me a casual but interested glance.

"My Dear Elizabeth,

What a pity you were not able to accompany Michael to London, but he expressed sympathy for the entire Tyrone family. Harry's funeral was a smashing success! Everyone who was anyone was there. Of course, after words at the cemetery were said, we all came back here and had a gala time of it.

I am indeed grateful to Michael for suggesting that David come with me to Venice. He was an indispensable jewel through all the travails of getting Harry's body home. But it has been Michael who has been my strength through the ordeal in London. He's been such a love! I don't know what I would have done without him.

It was naughty of me, I know, to let him take me to dinner, the theater, and all those other divine places so soon after poor Harry's funeral. But Michael can be *so* persuasive! I guess you already know that. Poor David was a bit put out by my spending so much time in Michael's company. But that really isn't any business of his, now is it? After all, your being my dearest friend, it was only natural that I would spend time with someone who is almost like family to me.

Oh, how I chastise myself for remarking how repugnant I found Michael's scar. Remember at your eighteenth birthday ball? I find it quite dashing now. It gives him an aura of almost brutal virility. How lucky you are, Elizabeth, to have Michael for a husband.

I am looking forward to having you and Rose visit me in the near future. Michael said he would see what he could do to arrange it. You can count on me to make sure there is a full calendar of social events to keep both of you busy and properly dazzled.

Must say 'ta' for now. There is a lavish gala at the Cavendishes' tonight and I must have my rest. Give my fond regards to everyone at Dunwick.

Maude"

I was stunned! Michael had been in London all the time we'd thought he was in Belfast. At least I had believed him to be in Belfast. Why hadn't he let me know he was going to attend Harry Payne-White's funeral? And, more important, why had he regaled the widow so sumptuously? The questions were obvious and so were the answers. Michael had chosen my replacement, a woman more to his liking and temperament.

Drained of all emotion, I could feel neither jealousy nor anger as my eyes stared blankly at the letter in my hands. If Michael intended to do away with me, I wanted it done quickly, for death seemed preferable to this slow erosion of my sensibilities, pulling me into a void where neither pain nor joy existed, a vacuum where life itself was meaningless. All hopes and dreams of winning Michael as a loving and caring husband were ebbing, sinking into the emptiness of painless apathy. A voice somewhere in the distance called my name and I sighed deeply.

"Elizabeth!" Rose repeated with urgency.

"Hmmm?"

"I thought for a minute you had fainted with your eyes open. Has the letter brought bad news?"

"No . . . no . . . not at all. Just Maude's usual chatter," I murmured.

"Well?"

"Well what?" I asked, my thoughts still straying.

"What did she have to say?"

"Nothing much. You know Maude. Here . . . " I handed her the letter. "Read it for yourself."

I watched with a steady, focused eye as Rose read the letter. I watched for any change of expression that might signify she had already known Michael was in London. When she was finished she frowned and stared off into space. It was several minutes before she spoke.

"I don't understand it at all! If Michael was going to the funeral in London, why didn't he take you? Did you know he was going, Elizabeth?"

"No," I replied. "I thought he was in Belfast."

"So did I. Sometimes Michael baffles me." She paused

318

and drew in a breath as she handed the letter back to me. "Imagine! Thinking of a funeral as a smashing success. How grotesque!"

"Maude has a peculiar sense of humor, I'm afraid."

"Are we really going to London, Elizabeth?"

"Seems like it. We'll have to wait until Michael comes home to know with any certainty."

Rose smiled wanly and sighed. "Maude has a way with men from the sound of her letter. But David is always so gallant, no matter who he is with."

"Ever since I've known her, Maude has had the ability to draw men like fleas to a dog." Rose gave a little laugh. "Well . . . I didn't mean it like it sounded." I started to smile myself. "If we do go to London, we'll have to learn her secret."

"Oh, Elizabeth."

Driven by sharp gusts of cool wind, dark rain clouds scudded across the sky, leaving shadows to dart around the landscape.

"I think I'll go inside, Elizabeth. Our promising day has become threatening. Are you coming?"

"I'll join you later, Rose. I'm going to take a walk to the stables and see what Uncle Jack is up to."

I decided to stroll along the hedgerow path to the stables, breathing the fresh sea air and watching the field flowers bend in response to the snap of a quick breeze. Though it was a straight lane, it gave one the sensation of wandering through a green maze, and I found it childishly delightful. I walked along, my head swiveling as I gazed at the high tops of the hedgerow. I should have paid more attention to where I was walking, for I stumbled on a protruding rock, causing me to fall against the rough branches and leaves of the hedge. As I did, a shot rang out and I felt the rush of air whir past my ear as my hand clutched my throat in terror. Someone had taken a shot at me!

Panic-stricken, I quickly righted myself, lifted my skirts, and flew down the path. I didn't dare look back lest my would-be assassin take another shot. Fear propelled me down the path until I reached the end. I ducked around the wide end of the hedge, my hand to breast as I gasped for air. I couldn't help myself—I had to peer around the hedge to see if anyone was on the path following me. It was deserted. With fright still lingering in my heart, I lost no time in getting to the relative safety of the stables.

In the company of the stablemaster and one of the grooms, I relaxed and casually questioned them regarding the sound of a shot. They replied that they had indeed heard a shot and assumed it was the gamekeeper trimming the rabbit population. Relieved at having escaped any serious injury, I petted several of the horses then went outside, wondering where Uncle Jack had gone. I gazed up at the sooty sky and prepared to make a dash for the house.

The ground trembled beneath me, and I looked toward the entrance of the stableyard to see Michael astride the great black stallion, his cape flying behind as he thundered toward me. When he saw me, he reined the horse in so fiercely, the animal reared, its nostrils flaring as it whinnied in surprise.

Though Michael was a large man, he slid off the horse with the ease and grace of a ballet dancer. He smiled crookedly at me, and all my despair and fears melted like snow under a hot summer sun. In eagerness, I smiled back.

"Elizabeth," he said, taking my hand in his while holding the reins in his other hand. There was a genuine ardor in his greeting that puzzled me. But I found it so heartwarming, I didn't question it. "And what brings you to the stables? I can see you are not dressed for riding."

"I was looking for Uncle Jack."

"Ah . . . I had hoped you had come to welcome me home."

"I didn't know when you'd be coming home," I said curtly.

"An oversight on my part."

"And how was London? Maude?" There was a twinge of sarcasm in my tone.

"London?" He looked at me with dark scrutiny.

"I received a letter from Maude telling me all about the funeral and how accommodating you were. It was quite a surprise to learn you were in London when we thought you were in Belfast." There was a growing edge to my voice, which I thought was probably a delayed reaction to being shot at. I thought it best not to tell Michael about it until I'd had a chance to reflect on the incident.

"I should have let you know, I suppose. But it was a totally unexpected trip. An event in Belfast necessitated a trip to London."

"And trips to dinner and the theater?"

"My little sparrow has developed talons." He smiled and gripped my hand firmly in his large, powerful hand as we continued toward the open door of the stable. "I find it hard to believe you are jealous of Maude."

"I'm not," I replied defiantly. "I would have preferred to learn of your activities from you and not my friends."

"I didn't know my comings and goings were of any interest to you. I shall try to keep you informed in the future." He handed the reins to a groom and we headed for the house as a few sprinkles of rain began to create dark spots on the dry earth. "Best we hurry, Elizabeth. A storm is brewing."

He cupped my elbow and, with insistent pressure, pushed me along. We entered the foyer minutes before great drops of water thundered down. He undid the ties to his cape, which, along with his frock coat and gloves, was taken by a servant. Michael seldom, if ever, wore a hat. I gasped to see a pistol tucked in the belt of his tight, fawn-colored pants.

"Michael! What is the pistol for?" I asked, shakily wondering if it was the weapon that had been aimed at me in the hedgerow.

"Oh . . ." He looked down at it as if he had forgotten it was there. He pulled it out and laid it on one of the foyer tables. "For protection when I travel the roads alone. There are a number of scallywags about these days. How have things been at Dunwick?"

"Well." I saw no purpose in telling him about my travail in the tomb. Tattling on Callie would accomplish nothing except increase antagonisms. Suddenly, Michael's face tightened as though in pain. I reached out and tenderly touched his shoulder. "Is your shoulder bothering you?"

"No. It is quite healed." A strange look settled on his countenance, his dark eyebrows knitting together as if some thought kept eluding him. He pressed the bridge of his hawkish nose between his thumb and forefinger, shutting his eyes tightly as though trying to recall a forgotten moment in time.

"Are you all right, Michael?"

"Quite . . . quite. However, the journey has been long and tiring. A hot tub and a rest is in order before dinner. So, if you'll excuse me, Elizabeth . . ."

As Michael ascended the staircase, I glanced at the pistol on the foyer table. Had Michael fired it at me in the hedgerow? The incident certainly wasn't one of Callie's pranks. Callie couldn't possibly handle a pistol. Then, a peculiar thought entered my brain. Callie couldn't, but Mrs. Meehan certainly could. She was a woman of unusual capabilities, and it wouldn't have surprised me if she was adept at handling pistols. No . . . women didn't use pistols. It was a man's weapon. I was trying to rationalize away the idea that Michael had both opportunity and weapon. He could have reached Dunwick earlier by a back road, seen me wandering toward the hedgerow, and when I was in the path, fired, then remounted his horse to dash around to the main stable entrance. Hadn't the men in the tearoom said it was to look like an accident? It could have been put down to a stray bullet from the gamekeeper as the stablemaster suggested. Thoughts, ideas, suppositions whirled in my mind like mad dancers spinning to a cacophony of crazed tempos.

After a hot, scented tub, I chose a gown of pale blue silk brocade to wear to dinner. It was daringly low-cut with narrow, off-the-shoulder sleeves. Clara piled my hair in a swirl atop my head, teasing wisps of curls to frame my face. A single strand of pearls and matching earrings were the only jewelry I wore.

"Well, well, Elizabeth. Aren't you a vision tonight, isn't she, Michael?" Uncle Jack declared, pulling a chair back for me at the dining room table.

Michael surveyed me with cool detachment. "Elizabeth, why didn't you tell me about Callie shutting you in that old tomb?"

"I can't swear to the fact it was Callie. I saw no one," I replied.

"I have warned you about roaming around on your own, Elizabeth. I hope you'll be more prudent in the future. What morbid reason did you have for going there?" Michael asked.

"I was taking a walk and came across it. I suppose curiosity got the better of me."

"Are you sure you saw no one during your walk or at the mausoleum?"

"Quite sure."

"Of course, it was Callie," Uncle Jack interrupted. "Michael, that child is getting a bit out of hand. It's time

323

you considered special schooling for her."

Rose remained mute. I could see she abhored discussions which might lead to unpleasant controversies. She drew aloofness about her like a snug cloak.

Michael made no comment. He focused his attention on his soup, spooning it into his mouth in a measured pace. The rest of us followed suit and quietly tended to the food before us. Finishing his soup, Michael sat back in his chair, dabbing at the corners of his wide mouth with his napkin. I knew he was staring at me, but I couldn't bring myself to meet that gaze.

"I shall have to think about Callie, Uncle Jack. It is a decision I cannot make lightly," Michael said before draining his wineglass.

"I wouldn't put it off too much longer, my boy. The child is fast approaching young womanhood and it would be to Callie's advantage to have closer supervision," Uncle Jack said.

"Did you see David Cooke while you were in London, Michael?" Rose asked in a desperate effort to change the subject.

"No," was Michael's curt reply, his voice stern and frigid.

"Didn't you see him at the funeral?" Rose persisted.

"I did not attend that spectacle."

"There was quite an article about it in the paper. It was described as one of the most lavish funerals London has seen in some time, not counting royalty of course," Uncle Jack stated.

"It was a gaudy display of wealth from what I understand," Michael replied, cutting the duck meat from the bone. "Elizabeth, I spoke to Mrs. Payne-White concerning a proposed visit to London for you and Rose in September."

"She mentioned it in her letter to me."

"Right now, London is much too steamy to be enjoyed. I hope neither of you have any objections," Michael said. "Do you, Rose?"

"No, Michael."

I had the feeling it wouldn't have mattered if we did. In Michael's mind the issue was settled and he would calmly override any objections.

Michael surprised me by joining us in the drawing room. Since he'd been away so long, I was sure he would hide himself in the library and busy himself with neglected paperwork. He sank into a well-padded chair like a man weary of the burden of living. His taut face softened as I filled the room with the soothing strains of Chopin's lighter compositions. As his eyes closed and a faint smile played at his lips, I wondered if he was remembering his sojourn in London or devising a new plot to rid himself of me.

"Are you going to spend this beautiful morning with your nose buried in a book?"

Michael stood on the terrace, slightly behind me and off to the side. Were it not for the hint of an upward curve to his mouth, he would have aroused fear in anyone viewing his formidable stance. He had been home for two days and I found his attentiveness and solicitude a little disconcerting. It was not like Michael to openly display devotion to me. It made me uneasy as I wondered about the sudden change in attitude. Did he have some scheme in mind? A tremor knotted my stomach as a long-forgotten Latin phrase echoed in my brain. *Suaviter in modo, fortiter in re,* gentle in manner, resolute in execution.

"Uncle Jack was telling me how you do nothing but talk about visiting Rathlin Island and, expressly, how much you would like to go again. It is still quite early in the morning and the weather promises to be perfect. If you hurry, we could be there by early afternoon," Michael said, coming closer to me.

"We?"

"You and I. Or do you have some objection to being in my company?"

"Why . . . why . . . no," I stammered, astonished at Michael's amiable manner. After almost a year and a half of marriage, I had resigned myself to the fact, that Michael's ardor for me had waned. He seldom came to my bedchamber, leaving me to my own devices for the most part. For Michael to abruptly shift his attitude and actually ask me to spend some time with him alone was a shock with frightening overtones. I couldn't stop the thought from entering my mind that Isabel was drowned in that short stretch of sea between Ballycastle and Rathlin. Was this what Michael had been planning all along?

"You don't sound very enthusiastic, Elizabeth. I thought you would enjoy it."

"I'll go and change. Excuse me." I rose, went through the French doors and was halfway down the mirrored hall when I heard Michael call out.

"Have your maid put a few things in a satchel for you. We may be gone a day or two."

I hesitated. Something was wrong. This wasn't the Michael I knew of late. I turned, but he had left the terrace.

The trap was waiting, my satchel already placed in it. Michael paced the white-pebbled driveway, head down in solemn thought, hands laced behind his back. He looked up as I came down the steps, worry etching deep furrows on his brow.

He put his strong hands around my waist, preparing to lift me into the trap, but our eyes caught and he paused. Those ebony eyes searched mine as if looking for an answer to an unasked question, piercing mine as they did that first night when I saw him from the landing at our London house. Those early courting days came rushing in on me, and I smiled warmly at him as I placed my hands lovingly on his broad shoulders, ready to surrender my very being to him. Swiftly, my feet left the ground and I was in the trap.

Conversation was minimal all the way to Ballycastle. It was with relief that I boarded the boat to be regaled with tales of the sea by a garrulous captain. I found the old man most amusing, but Michael's thoughts seemed to be elsewhere as his eyes strained, with visible anxiety, to make out Rathlin's harbor, Church Bay.

I was totally unprepared for the surprise to come as we climbed into the carriage waiting for us at dockside.

"I never did give you a proper wedding present, did I, Elizabeth? Well, knowing your fondness for this island, I have found what I think is most suitable," Michael said as the driver urged the horse toward a familiar path.

The carriage stopped in front of Sean's house, and then, with a wide sweep of his hand, Michael said, "There . . . Elizabeth. Your summer home."

Completely bewildered, I looked at the cottage, then at Michael.

"Whatever is the matter, Elizabeth? I thought you would be thrilled." His face clouded.

"I believe someone lives here already, Michael."

"The artist, you mean?"

I nodded.

"I believe he moved to London some time ago. Uncle Jack told me how fond you were of this cottage, so I thought, as long as it was empty, I'd make you a present of it."

"You didn't force him out, did you, Michael?"

"Elizabeth! I'm not the sort of man who would evict someone from his home because I desired it. Don't you want the place?"

There was such a pleading expression in his eyes I didn't have the heart to tell him that it was Sean's company I was fond of more than the cottage. I put on my best smile. "It's lovely, Michael. And it was thoughtful of you to purchase it for me. Thank you very much."

He assisted me out of the carriage while the driver tended to the satchel. As we started up the short path, a neat, stocky woman, somewhere in her mid-forties, opened the door and smiled in greeting.

"Ah, Mrs. Dean, I see you made it all of a piece," Michael said.

"Yes, sir," she replied, bobbing a small curtsy. "Alfie's out back. He'll be here shortly to tend to your luggage."

"Mrs. Dean, I'd like you to meet my wife, Lady Tyrone."

"Pleased to meet you, my lady." Again, she bobbed. "I have a bit of tea ready for you and your lordship."

"Thank you, Mrs. Dean. It will be most welcome," I said.

The parlor was exactly as I remembered it. Nothing out of place. The only things missing were the violin, easel, and artist's accouterments. In the easel's place, by the window, was a highly polished mahogany table crowned with a vase of white roses. Two mahogany chairs, whose seats were covered with finely stitched petit point, flanked the table. I went over to the piano and trailed my hand across the keys, hearing only the merry strains of Sean's violin.

"Well, Elizabeth, are you pleased?" Michael face radiated such expectation I couldn't disappoint him.

"Of course, Michael. Very much. It's lovely. I'll have to talk Rose into coming to the island to see the cottage."

"Have you ever been upstairs?"

"No."

"Come along then, before Mrs. Dean brings the tea."
The second floor was laid out much like the down-

stairs except for two large, low-ceilinged bedchambers and a lavatory. Michael had to stoop to enter.

"You may choose whichever room you prefer, Elizabeth."

"This one is fine," I said, removing my bonnet and jacket and tossing them on the bed before we went downstairs.

Mrs. Dean had removed the vase of roses and set the table for tea. There was a plate of ham and watercress sandwiches along with a steaming pot of tea nestled in a cozy.

"I understand Mrs. Dean is an excellent cook," Michael claimed, holding my chair before taking his own seat.

"Are the Deans local?"

"No. I brought them from London. A bit down on their luck, they eagerly accepted the position, even though they'll be more or less isolated. But they've always wanted to live where the air was fresh and where there was land enough to grow vegetables and flowers."

"Will they be living in?"

"No. Their home is in a small cottage down the lane. Their chores here are finished after the evening meal. Of course, when no one is in residence, their only obligation is to tend to the grounds and see that the house is in order and good repair. Would you care to go for a walk after tea?" Michael asked.

"Yes. That would be nice."

I was still having difficulty understanding Michael's change of heart. It was clear our arrival here was expected, yet back at Dunwick, Michael had made the trip appear as a spur of the moment venture. Why? I was so baffled by it all, my mental capacities were fast becoming exhausted.

Wherever we walked the views were ravishing. The bold shores rose quickly into impressive cliffs. I studied Michael's handsome, sharp-boned face as he stared out to sea, and my heart was rife with conflicting emotions. His black hair whirled about in the capricious sea breeze and his eyes narrowed in close scrutiny of the vast ocean as if he were seeking a definite wave, a particular crest. Suddenly, his examination was at an end. He took my arm and led me back to the cottage.

I was exceedingly grateful to Mrs. Dean for the hot tub she had prepared for me in the upstairs water closet. I vigorously washed the salt spray from my hair and scrubbed the grime of travel from my body. Brushing my long hair until it shimmered in the soft light of the oil lamp, I silently thanked Clara for packing one of my prettier frocks, a pale yellow lawn with yards of material and a tight bodice trimmed with white lace.

Michael, who was already seated at the table, sipping wine, rose as I entered.

"Have I ever told you I think you are a lovely woman, Elizabeth?"

"I don't believe you have," I replied, thinking he must have had more wine than usual.

He took his place opposite me as Mrs. Dean entered with two steaming plates of soup. The rich, creamy potato soup was followed by a tasty poached salmon covered with savory egg sauce. My eyes widened in delight as she carried in the main course on a silver salver — a succulent goose stuffed with a potato, sausage, and herb dressing that was a treat for the palate.

"Oh, Michael, you are right. Mrs. Dean is a gem in the kitchen. Uncle Jack would be in heaven," I said, enjoying the meal and trying to make conversation.

"Uncle Jack finds anything he can put into his mouth savory," Michael said with a trace of humor.

Mrs. Dean's face fell in dismay when I declined the jam cake she had made for dessert. But her expression quickly changed to a beaming glow of pride when I used

330

every superlative I knew to praise her cooking.

Michael poured himself a large whiskey, then sprawled in a large wing chair. I sat at the piano and commenced to play a light Chopin etude.

"No Chopin tonight, Elizabeth. I would prefer Beethoven or Mendelssohn. Maybe some Schumann."

"I didn't know you had a liking for the German composers."

"It varies with my moods. I know Rose prefers Chopin or Liszt. She has so few pleasures I don't feel I should impose my musical preferences on her," Michael explained.

When I began to play, he laid his head against the back of the chair and closed his eyes, occasionally rousing himself to take a sip of his whiskey.

Mrs. Dean came in to ask if we wished anything else before she and her husband left for the day. I looked at Michael, who, with eyes still closed and whiskey finished, seemed content never to leave the chair. I whispered a "no" to Mrs. Dean.

I continued to play as the night deepened. After a while I began to wonder if Michael had fallen asleep, for his hand, which loosely held the empty whiskey glass, was dangling over the edge of the chair's armrest.

My unspoken question was answered as his body suddenly tensed and his dark eyes flashed open. He reached into his vest pocket, pulled out his watch and, sitting erect, studied it.

"It is late, Elizabeth. You must be tired. I'm sorry if I kept you playing later than I should have."

"Playing the piano is never a chore for me, Michael."

"All the same, I think it best if you retire for the evening."

"And you?"

"I'm going to read for a while," he said, rising and going to the sideboard to pour himself another whiskey.

"This is an excellent opportunity to catch up on some reading, a pleasure in which I haven't indulged for far too long."

"Good night, Michael."

If he answered me, I didn't hear him. Preparing for bed, I pulled the combs and pins from my hair, letting the long auburn tresses cascade down my back. Then I slipped into a white linen nightdress.

Sleep eluded me as I lay quietly on the bed, straining to hear Michael's footsteps ascending the stairs. Nothing. All was hushed. I went to the door, opened it and left it slightly ajar, noting there was no sound at all from downstairs. Then I heard something — a faint click of the outside door. I darted to the window and peered into the shadowy night. The moon was sporadically obscured by shifting clouds.

For a brief instant the moon was unmasked by a trailing cloud, and I saw Michael's tall, cloaked form striding toward the stable at the back of the house. Then, all was bathed in an impenetrable inkiness. I could see nothing. Only the steady, rapid beat of a horse's hooves, at first pronounced, then fading, broke the eerie stillness of the night.

Where could Michael be going at this time of night on this small island? Was he heading back to Dunwick, leaving me to enjoy the delights of the cottage by myself? Or was he flying to the comforting arms of some island maiden? After all, Michael was a frequent visitor here. Or was he plotting my death? I should have realized he had an ulterior motive in bringing me to Rathlin. He obviously hadn't come here to be alone with me; there was a deeper motive behind this little sojourn. The gentle manner, the gift of the cottage — it was all a façade. His show of tenderness and love had been nothing more than ruses to lull me into his power, to gain my confidence and trust. But why? Had the time come for me to be

332

disposed of? I recalled the tearoom conversation all too vividly. "He can't wait much longer." And the shooting in the hedge. Oh, how I wished I was back at Dunwick, where Uncle Jack and Rose afforded me some sense of security. I crawled into bed trembling, my heart sinking in fear and unhappiness as it so often did since that day a shot was fired at me, and I wondered who or what Michael Tyrone really was.

The days were passed in various activities depending on the weather. There was a tension about Michael that spread itself between us like an ever tightening skin over a drum. He was perpetually preoccupied as though an arduous task lay before him, weighing him down with its complexity. And as his anxiety increased, so did mine — especially during the nights, when believing me to be asleep, he would ride off into the night like an avenging demon.

Three days had slipped by when the morning dawned in pewter tones. The porridge, which I covered with brown sugar and heavy cream, was hot and exceptionally delicious. The golden eye of my egg stared boldly back at me, guarding the two sausages hugging its white rim. After the first day at the cottage I had come to take it for granted I would breakfast alone. Michael's late-night wanderings caused him to sleep until shortly before noon.

I poured myself another cup of hot tea and, holding the cup with both hands, my elbows resting unceremoniously on the table, I raised it to my lips as I watched the green trees yield to a slow breeze, their lacy fingers patterned against the slate-colored sky.

"Elizabeth."

The scalding tea slid down my throat too quickly, and I started to cough.

"Well, now. I hope the tea isn't all that bad," he said, gently patting my back in an effort to ease my distress.

I shook my head, waiting for the constricting spasms in my throat to cease.

"We'll be leaving for Ballycastle this morning. I've instructed Mrs. Dean to pack for you," he informed me as he took his seat.

"Why didn't you tell me last night? I would have been prepared," I said after clearing my throat and regaining control over my voice.

"I wanted you to rest well and not be concerned with the journey home," he replied as Mrs. Dean placed a bowl of porridge before him, which he promptly waved away. "Several rashers and a couple of eggs will do nicely, Mrs. Dean."

She promptly left, returning moments later with the food he'd requested and a fresh pot of tea.

"But Michael, the weather doesn't look very promising," I protested, agitated that again he had not consulted me and wondering what he was up to now.

He looked out the window, assessing the sky. "We'll make it to Ballycastle long before the weather gets really bad. I have to be back at Dunwick before nightfall. Besides, you should be quite a sailor by now." A smile was on his lips, but not in his eyes. His eyes were hard, betraying a stony resolve. There was no question that we would be leaving today, even if a gale should whip the sea.

The leaden sky withheld any promise of clearing as Michael aided me into the carriage. A strong breeze licked at the edges of my skirt.

After placing our luggage in the carriage, Mr. Dean took the reins and proceeded to Church Bay, where the boat was waiting for us. The captain cast a wary eye to the heavens, but did not question Michael's determination to leave Rathlin Island. A glance passed between them as if an unspoken pact had been made. The licking breeze had now turned to gusting flurries. Michael's

334

hand tightened on my upper arm as he helped me into the boat.

As the boat heaved in the rapidly swelling seas, I gazed back at the dimming outline of Church Bay. Rathlin Island disappeared as, without warning, the wind blasted in gale force and the rise of the sea loomed high above the boat. The constant up and down pitch sent terror pulsing through my heart. Each time the boat plunged lower into the watery depths, it rose higher on a foaming crest. At any moment, I thought, those peaks rising with terrifying power would engulf the frail vessel and drive it to the bottom of the ocean.

I looked across the deck to see Michael coming toward me, his eyes glowing with a rapacious, demonic intensity. Fear totally possessed me and I started to back away from him.

"Elizabeth!" he cried. "Don't . . . don't move."

My movements only increased his urgency and he raced unsteadily across the wet, slippery deck, a crazed expression on his face. I did not want to die a watery death like Isabel. I wanted to live! I hastened my backward steps as Michael lunged at me, again crying my name. I could feel the wet wood of the rail press painfully into my back as his hands roughly grabbed my shoulders. My hands and arms flailed at him, uselessly, for he was a powerful man with a tenacious will. I shut my eyes and went limp, expecting to be tossed into the dark, turbulent sea at any second.

But the boat shifted in the restless and capricious sea and I found myself falling to the deck, trapped in Michael's arms, our bodies skidding uncontrollably over the slippery boards as the sky opened up to unleash slashing sheets of rain. Our rolling suddenly stopped as Michael's head hit a mast and his arms went limp. I circled my arm around the mast and held onto Michael with the other. It seemed I hung on like that for an eternity as my body grew numb in that awkward position and my eyes finally closed.

Suddenly, everything was still. I knew we were at the bottom of the sea and I knew I was dead, for I could no longer move or see. When wet, brawny arms lifted me, I was sure that Poseidon had come to claim me.

My eyes fluttered open at last to see a cheery, rotund face smiling down at me. "Where am I?" I asked anxiously.

"You're at the inn in Ballycastle," the woman said. "I be Jean Murphy. Me and my husband own this place. They brought you here the minute the boat from Rathlin Island tied up at the pier. You've had a right time of it, you have. But none the worse for wear, I expect. Some good hot lamb broth and you'll be as fit as ever."

"Michael . . . my husband?" I murmured as the events poured into my mind.

"Fine . . . just fine. His head is a pounding, but he's all of a piece. Imagine! Trying to cross in this weather. His lordship should have known better." She shook her head in remonstration. "I'll fetch the broth for you now."

I was in my nightdress and was covered by mounds of down-filled comforters as I stretched in the bed. Someone had loosened my hair and rubbed it dry. My rain-stained traveling frock lay over a wooden chair and my satchel rested on the floor beside it.

The woman returned with the hot soup, which I eagerly devoured, enjoying the warmth it spread through me. The woman was right. The soup definitely had restorative powers. I handed her the empty bowl and proceeded to get out of bed.

"Would my lady like me to help her dress? His lordship is chomping at the bit to leave," she said with a grin.

"No. I can manage. I do want to thank you for your kindness though."

"His lordship had already seen to that. And quite handsomely, I might add. Well, I'll just take that damp frock and wrap it for you. Do you have a dry one?"

"Yes. At least I think so, if the water didn't penetrate my satchel."

"From what I gather, your luggage and other cargo were below deck and quite safe from the water. I'll be leaving you now, my lady. Don't hesitate to call if you need anything at all," she said, throwing the wet garment over her ample arm.

I slipped out of the nightgown and stepped into my chemise, put my arms through the straps and searched for the hook on the back.

"Need some help?"

I knew it was Michael, and felt my face flush from embarrassment. I trembled at the touch of his warm fingers on the bare skin of my back as he moved my hair to get at the fastening.

"There . . . " he whispered, his hands briefly caressing my shoulders.

I bent over the satchel, pulled out a couple of petticoats and quickly threw them over my head to fasten them at my waist. I felt extremely awkward, never having dressed in front of a man before. But, not wanting Michael to think me a prude, I tried to appear casual and urbane. Even though it wasn't very suitable for traveling, I removed the pale yellow frock from the satchel and slid it over my head. Having tugged it into place, I once again fumbled with the hooks at the back. I could sense Michael shaking his head before he deftly completed the fastening.

"Are you ready now?" he asked, impatience surfacing in his voice.

After quickly brushing my hair, I secured it at my

nape with a matching ribbon, unmindful of the loose tendrils curling about my face. I didn't dare take the time to dress it properly.

"I'm ready," I announced.

He plucked my nightdress from the bed and stuffed it into the satchel. With one hand at my elbow and the other gripping the satchel, he escorted me to the waiting trap, in which a large bundle of wet clothes lay neatly wrapped.

My mind was whirling with the ordeal on the boat, and on the way home I stole frequent glances at Michael to see if there was any readable expression on that sharply chiseled face. But those black eyes were inscrutable and his countenance impassive. I had no way of knowing what he was thinking or feeling.

Would he try again? That was the question which plagued me. Deep down, I knew he would. It was just a question of when. Michael had indeed made his move but failed. I had found some measure of truth at Rathlin. My fate was to be the same as Isabel's and the banshee of Dunwick could be put to rest once again.

Fifteen

"I don't think I can take much more, Elizabeth," Rose moaned as she stood in the midst of her bedchamber, where frocks and gowns were scattered about, waiting to be placed in a trunk or hung back in the closet. She whirled about, picking up one, then discarding it in favor of another.

"Oh, Rose . . . really. You're making much more of this than you should. After all, it's only London." I couldn't help but laugh. She looked so at sea.

"Only London! Only London!" she exclaimed, her voice a little high-pitched. "I've never been farther than Belfast. Oh, Elizabeth, do help me decide on what to take. The problem is reaching monumental proportions. I can't even decide on what handkerchiefs to take."

"Ten gowns, ten day-frocks, a cape, a riding habit— oh, you don't ride, do you? No matter. Anyway, appropriate undergarments, nightdresses, shoes, hats, gloves, and toiletries. It's simple!" I declared laughingly.

"Will that be enough for a whole month, Elizabeth?"

"They do have shops in London, you know. If you find there's something you forgot, we can purchase it in London. Now, we had better get your things packed or we'll never get to London," I said firmly, but with amusement in my eyes.

Rose shrugged in despair, but as we started to make order of the chaotic room, with the aid of her maid, her enthusiasm returned.

"Do you think we'll see David in London?" she asked.

"I don't know. Maude didn't mention him in her last letter. But Michael told me that Sean, my artist friend, has moved to London. I do hope we can find him. I know you'd like him as much as I do."

As we chatted, the trunks were being filled, and before we knew it, our packing was completed as we prattled on.

At dinner, Michael gazed at me with tired eyes. I felt a small sense of relief knowing I would be out of his reach for an entire month, but deep in my heart it gave me little pleasure.

Instead it posed too many unanswerable questions. If Michael was indeed trying to take my life, why was he allowing me to go to London? Did he need time to conjure up a new scheme? Or had he conspired with Maude for me to meet my demise in London? Instead of fleeing from death, was I running straight into its arms? I was pondering these questions when Uncle Jack's booming voice derailed my thoughts.

"Well, ladies, are my two flowers of Ireland ready to dazzle London society?" Uncle Jack asked.

"I'm afraid London society will dazzle me," Rose exclaimed.

"Michael, has the house in London been readied for our arrival?" I asked. I had almost said "my father's house," when I realized it now belonged to Michael.

"You, Rose, and your maids will be staying at Mrs. Payne-White's while you are in London. She preferred it that way, saying it would be more expedient. Besides, the London house is otherwise occupied for the time being."

"Oh? Maude never mentioned it."

"Believe me, all arrangements have been made." The tone of his voice indicated that the subject was closed. I didn't pursue it, although I was curious about who was in the London house. I would have to make a point of casually dropping by.

"I do hope I'll have enough to wear and that my clothes will be suitable from London," Rose lamented, her smooth brow crinkling with worry lines as she idly pushed a potato around her plate.

"You'll be elegant, Rose. You and Elizabeth both," Uncle Jack said with genuine sincerity.

Michael remained silent throughout the rest of the meal, excusing himself when he had finished. Claiming he had a pile of paperwork to attend to, he quickly headed for the library.

Although we retired to the drawing room for our routine evening of music, Rose and I were too excited to concentrate on our usual pursuits. Instead, we spent the evening discussing some of the main attractions we hoped to see while in London, with Uncle Jack contributing anecdotes to the general discourse.

London hadn't changed. It was still bursting with vitality and hummed with the steady work a day rhythms of city life. Rose's eyes widened in awe at the architectural maze London afforded, her head bobbing every which way at the cacophony of sounds slicing through the air from every direction as our carriage made is way from Euston Station to Maude's elaborate residence on Prince Albert Road.

"Darlings! At last!" Maude cried, dashing from the drawing room into the ornate, marbelized foyer. "I've been so anxious regarding your arrival. I really expected you yesterday." She perfunctorily hugged each of us.

"We missed our train connection in Liverpool," I ex-

341

plained.

"Well, you are here now. Poor dears! You must be exhausted. Come! I'll show you to your rooms, where you can refresh yourselves and have a rest before dinner."

"Have you seen David Cooke lately, Maude?" Rose asked, anticipation lighting her eyes.

"He became a trifle miffed when Michael appeared during my bereavement, and I haven't seen him since. Perhaps he's traveling again, working on an article or some such thing," Maude replied with an air of boredom.

Rose looked thoroughly dejected, as though the London trip was already a disappointment, while Maude chatted away as she led us to our rooms.

True to her word, Maude saw to it our every moment was occupied with a round of teas, theater, shopping, evening soirees, and a notable ball—all whirled through inside of a week. I was beginning to wish Maude wouldn't play the dedicated hostess quite so fervently. There were places in London I wanted Rose to see. I wanted her to remember more than one long social whirl.

One morning as Maude began to plot the activities for the day, I interrupted her. "Maude, I think for a change, Rose and I would like a quiet day. The British Museum, the Tate, the National Gallery, Westminster Abbey. Rose has never seen historic London."

"Oh, yes, Maude. I would like that," Rose concurred.

"How dull!" Maude exclaimed, but her face suddenly brightened. "I'm glad you mentioned the Tate. They are having a special showing of paintings by a new artist who is fast becoming the rage of London. He is a countryman of yours, I believe. Mysterious fellow though. Very aloof. I've sent him invitation after invitation to balls and teas, but he always declines. No one even knows what he looks like, for he will not be enticed to attend any social function."

My heart leapt and I wondered if it could be Sean. "The Tate Gallery isn't too far from Westminster Abbey. We could take in both today. What do you think, Rose?" I asked with an excitement surging through me.

"I'd like that very much. I've never seen a truly great cathedral," Rose said, her brown eyes shining.

"I'll instruct the driver as to your preferences," Maude said coldly.

"Aren't you coming with us, Maude?" I asked, realizing she was a bit put out by the abrupt change in plans.

"No. I've seen the Abbey and find the Tate boring."

I had been to the Abbey several times when I was a child, but seeing it again through Rose's eyes was a revelation. She managed to position us with a group of people who were being given a guided tour through the great cathedral. I was amazed at the guide's historical expertise, and learned not only the special features of the Abbey, but facts of British history my tutors had never mentioned. Lost in rapture and absorbing every word, Rose lovingly touched each relic, stone, piece of wood, statue, or tomb the guide discoursed upon before going on to the next point of interest.

We spent two hours in the Cathedral and Abbey, drinking in every Gothic splendor, from the Royal Chapels to the kingly shrines, from stained-glass windows to the soaring, vaulted ceilings.

Emerging into the bright sunlight, we both felt we had gone back in time and tasted a regal past that would never be regained. The weather was so splendid we decided to send the carriage on to the Tate to wait for us while we strolled along Millbank Walkway beside the River Thames, stopping on occasion to study the bridges or watch the boats.

At the Tate Gallery I received a most delightful shock as we entered the special section housing a new exhibition.

"It's Sean!" I cried, then quickly put my gloved hand over my mouth as art devotees turned to stare at me. "It's Sean, Rose. The artist on Rathlin Island I told you about," I cautiously whispered.

"How do you know? We can't see the signature from here."

"No one depicts light with the passion Sean does. And those scenes! I've seen them on Rathlin. His paintings so fresh and vibrant as one color refracts and enhances the other colors to give a special life to the scene."

"They are dazzling and so . . . so . . . intense," she said as we moved closer.

"Michael told me Sean had left Rathlin for London. Oh Rose, I must find him."

"Maude must know where he is. She said she sent him invitations," Rose said.

"Would you mind if we limit our tour of the Tate to this section? I'm anxious to return to Maude's to see if she has Sean's address."

"Of course not, Elizabeth. With your adulation of the man, I must confess that I've become obsessed with meeting him," Rose said with a smile.

We walked around, studying each of Sean's paintings with care. Some were very familiar landscapes of Rathlin, others unfamiliar. I smiled with remembered warmth when I saw the painting of the violin and piano. I could almost hear the music.

The carriage was waiting for us on Bulinga Street, a side street off Millbank. In my anxiety, I started to dash across when Rose's shout halted me and I looked up to see a speeding carriage bearing down on me with what appeared to be deliberate intent. For a second I froze, until Rose's persistent shouts rallied me and I threw myself out of the way. The wheels missed me by just inches as the racing carriage rattled over the hem of my skirt.

"Oh, Elizabeth! You were almost killed!" she cried,

reaching my side at the same moment as the driver of our carriage, who assisted me to my feet. "Are you all right?" Rose asked.

"I don't think there are any broken bones," I said, managing a weak smile despite the unspoken fear that gripped me. There was something familiar about the driver, but it had all happened so fast I hadn't hadn't seen his face. The wild, bolting horse had commanded all my attention.

Rose held my hand all the way back to Maude's as I sat in silence. Was death going to follow me forever? At least I knew it couldn't have been Michael. He was at Dunwick. But he could have hired someone. No . . . he wouldn't want anyone knowing . . . there was too much chance of blackmail. I had to stop this foolish debate. It was an accident, I told myself, yet I breathed a lot easier when we reached Maude's

Her butler informed us that Maude was entertaining a guest in the drawing room and was hoping we would join her. Rose looked at me with a hopeful glint in her eyes as we proceeded to the drawing room.

Both the accident and Sean vanished instantly from my mind when I was the powerful form of my husband rising from a settee.

"Look who just walked in minutes before you," Maude said, a broad smile on her face.

"Michael . . . what are you doing here?" I asked sharply, not meaning to sound so harsh, but I was so astonished to see him, the question spilled forth spontaneously as he came toward us with a grim expression

"I've come with bad tidings. I'm sorry to tell you and Rose that you will have to come home immediately," he replied solemnly.

"Uncle Jack?" I half whispered in dread.

"No. It's Callie."

"Is she hurt?" I asked with concern. Remembering

345

Callie's cruel pranks, I couldn't pretend any great fondness for the child. But she was still a human being, a young child, and Michael's daughter. I certainly didn't want any harm to befall her.

"I'm afraid she is dead," Michael announced soberly.

My legs buckled and my brain fogged as Michael led me to the settee while Maude assisted a quietly weeping Rose to a chair.

"Oh Michael . . ." I moaned when my senses returned. "How awful . . . how awful . . . how awful." For some time those were the only words I could manage as tears began to trickle down my cheeks.

Michael insisted we leave for Dunwick immediately, without bothering to pack our luggage as it would only impede our progress. It was on the journey home that we learned the circumstances of the tragedy.

Callie had been racing her pony, urging it to jump greater and greater heights over a jumping bar. Suddenly, she pulled the pony from the bar and, with the heavy use of her riding crop, sped the animal over the field toward a stone wall, screaming for the pony to jump it. The pony balked as he approached the wall and, digging his forefeet into the turf as he came to an abrupt halt, he tossed Callie over his head, smashing her young body into the rough stones.

Michael informed us that Mrs. Meehan had become hysterical, wailing that Callie was only injured as the groom carried the child's body into the house. When the doctor arrived and confirmed Callie's death, Mrs. Meehan became rigid. Without another word, she left the child's bedchamber, went to the library, took Michael's pistol, then went to the stable and shot the pony.

Saddened and horrified by the tale, Rose and I remained silent for the rest of the trip home.

The funeral was small and somber. Rose and I quietly cried, and I noticed Uncle Jack wiped away a stray tear or two. Only Michael baffled me. I had expected to see some sorrow etched on his face, at least in his eyes. But he looked relieved, almost as though a great burden had been lifted from him. She was his daughter and there should have been some compassion I thought.

A chill went through me when I glanced at Mrs. Meehan. She was continually staring at me with a hatred that spoke of her twisted belief that I was the cause of Callie's accident. I suddenly thought again that Mrs. Meehan was indeed capable of using a pistol.

When all the mourners had left the house, Rose, looking strained, went upstairs while Uncle Jack poured himself a very large whiskey and sprawled in a chair in the drawing room. I watched Michael pour himself a drink before I went out onto the terrace. A foggy dusk mantled the land and nothing looked real as I gazed over the fading flower beds to the pool, then to the bench where Callie had first frightened me. I wiped a stray tear from my cheek.

"You shouldn't be out in this damp air, Elizabeth. You might catch a chill," Michael said as he walked over to the stone balustrade and stood next to me, whiskey glass in hand.

"I'm all right, Michael." I continued to stare off into the distance. I was desolate and without words. But Michael's odd detachment hung on me heavily until I could stand it no longer. "Oh Michael . . . I'm so sorry."

"Don't be." He took a long swallow of the whiskey. "Perhaps it was all for the best. Callie was fast approaching womanhood. It was one of my greatest fears that the mind of a four-year-old dwelling in the body of a woman might have caused her great suffering and ultimately destroyed her in a far more hideous way. I worried constantly about her well-being if anything happened to me."

He took a long pull on his whiskey and gazed into the

fast approaching night. Now I understood why Callie had so deeply troubled him.

"She is safe from all hurt now, Michael," I said soothingly and placed my hand on his arm.

He looked down at me in silence for some time before saying, "I want you and Rose to go back to London and finish your holiday."

"Oh Michael . . . under the circumstances I don't think we should. It wouldn't be right!"

"I insist."

"Really, Michael, I don't think going on holiday so soon after this tragedy is the proper thing. The whirlwind socializing would seem out of place. I'm sure Rose feels the same way."

"Nonsense. Stay here a week or so, then return to London. I will not argue the point, Elizabeth. And Rose will see it my way. Now . . . let's go inside. There's a definite chill in this dampness."

I was quite surprised when Rose offered no resistance to Michael's suggestion. In fact, she appeared pleased to be going back and chided me for being so gloomy, saying Callie's death was the will of God and that the child was with the angels where she would at last find happiness and peace. So we returned to London, against my wishes.

"Oh, my poor dears! How awful it must have been for you. I'm so glad Michael talked you into returning to London. I'll soon have you thinking of life in much brighter terms," Maude said as we sat down to a delectable luncheon in her dining room. "I didn't plan anything for last night, thinking you'd prefer to rest after your journey."

"That was very thoughtful of you, Maude," I said rather listlessly.

"Lord and Lady Trumble are having a musicale this afternoon. Everyone of note will be there and a number of eligible young men." Maude stressed the last part of her sentence, looking directly at Rose.

"Maude, before we had to return home, I saw the paintings in the Tate and I know they are the work of my friend Sean. As you've sent him a number of invitations, I was wondering if you'd give me his address." I was bewildered by the look of amazement on Maude's face.

"Why . . . don't you know, Elizabeth?"

"Know what?" I asked.

"That the artist is living in your old house here in London. You still own it, don't you?"

I gaped at her, then mumbled a "yes" as I tried to assimilate the unexpected news. Michael had given me the impression he didn't know Sean, but evidently he must have known him well enough to give him the use of the house in London. Maude's voice barely managed to intrude on the thoughts spinning in my head.

"Elizabeth . . . you must get him to attend a soiree for me. I'll throw the largest gala London has seen this season. Do promise you'll talk to him," Maude pleaded, excitement animating her face.

"I'll do what I can. He likes his privacy," I said, quickly finishing my tea. "I won't be attending the musicale, Maude. I'm most anxious to see Sean again."

"What a shame! It promises to be a lively little affair. But I'll forgive you if you get your artist friend to attend my gala. Oh, I'll be the talk of society. What a coup! You go ahead, Elizabeth. I'll take good care of Rose and make sure she meets a few of the more interesting men," Maude said.

"Maude, if you don't mind, I'd rather go with Elizabeth. She has talked so much about this Sean, and now that I've seen his paintings, I am eager to meet him," Rose said.

"I'm devastated," Maude exclaimed, pouting. "Deserted by all! Oh well, if it's the price I must pay to have this artist as an honored guest, then pay it I must. Perhaps your combined persuasive powers may sway him. Go . . . go . . . but return with favorable news."

After giving the driver my old address, we sped through the streets of London swiftly, but it still seemed to take an eternity to get there.

"Why . . . Miss Elizabeth," a stunned Charles greeted me as he opened the door and led us into the foyer.

"It's good to see you again, Charles. How have you been?" I asked and, after he replied, I introduced him to Rose. "I would like to see Sean. Is he in?"

"Yes, he is, Miss Elizabeth, but I'm afraid he is not receiving visitors."

"Will you tell him Elizabeth is here? I'm sure he'll see me," I said with conviction.

Charles looked at me warily. "He doesn't receive uninvited guests, Miss Elizabeth. But I will tell him you are here. I must ask you to stay here in the foyer until I have his reply."

I looked around at the familiar entry with the strange feeling that I no longer belonged in this house. My home was at Dunwick and a peculiar longing to return there washed over me.

It was only a matter of moments before Charles returned and was leading us to the drawing room. "Lady Tyrone," he announced, then quickly retired, closing the doors behind him.

"Sean!" I cried and the wheelchair spun around. I expected a look of welcoming delight to cover his face. Instead, there was an expression of fearful horror. Rose gasped in agony and I had to put my arm around her waist to stay her swaying form.

"Rose . . ." His gentle voice was suffused with pain as he sat motionless. "Rose . . . I . . . I didn't want you to

350

know." His wounded eyes turned to me. "I thought you were alone, Elizabeth."

In my bewildered state, all I could do was stare at Sean, whose gaze had returned to Rose. Suddenly, Rose broke away from me and rushed forward, tears starting to spill from her warm brown eyes.

"Oh Jamie . . . my Jamie," she cried, sinking to her knees before him. She laid her head in his lap, her body shaking uncontrollably with racking sobs.

"I never wanted you to see me like this, Rose," he murmured as he tenderly stroked her hair. "It would have been better for you to think me dead. I am no longer a whole man."

I felt like an interloper who had stumbled into a secret and private dream. I quietly left, knowing my absence would go unnoticed. Instinct told me they needed time to be alone—completely alone.

I wandered down to my father's old library. Nothing had changed; yet everything was different. I was a different person. I traced my fingers over the spines of some leather-bound books, thinking the physical contact might engender a certain nostalgia. It didin't. More than ever, I wanted to go home to Dunwick. I wanted to run from this place. But I didn't know if it was the house itself or the strength of the love I saw between Rose and Sean that made me unable to face my surroundings. Oh, if only Michael loved me with same intensity that Sean loved Rose. If only I could see the same unwavering devotion in Michael's eyes that was so blatant in Sean's.

I slid into one of the large, leather wing chairs and closed my eyes, letting an image of Michael form on my lids, trying to picture on his face, in his eyes, the love and passion for me that once was in evidence. I must have dozed off, for a crisp voice was repeatedly calling my name.

"Miss Elizabeth," Charles persisted.

"Oh Charles . . . yes . . . what is it?" I asked, trying to bring my sleep-clouded eyes into full focus.

"Mr. McGregor requests your presence in the drawing room."

I rose and obediently followed him. I was relieved to find that Rose's tears had stopped. She and Sean were smiling broadly.

"As usual, you have been most considerate and tactful, Elizabeth. Rose, do you wish to explain, or should I?" Sean asked as they held hands.

"You do it, Jamie. You have a way with words that I lack," Rose replied, never taking her adoring eyes from him.

"Well, Elizabeth, to be as brief as possible," he began, reluctantly taking his eyes from Rose. "As you might know, Rose and I were childhood sweethearts and as we grew to adulthood we really fell in love and vowed to marry. Business took me to Rathlin Island, and while there I met with a terrible accident which left me as you see me, paralyzed from the waist down. But that you already know. Anyway, I couldn't go back to Rose half a man, unable to give her children, unable to support her. I couldn't bear the thought of her love turning to pity, or that she would be forever tied to a cripple. I contacted Michael, swearing him to secrecy. He obtained an army of the finest physicians to examine me, but they all said the same thing. The damage was permanent and beyond cure. Not one of them offered any hope of recovery. Michael tried to get me to return to Dunwick, but I was adamant. So, he purchased the cottage for me on Rathlin, along with a piano, violin, and art material. I began to paint under the new name of Sean. It was Michael who took my paintings to London and sold them. I am indeed grateful to him, even more grateful that he kept his vow and never told Rose.

"Now I realize how foolish I was. Very foolish. I've

never stopped loving my Rose, and now I know she loves me too, and always will, regardless of any handicap." He smiled warmly at Rose and covered their joined hands with his free hand. "And now my fair Rose has consented to be my wife."

"How wonderful!" I cried, rushing to give Rose a generous hug, then stooping to kiss Sean, who I had now come to think of as Jamie, on the cheek. "Now you truly will be my brother. I'm so happy for the both of you, for all of us."

"We plan to hold the wedding here in London as soon as possible," Rose said.

"We hope Michael and Uncle Jack can make it," Jamie said.

"Oh yes, I do want Michael to give me away," Rose blurted.

"I'll telegraph them immediately." An odd thought entered my mind and I laughed. "Oh Rose, here we've been shopping so haphazardly when all the while we could have been shopping for a wedding gown and a trousseau."

"It was providence that made you want to go to the Tate Gallery," Rose exclaimed. Obviously, clothing was the furthest thing from her mind at that moment.

"Oh Jamie . . . we saw your exhibition there and it was wonderful. Most of the paintings I had never seen before. And from what Maude Payne-White told us, you are the rage of London's art world right now," I said.

"I must confess it has gone quite well. Not only are over half the paintings sold, but I have received a number of commissions that will command substantial fees. I'm now in a position to give Rose whatever her heart desires."

"You're all my heart desires, Jamie." She leaned over and they kissed tenderly.

"And now that you've consented to be my wife, life

has given me everything a man could possible hope for," Jamie said.

"Consented? Why Elizabeth, I practically had to beg him to marry me!" Rose exclaimed, her eyes twinkling with pure joy.

"Dear me! Look at the time! Maude will think we've been abducted," I stated, reluctant to break up the reunion.

"Rose is staying to have dinner with me, Elizabeth. Don't worry, she will be properly chaperoned. Besides Charles, there is a housekeeper, a cook, and a maid living here. And I'll see to it she is delivered to Mrs. Payne-White's house at the proper hour and quite safely."

"Well . . . good-bye for now, you two. First thing in the morning I'll get that telegram off."

Riding back to Maude's, a thought kept tugging at my mind, but I couldn't quite bring it to the surface. I was glad when her butler gave me a message that she was dining out, then would proceed directly to the theater, where I could join her if I wished. I didn't wish. I wanted solitude to pull from my mind that piece of puzzle that had a strangle hold on me.

After a solitary but superb dinner, I went into Maude's library to compose a telegram to Michael. As I stared at the blank sheet of paper, I plucked a memory from the depths of my mind. Isabel's diary! Something was wrong . . . very wrong.

Sean was certainly Rose's James McGregor, but he was also Isabel's lover, prepared to flee to America with her. But he appeared to be truly in love with Rose. Had he toyed with Isabel? Pretended to be captivated by her? No. I really didn't think that. From what I gathered about Isabel, she was too sure of herself and too astute to be duped by a man, especially a young one. Jamie, being so young, had probably been easily infatuated with the dazzling Isabel, even though he really loved Rose. I

354

then recalled how Isabel had stated in her diary that Michael knew of the liason and she feared for her life. Did Michael murder Isabel, then try to kill Jamie? Failing to do that but rendering Jamie paralyzed, did Michael try to atone by seeing to Jamie's every need? Or had Jamie witnessed Isabel's murder and was now blackmailing Michael? I had to have some answers—and soon—or I would go mad.

The days flew by in preparation for the wedding. I had never seen Rose happier. She glowed with a new-found youthful exuberance. And Maude was in her element. The dinners and frequent visits between the Payne-White residence and the home of the voguish artist put Maude in a state of fevered euphoria. At times, she bordered on the melodramatic, describing her coup of the decade.

Rose's happiness turned to absolute bliss when a letter arrived from Dunwick stating that Uncle Jack and Michael were on their way to London.

The wedding itself was quiet and simple, yet had a grandeur about it that was most notable. Rose was a radiant bride and Michael was so handsome, my heart jumped every time I looked at him. Maude insisted on giving the reception, personally handling every detail. It seemed like the cream of society had an *en masse* invitation, which I imagined would provide Jamie with more commissions than he could handle.

I was surprised, and secretly pleased, that Michael paid little attention to the glamorous Maude. At the reception, his manner toward her was one of polite reserve, and he appeared far more interested in talking to a particular group of men. I scanned the room for a sign of Uncle Jack, whom I had last seen charming a circle of splendid dowagers.

"Elizabeth, my dear, what an absolutely grand reception this is," Uncle Jack exclaimed, coming up behind me. "I haven't been to a do like this in ages. Maude is a superb hostess. And look at our Rose. Beaming with happiness. Never leaving her new husband's side. Ah . . . youth! By the way, have you seen Michael around?"

"He's on the other side of the room, talking very seriously to a group of men," I replied.

He craned his neck. "He seems quite engrossed. I think I'll indulge in a bit more caviar and duck. Have you tasted the duck, Elizabeth? Superb, positively superb! And first-rate whiskey! Excuse me, my dear."

As Uncle Jack graciously elbowed his way to the large buffet, I saw Maude looking around, a bored expression on her face as a portly old gentleman prattled away, thinking he had her undivided attention. I knew that look of Maude's and decided to rescue her.

"Excuse me, sir . . . Maude, I simply must talk to you," I implored, taking her arm and steering her away from the befuddled gentleman.

"Elizabeth, you are a dear. I was plotting my escape when you liberated me. If I'd had to listen to one more story about the Crimean War, I would have screamed. Good Lord! That was almost sixteen years ago. Oh, do look at Rose and James. They make a handsome couple and it's obvious they are deeply in love. How refreshing! Will they be going on a wedding trip?"

"Of course. Why shouldn't they?"

"Well, I just thought . . . him being . . . well . . ." Her voice trailed off, giving up the verbal struggle.

It was the first time I had ever known Maude to be at a loss for words, and I had to laugh.

"You're laughing at me, Elizabeth!" Maude exclaimed petulantly. "I thought it would be difficult for him to get on and off trains, in and out of hotels and the like."

"Charles is going with them. It won't be as difficult as you think."

"Where are they going?" Maude asked.

"To Paris first. Jamie wants to see the works of a new

group of painters who call themselves impressionists. He's quite enthusiastic about it. I also understand he'll be taking some of his paintings to the Durand-Ruel Gallery at their request. They are most anxious to exhibit them. Then they'll go to Venice for a while," I informed her.

"Speaking of impressionists, I heard that one of them — I think his name is Manet — caused quite a scandal a few years back with a painting call "Olympia." A nude woman. Imagine that!" Her laughter tinkled like tiny silver bells. "Where are they going to live when they return? Here in London?"

"Yes. In our old house. They'll probably come to Dunwick for the summer months, although I'm trying to convince Jamie that he and Rose must see the Lake District. So much beauty there to paint. But the way, did you ever hear from David Cooke again?" I asked.

"No. And I'm a bit surprised."

"Why?"

"Well, someone said they saw him in London a few weeks back. If he was here, I can't understand why he didn't contact me. He seemed to enjoy the lifestyle I had to offer. Oh well, there are scads of David Cookes about. They may not be quite as handsome as the original, but they are witty, charming, and willing to be of service. Tell me, Elizabeth, how is our dear Michael doing? I haven't had much opportunity to speak with him what with all the preparations for the wedding and all these people to attend to."

Before I could answer, a strong hand was placed at the small of my back and I could feel the warmth of Michael's body touching mine.

"Well, Michael, your ears must have been burning. I was just asking Elizabeth how you were," Maude said, a brilliant, coquettish smile lighting her face.

"I'm as well as ever, Maude. I wish to express our

357

deepest gratitude for the excellent reception you have provided for my sister and her husband. A very commendable affair," Michael said.

"It was my pleasure. Besides, James has promised to do a portrait of me. How long will you be in London, Michael?" Her voice became seductive, her eyes entreating.

"We shall be returning to Dunwick as soon as Rose and James leave for Paris, which I believe is the day after tomorrow," Michael replied.

"We?" Maude queried. "You mean you and your uncle. Elizabeth and I have hardly had much time together and there is so much to catch up on."

"I mean the three of us," Michael said quietly.

"Oh . . . must you, Elizabeth?" Maude asked, trying to look mournful.

"I . . ."

"She must. Dunwick is a lonely place without her," Michael stated emphatically.

"Pity!" Maude responded with a sudden coolness. "Oh, there's Lord Wilkles. I simply must talk to him. If you'll excuse me." She started to walk away, but turned to face us as if seized by an unexpected impulse. "Tomorrow night I shall have an intimate farewell supper party for the newlyweds and, of course, the Tyrone family. I'll expect you at eight. Ta!" She swirled off into the crowd.

"I could never understand how you came to choose Maude for your best friend. The two of you are at opposite ends of the pole," Michael said.

"Perhaps that was the attraction in the beginning, but she's not my closest friend anymore," I offered weakly, for Michael's arm had slipped about my waist and he was drawing me close to him.

"Would you rather stay in London?"

"No. I don't want to spend any more time with Maude. I'm ready to go home to Dunwick. I only came because of Rose. I'm glad I did now. If I hadn't, she and Jamie might never have found one another."

He looked at me long and hard, and a dark shadow crept over his face. "If there is anything you particularly want in London, you had better get it tomorrow. I don't think you'll be coming back here for some time."

I glanced up at him quizzically and wondered what meaning lay behind his statement. Would I never leave Dunwick again? Would I be ensconced in the tomb beside Isabel's empty coffin?

Sixteen

Dunwick was bathed in sunlight, all rosy and golden as it loomed on the horizon ahead of us. I did not know what fate awaited me at Dunwick, or if Callie's banshee would indeed claim me. But I did know I loved my home at Dunwick as much as I loved its lord.

Once inside, we quickly dispersed, Michael to the library, Uncle Jack and I to the upstairs. One of the other maids readied my bath, for I had told Clara to take the rest of the day off after the tiring journey from London, knowing full well she could hardly wait to tell everyone downstairs about the sights she had seen in the city.

The warm bath washed away the ache and grime of traveling as I languidly let the water soak into my pores. After brushing my freshly washed hair to a glossy sheen, the maid did a respectable job of styling it before assisting me into an amber-colored taffeta gown that sparkled with hints of gold when the light caught it. It was a gown I'd purchased in London and it made me feel quite regal.

Both Michael and Uncle Jack rose when I entered the dining room, smiles of admiration on their faces.

"London seems to have had a good effect on you,

Elizabeth." Uncle Jack grinned. "You look positively radiant."

"Thank you," I said as we took our seats.

After the soup, we were served a succulent roast loin of pork surrounded by mashed potatoes and brussels sprouts. Michael carved and we ate the delectable meal with relish.

Filled to capacity I was grateful for the glass of sherry Michael handed me when we retired to the drawing room. Uncle Jack lit his pipe, picked up his whiskey and implored me to play some Chopin for him, claiming his ears were starved for some soothing music. I glanced at Michael as I made my way to the piano. He was staring down into his whiskey, his expression one of dark brooding.

After a polonaise and a few etudes, I looked up to see Uncle Jack dozing and Michael gone. I gently woke Uncle Jack and informed him I was going to bed. He mumbled something about walking upstairs with me before his head fell back against the chair, his eyes once again closed, his breathing deep and heavy.

I didn't realize how much I would miss Rose until Uncle Jack and Michael left shortly after breakfast the next morning. I tried to busy myself with the household accounts but soon had them in order, which left me wandering about the house like a stray orphan. Having dinner alone did nothing to bolster my flagging spirits. The piano was my only diversion, but after a few pieces I found my heart was not in it. I stopped playing and was about to retire when Uncle Jack and Michael entered the foyer in rare spirits.

"Ah . . . Elizabeth. Do play a merry tun for us," Uncle Jack said as he came into the drawing room with Michael close behind him. "Perhaps a song or two we can sing. Eh, Michael?"

"Yes. I think that might be in order," Michael agreed, going to the sideboard, pouring two glasses of whiskey, then bringing them to the piano where Uncle Jack already stood.

Though it was late, I happily complied with their wishes, for I didn't want to dampen their festive mood. It was so rare to see Michael in a mood akin to happiness. His deep baritone voice blended quite pleasantly with Uncle Jack's mellow tenor as they sang song after song.

Suddenly, Michael's carefree mood vanished and he became sullen. He slammed his empty glass down on the piano and stalked from the room. Uncle Jack shrugged and went to pour himself another whiskey after I kissed him on the cheek and murmured good night. In the foyer I heard the slam of the library door.

I screwed up my courage and marched toward the library. After rapping at the door, I turned the knob and entered.

"Michael?" I said quietly.

He lifted his head and looked at me with weary eyes, then irritably asked, "What do you want, Elizabeth?"

"I would like to talk to you about Mrs. Meehan if you have a moment."

He leaned back in his chair and pinched the bridge of his nose. "Well, what is it?"

"From the beginning, it has been evident that Mrs. Meehan holds no great love for me. And to be honest, it makes me uneasy to have her in the house, especially when I'm here alone so often. I feel now that Callie is gone, Mrs. Meehan serves no purpose in this house. I would greatly appreciate it if you would pension her off. Really, Michael, it would very much please me if she left Dunwick for good."

He drew a long breath, then exhaled slowly. "Quite

frankly, I had forgotten about Mrs. Meehan. You're right of course. I'll take care of it. Naturally, I'll have to give the woman two weeks' notice so she can make whatever arrangements she wants. But she'll be well compensated and I'll see that she has a small annuity from Dunwick. Can you bear her presence for another two weeks, Elizabeth?"

"If I must. You won't forget, will you Michael?"

"No. I shall speak to her first thing in the morning. Is that all, Elizabeth?"

"Yes. Thank you, Michael."

Alone in my bedchamber, fully prepared for bed, I brushed my long auburn hair until it was free of all snarls. As I looked at myself in the mirror, I thought my face had become a little fuller and more attractive. I rose and went to the window, my silk-and-lace nightgown fleetingly clinging to my slight body with a delicate caress as I moved. The full moon stared back at me from a cloudless sky. I released a long, loud sigh that seemed to echo around the room with a ghostly reverberation. Turning off all the lights, I climbed into bed and lay with my eyes open, watching the opalescent shimmer of shadows cast by the moon.

An eerie restlessness stirred within me. A craving, a desire that defied explanation. I felt like a boiling tea kettle on too hot a stove, whose steam vents were all closed. It was as though there were a demon in me that wanted to escape, but couldn't find an outlet and the pressure was becoming unbearable. With sleep forgotten, I went once again to the window and, lost in thought, hugged myself as though a chill breeze had danced over my skin.

An involuntary spasm shook me as two large hands came down on my shoulders and warm lips nuzzled my neck and shoulder. I was immobilized, unable to discern

363

reality from dream. The two small buttons on the back of my nightgown were quickly undone and the silken garment was eased from my shoulders. It slipped to the floor, emitting small sparks of light in its passage. His hands moved over my body with infinite care and I trembled with anticipation. When he pulled me back against him, I realized he, too, was without clothing. The sinewy body and the thick mass of hair pressing against my back left no doubt in my mind it was Michael. He slowly turned me around, but before I could speak, his wide lips covered mine and he embraced me tightly.

Sweeping me up effortlessly, he carried me to the bed, his lips never leaving mine. My heart pounded and my blood warmed as I recalled the night that Michael first bedded me and the sensations of sheer pleasure it had brought me. With wavering timidity, I reached out for him and, as if sensing my growing desire, he came to me gently, his kisses, his caresses invoking deeper and deeper responses in me until I was returning his ardor in kind. Soon, flesh melted into flesh and the only sounds in the room were the beating of two hearts, rapid breathing, and the rustle of sheets.

As if the night were endless, Michael took me again and again, our frenzy mounting each time with mutual need. Finally spent and sated, Michael drew me to him without a word, kissed my forehead, then stroked my hair, my head in the crook of his arm as I fell asleep.

The brilliant light of dawn roused me and I happily stretched in bed, the only disappointment being Michael's absence. I dressed with haste and rushed down to the dining room, where Uncle Jack was eating breakfast and reading the paper.

"Has Michael been down yet?" I asked, my cheeks flushed.

"Ages ago, my dear, ages ago. Dashed out of here as

though fire was licking at his boots," Uncle Jack replied, putting his paper aside.

"Did he go to the stables to wait for me? I'm afraid I slept later than usual this morning."

"He went to the stables, but not to wait for you. He was mumbling something about Belfast and how he didn't know when he'd be back," Uncle Jack said.

"I see." Disenchantment and frustration washed away my earlier look of joy.

"There . . . there . . . Elizabeth. He'll be back. Besides, am I not every bit as charming and handsome as Michael? No. Don't answer that. But I do know I'm jolly good company, am I not?"

"Of course you are," I assured him, softening under the warmth of his engaging smile.

For three days Uncle Jack did his best to keep me entertained until a message from Michael came from Belfast, requesting Uncle Jack join him there. When he left, Dunwick took on an elusive aura that unsettled me. And what was particularly bizarre was Mrs. Meehan's increasing presence in the lower part of the house. Even though I didn't see her all the time, I could feel her eyes on me, watching me, following me. The very house suddenly seemed saturated with hatred. At night her tread sounded up and down the corridors of the west wing and I took to locking my door. I felt exceedingly vulnerable without Uncle Jack or Rose around and I couldn't wait until she was gone from Dunwick.

Then it began. Muted laughter echoing through the upstairs corridor at night, sending chills along my spine, for the sound was akin to Callie's weird, maniacal laughter. Reason told me Mrs. Meehan had initiated a war of nerves against me; that it was not the cries of a banshee. Still, my anxiety grew in intensity instead of abating. I soon found myself lying awake waiting for the eerie laughter to commence, then running to the door and opening it a crack to peer out, only to see a deserted corridor. My nights became sleepless horrors and when I did doze off, it was only to be awakened again by that chilling laughter. Of course, when I questioned the servants, they hadn't heard a thing and knew nothing about it. Though I knew Mrs. Meehan was lurking about, I could never catch her.

One day after breakfast, I went to the upstairs sitting parlor to plan some menus for when Michael and Uncle Jack returned home. While they were away, I'd told cook not to fuss just for me. There on the desk was a note with the carefully printed words:

"The moon, by driving clouds o'ercast,
Withheld its fitful gleam;
And louder than the tempest blast
Was heard the banshee's scream."

This was too much. I promptly sent for Mrs. Meehan. She seemed to glide into the room, her black mourning frock emphasizing her gaunt, pallid face on which was registered a perpetual expression of disdain.

"Yes, Lady Tyrone. You wanted to see me?" she asked in icy tones.

"I would like an explanation for this," I demanded, holding up the paper for her to see.

She studied it for a moment, her blue-veined skeletal hands, seemingly bloodless, clasped against her black skirt. "I have no idea what it could be, Lady Tyrone."

"You didn't place it on my desk?"

"I don't make a habit of coming into the west wing unless I'm ordered to do so, Lady Tyrone." Her voice was abnormally calm.

"Then I suppose you've heard no laughter during the

night," I tossed at her, even while knowing any attempts to pry information from her were futile.

"I've heard nothing, Lady Tyrone."

"Thank you, Mrs. Meehan. You may go now." What was the use? She would never admit to anything, and I was only playing into her hands by expressing my concern. A derisive smile forced on her thin, bloodless lips as she left the room, a smile that pulled my nerves taut.

Early afternoon brought picture cards and a letter from Rose. I eagerly opened the letter after a swift perusal of the cards. The letter overflowed with love and happiness. Obviously quite taken with Paris, Rose described it in glowing terms. She went on to say how Jamie's attitude toward his handicap had been changed considerably by the camaraderie he found in Paris. He was no longer shy about being seen in public and they were doing quite a bit of entertaining, especially other artists and writers. They had even begun to frequent the theater and ballet. When I had finished the letter, my eyes were blurred with tears of joy.

At dinner I listlessly ate my small shepherd's pie. I had been alone in the house with only Mrs. Meehan and the servants for more than a week, and if Mrs. Meehan had declared war on my nerves she was winning. Again I wished she was gone. I consoled myself with the fact that she would be, very soon.

I went into the drawing room and played the piano, more out of habit than desire. In the spacious room, the music took on a haunting quality, a dirgelike sadness which I couldn't seem to control. Even a gavotte or a saraband by Bach lost its crisp liveliness under my fingers. Fatigue had made me careless and, rather than continue playing in a slovenly manner, I went up to my bedchamber, determined to read myself to sleep.

I had scarcely begun to read when I dropped off into a

deep sleep. Then, I began to toss and turn, trying to escape the dreadful laughter that rang in my head. Soon, my ears became flooded with the wild, vibrant sound, forcing me awake. I bolted upright in the bed, rigid with fear as I realized those horrendous cries were right outside my door.

Taking my robe from the chair, I slipped it on, tying the sash as I made my way to the door. I quietly slipped the latch and turned the knob, then swiftly flung the door open. There was no one there . . . nothing! I stepped out into the corridor and glimpsed a diaphanous figure racing away from me, its gauzy apparel billowing behind. I was angry and, this time, I was going to catch Mrs. Meehan in the act. Pulling my sash tight, I briskly followed the disappearing form down the dimly lit corridor.

Suddenly, the object of my pursuit vanished into the east wing. I trudged on, quickening my pace. I was resolved to trap Mrs. Meehan with that ridiculous costume on and make her confess to her heinous deeds. I stood before her door and was about to fling it open when the hall whirled around me and I sank to the floor in an inky cloud.

As my eyes fluttered open, I became aware that my head was pounding furiously. At first, I thought my eyes were playing tricks, for I couldn't seem to focus them properly. I soon learned my hazy vision was due to the dimness of the room, which was filled with ominous shadows cast by the eerie amber light of a turned-down oil lamp. My head throbbed as I sat up with the instinctive knowledge that I wasn't in my own room. My fear turned to horror as I found myself staring straight into the malefic face of Isabel. The portrait seemed to be alive in that peculiar light, and it looked as if it were about to speak to me at any moment. I wanted to scream, but sheer panic constricted my throat as I scrambled off Isabel's bed and raced back to my own room, praying there was no banshee behind me. Closing and locking my door, I climbed into bed and lay there wide awake and trembling, waiting for the morning.

If Clara noticed my exhausted, nervous state the following morning, she said nothing and went about her duties as though everything were perfectly normal. But to me, nothing was normal. Dressed in my riding habit, I stared out the window as Clara left. I heard the door open and close again quickly.

"Did you forget something, Clara?" I asked, not bothering to turn around.

Suddenly, a silk scarf was thrown around my throat. Automatically, my hands flew to my neck to relieve the terrible pressure and let some air reach my lungs.

"You got away from me last night," a familiar male voice said. "But this time, I assure you, Elizabeth, you won't. I'll finish the deed once and for all." His warm breath fanned my ear as he held fast to the scarf.

"What are you doing?" I demanded in a hoarse whisper. "Why, David? . . . Why?"

"Oh yes . . . I want you to know why. Actually, I never meant to kill you, but soon I had no choice. You see, my dear Elizabeth, your father eluded me. I saw him get off the train at Penrith and, thinking it was the ideal place to reap justice, I got off too. Unfortunately, I didn't see him get back on. Not finding him registered at any of the inns, I was dashing back to catch a train to London when we had our fortuitous little meeting. I thought it might be beneficial to my cause to develop a relationship with you. And when I learned you were Michael Tyrone's new bride, I couldn't believe my good fortune," David Cooke said.

"I don't understand. What have Michael and my father

369

to do with all this?" I managed to ask as the scarf slackened just enough to let me breath.

"Your father ruined my family. My father had a thriving business and we were fairly well-to-do until one of your father's little business deals wiped us out. My father committed suicide when he lost the business, and my mother died of a broken heart. I was forced to do menial labor to support myself, and my sister had to marry beneath her station in life in order to survive. I vowed revenge at whatever the cost." He laughed in a strange, yet familiar way. "Your father had to go and die of natural causes. But I wouldn't be cheated. I had you. At Dunluce I thought my revenge had come to fruition, but you refused to comply."

"It was you—and not Callie—who was behind all my mishaps!" I gasped, working my fingers deeply between my throat and the silk scarf.

"My dear Elizabeth, I wouldn't dream of taking all the credit. I had nothing to do with your being sealed in the tomb. Callie did have a few tricks of her own, you know. And she really must be credited with the cord across the staircase, for I stole that rather original idea from her. When Rose told me what the little monster had done to her teacher, I thought the notion quite clever and decided to try it on you. You know, Elizabeth, you have a tenacious way of clinging to life. Escaping from your bedroom at just the right time . . . leaping from the path of a carriage. You're a very agile woman, Elizabeth, very agile. However, I don't think your agility will save you this time." He tightened the scarf.

"Michael . . . what has . . . Michael . . . to do . . . with this?" I asked, trying to pull the garroting scarf from my neck.

"Ah . . . the great Lord Tyrone. He has interfered in my business for the last time. But all that has nothing to

370

do with you. There's no more time for talk, Elizabeth." Again the scarf tightened.

"Wait . . . the laughing . . . the specter in the corridor last night . . . you?" I had to stall. I needed time to think.

"I was good at it, wasn't I?"

"I thought it was Mrs. Meehan," I said weakly, knowing time was running out. If only Clara *would* come back for something!

"Ironically, this whole business would be over now if it weren't for Mrs. Meehan. You'd be dead. Suicide by hanging yourself in Isabel's room. The reason being you knew Michael Tyrone still loved his first wife. But now I'll have to kill you, then carry your body down to Isabel's room, where the suicide scene has been fully staged."

"The servants . . . Mrs. Meehan will hear you."

"You forget, my dear Elizabeth, I know the routine of this house like the staff itself. There are no servants on this floor at this time of day. As for Mrs. Meehan . . . well, she'll never hear anything again."

"What do you mean?" I asked, my anxiety rising.

"Last night she came upon me as I was placing you on the bed and putting the scarf to your throat. I turned toward her, the scarf stretched taut in my hands, but the foolish woman pulled a pair of scissors from the pocket of her robe. I shoved the scarf back in my pocket and went for her. She put up a brilliant defense, slashing the scissors through the air as I approached. But I was a little faster and caught her wrist, twisting it until the scissors fell to the floor. When I stopped to pick them up, she made a dash for the door. Again, I was quicker and plunged the scissors into her back. Unfortunately, you escaped to your room while I was putting the old lady back in her room."

"David . . . why did you wait so long? Why the taunting laughter?"

"Call it a sadistic quirk. I thought it quite ironic to pass on the terror and agony my father went through for so many months. Be thankful I limited your anguish to a week or so."

"And Rose? You seemed to genuinely like her." I was running out of questions. I had to think of more questions that his ego couldn't let pass unanswered.

"Ah, Rose. With both you and Michael out of the way, I intended to court Rose. She's a docile little thing, and with my charm and persuasive powers, I would have convinced her to be my wife. Then, not only would I have had the Tyrone fortune at my disposal, but yours as well. Yes . . . I would have had it all. That would have been true poetic justice. But again you interfered, Elizabeth, ruining all my plans for the future by bringing Rose to her long-lost lover. You're just like your father, bent on destroying the Cooke family. Well . . . that was your last question, Elizabeth. You don't even have time to say good-bye."

As the scarf jerked tightly about my neck, I lifted my booted foot and brought it down on his toes with all the force I could command. As a groan of pain escaped his lips and his hands left the scarf, I raced to the door, flung it open and ran down the corridor to the marble staircase. I could hear him behind me, hard on my heels. As I reached the next to last step, his hand caught my wrist.

"Mr. Cooke!" bellowed a deep, resonant voice.

Startled, David let go of my wrist and I raced to Michael, throwing my arms around him.

"Why, if it isn't the lord of the manor himself," David sneered, as he threw himself against the wall of the staircase and reached for an antique sword. "I thought they had taken care of you in Belfast. Well . . . in a way I'm glad they didn't. Now I'll have the privilege of making up for the time that I botched it."

As he came toward us, brandishing the gleaming sword, Michael pushed me aside and darted to the wall by the entrance, where he grabbed a similar shining sword. Each man had to use both hands to hold the heavy relics of a knightly era as they postured at one another.

David raised his sword as if to cleave Michael in two, but metal struck metal, the clash reverberating through the house like ancient chimes. Michael sucked in his stomach as David's sword slashed at him. Light flashed from Michael's sword as he retaliated, missing a grinning David by inches. I screamed when David knocked Michael's sword from his hand and moved in for the kill. But Michael quickly rolled to one side and reached his sword in time to fend off David's lethal blow, then sprang to his feet.

Michael's angular features were set with raw anger and deadly determination as he began to stalk David with his glinting blade. If there was any fear in David, he never showed it as Michael's swinging strokes became fiercer and increasingly swifter. Servants began to line the foyer as the brassy clang of the swords echoed to the lower floor. One maid swooned while another screamed in fright.

As Michael began to back David up the marble staircase, a satanic look distorted David's normally handsome face and the gleam in his eye was more than evil; it was demoniac. When David made a frantic thrust toward Michael's abdomen, his foot rocked on the edge of a riser, causing him to lose his balance, and his mouth gaped hideously as he impaled himself on Michael's upturned sword. Michael swiftly withdrew the bloodied weapon, and David's body rolled lifelessly to the bottom of the stairs.

Michael dropped his sword, looked at the body of his foe with aversion, then called to one of the servants to go for the constable. He slowly walked toward me and I threw myself into his outstretched arms. Tears spilled from my eyes as he led me into the drawing room.

"I think you could do with a bit of brandy about now," Michael said as I slumped onto the divan.

"It's so ghastly . . . all so ghastly," I said between sobs. "Mrs. Meehan . . . you . . . all of it."

"What about Mrs. Meehan?" Michael asked, handing me the glass and sitting down beside me as he sipped his brandy.

"He killed her, Michael." The fiery liquid seared my throat and splashed fire in my stomach.

"What?" he roared. "Killed Mrs. Meehan? Whatever for?"

"Last night he dragged me into Isabel's room intending to murder me, but Mrs. Meehan came in and he killed her. I escaped when he was taking her body back to her room."

"He was a madman and a fanatic. I know why he wanted me out of the way, but why you, Elizabeth? Why you?"

Between sips of brandy, I slowly related David's reasons for wanting me dead. As the liquid began to course through my blood, a certain calmness came over me. "And you, Michael . . . what did David have against you?"

"David Cooke was an ardent member of the Sinn Fein, an organization that believes Ireland's independence can be achieved only through violence. He was most certainly not a travel writer, nor a journalist. His main purpose in going to America was to secure funds to help promote

Fenianism. I don't believe in violence, Elizabeth. I support Home Rule, and now that Gladstone is Prime Minister again we at least might stand a chance of some reform. But that is another topic. As far as David Cooke goes, he was aiding in the purchase and smuggling of weapons into this country. Along with a small group of men who feel the same way I do, I have been thwarting Mr. Cooke's efforts by confiscating his armaments whenever we hear that another shipment is about to be smuggled in. He sorely wanted us out of the way, especially me," Michael explained.

"Is that why you made all those trips to Belfast and the late-night outings on Rathlin?"

"Some of it was business in Belfast, but most of the time we were at points along the shore where we knew the weapons were to be unloaded. Rathlin Island was their favorite place for delivery. I never dreamed Cooke was out to harm you, Elizabeth, or I would have finished him off when I first learned who he was."

"When did you know, Michael?"

"Seeing how interested you seemed in him, and he in you, I hired a detective to investigate him. I knew his father had been ruined in business due to bad investments, but the detective never mentioned your father and, at the time, I really didn't care about his father's status. The detective made his report while Cooke was staying here, and it galled me to have a member of the Sinn Fein under my roof."

"And that's why you wanted him to leave?"

"Yes. And I didn't want any relationship developing between you and him, or between Rose and him."

"But if he was so interested in this . . . this Fenianism, why did he go with Maude to Paris and Venice?"

"There was money waiting for him in Paris for the cause. The French have always been anxious to see an

Irish Free State. And then, there was Maude herself. I'm sure he was handsomely paid for any small services rendered." Michael's lips twisted in a contemptuous smile.

When I questioned him further, Michael went on to explain the differences, politically and morally, between Fenianism and Home Rule. I listened with fascination and a growing insight into the world in which I lived. A light luncheon of sandwiches, cakes, and tea was served to us in the drawing room as Michael continued to expand on politics like a man obsessed. The lengthy discourse was interrupted by the arrival of the constable, his men, and the coroner. Michael instructed me to stay in the drawing room while he attended to the waiting gentlemen.

It seemed to take forever for the constable to go over it all with Michael and for the bodies to be removed. I wished I'd had another glass of brandy when I saw the formidable and whiskered constable come into the drawing room with Michael at his side. After the amenities, he asked me to relate all the events connected with David's and Mrs. Meehan's deaths.

Slowly and carefully, I described all the episodes that were related to David and me, from the incident at Dunluce to the present, with special emphasis on the events of the previous night and that morning. When I had finished, he asked me several questions, then asked Michael's permission to question the staff. Readily agreeing, Michael followed the constable out of the drawing room.

I went to the sideboard and poured myself a small brandy with trembling hands, then walked over to the windows and stared out onto the terrace. The sun was beginning to dip in the sky, turning the gray stone to gleaming gold. I tried not to think of David, Mrs. Meehan, Callie or Isabel—but they were all there in my mind, intermingling like evanescent dancers in a ghostly pavane. Even the brandy wouldn't make them go away. Perhaps there was a banshee after all, a banshee that invaded minds like David's or Callie's and turned them into the devil's creatures.

"Elizabeth . . . are you all right?" Michael asked as he poured himself another brandy.

"Yes," I replied, going to join him on the divan. "Are they still here?"

"No. They've all gone now."

"Will there be trouble for you?"

"No. There'll be no trouble. The servants corroborated our version of the fight between Cooke and me. We will have to appear at the inquest, but I'm sure you'll weather it. It's only a formality."

The brandy had seeped well into my bloodstream, making me daring and perhaps a bit giddy. "Michael, I've read the letter my father wrote to you and I will give you a divorce any time you wish."

The surprise in his eyes was genuine. "Do you wish a divorce, Elizabeth? Have you found a young man to your liking?"

I gasped. "Why no, Michael. There's never been anyone but you. I . . . I thought . . . well, I'm not beautiful like Isabel or Maude. I'm not even pretty. And a man like you . . ." I couldn't continue.

"And a man like me what?" He set our brandy glasses down on the low table in front of us, then took my hands in his.

"Oh, I don't know. You were practically blackmailed into marrying me in the first place," I sputtered.

"No one blackmails a Tyrone into doing anything he doesn't want to do."

"The money then?" I asked meekly.

A warm smile broadened on his wide lips. "I would

never marry a woman for her money, Elizabeth. I value my independence and freedom far too much for that. In fact, I was quite incensed when I read your father's letter. In a cold fury, I went to London, fully intending to break off all business and personal relations with your father. Then I saw you leaning on the railing, smiling down at me with those large china-blue eyes, and I remembered the little girl sitting on my lap, winning my heart and love as she smiled at me so long ago, her young face shining with beauty and innocence. I accepted your father's offer without hesitation. I had hoped you would come to have some affection for me in time.

"In the beginning of our marriage, I thought you were coming to love me, but after a while whatever love I had seen in your eyes seemed to turn to fear," Michael said.

"You were the one who changed, Michael. You became distant, almost aloof. It was as though your feelings toward me had altered. I couldn't seem to reach you. Quite frankly, I thought you were trying to kill me."

A feeble smile flickered on his lips. "My poor Liza. How could you ever think I would dream of harming you in any way? Granted, I have been more than irritable of late. The Fenian business, the squaring away of your father's enterprises, plus my own business concerns, have weighed heavily on me. But things are coming under control now. I can understand that you felt I was shutting you out. I didn't want you involved in the Fenian business lest there be retaliations. But how could you think I wanted to kill you?"

"Oh . . . a lot of little things, but mostly because of the time I was shot at in the hedgerow and the time on the boat coming back from Rathlin. I thought you were going to push me off," I explained sheepishly.

"Look at me, Elizabeth," he ordered, lifting my chin

with his finger. "You don't truly believe I meant to shoot you or to toss you overboard. I had just come riding in when you came out of the hedgerow. I didn't even know until now someone, undoubtedly David, had shot at you. As for the incident on the boat, I saw you edging perilously close to the railing and, with the boat rocking so precariously, you could have lost your balance and been taken by a wave. I went to pull you back and hold onto you."

A sob rose in my throat and tears welled up in my eyes. "Oh, Michael. I love you so much . . . so much," I blurted, losing all sense of pride.

He pulled me into his arms and cradled my head against his broad chest. "I've waited a long time to hear you say that, Liza, my own Liza."

"I've always loved you, Michael, didn't you know that?"

"As I said, I was never really sure."

"Did you love me from the first?"

"Didn't you know I did when we danced at your birthday ball? Even as a little girl, you fascinated me. Those large, wondrous eyes would stare at me in awe, making me feel very much the man, even though I wasn't quite twenty-one. At your eighteenth-birthday ball, I found a sweet, unassuming woman who enchanted me. Then and there, I knew that I wanted you for my wife and mistress of Dunwick. I could only pray you would come to love me before some young man captured your heart forever."

"Then why didn't you come to the Lake District with me?" I asked.

"Initially it was Callie who brought me back to Ireland. While there, I was needed to help track down a new shipment of arms. Believe me, I would have preferred to be with you, but I had committed myself to the cause of peaceful change in Ireland."

"Why did you stay away from my bed for so long if you loved me?"

"Having to leave you to tend to business matters after making love to you was becoming more and more difficult. I found it easier to take care of things if I didn't touch you."

"Then why did you make such tender love to me the night before you left for Belfast?"

"I knew the venture was going to be dangerous, very dangerous, and I wasn't sure if I'd make it back to Dunwick alive. I had to feel you in my arms, feel your flesh and know your body once more in case I didn't return," Michael said, putting his arm around me and drawing me to him, kissing my forehead gently. "All will be different now, love. I will no longer take an active part in preventing the gun-smuggling. Instead, I have pledged financial support, and I have hired very capable people to help run the businesses in London. So you'll be seeing a lot more of me. I hope you approve."

"You know I do."

We embraced, kissed, and sat on the divan in each other's arms.

We sat for some time like that, Michael lost in his thoughts while I basked in the glow of our love. I thought of Rose and Jamie and I knew exactly how they felt. But thinking of Jamie also brought to mind the discrepancy between Isabel's diary and Jaime's version of their relationship. I sat up suddenly, disengaging myself from Michael's comforting arms.

"Michael, I found and read a diary Isabel had written," I said somewhat breathlessly.

"My, you have been a busy little devil. I didn't know Isabel kept a diary," Michael said with a lazy smile.

"In it, she wrote that she and James McGregor were lovers and they were going to run away to America.

380

I . . ."

Michael put a finger on my lips. "I'm going to tell you about Isabel and James, but under no circumstances are you to tell anyone else, especially Rose. Promise?"

"I promise, Michael."

"I had warned James about Isabel, her whims, her need to constantly augment her male conquests. But he was young, impressionable and, I daresay, totally naive regarding women of Isabel's ilk. He plunged headlong into Isabel's web like a blind and deaf man. It wasn't long before he learned the difference between love and infatuation. You see, he always did love Rose. Isabel's flirtatious attentions only flattered his ego.

"They met in a deserted fisherman's shack on Rathlin Island on that fateful day. Isabel informed him she was leaving me and wanted him to go to America with her. She showed him the money she had obtained and the Tyrone jewels. James was appalled to think she'd steal the Tyrone jewels without a twinge of conscience. He upbraided her, then told her he was deeply in love with Rose and wanted nothing more to do with her. He started to walk away. But one did not walk out on Isabel.

"Carrying all that money and jewelry, Isabel had brought a pistol with her for protection. Infuriated by James's rejection, she pulled the pistol from her skirt, aimed and fired, hitting him in the back. He lurched forward, then fell on the ground. Thinking she had killed him, she left him there alone, then paid one of the islanders a huge sum to take her back to Ballycastle — despite a raging sea. A farmer, hearing the shot, soon found James while Isabel and the hapless boatman were taken by the sea. The fetched me from Dunwick and I took James to London, where every specialist examined him. The bullet had penetrated his spine and there was

381

nothing they could do. James refused to stay at the hospital, where care was available, and he wouldn't come back to Dunwick with me. He insisted on living by himself on Rathlin Island as punishment for his being unfaithful to Rose. Between the success of his paintings and his fear that you might bring Rose to the island, he implored me to find a flat for him in London. Your house was ideal," Michael concluded.

"Our house," I corrected. "How could Isabel do such a thing? Poor James." I sat quietly for a moment, then frowned. "I thought you loved Isabel very much, so much, in fact, that you couldn't bear the mention of her name."

"I was very much infatuated with her when I was young — very young. But I soon realized how superficial, shallow, and self-centered she really was. But it was too late. She was my wife. I turned my attentions to work and politics."

"Did Maude ever mean anything to you?" I asked, a little fearful of the answer.

Without warning, the room was filled with Michael's deep baritone laughter. "Haven't you heard one word I said, my sweet Liza? I came to loathe Isabel, and Maude is nothing more than a mirror image of Isabel, a kindred spirit," he said, kissing my cheek fondly before his lips covered mine with a deep urgency as he strongly embraced me. Suddenly, he held me at arm's length and murmured huskily, "I think this had better wait until we are in our bedchamber."

"Our bedchamber?" My eyes sparkled with delight and my senses sharpened with anticipation.

"Yes. My bed has been without a woman for far too long, especially one of great beauty," he said, surveying my face eagerly.

"You think me beautiful, Michael?" I asked as my

382

eyebrows arched quizzically.

"In my eyes, you are the most beautiful woman in the world and I love you dearly." He was about to kiss me again when a maid announced that dinner was served. "Come, Lady Tyrone." He stood and offered me his arm.

"Michael, can we have Isabel's old room dismantled?"

"We'll have the entire east wing redecorated. It's time new life filled this house."

"By the way, where is Uncle Jack? Didn't he come back with you?"

"No. He'll be here tomorrow, though. We have the entire evening to ourselves. And many more, I trust, as Jack divides his time between here and the McGregors'."

As the years passed, Dunwick was once again filled with wailing, and occasional screeches echoed about the house. But they were the cries of our children, for the banshee of Dunwick had been banished forever.